MARS WARS

Abyss of Elysium

DENNIS CHAMBERLAND

Other Books by Dennis Chamberland

Consuming Fire

Proverbs for My Children

Aaron Seven - Quantum Storms

By Dennis and Claudia Chamberland

The Proxima Manual of Space Exploration

Coming:

Aaron Seven - Abyss of Space: The Parallel Novel to Abyss of Elysium

All books are available either in hard copy or in nearly every popular e-book format from:

QuantumEditions.com

MARS WARS

QUANTUM EDITIONS
ORLANDO – CHATTANOOGA – WASHINGTON D.C.

Abyss of Elysium

Dennis Chamberland

Cover art by Christopher Chamberland
Interior illustrations by Brett W. English and Peter D. Chamberland
All photos and maps obtained from the public domain – National Aeronautics and Space Administration and the U.S Geological Survey.

A Quantum Editions 1st Edition

Persons and places described in this novel are strictly fictional. Any characterization, likeness or relation to any person living or dead is strictly coincidental and unintended. The author endeavored to make this story as scientifically and technically realistic and detailed as possible. However, any policy, idea or concept stated herein is solely based on the opinion of the author and is not related in any way to anyone's actual endorsement of any organizational or privately sponsored practice or any national procedure, plan, guideline or process. Concepts and ideas stated herein were solely developed to move a fictional story along a predetermined path to an imagined conclusion. Quantum Editions is a registered publisher – R.R. Bowker and Books in Print

Library of Congress Cataloging-in-Publication Data
Chamberland, Dennis, 1951-
Mars wars : abyss of Elysium / Dennis Chamberland.-- 1st ed.
p. cm.
1. Mars (Planet)--Fiction. 2. Space colonies--Fiction. 3. Space warfare--Fiction. I. Title.

PS3603.H337M37 2004
813'.54--dc22

2004002070

ISBN 1-889422-03-7

To

William M. Knott III

NASA Scientist, Boss, Mentor, Friend

And to the Kennedy Space Center's
space life sciences team he founded
and led so brilliantly.

The very best and the brightest,
carving out the path to tomorrow's worlds,
whole new human civilizations and frontiers -
blazing that single path that everyone else must follow.

And in Memory of

Richard S. Young

NASA Program Manager for the
Mars Viking Missions

Who sat with me for endless hours on countless
pre-dawn Cape Canaveral mornings
teaching all-things-Mars.

He left a legacy of exploration and discovery.

He also left the world another Marsphile to take his place.

Human beings are not easily satisfied. There are always new adventures to be dreamed, unexplored regions to explore, and new frontiers to be settled. Just as humankind left low earth orbit for the moon, so they will leave earthly and lunar orbits for Mars.

In this work, Dennis Chamberland weaves a tale of adventure, exploration and settlement, all rolled into a single sci-fi story of interplanetary destiny. It has been said that life is what happens after you make plans. So it is that missions are what happen after you train. After all, training for space missions is little more than training for the unexpected. In *Abyss of Elysium,* Dennis has written a story that goes well with that maxim – complete with mystery, intrigue, adventure and emotional impact consistent with the full expression of historic human destiny. Between these pages, exactly as in reality, few aspects of any mission go according to best laid plans; but in the end, this reality is what makes true discovery and exploration authentic adventure.

Dennis is a space systems engineer who brings more to these pages than just an ability to tell a good story. He imparts to the genre wide, professional experience which lends credence to a captivating tale and weaves uncommon reality into a story of likely proportions. Here he describes an alien world of deep cold; one whose atmosphere is but a small fraction of the earth's, but paradoxically is capable of spinning winds and storms of hundreds of kilometers per hour and twisters capable of intense destruction.

One true nugget found inside this book is Dennis' insight into advanced space life support systems and the engineered structures that work quietly to keep everyone alive in space. Every astronaut would like nothing more on any given space mission than to concentrate entirely on the assigned tasks and let the silent and invisible systems work their automated magic in the background. But as I found out on my own mission, the most important human talent not duplicated by the robot is the ability to react properly to unforeseen circumstances and to pull things together, even out of imminent disaster. My colleagues on Apollo 13 discovered just how important those invisible systems are when the nominal mission plan goes south. Intense and effective planning and training usually leads to relatively uneventful and successful missions. But sometimes it leads to just making it back home alive after a bad day. Either way, the object is to make the number of successful landings equal to the number of successful launches, and the bean-counting of mission success is always secondary to the glorious reality of homecoming.

Dennis has created a whole new world on Mars. The tale is fiction, of course, but it is a good one, woven together with fact and sound engineering, and it is a memorable account that will keep you turning the pages until the end. It is the kind of story that will lead to real life imitating fiction one day; a kind of irony of facts that lead to fiction later turning into a new reality. It is a book seeded with accurate science and laced together with all the human characters and their unscientific emotions that ultimately lead to the founding of a new society on a distant planet spinning millions of miles away in space.

Dennis has his own real-life experiences with such adventures in the space analog - undersea habitat he designed, built and commanded on seven missions over two years. He found out for himself just how things go as real life interposes itself on the carefully crafted plans of bureaucracies and men. But I'll leave it to Dennis to unfold that particular story in his time. Until then, it is off to Mars now and down into the *Abyss of Elysium*.

Scott Carpenter
Vail, Colorado

"There can be no discovery without first engaging the mind. But discovery alone is empty and impotent without likewise engaging the heart. It is inside these fleshy chambers of heart and mind that a critical mass is formed by the breathtaking fusion of sheer, brittle intellect and tender human emotion. It is from this astonishing unity that the energy of every great discovery and every magnificent achievement is created then released to the world as the pure light of creative genius."

Dennis Chamberland
In Remarks to the Harvard Club of New York
October,1991

THE ELYSIUM DESERT
MARS

ithout warning, out of season and just out of view, an enormous dome of high pressure air, millions of square kilometers in area, collapsed. As the super-cooled gas fell from the high atmosphere, it poured down the slopes toward the deserts and began to turn, deliberately following the rotation of the planet. Quickly its circulation became self sustaining and in the thin, cold environment of the red planet it reached speeds of over three hundred kilometers per hour. Scourging the Martian landscape, it picked up dust particles from the sandy slopes and tortuously wrinkled gorges. Gaining momentum as it fell across the landscape, the huge gyre tightened, accelerating and drawing up even more dust in its powerful maw as it expanded into a fully developed redwind.

Some distance away, just over the horizon, unaware of and unprepared for the approaching wall of wind, Colonist Peter Traynor rested on his knees in the fine orange sand and surveyed his land of paradise. He was protected from the near vacuum and bitter, deep cold by his pressurized suit and bulbous helmet. As he knelt on the red desert, his bright, white suit contrasted with the ruddy sands, his face nearly invisible through the gold, rounded visor of his helmet.

His eyes scanned the vast Martian plain, sprawling across the planet's equatorial deserts to form this place called Elysium. Unlike its mythological namesake, it bore no resemblance to a paradise at all and offered no perfect eternal repose for the dead. Its expansive regions were no more than desiccated wastelands; immense boulder fields whose only travelers over the epochs of geologic time were, until now, endless parades of dunes hurried along by the thin Martian winds.

Yet, it was this bizarre world, this Elysium paradise, for which Peter Traynor had sacrificed everything. He vowed that this was his new home, his new life which he would never leave again, not even for the planet of his birth.

The knees of his white suit cut into the powdery sand that had already soiled and discolored it. He sighed contentedly at his complex and dangerous world, this planet he was claiming with his sweat and muscle for himself and his children to be.

Peter glanced some ten meters to his right where Ashley Alcyone worked steadily, also kneeling in the sand. They were coworkers who shared a common dream to live out their lives on Mars. They also shared their lives. Meeting during training, they had fallen in love and had been secretly married just before leaving for Mars rather than wait for a future mission when the planet was deemed suitable enough to support families. Soulmates that shared the same awe and fascination for this bizarre paradise, they planned to spend their lives together here.

Peter finally returned to his task, driving the seismic probe into the stubborn soil with a rubber capped spike driver. This probe was especially stubborn. It felt almost like he was driving it through steel.

Tunishiawa See, known as Toon to all his friends, was the chief computer engineer at the American base. He worked outside the Mars All Terrain Vehicle, known as a MAT, located some 50 or 60 meters away, wiring probes for Peter and Ashley.

Peter stopped to rest his arm again. Setting this particular seismic probe was more difficult than any of the others. He looked at the marred head of the instrument, now misshapen with frequent hammer blows. It perplexed him that a device designed to pass through the upper sediment with relative ease would be so stubborn.

But this moment of inattention to the task at hand may have saved their lives. Peter looked up at the slight motion on the horizon to recognize the approaching redwind, swift and unrelenting, bearing down on them at 300 kilometers per hour.

For eons, such redwinds were the single most profound agents of change on this planet. Now, this wind, in the blink of a human eye, was about to change her newly-arrived inhabitants lives as well.

"Redwind!" Peter shouted, immediately looking toward Ashley.

He could see her helmet rotate up just as he dropped his hammer and rushed toward her.

"Ashley, get... MAT hurry!" he warned through a broken transmission. But she needed no encouragement. Dropping everything, she sprinted as fast as possible toward the MAT. Peter watched from a distance as Toon arrived at the MAT first and switched on the high intensity navigation beams. Still hanging half out of the door, Toon kicked its electric drive into gear. Operating the drive with his hands, he swung the MAT around to face Peter and Ashley just as he was engulfed by the cloud front.

Peter and Ashley collided blindly and fell to the sand in the gathering, blood-red diffusion of light. Their hands grasped for each other on the ground. Peter felt for her shoulders, able to see only parts of her Environmental Protection Suit, or EPS, through the whipping, swirling dust and gathering blackness. He felt her struggling to sit up and forced her shoulders to the ground.

"Ashley, stop; stop for a second!" Peter shouted into his lip mike.

Her body partially relaxed as he gripped her shoulders. Straddling her he pressed his face plate to hers. He could just barely see her face, dimly illuminated by the green lighted indicators in her helmet. The dust quickly curled across their mated face plates, blurring further his muted vision of Ashley. He could make out her eyes, wide with panic, flashing about through nearly total darkness. He forced her helmet down as she tried to push him away.

"Ashley, look up at me! Ashley, look up!"

Finally Peter could see her eyes focus. Her body relaxed immediately as if the clear sight of him had ended her claustrophobic vertigo. She gasped several times then closed her eyes.

"Okay, now what," she asked calmly and more characteristically.

"Are you okay now?" he yelled into his lip mike.

"Yes… I'm fine," she replied haltingly.

"Keep talking, guys, I should be heading straight toward you," Toon said excited but reassuringly over the common communications circuit.

"Toon, stop the MAT! You'll run us over!" Peter yelled again.

"Okay, I'm stopped."

"Now let's all just relax for one second while we get our bearings," Peter instructed. "Toon, we're lying on the ground together about 50 meters from where the MAT was parked. "You were able to point it in our direction before you lost us, right?"

"Yes."

"How far do you estimate you are from us now?"

"About 15 meters."

"Can you guess what your error radius might be?"

"No more than 5 meters."

Peter focused on the facts, still astride Ashley, holding her tightly to the ground. Already the dust clung to and coated their visors. He still held her hands, tightly folded across her breasts. He sat upright in the swirling murk and breathed hard, straining to see, feeling lost but still in control.

"We're going to come to you," Peter stated with finality. "Toon, I want you to turn the hi-beams on."

"They're already on, Peter."

"Ashley, I'm going to stand up. You keep a hand on me. Don't lose me. When I'm all the way up, feel along my leg until you reach my tool belt in the back. Lock your hands around that and don't let go. If you do lose me, stop immediately where you are and kneel on the ground."

Peter slowly stood up against the Martian wind. Although it whipped by him at hundreds of kilometers per hour, he had no trouble standing against it. The Martian air was so thin, nearly a vacuum by earth standards, that even such a velocity offered little resistance. This wind in a near vacuum served only to magnify the deep cold of the Martian air, mixing and robbing the lower layers of the energy of captured sunlight near the ground.

The wind exerted a steady, even pressure against him. Unlike even a mild earth wind, here there were no violent gusts to upset him. The Martin redwind lent a nearly even, horizontal pressure.

"Okay, Ashley, I'm standing now. Come on up."

He could feel her hands work up his legs from behind. He reached a glove behind him, groping to assist her but she couldn't see it. Running her hands along the seat of his pressure suit she found his belt and pulled herself up.

"Okay I'm up. Nice buns."

"Get a room!" Toon snickered over the circuit.

"Both hands, Ashley," Peter added firmly with no trace of humor. He could feel her grip his belt tightly. He raised one arm and wiped the dust away from his visor with his glove. The minute, microscopic powder fell away in streaming, fine lines and drifted around his visor with the wind. Immediately it began to accumulate again.

Quickly he summarized the situation. He had chosen to walk to the MAT as the less hazardous of the available alternatives. His reasoning was obvious: they were slower and more deliberate than the MAT and had less mass so that any chance encounter would not be as dangerous.

Visibility was as near to zero as possible and what sunlight existed was quickly diminishing in the building cloud. Even the MAT's high intensity navigation beams would have no more than a meter's range in this dust, if that. Peter knew their chances of walking, unassisted, squarely into the MAT were less than 50-50. In this soupy darkness they could walk within an arms length of the vehicle and miss it all together. They would have to rely on an assist from the MAT's weak external sound system called the ESS.

"Toon, is the ESS operational?"

"Yes, but I seriously doubt if it's going to carry very far here," Toon replied skeptically.

The ESS was used only in the pressurized environment of the domes for calibrating and setting the navigation instruments. The atmospheric pressure of Mars was so low that sound, for all practical purposes, did not transmit in its near vacuum. Outside communications were carried on exclusively by the suits' radio transmitters. But Peter had a theory.

"Let's see how well the wind and dust particles in the air carry the sound. Toon, can you whistle through your teeth?"

"Sure, man. Like this?" Then he cut loose with a shrill, high-pitched, painful whistle that penetrated their ears like a shot.

"Oh, man!" Ashley complained. "Turn off the transmitter next time, Toon!"

"That's right," Peter agreed calmly and slowly in a measured voice. "Turn off your transmitter and whistle into the ESS mike. I'll see if I can hear you."

In windless conditions at near vacuum, this would have been an exercise in futility. But in the artificial pressure created by the rushing flux of wind, some limited sound could carry – or at least this is what Peter hoped.

With that Peter touched a switch on the sleeve of his suit which activated the outside microphones located on both sides of his helmet. Immediately he could hear the faint Martian wind rustling across them.

Like the ESS, this system was normally used only for verbal instructions in the pressure of the domes before entering the airlocks. Even at several hundred kilometers per hour, the wind hardly created an audible sound on the mikes. In the background he could barely hear the nearly inaudible clicks and pops of tiny soil grains. Closing his eyes to focus, and straining to hear through the steady din, Peter picked up the feeble hint of a whistle.

"I think I heard you, Toon. Wait five seconds, then whistle again, three times, two seconds apart."

Peter placed his hand over his left mike and turned the right mike in the direction he thought he had heard the whistle. By moving his head a few degrees every time he heard the whistle, he finally focused on the loudest sound.

"Toon, try to make your whistles the same each time. I'll aim toward the direction of the loudest. If your lips get tangled up, let me know. Be sure the ESS is cranked all the way up. Now, one more time so I can focus on your direction."

This one Peter definitely heard. It was faint, near the threshold of his hearing, but audible, nonetheless.

"Okay, Toon, we're walking in your direction."

Peter paced off 10 meters, slowly, feeling Ashley's tug on his belt. Then he stopped and said, "Three more times, please, Toon."

This sequence was still faint, but louder and more distinct than the last set.

The sky around them had darkened almost completely and Peter also noticed the strip heaters in his suit were on almost continually now. He quickly calculated that at this rate, the power packs wouldn't last another half hour. The swift wind had captured the profound cold of the high atmosphere and it now rushed around and encapsulated them. It was absorbing any heat energy in its dark, onrushing path.

He paced off another six steps and ran broadside into the forward part of the MAT.

"We're here, Toon."

"I heard the bump. Starboard side hatch is unlatched."

"Thank God," Ashley sighed, obviously relieved. They worked their way around to the starboard hatch by feel.

"Go ahead, Ashley. You first," Peter offered.

A few seconds later they were both securely inside the vehicle with the hatch dogged closed. "Pressurize this pig," Peter ordered. Moments later the blue 'PRESS OK' light glowed on the panel as the trio unlatched and removed their dusty helmets.

"Well now, guys, how about this for an end-of-the-day surprise?" Toon asked with a wide smile.

"Thanks, Peter," Ashley said from behind. Peter could feel her place a hand on his shoulder.

He turned to watch her brush a few misplaced hairs out of her youthful, gray eyes. They reflected clearly back to him. Somehow, he mused, she was able to preserve her consummate appearance even in emergency situations. Her face bore the strength of French Scandinavian ancestry, her light brown hair tucked neatly under a cotton cap. There was a spray of light freckles across her slight nose and he knew well there was a set to match across her bare shoulders.

Peter surveyed the interior of the craft now completely covered with a filmy, thin layer of the fine Martin sand and soil. "I'm afraid we've messed up your MAT, Toon," he commented. "But I'd much rather be in a dirty MAT than outside in a redwind looking for one."

Toon had become close friends with Peter and Ashley before they had departed Earth. They frequently shared work assignments, even though the tasks themselves may have been outside their fields of expertise.

Toon's face was rounded; his Japanese eyes seemed to always be laughing, infecting everyone he encountered with an instant friendship and confidence. Down low on his chin was a fine patch of black fuzz that swept up beside his laughing smile and seemed to accent the perpetual grin that initiated so much natural, intimate familiarity.

"What do you say we get out of here, like *right now*?" Ashley suggested, giving way to a touch of anger she betrayed with her voice that she obviously felt toward herself for loosing her cool in the storm. Only Peter noticed, and even though they were intimate companions, even such slight embarrassment, he knew, would hurt her fiercely independent ego.

"Agreed," Peter replied. "Plug in the NAV CART and let's go home," he said, referring to the Navigation computer.

A moment later Peter saw Toon's face disfigure in distress.

"Toon, you did plug in the nav-cart didn't you?"

"Of course. But something's not right."

"What?" Ashley asked with a heavy accent on the "t," pulling herself up between the front seats.

"It won't respond to the interro-gate," Toon said in a low voice, referring to the console mounted computer key-board, as he hammered out the code again and again.

Peter turned back to look at the cargo bay wall where the logic circuits were plugged into the master computer.

"Oh boy," he mumbled.

"I don't like the sound of that," Toon commented with a deep sigh, looking straight ahead out the dust coated windshield.

"Toon, it's crushed. Looks like you crunched it when you tossed your tools into the afterbay."

"That's great... just great!" Toon said with acerbic disgust.

Peter anxiously looked back to assess the full damage, and attempted to piece things back together if possible, but it was too far gone. The little plastic plug-in module lay in several large and not-so-large pieces in his hands.

Now they were essentially stuck. The nav-cart's memory could have instructed the auto-pilot to precisely back-track their previous movements, hands off. The route to the site, which had been carefully stored in its memory was now irretrievably gone.

Toon was the head "PT" or "professional twidget," of the colony's computer engineers. He cultivated his reputation as a certified world-class genius of his craft as well as a die-hard perfectionist, demanding and giving "the standard," as he was so fond of drilling into those who worked for him.

Peter could see Toon was sick and had an instinctive feeling that this was a mistake Toon thought he would never live down, provided he lived at all.

"So we sit this one out," Ashley commented, unhappily falling back into her seat. She was a biologist, not a geologist and most especially not an engineer, and frequently reminded everyone around her of that fact. She had come along to get away from the claustrophobic domes and to help Peter out in his unending search for water deposits. It was obvious now to Peter's considerable discomfort and embarrassment that this ride was far more than she had bargained for.

"Unfortunately, it' not that simple," Peter said, staring at the dust, flowing and sweeping across the MAT's windshield and windows.

These monstrous storms swept across the barren plains and highlands as enormous, ugly clouds of reddish-orange sand and dust. The onrushing, deadly clouds, capable of bearing a hundred thousand tons of red dust were called redwinds by the colonists. This unpredictable redwind engulfed everything before it, including sunlight, at hundreds of kilometers per hour and devoured the sky in seconds. A redwind could last for minutes over a few square kilometers or an occasional monster redwind would engulf the entire planet for months.

The art of forecasting them in these early days of colonization was virtually nonexistent. After only three months on Mars, the colonists had lost two of their number and a MAT to a redwind. It had tumbled blindly off a cliff in one of the unpredictable storms.

Peter watched Ashley pinch the bridge of her nose, squinting her eyes closed, as though she wasdeveloping a headache. Then she opened her eyes and returned his gaze, looking into his eyes, sudden and steel gray; not perfect but absolute. Framed in a strong face, those steely eyes were his greatest asset and seemed to compel trust and sincerity. From under his white cotton cap, a lock of blond hair fell across his forehead, damp and dirty red.

Peter looked away from Ashley and ordered, "Toon, contact Base Camp and report our situation. In the meantime, maybe we can figure something out."

"You sure that's a good idea, boss-man?" Toon asked suspiciously, in typical form merging his weird sense of humor with a serious question and the perfect accent of a Civil War slave. "Them folks dey ai't a gonna be happy wid us-ins." No one in the inner solar system could mimic the incredible multitude of voices and a virtual encyclopedia of accents like Toon.

"Just do it," Peter replied with mounting exasperation, obviously not amused.

Toon hesitated, then with a slight glance to Ashley, flipped some switches to start his transmission, announcing, "MAT12 to base, over."

"Go ahead, guys. We've got you plotted in the middle of some red trouble, over," the BC1, or Base Camp, Command Center watch officer replied. "Is everyone okay there, over?"

"We're fine, base," Toon replied. "However, our NAV CART is, ah, disabled, and we're trying to figure this one out right now."

"Roger, gang," the BC1 Command Center replied, followed by a long pause. "New procedures require you stay put till further orders from Lipton's office."

Toon looked to Peter with disgust. "That's all we need, you know that? I knew we shouldn't even have turned the transmitter on. Now we have no other choice but to follow Lipton's procedure."

"Alright, Toon, knock it off," Peter stopped him. "The man's in charge, okay? If he's an idiot, we'll just have to work around that. We're going by the book here, and that's it."

"Toon's right, Peter," Ashley added. "Lipton's likely to tell us to sit right here till our life support runs out just to save this MAT and his own butt. He almost got fired over the last redwind incident and he's going to call this one safe even if it means sacrificing us to save the machine."

"We can't stay here forever, Peter," Toon continued. "This isn't storm season, but you never know how long these things will last. We've got life support here for no more than four hours and it's at least 20 klicks back to base. If he orders us to stay till it slacks off, we may make it and we may not."

Peter sat back in his seat. They were probably right. Lassiter Lipton, the Director of the Mars colony project, was running scared with a politician's personality. Enhancing his political future *was* his leadership style. He had not had to make a life or death decision in the project yet, but a sickening feeling swept over Peter that this may just be his moment.

"We have to wait and see what the man says." Peter said with finality. He was true to his own worst fault; an inexplicable devotion to doing things by the book. Peter activated two jets and blew a layer of dust away from the forward view shield as if it would somehow blow the storm away. But the sky had darkened, if anything. Visibility was now no more than three or four centimeters. He reached to the panel and shut the navigation beams off and switched the interior to red running lights.

An unbearable 10 minutes of waiting was broken by the welcome crackle of BC1.

"MAT 12, BC1, over."

"Go ahead."

"Peter, this is Francis," the voice continued. Peter sighed with some belief. Francis Linde, meteorology department head, was also his best friend. But his greeting was followed by an uncomfortable pause.

"I'm sorry to have to tell you this buddy, but Lipton says to stay put 'till the redwind abates."

Toon gave Peter a killing look. Ashley covered her face with her hands.

"Your last message was garbled," Peter replied calmly, raising his voice artificially. "Do you have data from Orbiter One on the extent of this storm and reasonable projections of when it may abate?"

There was another extended pause.

"Er, roger, MAT12. This data is, ah, specific to your analysis unit 42 alpha slash MAT12 bravo. Can you switch to frequency 16 for a download, over?"

"What?" Toon asked, aggravated.

"Lipton doesn't have frequency 16 in his office. Switch over," Peter said quickly.

Toon had already acted.

"MAT12, you there?"

"Run it," Toon responded.

"Peter, Francis," the deep voice began quickly. "The orbiter shows the storm building over you. According to the only analysis program we have, the probability of it breaking up is 70 per cent. But the reliability of that program is so low that it isn't even statistically significant. Lipton knows that, but it doesn't make any difference to him.

"I'm coming after you," Francis stated with finality.

"No!" Peter responded instantly. "Stay where you are. Lipton's already going to have all our butts for this. I repeat, don't come after us; we're coming in on our own."

"Be careful, Peter. Be careful," Francis warned, his voice clearly angry.

"Roger," Peter replied, switching back to the primary channel. "Our transmitter is failing. We have just suffered a total loss of receiving capability. We believe we interpreted your last orders as not to, repeat, not to stay put until storm abates. We are coming in, as instructed. MAT12, out."

"Think Lipton will buy that?" Ashley asked.

"No. We all just bought ourselves one way tickets back to earth on the next shuttle flight outbound, which if I'm not mistaken, is scheduled to depart tomarrow."

Toon sighed. "Better that than dead, I suppose."

"Oh, we're not back yet," Ashley replied drolly.

"Or dead..." Peter reminded them with a fake half grin.

"We'll fight it, Peter," Ashley added, lacing her fingers over the metal neck ring of his suit. Her warm flesh against his skin caused him to shiver. Taking a deep breath, he grasped her hand over his shoulder, his analytical mind racing.

"Okay," Peter began, offering both of them their hand held notepad computers, "the object of this game is figuring out how to get back without smashing the MAT or falling off a cliff. Both of you draw the route we took to get here as best you can remember. Be as specific as possible. You have four minutes. After that we'll average our maps and start back." Almost reflexively, his eyes scanned the pressure and power read-outs.

"Go..."

As he drew his map, Peter considered their situation. It was not good from any viewpoint. If they made even a slight error along their route they could easily die. The impact of the MAT falling off of a cliff or even a rupture of the MAT's fragile pressure hull could kill them. Impacts on boulders or sliding into deep craters or depressions could also strand them. But even these risks were better than waiting around. Peter mused grotesquely that a spectacular death tumbling off the face of a Martian cliff would be better than a slow one, asphyxiating while freezing to death in the MAT.

Yet, Peter felt strongly that it was Lassiter Lipton who really controlled this life and death decision. As the Director of the colony, he had been blamed by the U.S. Administration for the deaths of the two colonists earlier. Lipton did not take this criticism well and instead of defending his position, he turned on the colonists. In a six page statement to them he declared that any other "endangerment of life or property would be worked with vigorous administrative action." To the colonists, this was so much bureaucratic whining. In more practical terms, the survivor's punishment would be a one way ticket back to earth.

But now that the MAT was stranded, ready to repeat a disaster that had greatly embarrassed him, Lipton's hand seemed invariably forced into this clumsy trade. It was clear to Peter what Lipton's strategy was. If they did die awaiting clear skies or rescue, Lipton could easily escape criticism on the basis that ordering the MAT to return to BC1 was too dangerous. His evidence would be the last fatal accident. He could also justify his decision because of the meteorological program's determined probability of dissipation, regardless of its reliability. Furthermore, it was not storm season or a year of a severe storm cycle. Unfortunately, even the science team would have a hard time arguing with any of these judgments.

The decision to defy Lipton was difficult for Peter. He described himself as a strict, by-the-book professional. Yet he had no desire for himself, his wife or his colleague to become Lipton's first fatalities. It was a clear and straightforward decision. The instinct to fight for his life and for his companions' far overrode any trust or respect he may have had for Lipton or the system.

Peter knew his theory did have one great flaw. If the storm did abate before they returned, Lipton would have them on clear charges of insubordination. The next flight back to earth was scheduled to leave in just one sol and they would be on it without defense. So the choice was the unacceptable possibility of death by asphyxiation, a not-much-better chance of blindly smashing up the MAT in the storm, or a one way ticket back to earth. All of these options were equally repulsive to Peter, but as Toon had correctly surmised, better they risk a return than inaction and slow death.

"Alright, gang, let's have your sketches," Peter quipped, breaking the silence. He collected the two other computers and lined them in a row across the dirty legs of his suit. Then he displayed a U.S. Geological survey quadrangle map with their last position marked. He looked at the three sets of convoluted lines and attempted to summarize them in his mind and relate them to the map.

"I think we may almost know where we're going," Peter said, satisfied with all the available information.

His voice was confident and direct. "Toon, you're the driver. Take it easy. The object of this exercise is to make a liar out of Lipton. Ashley, you can operate the gear up here and I'll supervise. Come on up here and sit on the console between us," Peter said, offering his hand to assist her to the now crowded front of the MAT. He strapped her between the two seats with a spare harness.

"Toon, what's the range on the docking probe?" Peter asked in reference to the MAT's significantly powerful sonic range finder. Although it transmitted an energetic sonic beam, in the rare Martian atmosphere, it had a very short, almost insignificant range. It was designed for use only under controlled conditions as a docking aid inside the pressurized domes. The present conditions were well out of its intended working parameters but Peter had an idea he could make it work nonetheless. He reminded himself that, again, he was relying on the pressure of the wind to carry the sound.

Toon responded with his estimate of the range. "Thirty meters or so, under the best of conceivable conditions. Under these circumstances, I'd say half that, although what affect the dust particles may have on transmission of the sound, I can't say."

"What's its spread at 10 meters?"

"A meter and a half, if I remember correctly."

"Good! That's all we'll need. Ashley, direct the forward echo finder at zero degrees ahead. Toon, what's the transmitter height above the ground?"

"About 2.5 meters."

"Go ahead and enter it just like that. Have it look forward and signal distances greater than 12.25 and averaging 7.75. That should cover obstacles and depressions greater than half a meter in height or depth. Cycle the alarm subroutines through three times before reporting status. Got it?"

"Cake..." Toon said, fingers already tapping out the details. As a master programmer, Peter knew it would be easy for him.

"Wake me up when you're finished," Peter jabbed him lightly.

"What's my job up here?" Ashley asked, putting her arm around Peter's shoulder.

He smiled at her and looked lovingly into her gray eyes. With his finger he wiped a smudge of red soil from the tip of her nose.

"You're going to lock our echo finder in at 12.5 degrees, but spin it 45 degrees either side of zero degrees relative as I instruct," he replied slowly, his eyes sweeping hers again and again. "Meanwhile I'll plot our position on the map."

Her eyes silently returned his message, "I love you."

Peter was the chief staff geologist for the American base and Ashley the director of space biology. She was a handsome woman, nearly the same age as Peter, in her early thirties. After the years of education leading to their doctorates and all their training, their careers, and their partnership, had begun later in life. But their mutual, long-repressed passions more than made up for lost time.

He forced himself to look away from Ashley then back again at her with a worried, thin smile. Their eyes briefly locked again tightly.

"I can handle it," she whispered.

"I know that," his lips silently returned.

"In fact, screw it up and I'm in charge," she warned in a loud voice, then lightly rapped Toon on his head with her knuckles. "Same goes for you."

Toon simply nodded, concentrating too intently for idle banter. His brain and fingers were working furiously to reprogram the MAT's tiny mind, too busy to take in the dribble around him. Minutes later he spoke, simply, "Done. We're ready to go."

"Super," Peter sighed, his worried eyes on the instruments before him.

Toon looked around to Peter's face. For a half-second they exchanged expressionless, male glances before Toon returned a thumb's up. His straight black hair fell in a neat row across the top of his expressive Japanese eyes.

"Life's tough when your finest hour may be your last," he quipped in his best British accent.

"Helmets on," Peter ordered with a half-smile and wary eye on Toon. He felt good about his team, but not so good about their chances either way. "Pressurize suits when ready."

"Let's move it," he continued. "Toon, turn this pig in a tight left circle and let's back-track as best we can.

"Ashley, rotate echo 15 degrees port."

Silence befell them as the MAT turned slowly to the left. Their eyes followed the echo finder numbers and gyro compass. "Stop," Peter ordered when they were pointed toward BC1. The safety of Base Camp One was only 20 kilometers away, but between them and security lay a deadly, jumbled landscape.

As Peter looked his instruments over, the voice of Lassiter Lipton broke the silence.

"BC1 to MAT12, Lipton here. In the event you can hear this transmission, I am ordering you to stay where you are. When the redwind clears sufficiently, we will be sending a team after you, if that becomes necessary." He repeated his transmission, asking, "MAT12, can you read me? This is the Director, over."

"Who pulled his string?" Peter asked of no one in particular, clearly agitated at the interruption.

"Now that's real Caucasian of him, granting us permission to stay here and suffer a touch of anoxia, don't you think?" Toon inquired.

"Respectfully request permission to crank on the squelch till the clown disappears," Ashley asked of Peter.

With just a second's hesitation, he replied, "Granted. Straighten us out, Toon, and slow ahead, 25 meters."

Ashley reached up to the overhead console and eliminated all communications from BC1. Peter rationalized that they would need the silence to navigate and grope through the deadly darkness. The fact that Lipton's voice made him nauseated probably had something to do with the decision, as well.

"I'm at 25 meters and stopped."

"Turn to 40 true for 135 meters. Ashley, rotate echo dead ahead."

Two minutes later, their warning beeper sounded.

"Stopping," Toon cautioned, "Obstacle."

"Estimated distance?" Peter queried.

"Five meters."

"Backtrack three, turn to pass on your port, then ahead slow. Ashley, track it with your beam."

This relentless pattern continued for nearly two hours as they successfully maneuvered through the desert. As the MAT reached the outskirts of the most perilous part of their trek they were finally poised to run a more straightforward 12 kilometers back to BC1. The storm showed no signs of letting up.

"I was hoping we could get some slack from the weather for this phase," Peter noted, straining to see out of the opaque forward view shield.

"You mean we've come through the worst part and you'd give the contest to Lipton?" Toon asked.

"Yeah, you're right," Peter admitted. But he could not bring himself to actually hope that the redwind continued.

"So what's next?" Ashley asked. "How about a land speed record, or, how about..."

"..rolling off the next cliff," Peter finished drolly as he looked at the map. He felt he had an excellent idea where they were within 10 meters or so. The chief worry on this leg of the journey would be dodging boulders or rolling down a dune or other embankment. "250 meters at 45 degrees, and let's pick up the speed a little."

At the higher speed, the ride became noticeably rougher, even with the MAT's independently suspended wheels and balloon tires. Their echo finder could only warn them of rocks larger than half a meter in diameter, so, their movements were violent and lurching.

"Let's slow it down," Peter finally said, holding himself away from the forward panel with both hands and feeling his seat harness cut into his shoulders.

"Not too much slower, Peter," Toon offered. "We've only got two hours of life support remaining and at least two hours of distance left."

Peter nodded and resisted the urge to change the speed control lever. The darkness was devouring the MAT's batteries, the heaters struggling to keep up with the bitterly cold wind outside. But Peter also worried about the incredible beating the vehicle was taking and its constant lurching. They would not survive a breakdown.

An hour later, the lurchings became less severe as they moved away from the chaotic Fossae. These features were long and narrow depressions that lay across the desert preventing them from making a straight line path across them, even though they were now on the somewhat less bolder-strewn sands and dunes of the vast Elysium desert. The storm itself had not abated. Peter thought, optimistically, winning this one now appeared to only be a matter of surviving the trip home.

Peter eyed the radio and moved his hand to the squelch control. Ashley and Toon both gave him homicidal stares. He spread his palms apart and nodded his helmet in understanding. Then he increased their speed. They maneuvered silently for about ten more minutes. The now infrequent alarms, stopping, and turning tactic were affected wordlessly.

"Toon, bring up the life support summary on monitor three," Peter ordered.

Toon momentarily took his eyes off the echo finder to bring up the life support system data and the rest happened too fast to manage.

The warning beeper sounded as the MAT's left front tire struck a large boulder. The MAT lurched to a half stop as its gears caught the rock and rolled over it, which caused the whole vehicle to jerk, unbalanced, to the right. The right wheels caught on the edge of a crater wall, then slid down a steep embankment. There was nothing to stop the vehicle's backward slide down the sandy slope. Seconds later the rear wheels struck another bolder and the vehicle began to roll end over end until it reached the bottom of the crater where it came to rest on its top. As it finally crunched to a stop, its pressure hull breached with a slam, a groan and a penetrating hiss.

Their air rushed nearly instantaneously out of the fractured vehicle and as it did so, the moisture inside immediately condensed into a frozen fog, coating their faceplates with a sheen of red dust and ice. The three of them had slammed about their seats and into each other as the MAT rolled and now they hung upside down, blinded by the ice on their helmets.

"Ashley, Toon...okay?" Peter asked in a series of grunts, his breath knocked out of him.

No reply.

With the ensuing silence and darkness, Peter succumbed to a momentary onslaught of vertigo as he hung upside down, swinging from his seat restraints. He clawed and jabbed at his quick release mechanism, then dropped the 15 or so centimeters onto his head against the inverted ceiling of the MAT. He fought to regain his balance, frantically seeking his orientation and vision. In near panic, he scratched the ice off his faceplate with his gloved hands. Then he rose up on his knees to find the inverted figure of Ashley in front of him. She hung motionless, her hands across her chest, gripping her harness tightly.

Peter scratched the ice off her faceplate and peered inside. With the dim lights of her helmet instruments, Peter could see her staring back at him, unmoving. He feared she must be dead. He grasped her helmet and forcefully shook it.

"Ashley! Ashley!"

She looked back at him, upside down, and smiled an inverted grin. Then she moved her lips. He shook his head. There was no power. The MAT was dead. There were no communications. They could not talk…

She moved her hands along the breast of his suit and toggled a switch. "If I'm not mistaken, we're basically outside now, ace," she said, her voice now ringing clearly through his helmet.

His head clearing from the near panic of the moment, Peter realized that he was disconnected from the MAT's power and he had to rely on his suit's power pack now. As Ashley had informed him, with the MAT's pressure gone, they were, in effect, outside.

"Toon!" both cried together as one, Ashley simultaneously releasing herself from her harness.

Toon, still hanging inverted, had already scraped the ice from his visor and was struggling to turn on his suit communicator. Ashley reached through his harness and toggled the switch.

"Toon, you okay?" Peter asked.

"This is great, just great," Toon complained with wide eyes and a crazed smile on his face. "....upside down on a Martian desert in a full blown, freakin' hurricane, ... unemployed, no less, and we'll probably freeze to death before Lipton actually gets to pull the plug himself!"

Peter slapped Toon's harness quick release causing him to fall with a thump down onto the MAT's inverted roof. "Now you can scratch 'upside down' off your list," Peter said with the most arid amusement he could muster.

The three of them sat in silence for a full five seconds looking blankly at one another.

"In case anyone was wondering, this vehicle is totally screwed up," Toon observed first, and then Peter saw it too, eyeing the sand and dust drifting through the fractured canopy's three centimeter crack.

"How badly? Can we turn it over, patch the hole and repressurize?" Peter asked in an artificially brisk voice, desperately trying to assess their situation.

"No way," Toon began, waving his hands, embellishing the obvious in a toothy grin. "She's too heavy to invert, the breech is too wide to patch, and then what? What if we did actually manage to flip her over; then what? I know! We could rig the odometer and claim it was ready to turn in for a new one!"

"In case you haven't been paying attention," Peter shot back angrily, sick of Toon's out of place humor, "we've got 30 minutes of air left, at best, on the suit packs and 25 minutes heat. If we could turn the pig back over, at least we could have another 20 minutes on MAT air and power."

"Oh, boys," Ashley whined mockingly, "let's be friends here. There may not be time for apologies later."

"You're right... Toon," Peter replied, as calmly as he could manage, placing his hands to either side of his helmet as if to force himself into logical thought, "what do we have to work with?"

Peter looked directly at Toon just as his face abruptly flashed into absolute astonishment; his features arrested, open mouthed. Peter continued to look at him, straining to comprehend his problem. Then he turned to look behind him at Ashley only to see her legs disappear backward through the open hatch of the MAT.

Toon lunged toward the hatch. "Somebody pulled her out," he said following.

"Toon, wait; Toon!" Peter shouted after him. All they needed was the three of them lost together or one at a time on the Elysium plain in a redwind. But after only a second and a half of looking around the MAT and finding himself all alone, he too quickly crawled out after them.

As soon as his body cleared the hatch, he felt the welcome grasp of hands on his shoulders and heard the voice of Francis Linde through his helmet, even though he could not see him.

"Peter!"

"Francis!" he bellowed. "I can't believe it..."

Francis grasped Peter's helmet and pulled him face to face. "Good God Almighty, son, I thought we lost you over the edge. We watched you go right over and tumble down the side. Scared the living hell right out of me."

Peter could barely make out Francis' profile through the diffuse dust. "You got Ashley and Toon?"

"Yeah; they're sitting safe in MAT1 as we speak."

"We're okay," Ashley's voice replied over the suit speakers.

"Let's get on back to BC1," Francis continued. "Lipton's already torqued to the max. You wrecked MAT12, I ripped his vehicle off to come get you, and if that's not enough, this redwind is going away even as we speak."

Peter felt a sinking feeling like he had never felt before. It would appear that Lipton had made the right decision. Had they followed his orders and sat it out, they could have made it safely back to BC1. Now firing them was just a matter of processing the documents. Their careers were over. The flight back to earth was only a matter of waiting for the next sunrise.

"Move it, pal," Francis prodded, pulling Peter's arm. If nothing else, Peter felt a surge of hope at the thought of escaping the redwind and at hearing the cool, intelligent voice of Francis Linde. Seconds later, he had stumbled up the steep incline of the crater wall clinging to a nylon line attached to MAT1.

"MAT1!" Peter cried, realizing it was Lipton's personal vehicle. And Francis had stolen it to come and get them. But how did Francis manage to maneuver about in the storm and find them wrecked over the side of a crater? How could Francis actually watch them drive over the edge?

Just as he saw the insulated wall of the MAT, a hand reached out for him. "Steady, Peter; you okay?" It was the voice of Geoff Hammond.

"Geoff, what...?" Peter began.

"Somebody had to come and get you guys," Geoff began. "We've been trying to reach you by radio for over an hour, telling you to stay put." Geoff's hands directed Peter toward the hatch of the MAT. "Now, open it and get in quickly. I'll close it after you. I have to stay and recover the line."

Peter felt an instant twinge of indignation at being treated like a refugee, but it quickly passed as he bolted into the already crowded MAT. He, Toon and Ashley were jammed into the two back seats.

Peter watched Francis turn around as far as he could and speak to them from the driver's console. "By the time we get back, this storm will be a bad memory. Unfortunately, Lipton will probably be leading the welcoming committee. For the first time in his idiotic life, he's called one right. And it's not like we don't have egg on our faces...."

"More like the whole chicken," Ashley added.

"We've been on the radio calling you for nearly an hour," Francis continued as they waited for Geoff to return. "When we couldn't raise you, we figured you'd either turned it off to keep from listening to King Tutt or... worse."

Peter felt stupid as he nodded and looked away from Francis. He was beginning to feel as though he had not done much of anything right. Turning off the radio for any reason, particularly in an emergency, was strictly against procedure and in hind-sight, mostly shy of common sense.

"Who can blame you?" Francis continued. "After the first ten minutes of his speech I finally got annoyed enough to come and get you. It was obvious to everyone and his cat that Lipton was going to trade you for the vehicle so his Washington buddies would have a little less to joke about at cocktail parties."

"So how did you manage to... appropriate his personal MAT?" Toon asked fighting back a smile.

"How do you think? I nearly had to drive over his silly deputy Hernandez to get it into the airlock. Now why steal Lipton's MAT, you may ask? Good question for which I have a good answer. Not having any suicidal tendencies to draw on, I rigged this up for our little joyride because it has high resolution terrain radar, better known as HRT!"

"What?" Peter howled, the rest of the party shaking their heads from the ear piercing volume in their helmets. Overwhelmed, he stammered, "Then he was going to let us die when he had the means to come and get us?"

"That's right, my friend."

"Why?" Ashley asked, looking to Peter as though she were just as angry as he felt.

"Because he thought no one knew he had it. He had the HRT sent in on a shuttle after the last redwind accident and one of his Marines installed it for him. *He* wasn't going to get caught in a redwind. He could have come and rescued you personally except for two good reasons."

"I don't think I want to know," Peter responded truthfully.

"Number one," Francis continued anyway, "he didn't want the colony to know he was the only one with HRT. He ordered his Marine to keep quiet about it. But when one of the techs was doing maintenance on the MAT, she found the forward sensor and traced it back with software. It's hidden in the navigation routine."

"So what's the second reason?" Toon asked.

"Lipton's a certified, card carrying coward. He wouldn't have come out for you in that storm if he were escorted by a thousand dancing girls tossing rose petals under the wheels. Face it, guys, our leader is a lousy transient wimp."

The hatch sprang open momentarily as Geoff bounced into his seat with a bundle of line coiled in his hands.

"Let's head back, team," Francis said. "Keep your pressure suits buttoned up, just in case. Peter, Ashley, see if you can strap yourselves together for the ride back. We only have a single harness for the both of you."

As he powered up the MAT, the forward console sprang into a brilliant, false color representation of the desert outside. The HRT showed the surrounding terrain as clearly as if there were no storm in progress at all.

"Selfish ass..." Peter began, admiring the display that would have escorted them back with complete safety.

"You're much too kind," Ashley replied.

"Listen, Francis, Geoff," Peter began, "we really don't know how to thank you...."

"Cut it out. You'd have done the same for any of us," Geoff replied sincerely.

Peter sighed and rested back against the seat as Ashley pulled the lap belt snugly around them. With a hiss she plugged their life support systems into the MAT. They only had eight minutes remaining on their personal packs.

Geoff was right; Peter knew he, too, would have come out after his friends. That concept alone painted the clearest distinction between Lipton and the colonists.

Francis and Geoff concentrated on the task of navigating home as the dust cleared from the sky. The atmosphere of Mars was so thin that as the wind velocity dropped lower than aerodynamic support velocity, the dust simply fell out of the sky. Even the smallest particles were lost quickly as there was little in the way of support from the thin atmosphere.

In minutes, the sky rapidly began to lighten, from black to a deep red, finally revealing the full, light-pink Martian atmosphere. Everything here was a part of the learning curve. This storm was a good example. It had been one of the shortest lived redwind on record. Peter was sure Lipton would be prepared to take full advantage of that.

Peter felt Ashley's body press firmly against him. He rested his gloved hands on her leg. She responded by laying her hand gently atop his. He knew the next hour was going to be the most difficult of his life. The colonists all defined survival itself in terms of whether they could make a go of it on Mars. At this moment he did not think the chances of the Colonists in this tiny MAT were very good. And he despised the man who was about to make that choice for them.

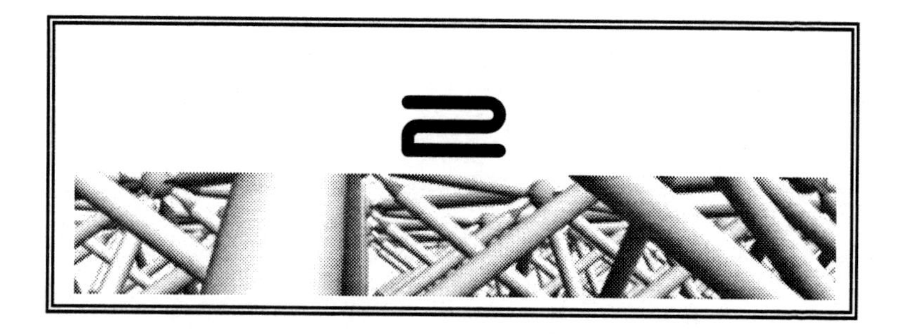

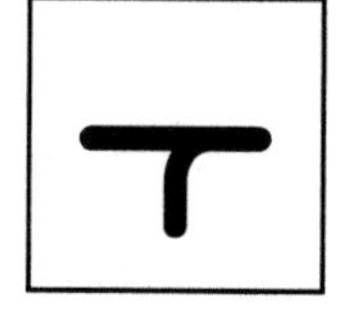

he MAT carrying the five colonists made its way back to BC1 at its top speed of 60 kilometers per hour. The sun was just beginning to set as the Martian "sol" transitioned into night, but the dust had already completely settled and there was sufficient light to see the well traveled southern trail named "Interstate 3," more commonly referred to as I3.

Days and nights on Mars were nearly the same as Earth days – but just slightly longer. Each Martian "day" was called a "sol". It was understood that the word "day" meant an earthy cycle of 24 hours, but the term "sol" referred to the Martian equivalent of 24 hours, 39 minutes and 35.247 seconds. The colony preserved the same time standard of hours, minutes and seconds as on earth, but their clocks just ran a little longer than on earth for each Martian sol.

"MAT1, BC1 control. We've got you in sight now at six kilometers south on I3," radioed the control monitor.

"Roger. We should be dockside, main terminal shortly," Francis replied.

The Director wants to see you in his quarters, right away," the control monitor informed them, his voice heavy with premonition.

A neutral "Copy," was all that Francis would return.

Peter's mood was black. In his view, a chance to be assigned as a colonist on Mars was one of the highest honors that could be bestowed on any human. Tens of thousands had applied for every one who actually got the nod to go. Even worse yet, no one had ever been fired or removed before. A handful had been unable to adjust and had given up and gone back to earth on their own volition, but no one had ever been fired and shipped back home in disgrace.

Base Camp 1 sprawled out before them across the Martian desert like a reticulated web: planned with careful forethought, uniformly engineered and purposefully executed. The original design consisted of a set of substructures that were to radiate out from the central dome in neatly ordered spokes. As it was constructed, the colony actually survived the demands to constantly change, and the plan retained its proposed regularity over the years of its construction. From the expensive lessons learned in the construction of the first International Space Station, BC1 was designed by an ingenious systems engineering plan that severely penalized politically inspired construction changes while encouraging and richly rewarding coherent system and design improvements.

BC1 had been established on the Elysium plains by the second American expedition to Mars. They left behind the base of their lander and a fair amount of un-recycled waste. Later colonists quickly made good use of the latter and fenced in the lander as a kind of shrine for future generations. It took nearly 50 years to establish a permanent presence on Mars, and BC1 was close enough to the relatively warm equator to have become the prime site for the full time American base of Martian operations.

The ability to survive on this planet long term was only now possible, although it still required periodic re-supplies from earth. The humans that had arrived on Mars determined to stay labeled themselves "colonists" because they had no plans to ever return to their home planet.

There were forty three permanent colonists at BC1, not including the fourteen part-time administrators, miscellaneous visitors and visiting scientists. The numbers varied, give or take a few, dependent on the assigned tasks and status of the supply ships. The population had steadily grown after each earth re-supply mission along with the authorization of more colonists. The restrictions seemed to be slowly

BASE CAMP ONE – THE UNITED STATES

Brett English

relaxing all along, dependent entirely on re-supply costs, government fiscal commitments and the drive toward the long sought after goal of self sufficiency - the much longed for sol when they would require no more life giving supplies from earth.

The MAT receiving doors of the main terminal gaped open for the vehicle as they neared and centered on the strobing medium queue, now brilliantly flashing in the gathering darkness. Francis dutifully, and according to procedure, turned the simple docking procedure over to the onboard computers. As elementary as such a maneuver was, the cost of repairing even the most simple of damages to a MAT was so overwhelming that no chances were taken at all.

This realization occurred to Peter like a physical blow. He had not even returned with his MAT at all, leaving it ruined in the Martian desert after clearly and unarguably refusing to follow orders and who knew how many procedures. It had been drilled into all of them again and again: procedures and orders are the stuff of life. Unquestioning obedience was equivalent to survival. Peter had failed the test, and now he would face the consequences.

The MAT receiving doors slammed shut behind them and the air rushed into the airlock. As the standard blue PRESS OK lights glowed on the outer panel, Francis cracked the door valve and a final hiss signaled the pressure had been equalized.

The window outside the airlock was crowded with faces. Peter could see Fabian Gorteau, the Nobel Prize winning physicist standing at the front of the group which seemed to be made up exclusively of colonists. One lone face, however, was not that of a colonist, but one of Lipton's Marine guards.

Francis turned around to face them. No one outside or in had made a move to open the doors. "Listen," he began, "we're all in this together, got it Peter? We're in this as a team. Let me handle Sir Thomas," he said, using the irreverent nick-name they had hung on Lipton.

"No, wait, Francis, no," Peter said. "I made all the decisions, and you only came out to fix what I started. There's no way you're going to take the rap for this, period - you, Geoff, Ashley or Toon. I take full responsibility."

"Sorry, but Francis is right. We're a team," Geoff insisted.

"That's right," Toon added.

Peter felt Ashley squeeze his hand tightly as he reflected on how quickly things had spiraled out of control.

BC1 Leader Lassiter Lipton had been appointed to his job as a political favor by the previous U.S. president. When "the other" party came to power just prior to launch of the colony from earth, it was much too late to replace Lipton. He had already sunk too many fingers into the political and scientific pies of the mission. Yet, with no specific scientific credentials, he was clearly unqualified for the job. Lipton made an attempt to cover this by personally hiring a group of "scientific advisors." These so-called advisors turned out to be a lawyer who specialized in space treaties, a nutritionist friend-of-a-friend who brilliantly erected a diet program empire, and a real estate whiz who had contributed royally to the President's ill-fated reelection attempt but was a veritable prodigy at cultivating his own connections. Although powerful, Lipton was becoming the controversial meat of the invisible but formidable Washington social circle gossip.

Lipton's selection of his odd gang was not quite so popular in the scientific community. Fortunately, Lipton offset his initial error by acquiescing to the National Academy of Sciences whom he allowed to select the colony department heads; a decision he quickly regretted.

Yet when it came to manipulating the bureaucracy, Lipton had no equal on either planet. He could name his price or call any shot by adroit manipulation of the system or simply by stalling it. He had no peer when it came to maneuvering with under the table politics, or funding. Only the threat of exposing his own lack of technical knowledge successfully steered Lipton clear of the science of the colony. Sorely tempted as he was to make his own inroads into the mission's scientific objectives, he was intelligent enough to keep a watchful distance. Recognizing this, the true scientific contingent of the mission was able to somehow secure their end of things and keep him out whenever possible. It was an uneasy, unspoken truce, and a very unstable one at that.

When the pair of colonists panicked in a redwind and tumbled to their deaths off a Martin cliff, a newly inaugurated Administration in Washington quickly took action to fire a full volley at Lipton in an undisguised attempt to force his resignation. Lipton, in true character, chose to draw on political favors and pull various strings until the pressure stopped. This left his personal culpability essentially unchallenged. He saw the scientific cadre as responsible not only for the accident but guilty for not coming to his defense. Isolating the administrative arm from the scientific branch had created gross rifts in the colony, and both sides were guilty. Unfortunately, the colony was thus rendered unstable both politically and administratively.

Lipton's decisions became conservative and self protective in the extreme. Up to now they had affected only the bureaucratic end. Lives had not been endangered by his ongoing, personal quest for more control and political security. But the stakes had been raised and everyone's hand called in. Unfortunately, now it was Lipton who held the trump.

Peter watched from his seat in the crowded MAT as Fabian Gorteau finally made the first move and opened the airlock door. As it swung away, he stepped into the airlock and popped the canopy on the MAT. The Marine guard moved in closely behind him, following right on his heels.

Gorteau stopped in his tracks, then swung around and faced the young, fresh-faced Marine. "Son, you are interfering with this procedure," he said sternly, aiming his entire polished, professorial demeanor toward the Marine over his bushy eyebrows. "Please, step out of the airlock."

The Marine looked momentarily intimidated. Then he collected himself and replied in an artificially deepened voice, "I have orders to escort this party to the Director's office without delay."

"Yes, son, and so you shall," Gorteau assured him. "But not before the scientific community of this colony assures ourselves that this party is in good health. Now if you'll kindly step out of this area, I give you my word you shall have the pleasure of their escort in a few moments hence."

The Marine started to respond, looked over his shoulder at the others, then backed away. "I'll be waiting at the main passageway," he replied, trying not to look intimidated.

"Thank you, corporal," Gorteau said patiently as the Marine walked away, then offered his hand to those in the MAT and assisted them out.

Peter was the last out, and Gorteau seemed to be waiting for him. For a moment, Peter feared it would be Gorteau to fire the first volley. Gorteau was the president of the International Union of Planetary Scientists and a member of nearly every other major scientific body on earth. He was also elected to be the spokesman for the colony scientific cadre, a position he held without rival or competition.

"My boy, we are happy to see you alive," he said to Peter, embracing him. "You did the only thing you could do under the circumstances, and all of us give proper thanks to God for your safe return." He stepped back and looked reflectively at the five of them coated with Martian dust. With their helmets off, their faces were streaked with sweat and red dust, and they were all obviously fatigued. Gorteau felt a wave of sympathy for them.

"I am afraid that you are about to walk into the most convoluted, illogical, politically motivated thrashing you have ever had to endure. And I am fearful that something professionally tragic will probably come about as a result of all this in the short term. Lipton has been waiting for some happenstance to reduce the prestige of the colony's scientific team, and I am afraid this is going to be his golden opportunity. I can do nothing to stop whatever reproof he may levy on you, but I can promise you that we shall fight it for all we are worth. And I can also tell you that if he returns any of you to earth, that you have my word that you shall be reinstated here at a subsequent date, and I will stake my personal reputation on that promise!" he said resolutely, slapping his fist into his palm.

Then Gorteau looked into Peter's eyes and grasped the neck ring on his suit, tugging it toward him. "Now go on and listen to the oddest collection of pathetic logic you will ever hear strung together in a single discourse. But also remember that his wretched wisdom has little meaning in the long term, and that, after all, the truth has always, and shall always, endure. We are with you all in spirit."

Peter sighed and forced a thin smile as he answered, "Thank you, sir," truly moved by this level of support. Although he was in his mid sixties and Peter half that age, somehow the age and wisdom of Gorteau seemed substantially greater.

The crowd of colonists that had managed to squeeze into the airlock applauded at Gorteau's speech. But Peter realized it was Lipton who stood directly in the way of independence for all of them.

True self sufficiency from this tyranny was the only way the colonists secretly believed they could relax the strangle-hold of government bureaucracy on their lives. The permanent colonists viewed the overwhelming number of regulations as unnecessary and intrusive. Yet their lives were entirely dependent on re-supply from Earth every two years. A study initiated by the colonists themselves had projected when the colony would become self sufficient: some ten Martian years ahead. The two central issues cited in the non-political Bronson - Chaikin

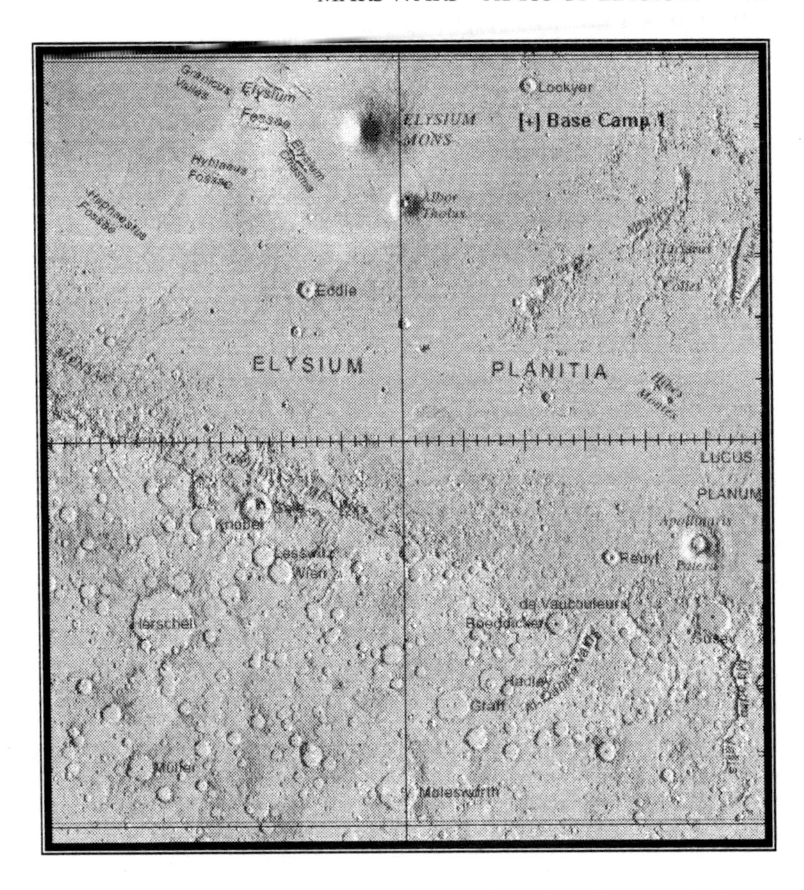

Report were energy and water, without which the colony periodically literally ran down. With enough water and energy, the colony could produce all the oxygen, crops and raw materials they required to cut their links with the re-supply ships. Of course, as all colonists of history had discovered, the doors of trade would be necessary and welcome as a factor in the quality of their lives. But the Mars colonists were feeling the uncomfortable encroachment of a massive, earthly bureaucracy breathing constantly down their necks. The focal point of that complaint was Lassiter Lipton.

No single colonist really thought much about independence in the political sense, but they longed for the ability to govern themselves as an independent organization. They looked forward to the sol when they at last waved a long good-bye to the likes of Lipton and his entourage and got on about the business of developing their own rules to live by. Lipton was not so much a tyrant as he was a symbol for their lack of autonomy, as individuals and as a colony. Lipton represented the chain that shackled them to earth. He represented the central threat to their ultimate permanence.

Few colonists cared whether or not they were called U.S. citizens. They all had loving memories of their country, but it was hundreds of millions of kilometers away in a long, sweeping interplanetary orbit and they had long since left the earth for good. Now they were first generation Martians and they were fiercely proud of that.

It was that very thought process that forced the rift in BC1. The U.S. government had set aside separate housing for the colonists, so that they were each assigned their own living units. These were constructed apart from the temporary administrators and visitors quarters. Inadvertently or not, this caused the two groups to develop socially isolated viewpoints. Though there were notable exceptions to this, principally among visiting scientists and the colonists, the two groups usually went to great lengths to remain apart. The only common meeting places were generally the offices and laboratories. Even here there was back-biting and resentment between groups. The personnel officer, Lisa McConnel, herself a "transient" (this was the kindest term the colonists used for the temporary personnel) was constantly engaged in mediating disputes between the groups.

Not many of the transients thought much of life on Mars. The colonists had frequently expressed between themselves that one either loved Mars or hated it and it took no longer than four weeks to sort it all out. Yet a stint on Mars was a career boosting guarantee for a transient. Whether one made the four to six year career round trip with one of the multi-national space agencies, or under the auspices of industry or a university, time on Mars rated the highest financial and professional rewards upon return to earth. Most of the transients were after this reward; few of them could understand the colonists' way of thinking. The transients had their own view of the colonists, referring to them irreverently as "squatters". They generally viewed them as oddballs, idiosyncratic and whining.

To most transients, time on Mars was a sentence to be served. In their thinking, Mars was the bleakest of bitterly cold, lifeless deserts, and in their point of view, only the most deranged could imagine remaining there for life. As the weeks passed, to those who longed to be earth-side again - those who crossed each sol off of their calendars - the thinking of the colonists became more bizarre after each passing sol.

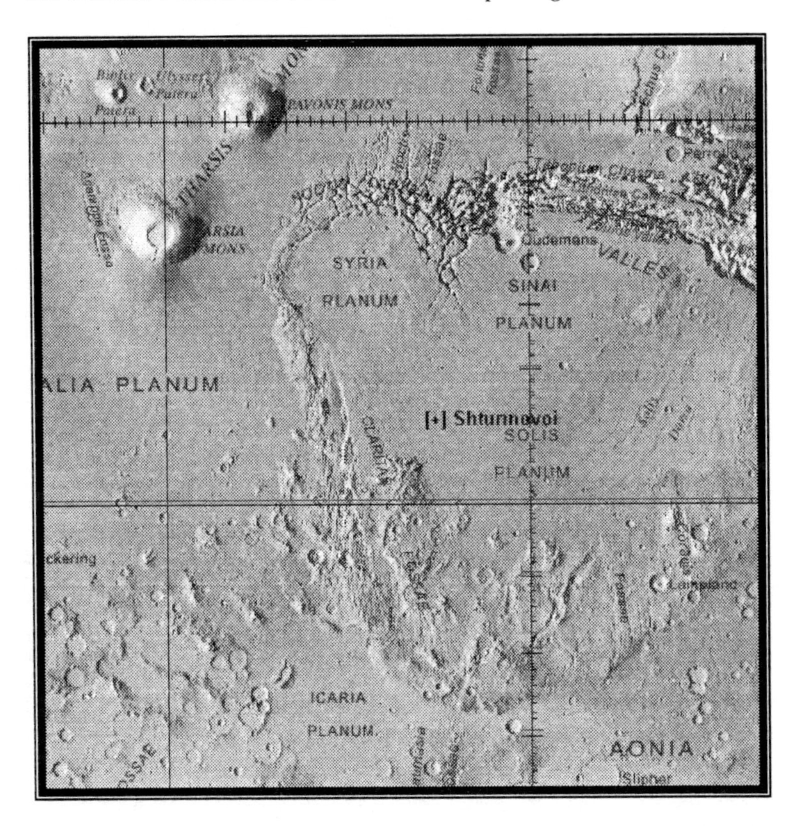

But Mars was not inhabited by the American base alone. The Reunified Soviet Empire – or RSE nations – had also set up a base on Mars some half a decade after the permanent American presence was established. Their base was named Shturmovoi, after the famous Russian gold fields, and was located some 2065 kilometers southeast of BC1 across the southeastern fringe of the *Amazonis Planitia,* skirting just south of the Tharsis mountain range and located near the center of a feature called *Solis Planum.* The residents of BC1 called it "Sun Lake" because of its historic legacy, not necessarily because of its direct Latin derivation.

The various Latin names for the Martian features were not all friendly to the English tongue, so the Martian geologic features began to take on more palatable names such as Sun Lake. The huge, cavernous *Valles Marineris* was simply christened "Mariner Canyon". *Amazonis Planitia* became the Amazon Plain and so on.

The Soviets intentionally arrested what they laughingly referred to as "the colonization nonsense" from the outset by rotating everyone off Mars without any exceptions. There were only a few radio exchanges between the RSE base, which the colonists referred to as the "Little Kremlin," and BC1 due to the political tensions on earth, and the distance between the bases was greater than any Soviet or American vehicle was nominally designed to safely cover.

At BC1, a re-supply ship had just arrived in orbit three sols earlier. The colonists were always excited at the arrival of each new ship. To the colonists, the transients would finally leave and take their poisoned perspectives with them. The fresh transients were usually easy to live with for awhile, and for the first few weeks, they were almost always wide eyed and pleasant.

Peter raised his hand at the crowd. "Excuse me folks, but I believe we've got a date with destiny. There's a Marine guard somewhere out there who doesn't think we colonists can find our way over to the executive suites. So if you'll excuse us..."

"Tell Sir Thomas he can go take a walk outside in his BVD's, Peter!" said a roughened voice in the crowd.

"I just may do that, Louie-Louie," Peter replied to the roguish looking facilities engineer whose real name was Louis Louis. Any other messages from the motley, disorderly masses?" Peter continued, obviously enjoying it all. Several responses were delivered all at once; a mingled, irreverent assortment of suggestions, some of which were anatomically improbable.

Francis, Ashley, Toon and Geoff were soon laughing despite themselves, enjoying the spectacle of Peter directing the crowd so expertly.

"Well then," Peter finally sighed, "that settles it! It's off to the dungeon." Offering his arm to Ashley, he inquired, "Shall we?" Accepting Peter's arm, Ashley looked at Gorteau.

"It seems you are in good hands, my dear," he said with a smile that was not as light-hearted as the mood of the crowd.

Five minutes later, the Marine escorted them into Lipton's office, executed an about face and stood, hands folded behind him, at the door. Peter looked about him at the immaculate room. Hung on the walls were the evidences of Lipton's career: his Harvard Ph.D.; his commissioning certificate in the U.S. Naval Reserves; photos of a white water rafting trip with the former President; and a hand written note from the Chief Executive, asking him to accept the appointment as Director of the Mars Base. All were framed in clear, polished glass. There was nothing out of place here. Everything was ordered and correctly positioned; no dust, no lint, no disorder of any kind except the five of them, a stark contrast to the image of the office.

Francis was not going to be intimidated. "Well, I don't know about the rest of you, but I'm going to have a seat," he said as he sat down squarely in a white cloth-covered chair, a cloud of micro-fine red dust rising around him.

Ashley smiled at him, sighing, "Oh, why not?" then also sat down on a pristine cloth couch. Her eyes closed briefly, savoring the comfort of the deep cushions.

"Can you imagine hauling that useless thing over 220 million kilometers of space?" Toon asked, eyeing the couch.

"Well… as a matter of fact…" Ashley sighed sincerely, her eyes still closed. Peter and Toon joined her on the couch at once.

Peter looked at the walls then back to the rigid Marine who did not even shift his eyes. Here stood a living tribute to Lipton. The Marines stationed at BC1 had always been a sore point with Peter and the colonists. Lipton's position was equivalent to an ambassadorship, hence he rated Marine guards. But the usefulness of Marines on Mars was a joke, at best, as they served only as ceremonial stewards. Yet the cost of each human in the colony was quite extravagant in every respect, especially in the life support equation. Ceremonial humans were a cost far greater than Peter felt they could afford.

As Peter reflected on this, Lipton entered the room, and the Marine guard snapped to attention. "At ease, corporal," Lipton said smoothly. He briskly approached his desk from behind them, holding a folder in front of him. PERSONNEL: CONFIDENTIAL was stamped on the front in red ink. Without sitting down, he laid the folder on the desk and walked around to its' front, facing them. He wore white pants and a navy blue, double breasted jacket, his eyes framed in silver rimmed glasses. His black hair, just rimmed with the right amount of silver, was slicked back and flawlessly in place. This vestment was known throughout the colony as "Liptonesque."

Lipton was groomed for power, both figuratively and literally. Born the son of the United States Ambassador to China, he had been schooled and tutored for greatness. The way he carried himself in public, the way he spoke and moved his near-perfect features, the mode of his impeccable, starched attire, implied power and position. It was difficult not to feel intimidated in his presence. He had a precise vocabulary, and he used it circumstantially. He could perform individual surgery with his words and used them to terrify or solicit as he saw fit. He was the consummate confidence man.

Peter truly believed that had it not been for his greatest personality flaw, Lipton could easily have been President of the United States or Secretary General of the United Nations. But he was as trustworthy as a shark and a master manipulator. These flaws, despite his best efforts, he could not hide. His own political party felt the best place for him was on Mars. With Lipton safely millions of kilometers away, they all slept much better.

"First let me say how personally gratified I am that all of you are alive and unhurt," he began in his best pretentiousness, his voice lilting and calm; a voice that was all too familiar to all of them, and one which particularly grated on Peter. "I don't think the program could stand another tragedy, especially identical to the one before, when we lost two of your brothers."

Peter seethed with anger. Each word was uniquely Lipton, singularly arrogant and pompous. His clear reference to "your brothers" was meant to set the colonists apart, and yet it was Lipton who otherwise verbalized the solidarity of the community. It was one of Lipton's greatest assets, the ability to politicize one precept while actively driving the colony toward another. It was the intellect of a careful politician at work. Words were the essence of his vocation, while the manipulation of human behavior was exclusive of the evident truth.

"We have a grave situation here, and one that we need to clarify forthrightly," Lipton continued. "But, I'll skip the superfluous and get right to the point. There is a serious matter of either overt disregard for orders on all of your accounts or, at the very least, a blatant disregard for procedure. It has cost us an irreplaceable asset today and, frankly, all of you are lucky to be alive."

"Here comes the thrashing," Peter whispered quietly to himself.

Lipton moved behind his desk and sat down, looking up at them over his glasses. "I have listened to the recordings of all communications channels and it is useless for you to deny conspiracy to disobey a direct order, Dr. Traynor. The same applies to you, Dr. Linde. I won't bother to ask you for your defense, because that will come out in the ensuing investigations."

"Woah... wait a minute," Francis interrupted. "You may not ask for our side of the story, but I'm going to give it to you anyway."

"Francis, let me handle this," Peter began, holding out his hand to Francis.

"That is absolutely unnecessary, gentlemen," Lipton said, instantly taking advantage of the disparity between Peter and Francis. "To abbreviate these proceedings, let it rest; I already know the full story."

"You prejudged a meteorological condition which directly endangered these people's lives," Francis said angrily. "The Science department made the decision to go out and get them using the only device that could have saved their lives; your vehicle on which you hid the only HRT on the planet."

If Francis thought he had landed a significant blow on Lipton, he was mistaken. Lipton forced himself to suppress a flashing smile. These scientists were obviously amateurs when it came to judicious forethought, a term Lipton liked to use frequently.

"You have constructed your defense based on a number of faulty arguments," Lipton began, sitting far back in his chair, raising his hands to his chin, palms together.

"Point one: the high resolution terrain radar was installed by my technician to test the device in this environment. It had not been tested; in fact, it had not even been taken out of the hangar before today. I did not hide it, as you accuse; rather I was following flight hardware procedure which requires a whole battery of tests be successfully accomplished before equipment can be certified for use under normal conditions, much less an emergency where peoples' lives are at stake. Once certified and passed through normal process, more units would have been requested.

"These are procedures of which you must be intimately familiar. To use the term 'hiding' is somewhat fearful, and I am curious at what stresses may be responsible for that kind of erratic thought process in my senior meteorologist. The paperwork for the acquisition and installation is validated and available for your inspection, if you so chose."

Lipton sat silent for a moment to let the full impact of his statement set in. He had carefully crafted this defense long before HRT had even arrived in Mars orbit.

The only spontaneity in his personality was in linking his carefully crafted arguments; it was his greatest personal asset. Reality, even life, was a series of well constructed, carefully linked controlled events. Like an unfolding game of chess, Lipton's image of a successful man was of an individual who played the game as many steps ahead as it was possible to manipulate; it was, after all, judicious forethought personified.

"Point two, the meteorological event you say I had prejudged was an event whose probabilities of dispersion were predicted to be very high, and you, Dr. Linde, wrote the program. I'm not quite sure what that says for your professional confidence or your abilities as a meteorologist or both."

Francis' face turned scarlet as he sat forward in his seat. He looked for all the world like he was about to stuff Lipton in the nearest filing cabinet. But before he could respond, Lipton continued.

"Point three, the scientific community does not make life and death decisions here, I do. That, as you must know, is well documented in the compendium of procedures you took an oath to follow."

"That redwind program was written using earth based algorithms," Francis exploded angrily. "We were evaluating them here on the local conditions, and they had no statistical significance. That is something you should know and understand! And why didn't you volunteer your MAT and personal radar to help these people?"

Peter thought Francis was losing it. He had obviously fallen back on simple emotion to carry his argument, and it wasn't working.

"Are you relying on faulty meteorological instruments, Dr. Linde?" Lipton persisted. "Are you passing advice to the administrative chain of command based on these readings? And, again, for reasons that you well understand and are documented, you and I are strictly prohibited from using uncertified hardware in the environment."

"Those instruments were all we had," Peter spoke up, coldly.

"And Dr. Linde's prediction was incredibly accurate, was it not, given the presumed statistical unreliability of the product?" Lipton pressed, tossing his final ace on the table.

Francis sat back and sighed. Peter knew it was over. The only defense left was to cross the desk and choke the life out of Lipton. The advisability of that was not quite clear at this moment.

"I have carefully considered all the administrative options here, and have consulted my deputies on this issue," Lipton persisted, looking down at his desk and opening the personnel file with a slow, dramatic sweep of his hand.

Peter could almost feel his blood pressure rise, and felt Ashley stiffen beside him.

"Dr. Traynor, you seem to be the central antagonist in this unfortunate drama," Lipton began. "My staff and I feel that we have no choice but to deport you back to earth on the next flight, which, if I'm not mistaken, departs BC1 tomorrow morning. As for you, Doctors Alcyone and Linde, I cannot do without your services here, so you will be required to remain, but will be subject to a disciplinary hearing."

"No way, Lipton!" Francis said standing and pointing his finger at the man.

The Marine quickly interposed himself between Francis and Lipton.

"Your behavior is unprofessional, Dr. Linde. The matter has been decided."

"You haven't heard the end of this, Lipton. We will not allow you to ruin these people's lives."

"You and whomever else you are referring to have nothing to say in this matter. It's over and the decision has already been rendered," Lipton said calmly, still seated, looking up at the embittered Francis.

"Francis, let me...," Peter said, rising and placing a hand on his shoulder. "Say whatever you like now, Lipton. But I intend to see that a full blown investigation is launched into your behavior here at BC1 the minute I set foot back on earth. I have as many contacts on the Hill as you do. And if you think a redwind can stir up some trouble, wait till you see the cloud I send over your horizon!"

"Considering our lives were in imminent danger," Ashley said angrily, rising to her feet along with Peter and Francis, "and you didn't even have the guts to offer your vehicle and its radar to help us, even on a volunteer basis, well, I think your punishment is hardly fair..."

"Not fair, Dr. Alcyone?" Lipton interrupted. "Nothing in your actions of today speaks of fairness or equality or of thought for others or the equipment on which all our lives depend. Mr. Hammond was driving the vehicle which nearly struck my deputy..."

"I was driving, Lipton! And I regret I missed," Francis screamed.

"Don't bother with more deception; I have the videos," Lipton said, rising slowly, his voice painted with feigned fatigue. Then he looked at the Marine. "Corporal Tyler, ensure that Dr. Traynor and his belongings are on the lander in time for departure tomorrow morning."

"Just a minute, Lipton," Francis continued. "Send me back. If you're going to send someone, send me. No? Coward! If you send me back you know I'll be waiting for you when you get back to earth."

"And I'm leaving, too," Ashley added, "After all, he is my husband."

"Oh, I see; secretly married, are you? In violation of your contract? Not merely shacking up?" Lipton replied viscerally, a brief smile flickering across his face. Then he regained his control and backed away, having inflicted exactly the right injury at the point he intended.

"As you are aware, Dr. Alcyone, I alone determine seating assignments in the shuttle, and you will have to wait untill the next flight out to join your husband, some 24 or perhaps 48 months hence," Lipton said with a fully developed sneer, eyes flashing and boring into hers as he reveled in his display of power.

"You have one extra seat, and I intend to be in it," Ashley swore, her voice choking back emotion.

"If you make that threat once more, I'll have you incarcerated from now until the after the ship departs," Lipton said with some pleasure. "And that would mean no final, tearful goodbyes, now wouldn't it? Any additional comments from you, Dr. Alcyone?"

Peter took a step toward Lipton, fists clenched. The Marine moved again to check the threat.

"Let me promise you this, jerk," Francis screamed at Lipton as the Director folded his file and began to walk toward the door, "you will pay for this one way or another."

Lipton opened the door and walked out as Francis shouted, "Get out of my sight, Lipton!" Then he grabbed a glass sculpture off the table in front of him and sent it crashing against a wall.

The Marine, a full six inches shorter than Francis stepped up to them and warned, "I think all of you had better be leaving – now!"

Peter dumped his shock in a remarkable second of exquisite recovery and looked the Marine dead in the eye. "You know Corporal," he said evenly, "there's something I've been wondering about for years that has suddenly become very clear to me."

The Marine didn't respond, so Peter allowed the question to lie and ferment in the air until the Marine blinked.

"Now I know why a pantywaist such as your boss needs seagoing bellhops like you; no offense."

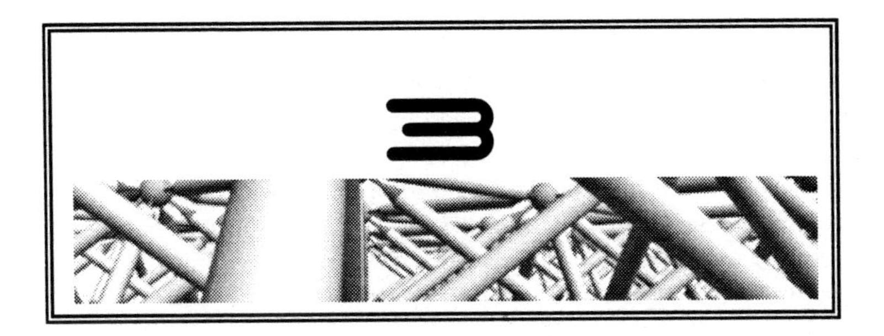

eter refused to engage in any discussions and walked quickly to his quarters. There he began packing his gear, tossing a few items toward his flight bag and smashing the rest against the wall. Minutes later, his communications console, tagged C2 by the colonists, lit up. He let it ping a dozen times before finally answering sharply, "Yes."

"Peter, I'm on my way," said Ashley, who severed the transmission before he could respond. When she arrived, Francis was standing outside Peter's door, his back against the wall, arms folded, wincing with every frequent thump, bang and crash from within. He had still not even changed out of his pressure suit.

"Francis," Ashley said, "go home and get some rest."

"No, I need to talk to him. I just wanted to give him some time to get it out of his system before I went in."

"Francis, go home. You can talk to him in the morning. Please," she said, then gently kissed him on the cheek. "I don't think we will ever forget what you did for us today. In case no one else noticed... you saved three lives, and you should know just how much we appreciate that."

Francis, choking with emotion, touched her cheek with the back of his hand, leaving a red smudge on her face. He nodded stiffly, forcing a weak smile.

"Dad?" came a voice from far down the passageway. It was Francis' son, Jack. He had qualified as a Mars colonist after receiving an advanced degree in astronomy.

"Dad, is that you?" Jack said, walking closer in the dim light. Francis' face looked worn and somehow older. The former Navy special forces member had taken beatings before, literal and verbal. But, somehow, this one hurt worse than usual. The reason was clear enough; he had lost his best friend, probably irrevocably. And the whole affair had come about because of someone he hated passionately.

"Jack, escort this man home, please," Ashley asked him.

"You okay, Dad?" Jack questioned. "Where have you been? I've looked all over for you." The lanky man in his late twenties looked genuinely concerned for his father. He had only once before seen his father in such distress and that was after the death of Francis' wife - Jack's mother.

Francis nodded. "Yeah, I've been right here. Let's go on home." Jack and his father walked slowly away, the son's arm draped lovingly over the shoulder of his father's filthy space suit.

When Ashley turned around to face Peter's door, it was already open.

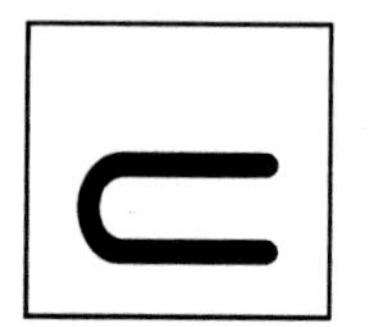

ome on in. You can watch me pack," Peter said, tossing a bag of climbing equipment over his shoulder and against the wall.

Ashley walked into Peter's room, closing the door behind her and began to cautiously step over the piles. The room was completely trashed. She looked at him but he would not return her gaze. Peter sensed that she did not know what to say or how to say it, so he sat down on the side of his bed, rubbing his hands together, and said nothing.

For three years they had been friends, lovers and secretly married partners. She had spent more nights in this small room than in her own. Now that he was leaving, she would be losing a major part of her life. But Peter knew that she could not follow him, even if she wanted to; Lipton controlled their lives right now. Peter had gained his one-way ticket out by trying to save all their lives. Ashley obviously agonized over the conflicts welling within her.

Peter had crawled out of his pressure suit, but still wore his cotton, insulated underwear. Ashley picked up a night shirt from the jumbled pile against the far wall, and removing her clothes, slipped it over her naked form. She touched the room's light controller and turned to faced Peter in the near darkness of the space. Her lithe form was embedded there as a fractal image; a muted, diffused shadow imposed gently against the darkness.

Peter looked up at her dimly illuminated shape. He stood and took three steps toward her. The pain assailed him at once, forcing him to stop abruptly. He wanted to speak the words that could somehow cause Ashley to leave with him. This pain was far worse than he could have imagined. Love consumed his soul and forced his mind into an irrational, emotional anguish he fought to control.

Yes, he must leave, but a part of him; a part of his vitality, would be ripped away from him and left behind. In a most literal sense, his soul was being left behind, hostage to a mindless, loveless bureaucracy and the political ravings of an indifferent system.

An ache arose in his throat and solidly arrested his speech. He could not speak at all, for if he dared to form the words now, they would come forth as sobs. He did not want that to happen at any cost. These emotions he would abide alone.

Ashley came slowly to him, and as she did, he could discern her fragrance, the sweet essence of her flesh and perfume, coalesced into an erotic, impassioned sense of intense and powerful enchantment. His sadness was not driven away by this new sentiment, it was made more profound. He wanted somehow, desperately, to comprehend how he could leave her, leave here, forever. The loneliness on the crowded planet of his birth would suffocate him.

His bitter thoughts were voided as she lifted her hand gently, fingers extended and closed, and stopped it inches from his face. Slowly, with a lingering motion, he extended his hand toward hers, matching her fingers with his, but not quite touching. With an almost imperceptible motion, he brought his hand so close to hers, he could feel the warmth of her fingers. Still, they did not touch.

Peter took a half step toward her and passed his lips across hers, also without touching, feeling again her warmth, her sweet breath, against his face. Ashley laced her fingers through his with a single, exacting motion. Then she kissed him, deeply, urgently, knowing the dawn would enjoin no more promises.

Peter interchanged part of his sorrow instantly for passion. He knew well that the night would not last forever, and with its climax, the pain would return more powerfully and more inescapable than before. As their lips touched, he could taste her tears blended with his own.

Just for a fleeting instant, before he was consumed by the fires of this oddly powerful fusion of sexual rapture and sorrow, the fear returned. In that final sentient second, he desperately prayed that he could chase it away; make the love last forever.

Yet, no matter how reality raged outside their bond, for now he was lost; lost to the passion and sadness that ravaged his reasoning. He commanded the fear away, from here where there was no reason, only purpose. Here in the brilliant darkness there would be no baleful red sky, no cold and distant sun, and no pain. In the darkness, fingers and naked flesh were his eyes, much more perfect, more consummate instruments of explicit detail. And with this vision of infinite definition, in this merciful world devoid of logic or hurt, he alone irrevocably commanded his destiny and bent time itself.

Without hesitation Peter altered his embrace, lowering Ashley gently to the floor and swiftly, forcefully slipped the night shirt away.

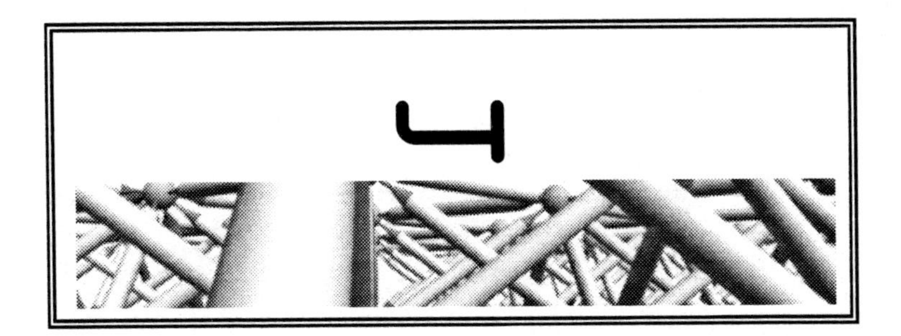

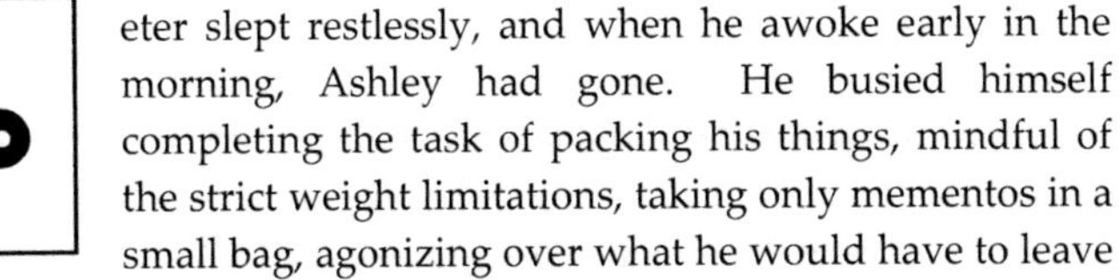

Peter slept restlessly, and when he awoke early in the morning, Ashley had gone. He busied himself completing the task of packing his things, mindful of the strict weight limitations, taking only mementos in a small bag, agonizing over what he would have to leave behind. He then went to work on his pressure suit; scrubbing the cloth, polishing the metal bands and cleaning the transparent visor.

If he was going to fly out, he was going to fly out looking his best. If he was going to feel miserable and defeated, he was not going to let anyone know. Besides, he mused, Gorteau had promised he would find a way for Peter to return. If there was any scientist on the two inhabited planets who could pull it off, it would be Gorteau.

Although it pained him greatly, Peter had no time to dwell on Ashley's absence while rushing to finalize the selection of his meager treasures. He tugged the last zipper on his single bag closed when the inevitable knock came at his door.

"Dr. Traynor, you have five minutes before we have to leave." It was the voice of the Marine.

"Let's go now," Peter offered, feeling a surge of oddly placed exhilaration as he slapped the door open with the palm of his hand and faced the surprised Marine.

"... Ah, er, you have five more minutes, Dr. Traynor..."

"Don't need it. Let's get a move on..," Peter said, noticing Gorteau standing with his back to the wall.

"Ah, Peter. Good to see you in such robust spirits!" the physicist said, slapping Peter's pressure suit. "My God, for a man on his way to exile, you look wonderful," he said, sizing Peter up. "And we won't waste precious time," Gorteau continued, solemnly turning his back on the Marine. Peter nearly had to suppress a smile. Gorteau was famous for his grand, embellished speech and body language when he was wound up.

"The power brokers have contrived to rob us all of talent and time, so we shall make the best of what we have. While you were resting, I took the liberty of contacting John Bakker Hamilton of the Princeton Space Studies Institute. I have arranged a visiting faculty position for you until we can return you here. Hamilton assured me you may pursue any path you like while there. The pay is commensurate with any similar faculty position. Is that to your liking?"

"Of course, but..." Peter stammered, truly surprised.

"I have also discussed your situation with several officers of the National Science Foundation and the American Academy for the Advancement of Science. They assure me, as I already knew, that they were all fully aware of the intolerable scientific situation here. I believe the word used most often in connection to this administration was "appalling", which I properly assured them was a gross understatement.

"Nonetheless, I have assurances from several members that the President is aware of the colony's situation and that your predicament will be brought to his attention in the coming weeks, as opportunity allows. No one I talked to seemed to think there would be any problems returning you here forthrightly. As you know, President Clarke would like nothing better than to see Lipton out posthaste."

"Dr. Gorteau, I really..." Peter began truly flattered.

"Don't be resistant, Peter. You deserve much better that what you've received. If the mob of incompetents who portend to call themselves bureaucrats can not reward you for your worth, then, by God, your own community will! Now, let us be off to the transport. I think your brief ambassadorship back to the home planet will do all of us good. While you are there taking care of some important diplomatic calls for the rest of us, we'll be here rooting out the kakistocracy."

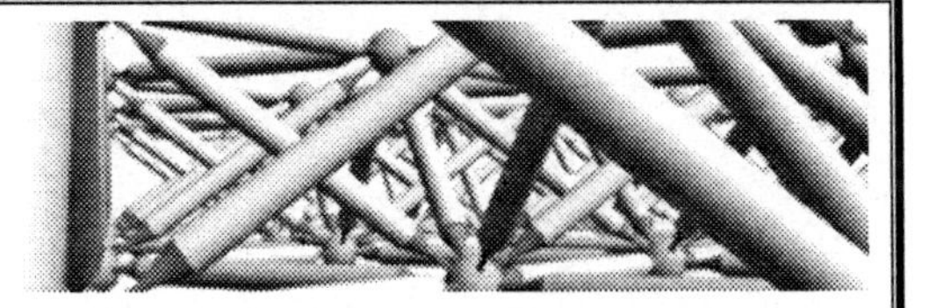

THE MARTIAN CALENDAR

January	**February**	**March**
April	**May**	**June**
July	**August**	**September**
October	**November**	**December**

S	M	T	W	T	F	S		S	M	T	W	T	F	S		S	M	T	W	T	F	S
1	2	3	4	5	6	7		1	2	3	4	5	6	7		1	2	3	4	5	6	7
8	9	10	11	12	13	14		8	9	10	11	12	13	14		8	9	10	11	12	13	14
15	16	17	18	19	20	21		15	16	17	18	19	20	21		15	16	17	18	19	20	21
22	23	24	25	26	27	28		22	23	24	25	26	27	28		22	23	24	25	26	27	28
29	30	31	32	33	34	35		29	30	31	32	33	34	35		29	30	31	32	33	34	35
36	37	38	39	40	41	42		36	37	38	39	40	41	42		36	37	38	39	40	41	42
43	44	45	46	47	48	49		43	44	45	46	47	48	49		43	44	45	46	47	48	49
50	51	52	53	54	55	56		50	51	52	53	54	55	56		50	51	52	53	54	55	

- One Martian year equals 668 Martian sols.
- One Martian sol equals 24 hours 39 minutes and 35.247 seconds.

- Martian Seasons at Base Camp One - On the Elysium Desert of Mars

	Duration
Spring	194.54 sols
Summer	177.10 sols
Fall	140.92 sols
Winter	156.04 sols

The Martian Calendar was developed by Dr. I. M. Levitt, former director of the Fels Planetarium in Philadelphia. The author acknowledges Dr. Levitt's kind permission to use the calendar in this book.

Gorteau talked as they walked toward the public passageways. Turning to the Marine he said, "Come on son, you're holding us up. Where is this planet's military presence when you need it?" Then he turned and flashed a wink at Peter.

The Marine sighed with exasperation. "... eggheads," he murmured quietly to himself, but loudly enough that Peter heard him.

Gorteau walked faster, obviously in a hurry. Peter matched his pace, but switched on his suit's portable air conditioner as he felt his body heat rise. Gorteau was spinning an elaborate plan to "short circuit the administration's objectives," laced with frequent winks. As he spun his wild tale, the Marine's eyes darted back and forth, as though he were struggling to remember the details of Gorteau's fairy tale to pass on to his superiors.

Peter could not help but reflect on this moment as a wild dream. He was marching to exile off planet on a moment's notice, being escorted personally by one of the century's greatest scientists who was spinning an outrageous yarn designed to provoke the government staff. Regardless of Gorteau's intentions, Peter could not help but burst out laughing loudly when the physicist got around to his plans to "...perform a grand prefrontal lobotomy by excavation of the treasures contained in the temporal lobes of the face on Mars."

"Laugh now," Gorteau mused, his back to the Marine, and fighting to suppress his own outburst, "but wait until Lipton sends an expedition to check it out!" He looked over to the Marine who was quietly mouthing "...face on Mars... temporary lobes..."

Peter was certain that such a juvenile abstraction on Gorteau's part must have been contrived just to lift his spirits, and it was working beautifully. Yet with this thought, he realized he had not considered Ashley's absence. He had almost reached his destination, and as he rounded the corner to the airlock vestibule, he desperately hoped that she would be there waiting for him.

She was not, but most of the colonists were. As the Marine saw the huge assembly of colonists jammed into the vestibule, he paused, and muttered, "... well kiss my ..."

"Peter, we wanted you to know just how much your service here has meant and how much your service as Mars' first envoy to earth will connote in the future," Gorteau enunciated loudly, hand outstretched at the group. They responded by cheering heartily.

The message console above the airlock door scrolled, "BON VOYAGE PETER - HE SHALL RETURN!"

Peter's eyes darted about the room quickly, scanning the faces for Ashley, who was nowhere to be seen. No rational words had been spoken in their final, libidinous encounter that Peter could remember. He loved Ashley more deeply than he had ever realized until this moment and wanted to at least tell her as much in parting. But it appeared he would not have that opportunity. They seemed to be parting under her terms of final recall, which he knew was surprisingly different for every woman.

The assembly pressed onto Peter, crowding out these final painful moments. Each seemed to have some final words of encouragement and a touch which he returned as long as he could carry a smile. He did not want to short change a single individual there. Yet, too soon, his burst of sentiment began to fade back again into the pain of missing his Ashley. But even as he thought about Ashley, Francis' face appeared from the pressing crowd.

"Peter....," Francis said, grasping his hand in a secure embrace. "Listen... I don't know how to tell you this..."

"Stop it, Francis. I know already...," Peter replied, gently slapping his face with his gloved hand. "Dr. Gorteau, has made plans."

"Yeah, I dialed the numbers for him," Francis replied immodestly.

"We're going to take care of Sir Thomas while you're gone, don't lose any sleep over that ass."

"Oh, I see. Shall I rent a two bedroom flat at Princeton?" Peter asked most sincerely.

"Not to worry. You heard the idiot yesterday. He can't do without my services. He'll wish he had...," Francis replied, his voice husky with hate and rage.

"Sir, you must depart now. We've already used up all the contingency time," the Marine reported. Peter looked to the faces of Francis, Gorteau and his friends.

"Guys, listen, thanks for everything...," Peter started, his voice choking. "Godspeed to all of you, and God bless you all."

"Godspeed to you, Peter," Gorteau said, grasping his hand one last time.

Francis grasped his hand and forearm tightly. "Take care, compadre. Things around here ain't over till their over."

Peter turned loose of Francis' grasp. Francis responded by gripping his hand and arm even tighter as if to reassure him. "Come back on the next ride or I'll kick your butt."

Peter could only manage a quick nod of his head, as he turned away toward the gaping maw of the airlock. The applause followed and continued as the Marine's hand slammed down on the door and it sealed closed, the air hissing out and carrying with it the spirit of his parting friends.

Peter glared at the Marine, who did not dare look at him or the crowd pressing at the inner window. To Peter, the whole affair had all the melodrama of a Nazi prison scene; the slamming of the door, the hissing of the escaping air, the crowd pressed to the window. Yet, even through this morbid thought, Peter managed one last theatrical smile and wave to those outside.

At last the airlock stabilized to the slightly lessened pressure and the outer door sprung open into the MAT hangar. Another Marine awaited him there, dressed in the spotless and shiny red and silver Marine pressure suit.

"Corporal Tyler releasing the prisoner to your custody, Lieutenant Quinton," Tyler reported with a sharp salute to the Marine officer standing at the open door of the MAT.

"Very well then, Tyler," Quinton replied, returning the salute.

"I'm not your prisoner, Marine," Peter informed him sharply, his voice giving way to a backlog of tightly packaged rage.

"If Dr. Lipton says you're my prisoner, then you *are* my prisoner," the officer replied flatly, tossing his helmet over his closely shaven head with an obvious and well practiced flip of his wrists.

Peter did not reply but leveled a long, murderous stare squarely at him. The Marine officer returned it with blue, piercing eyes. Lieutenant Quinton looked as if he were an old hand at brawls who realized the man in front of him was not going to back down without a confrontation. Peter knew that the Lieutenant had only arrived two sols ago as a replacement and it appeared that he was not sure if the crowd on the other side would come through the airlock to join any fray that might ensue. To Peter's supreme satisfaction, the Lieutenant looked away first.

Corporal Tyler appeared to have correctly sized up the situation as momentarily stable, caught the imperceptible nod from his superior and stepped back into the airlock.

"Whenever you're ready," Quinton said to Peter with impudence, looking at his watch, rounding the MAT to the driver's door.

Peter watched him with intense resentment, made him wait, then slowly donned his helmet. He turned and faced his friends and gave them a thumbs-up before he slid into the MAT. The Marine then made his point by depressurizing the airlock before Peter's door was fully closed, nearly jerking it out of his hand.

Quickly, Peter decided it was better form to give his friends a final salute rather than flash Quinton an extended middle digit, but it was a close call. The officer spun the MAT's wheels and headed down US 1 toward the Robert Crippen Spaceport in silence.

Peter popped the hatch on the MAT even before it slid to a stop at the base of the launch pad. The oddly shaped lander extended above them some sixty meters over the fused Martian soil, its composite carbon gantry arced around the ship. Peter was the last passenger to arrive. The others were already strapped into their seats.

Peter looked to Quinton and said, "Don't bother. I know the way." Then he slammed the hatch hard. He looked up to the bank of cameras and waved a salute to them. The image was undoubtedly the number one show at BC1.

The white room was a tiny anteroom sealed to the open hatch of the lander. It was pressurized to lander pressures, so Peter had to first enter an airlock followed by an air shower to remove any traces of Martian dust.

As he entered the white room, Peter removed his helmet to greet the two white room technicians, known as the "close out crew", and adjust his inner collar ring. They were not colonists, though one of them, Mark Teiner, had indicated an interest in staying permanently on Mars some weeks ago. They both greeted him with congenial smiles and hand shakes.

"Sorry to hear about your troubles, Dr. Traynor," Mark said sincerely.

"Thanks, Mark, I appreciate that."

"Don't have to take a leak, I suppose?" Mark inquired in a virtual whisper, turning his back to the other tech, now preparing the hatch for closure.

Peter looked at him with some surprise.

"No," Peter replied, in a mocking whisper, "I took care of that earlier."

"It's really no problem; really...," Mark said again, nodding his head almost imperceptibly toward the bathroom known as "the can".

"The can's locked and out of commission, boys," the other tech replied.

"Well, I guess that settles it then," Peter replied with finality, shaking his head and wondering about all this concern over his toilet habits. He lowered his helmet on his head and pressurized his suit. Just before he entered the lander's low hatch, he looked back to Mark, whose face was masked with total frustration as he stood staring at Peter.

"Never seen a real global *persona non grata* before, I guess," Peter mused to himself. And with that thought, Peter realized he was the first human ever to be involuntarily expatriated from a planet. That idea did not necessarily improve his outlook.

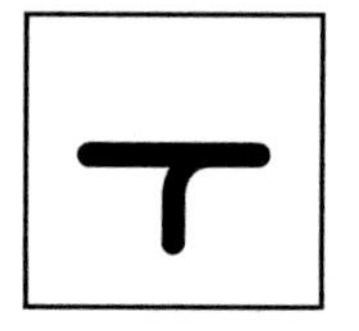

he earth shuttles came in cycles; one was continually in route, following a standard Hohmann trajectory. Each was piloted by a three member team. This shuttle, the U.S. Space Vehicle Robert H. Goddard, had just arrived at BC1 3 sols before and had ferried eight people down: three new colonists, three admin types and two United States Marines.

Meanwhile, back on earth, the next ship was being readied to leave outbound on its long trek out to Mars. That ship, the U.S. Space Vehicle Singleton, was a new design interplanetary shuttle that could carry double the supplies and passengers.

The vehicle that ferried passengers from the huge orbiter to the Martian surface and back into orbit was piloted by two astronauts and could carry a maximum of eight other passengers to and from space. One astronaut always remained in orbit with the mothership.

The passenger runs were made first, to and from the surface. Following the passenger runs, the personnel module was removed from the lander, attached to the orbiter and replaced with a massive cargo canister which was then landed by remote control at the U.S. Robert Crippen launch complex. These replenishment runs were vital to the survival of the colony. If one failed, with proper rationing, the colony could survive until the next supply ship arrived, but it would not be easy. Thankfully, not one had ever failed.

Once the cargo canister was unloaded, the lander was launched by remote control back to the orbiter. After docking in orbit, the ship departed for its cyclic visit to earth to pick up more supplies and exchange passengers before its next run to Mars. Two such ships were in constant motion between planets, each fulfilling its cyclic missions.

s Peter entered the lander's rear hatch, he stood on what would be the rear bulkhead of the ship when it was in the horizontal position, and, of course, the other passengers who were inclined with their backs to him, feet and legs above them. As he entered the tight fitting passenger module of the lander, he twisted his gaze upward to force an end to the simple vertigo of the compartment's vertical mounting. Peter walked on the rear bulkhead to the ladder he would climb to reach his rearmost seat, being careful not to step on the imbedded locker doors. These lockers held the personal possessions of the crew and passengers. As he climbed into his seat, Peter could hear one of the technicians latching the locker that held his own bag.

He lay carefully back against his seat and tugged the straps firmly around himself. His ears popped momentarily as the hatch was closed and sealed. Peter then plugged his suit into the ship's air and communications. The voices of the pilot, commander and launch control rang through his helmet.

"Affirm, launch control," the pilot relayed. "The last passenger is in and hatch is sealed. Launch minus eleven minutes and counting. We have 28 minutes remaining in today's window."

The launch window referred to the amount of time available to the crew to launch into the proper orbit to rendezvous with the orbiting mother ship. Each sol there was only a single window of half an hour to launch for a rendezvous that could be safely accommodated with their fuel load.

Peter sighed and regretted not having said a few parting words to Ashley; thirty seconds was all he needed. Now it would be at least 270 or more sols until he could procure a secure voice link to tell her the personal things he so desperately wanted to say. As he lay with his back to Mars, in the long minutes that followed, with his tender recollections of the evening just past, Peter cursed his brooding mood and what it had cost him. With a growing depression, he listened dispassionately to the dialogue around him that hastened the finality of this separation from everything he held dear.

"Minus six minutes and counting. All consoles report you are go for a nominal launch," the control center reported to the crew, followed closely by, "We have a hold at five minutes and 57 seconds. You have lost cabin pressure.... wait one... wait...wait...yes, your hatch is open, lander."

"Yep, the hatch is open. What the hell? I thought the close out crew was clear of the white room!" the pilot said, her voice betraying some anger, knowing they should be clear by now according to the procedures.

"Roger. The Personnel Accountability Console reports they're all accounted for and proceeding on their way back as we speak, post haste," control replied. "Suggest you see if you can fix it yourself and we'll hold the close out techs at the perimeter of the blast danger area. The hold should not affect the window."

Peter strained his helmet around to look at the hatch, just two meters below him. To his astonishment, he saw the interior handle turning. In a second, even as the pilot was still unstrapping herself to check the situation, the hatch opened, and the helmeted face of Ashley appeared.

"Ashley!" Peter cried with absolute amazement.

"What are you doing here?" the pilot asked, standing on the edge of her seat some four meters above Peter, seeing Ashley at the same instant.

"Just along for the ride, folks. Please keep your seats," she replied.

"Ashley!" Peter repeated again.

"You already said that, babe," she replied, calmly unlatching the number one locker at her feet and tossing it out the open hatch.

"What the hell is going on here? Now, what do you think you're doing?" the Commander roared as he, too, looked back at Ashley just as she tossed the number two locker out the open hatch.

"I'm lightening your load, Commander," she replied, slapping her gloved hands together. "You're fueled for a specific mass and since I'm coming along, well, I've just equalized your loading." She then turned the handle and sealed the hatch.

"Lander, control; please advise," launch control asked briskly. They, as well as the entire base, were watching through the cabin's mounted camera as Ashley sealed the hatch and began to strap herself in beside Peter. Throughout the halls of the colony, cheers rang out.

"Stowaway. Tossed out two lockers. Looks like we're going to miss the window." The Commander swore violently and unlatched his helmet.

Ashley squeezed Peter's hand as she lay back on her seat and looked over at Peter with a radiant smile. "I didn't get to say how much I loved you before you left," she said innocently, flashing her best girlish smile. Peter gasped, still propped up on his arm, looking down on her with wide-eyed astonishment.

The voice of Lipton came calmly through the communications net. "This launch attempt is not canceled. We'll miss the window if we have to remove her from the danger area. Bring the close out crew on back and continue with the count."

Ashley looked to Peter and winked. He then realized that his shrewd wife had this entire affair calculated to the minute, carefully timed to the individual action. And Lipton was apparently following her plan, whatever it was.

"We are in violation of our launch procedure, Mr. Director," the Commander warned. "I cannot launch..."

"You WILL launch if I direct you to launch," Lipton shot back tersely.

"We are in violation of multiple launch criteria here, Mr. Director," the pilot returned sharply.

"Pick up the count in 30 seconds on my mark," the launch director replied methodically, procedurally taking his orders from Lipton.

"Mr. Director, our extra passenger just tossed out lockers one and two," the pilot apprised control. These were widely known as the Director's personal lockers, containing Lipton's confidential mail and mementos. Ashley suppressed a guffaw. The rest of the colony did not bother, laughing loudly.

Lipton was livid.

"I hid in the can," Ashley mouthed to Peter. Then he realized that Mark had attempted to warn him.

"Pick up the count in ten seconds," Lipton said tightly. "You will launch this vehicle. We cannot risk the lives of every one in this facility due to the irresponsible actions of a few," Lipton said, already apparently beginning to formulate his plan to have Ashley and Peter jailed on their return to earth.

The Pilot took her seat and began strapping herself in for liftoff, shaking her head at the Commander who was spitting out unrepeatable half sentences detailing impossible human positions.

"Mark, minus five minutes, 57 seconds and counting," the launch director reported in a monotone.

"Minus five minutes; five minutes to launch."

The ship's four auxiliary power units (APU's) sprang into life, sending a high pitched whine and vibration throughout the ship. Peter's blood raced. He had hoped never to leave Mars again in his life, but as the moment of flight drew near, he gasped at the anticipation of liftoff.

Ashley squeezed his hand. He loved this woman, and, as far as he could tell, she had unquestionably given up her career, and perhaps her freedom, for him. The love he felt for her caused his face to flush with passion, oddly misplaced but blending with this moment of sheer, lip-biting apprehension.

"Minus three minutes and counting. All APU's up and running at 105 percent full power. All aero surfaces are powered and verified...," the pilot read off her checklist aloud.

"Standby, flight console...," warned a computerized voice from launch control. "Hold count at minus two minutes, thirty seconds."

"Crap! What now?" Lipton swore aloud.

"Loss of flight critical downlink," the communications officer reported.

"20 minutes remaining in launch window. Just over four minutes APU fuel remaining," the flight dynamics officer reported.

"We're sitting on a hot candle up here, guys," the pilot alerted control of the obvious.

"Give me a status, now, and hurry up," Lipton said tightly in his lip-mounted microphone.

"We have lost flight data downlink from CERTS-1 and CERTS-2," the communications officer reported.

"What do you mean the Earth sats are lost? How can they be lost?" Lipton demanded, speaking of the two deep space satellites that fed the colony all communications services from the earth, including certified flight data relay functions. Although 18 minutes delayed, the transmission was timed carefully to enable a coordinated data stream that was essential for a safe launch

"We've lost the downlinks, sir," the communications officer reported again. "I have no indication as to why."

"Launch director, switch over to the local flight units and pick up the count," Lipton ordered. He knew the ship and BC1 computers could handle the job as uncertified data, although it was not normally affected in that mode.

"Sorry, Dr. Lipton. I'm in a priority constraint condition. I'll have to have paper before I can resume the count," the launch director replied calmly, coining an antiquated phrase from the early space program. He knew his limitations and could act no further until Lipton signed a legal waiver of the constraint condition.

"Bob, fill it out and hurry up," Lipton demanded harshly of his deputy administrator, Robert Hernandez.

Hernandez's fingers virtually flew over his keyboard, generating the short document with Lipton electronically signing it even as Hernandez checked the boxes. Quickly they sent it electronically to the launch director's consol.

But as the bureaucracy plodded along in launch control, the pilot and commander of the lander were engaged in a rather colorful deliberation of their own.

Finally, the launch director satisfied that all was in order, continued, "Stand by to pick up the count on my mark. On my mark the count will resume at minus..."

"Whoops... wait a minute folks... hold it right here...," the Commander said. "Flight crew has decided to put the brakes on this mother, right here, right now."

"You can't do that," Lipton said on the network. "I have the authority to authorize proceeding with this launch and have already waived the constraint violation."

"Yeah, right," the Commander shot back dryly. "And I have the authority to back off any mission I see as potentially unsafe. Now why don't we just unload our little stowaway, repack our lockers, count all our marbles and try again tomorrow. Who knows, maybe we'll all wake up tomorrow and the local circus will have packed up its tents and gone home." Then he signaled the pilot with a thumb down to switch off the APU's.

"Pick up the count now!" Lipton screamed at the launch director.

"APU's powered off," the flight dynamics officer reported.

"Sonofabitch!" Lipton swore, slamming his headphones down on his console and stalking out of the room to the raucous cheers of the dozen or so colonists manning consoles in launch control.

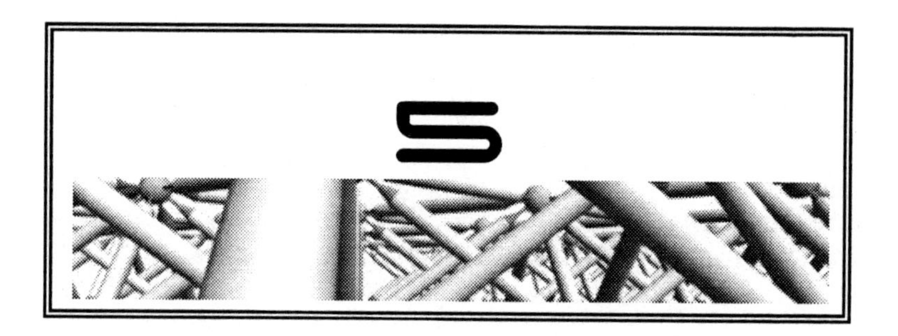

eter lifted his helmet off and looked quickly to Ashley. "What's going on?" he demanded breathlessly.

"Can't talk here...," she replied, removing her helmet, bracing for the commander who had just reached her seat on the way down.

"Okay, lady, let's have it. I want to hear this particular story real, real bad," Commander Cartwright began, braced against the bulkhead, hovering over and leaning on her seat.

"Sorry, pal. You're going to have to speak to my attorney on this one," she replied evenly.

"Well, let's hope you've got a good one, sister, 'cause you're going to need the best. You know, Siggy and I were just talking about you. As far as either one of us can determine, you're the first interplanetary space hijacker in history. That ought to net you at least four lifetimes in federal prison."

"Cool your jets, Commander. Or I just might have to stuff you in one of your lockers," Peter shot at Cartwright. Ashley looked with outright wonder at her usually mild tempered spouse.

"Yeah!" she added with a chuckle.

"Laugh now, my little space twins, but if I'm not mistaken, I just may have you both in leg irons on our way out of here."

"The close out crew is on their way back, Ian," the pilot reported, climbing down the seat rows, landing beside Commander Ian Cartwright.

"Plan B," Ashley returned. "Contingency."

"I need a beer... real bad," Ian said, looking at his pilot, Sigourney Michner, otherwise known as Siggy.

"Yeah," Siggy chuckled. "On this planet, you'll find it right next to the clown's tent." Then she looked at Ashley and Peter, still strapped to their seats and shook her head with a rigid, turned-down smile.

"You know," Commander Cartwright said, "I've flown at least 14 times, and not once, not one time, have I ever, ever encountered a pack of lunatics like this." Then he ducked out the hatch, followed by the pilot.

"He's right, you know," Peter replied to Ashley who kissed him deeply. "Plan B must be magnificent."

"It is," she replied with unexpected enthusiasm.

Close out crewman Mark Teiner arrived at the launch pad ahead of his fellow technician and passed Cartwright and Michner walking away from the elevator.

"When is transportation arriving to pick us up?" Siggy asked.

"Mike, give 'em a ride back to BC1," Mark suggested, walking backward, directing and pointing to his fellow technician.

"Don't you want any help safing the lander and unloading the passengers?" Mike asked.

"Come on back when you're done, for heaven's sake," Mark returned in an aggravated tone, turning and racing for the pad elevator. "I'll tell the safety console you're on your way."

As the astronauts and technician headed toward the MAT, Mark slammed the wire encased elevator door closed and sighed, "Whew!" He burst into the white room from the air shower, still fully suited, just as the first passenger slid out of the narrow hatch onto the white room floor.

"Back... get back in now!" he shouted.

"What the ...," the passenger replied, already frustrated and upset, his chance to finally get off the BURR, or Big Ugly Red Rock, as they referred to the planet, thwarted.

"Okay, go right ahead; breathe the air, go ahead," Mark warned, in his most condescending voice, looking out through his visor at the man.

The passenger, his own helmet in his hand, looked terrified and pressed his way back into the lander and closed the hatch.

Mark wasted no time in sliding a portable winch in front of the cameras; then he grasped the handles on the two flight lockers Ashley had tossed out of the lander and dragged them into the can, locking the door. He then plugged himself into the communications port and calmly announced, "Okay, folks, air quality is verified. You may now open the hatch." A bead of sweat dropped down onto his nose from his saturated head band.

The passengers filed out of the lander ahead of Ashley and Peter. The first two out were the Marines who had just been relieved and were headed back to earth: Corporal Pamela Hiraldo and Staff Sergeant Irving Brinker. Sergeant Brinker, short, black and stocky, known less affectionately as "Bupkis" (no one dared call him Irving), removed his helmet, exposing the ever-present, well-chewed cigar stub. The Marines had long since banned smoking, but Brinker insisted it was just decoration. He claimed he never lit his stub, and to anyone's knowledge, he never did.

"Now ain't this just peachy?" he began, walking over and standing toe to toe with Mark. "I got nearly two years on the BURR and you're tellin' me your rocket's broke? These civilian operations are all alike, know that?"

"Got that right, Sarge," Hiraldo agreed, her helmet tucked under her arm.

"If it weren't such a privilege serving in the Corps anywhere in the known universe, I'd probably be angry right now. Know that? You definitely do NOT want to see me angry. Now I ain't had no good booze, no good fights, no good sack time in two years, and you're tellin' me your rocket's broke...."

"Shower's a waitin', Sarge," Hiraldo offered, stepping into the air shower.

"And now I gotta go take another shower with Hiraldo," Brinker continued to ruminate, shifting one eye closed, and the other to the air shower, cigar poised to the near vertical. He sighed and hesitated before stepping into the air shower with Hiraldo, shaking his head and slowly latching his helmet into position, cigar still in place.

The other passengers filed out of the lander, their faces ashen and annoyed at this fantastically bizarre deviation from their plans. None of them were colonists and none wanted another minute on Mars, much less a full sol. Another 24 hours back on the BURR after being so close to leaving would be all but intolerable.

Ashley held Peter back until she could see the last passenger depart out of the airlock. Then she slid out of the lander's hatch and Peter followed.

"Mark, did we accomplish the contingency?" she asked, turning her back to the cameras.

"Barely," he replied, shifting only his eyes to the can, its door now clearly locked and sealed.

Ashley just smiled and looked to Peter. "Shhh...," she whispered without moving her lips, and then winked at Mark. "Thanks for everything, you're definitely in."

Peter rocked his head twice between Mark and Ashley and said nothing. The dumbfounded expression on his face said it all. Then he latched his helmet into place and looked to the can. "Can's really broke this time, right?" he asked sincerely.

"Yes, sir," Mark replied.

"Figures," Peter replied over the circuit, feeling the twinge in his bladder.

Four MAT's raced together to the pad surface and stopped almost simultaneously. The safety console operator was incensed. Nothing was going according to procedures. The lander was venting liquid hydrogen and oxygen, its tanks brimmed full. Making the ship safe (called safing) was not proceeding with any resemblance to procedure he knew about; discipline now totally gone. So he closed the screen on his safety procedure display, leaned back in his chair, and put his hands behind his head after simultaneously keying all his radio frequencies at once. "Okay, all you cowboy jocks out there at the rocket ranch, listen up. We got a hot bird sitting there and you folks are running around the pad beneath a million liters of rocket fuel. Go right ahead and entertain yourselves, but at least give me your names so that I can notify next of kin."

The launch director was equally outraged. "Who are all these people out there? Who authorized the close out tech to bring out the flight crew? Who authorized the other vehicles to follow the reentry team?"

"Great! I see you know about as much as I do," the safety console replied, palms raised.

Gorteau and Toon appeared out of one vehicle, Lieutenant Quinton out of another. The reentry team began to unload out of a vehicle and the fourth arrived to pick up the passengers.

"I'll stall him; you go up and get the lockers," Gorteau instructed Toon, eyeing the Marine officer who had just stepped from his vehicle.

Toon ran to the elevator and up the structure as Gorteau approached the Marine.

"Excuse me, sir; may I assist you in any way?" Gorteau inquired, his mind racing.

"No, doc, you can't, except to stay out of my way," the Marine replied harshly, turning his back on him and heading toward the elevator.

Gorteau pursued him. "You realize of course that you have no authorization to be here. This facility is not safed."

"I have my orders," Quinton replied, reaching the elevator. He jabbed the button repeatedly, turning his back on Gorteau each time the physicist tried to face him.

"We won't allow you to take our people into custody," Gorteau said flatly, finally abandoning hope of preoccupying the Marine.

Quinton turned and faced Gorteau, his face hard and framed with anger. "I'll take these people into custody, as I have been ordered to do. If you insist in interfering with my official duties, I'll take you into custody as well."

"Have you not heard of the most basic principal of law?" Gorteau asked sharply.

"Get out of my way, old man," the Marine replied, shoving Gorteau against the pad structure and heading toward the stairs. The elevator car obviously was not coming down.

"As a professional Marine officer, you should know the most basic principal of law," Gorteau called after Quinton as he had no hope of physically stopping him. It worked. Quinton stopped and turned to face him.

Gorteau continued briskly, taking advantage of the Marine's attention. "The most basic principal of law is that, ultimately, the ability to enforce your rules enjoins the reality of law. You can not possibly hope to incarcerate a majority of the people on this planet. And that is what you are proposing."

"Stuff it, professor," Quinton replied with a smirk, and turned to bound up the stairs.

Their only hope now was that Toon would pick out the right set of options at the top. Gorteau could not possibly keep up with the Marine, and with the weight of his pressure suit, probably would not make it anyway.

Toon reached the white room as Mark ripped the seal off the can's door and slid the lockers over to him. Toon tossed a large bag to Peter.

"Load them up and hurry," he said, breathlessly.

Peter, Toon and Ashley shoved the heavy lockers into the bag while Mark tied the white room doors closed with nylon rope.

"Hurry up," Toon warned as Peter and Ashley fumbled over the latch to the bag.

"What's in the lockers?" Peter asked.

"Later," Ashley replied as the Marine rushed into the air lock.

"I hate to drag up a useless and ugly fact at a time like this, boys and girls, but last time I looked, there's no other way in and out of here," Mark cried as the Marine kicked the air lock door open and attempted to burst through the lashed air shower door.

"Oh, but there is!" Peter said, eyes darting to the emergency escape hatch. "I hope our friend keeps his helmet on," Peter said as he crushed the glass plate to the escape lever with his elbow.

"Don't do it, Peter! Dump the air first!" Mark warned.

"No time. Get over here and button up!" Peter screamed.

He grabbed Ashley and Mark by the back of their collar rings, tugging them in front of the escape hatch as the Marine finally broke through the air shower door. Toon rushed up behind them, the heavy lockers draped over his shoulders. "Mark, pull it now!" Peter shouted.

Mark's hand pulled the ring and the explosive gasket disintegrated the door opening out to the escape net which sloped from the white room level to the ground. As the air in the white room exploded out into the rarified Martian atmosphere, they were sucked out, 60 meters over the pad surface. Peter intensely hoped they would actually land on the net and high enough up so that they would not be crushed when they finally hit.

They all separated in free fall, tumbling down in the agonizingly slow flight through Mars' fractional gravity. Eventually they all landed on the net, 15 meters down and rolled in a gathering pile toward the landing zone. Gorteau saw the incredible spectacle and rushed toward the MAT.

Quinton was already in a foul humor when his helmet slammed into the opposite wall as the escaping air propelled him about the white room like so much debris. His temper deteriorated even more, however, when he figured out his quarry had escaped.

Stunned, he sat against the wall as the room spun about him. Gathering his wits and shaking his head, he went through the cursory survival checks: suit pressure still good, visor not cracked, no severed arteries. With his head still whirling, he stumbled to his feet amid the trashed white room and looked out the gaping hole over the escape net. Seeing the group duck into an MAT, he simply rolled head first into the net and slid down to the pad surface.

The presentations broadcast on the various monitors scattered about BC1 had no sound, so when the white room air exploded outward in a soundless mist of cluttered vapor, it all seemed somehow surrealistic. The sheer vision of four bodies silently sucked out into the void was astonishing enough, but seeing the Marine bounce about the walls like a rag doll, then pull himself up and roll out through the hole was almost supernatural. The humans of Mars all watched what appeared to be the first planetary insurrection as it progressed in a stunning hush, all framed in incredible, soundless action.

Gorteau had the good sense to scramble out of the MAT's driver's seat and let Toon take the controls. Peter was the last in, dogging the hatch shut as Toon sped away toward the base down US1. As they headed out the gate, Peter could see the Marine's body tumble down the net.

"We're going to have company," he said loudly.

"We have actually survived our own plan," Gorteau said chillingly. "All these MAT's are designed to perform exactly the same. Unless our pursuer has some unknown capabilities, then the distance between us cannot significantly change." As usual, Gorteau was logically correct. As long as Toon could maintain the vehicle's progress at its maximum velocity, the Marine would not catch them on the road. And Toon was well known as the best MAT operator at BC1.

"What's in the lockers?" Peter asked, his voice giving way to near desperate curiosity.

"Lipton's booty; several million dollars in Mars' quartz," Ashley replied.

Mars' quartz was a common quartz with a light pink coloring. Although the supply on Mars was virtually unlimited, these stones on earth were black marketed at excessively exorbitant prices. The price recovered for these stones was usually higher than diamond. It was a silly gimmick, for after travel between the planets picked up, the stones would eventually flood the market and their price would plummet, rendering all the stones nearly worthless. Yet the scam continued and the U.S. government made their importation by federal travelers illegal. Since all travel to and from Mars was only made under federal orders, any imports from U.S. ships were considered contraband.

"How do you know that's what's in the lockers?" Peter asked.

"We had Mark ship them back to the laboratories last night after the Marine installed them in the lander. Then we scanned them with x-rays and NRI (nuclear resonance imaging) and recorded the data with certified time stamps."

"This isn't going to work," Peter said with a sinking feeling. "Lipton is going to claim you planted the stones."

"He can't. We also have the electronic logs of what time Lipton turned over his lockers to the Marine and what time they were delivered to the white room."

"But you could have opened the boxes anywhere in between."

"Not without the locker's security system recording the opening. Don't forget, these lockers are authenticated diplomatic pouches and can't be opened without the device recording the event."

"What about illegal search and seizure? What about unauthorized tampering of classified material? Surely you realize that you must have run afoul of at least a dozen legal issues here."

"It doesn't matter," Gorteau said. "When the State Department finds out what Lipton has been up to, they will quietly remove him from our midst. Even illegally gathered information on petty crime by a government official will be an embarrassment to them and they'll want him out before it leaks. This is the White House's big chance to rid itself of a great potential liability."

"How did you find out he was doing it in the first place?" Peter asked.

"Friends in low places," was all Gorteau would admit to.

"So, now we're all set," Peter remarked. "We've got a crazed Marine two minutes behind us; who knows what waiting in front of us; we just ripped off two confidential diplomatic lockers, wasting the white room in the process, and whatever other achievements in an already long and distinguished day. So what could be next?" he asked with a wide, toothless, fake grin.

"A hazard of contingency planning," Ashley replied, "is anticipating just the right amount of details. However, you'll all be happy to know that Francis is waiting for us at the end."

"Ah yes, Francis. And how did you manage to talk him into dumping two gigabit-per-second down links from the Earth Sats?" Peter asked, truly curious.

"Sorry, not our plan A," Ashley admitted truthfully.

"You mean you had nothing to do with that?"

"Don't look at me," Toon added without prompting.

"Remember," Gorteau recounted, "We're into Plan B. Plan A was to fly you back to earth so that you and Ashley could direct Lipton's termination party while we controlled the evidence here. We had no way of supervising the lockers upon their arrival on earth. The loss of the earth data links was not exactly on our list, though the possibility of a scrub was."

"Plan B," Peter added, understanding.

"Excellent," Gorteau replied as gratified as if he had just explained the theory of quantum electrodynamics to a freshman.

"So Francis was not in on your little plan?" Peter asked, truly surprised.

"Of course he was. But we don't know anything about dumping the earth links," Ashley replied, looking at Gorteau.

"Francis...," Peter mused aloud. He was the only one Peter knew who was actually capable of dumping the earth satellite data links. But he silently pondered the logic and even the wisdom of such a desperate plan. Such a serious act would be nearly impossible to explain away or justify and had almost frightening implications for the colony and lander. Just how frightening, he was about to discover.

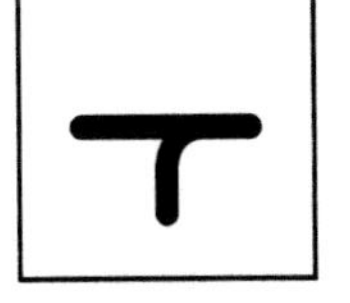

Toon gained 30 seconds on the Marine, opening his lead out to a relatively comfortable two and a half minutes as he slid to a stop inside the airlock. Francis operated the door controls internally and closed the air lock long before Quinton's vehicle threatened. In seconds, Peter, Ashley, Toon and Gorteau were inside, helmets off and embraced by every colonist who could make their way to them.

"Quiet; quiet, please!" Gorteau shouted at the assembled crowd. "We simply cannot allow these people to be taken into custody." The assembled colonists applauded their approval.

With his hand raised, Gorteau continued, "That will require that the colony restrict entrance into its areas. We will post guards immediately, and until further notice, accessibility will be controlled." The crowd cheered again.

"While this is necessary in the short term, it will soon become an intolerable situation, but until some aspect of control can be reestablished, it will remain in effect. We will have a community meeting of all colonists in one hour in the main dining hall."

With that, Gorteau, Peter, Ashley and Toon disappeared into the hallways of the central colony as Quniton burst through the airlock doors. Francis stepped in front of him.

"Excuse me, cowboy, but this area is off limits until further notice," he said, standing legs apart and arms folded in front of the officer who had just removed his helmet.

"Get out of my way," Quinton ordered in a slow, deliberate voice, his face bruised, a spot of blood caked over his right eye which twitched as he spoke. The colonists ringed Quinton and began to move closer. Quinton's head moved slowly to the right. Briefly he took his eyes off Francis as he considered his position. It was not good. Then his eyes shot back to Francis.

"You're about five seconds away from a long, unescorted walk back to Lipton's office," Francis warned solemnly, "...outside, in your underwear. You may be a Marine, but I'm a Navy Seal; and if you think that's a fair match, then you may make the first move."

"You're threatening my life," Quinton said impassively. "That's a felony."

"Indeed," was Francis' only reply.

Quinton glared at him, a murderous stare of detailed scrutiny. But Francis returned it coldly and neither man moved.

"Your five seconds are up," yelled a voice from the crowd.

"I'll be back to arrest the other criminals, and you," Quinton forewarned. And he added another malevolent threat never heard before on the planet in its short history, "And I'll be armed." Then he turned on his heel sharply and left.

The colonists cheered, but Francis shuddered to think of an armed conflict in this fragile colony. Mankind had brought along his genius to this red world. Now it seemed he had unpacked his lethal disposition as well.

obert Khun Hernandez embodied every executive's fantasy of an efficient, careful, intensely anal details man. The Deputy Administrator of BC1 was the consummate tracker, sorter and ultimate slayer of minutiae. He also believed in his boss, trusted him, knew his faults and did his best to cover for him when the time came. This was one of those times.

Hernandez had arranged a hastily organized meeting of the key BC1 administrators while Lipton frothed and raged in the privacy of his office. The six key administrators met in the Director's conference room. Their faces were masked with profound worry. They had a series of problems to deal with, each so extreme that any one of them could destroy BC1 and America's attempt at establishing a permanent base on another planet. Until Lipton became lucid, it would be Hernandez's problem to sort things out.

"Friends and colleagues," he began, "we face four problems in this descending order of importance:

"One: we have lost both communications links with the earth. We've not determined why and cannot effectively deal with the question until the professional staff makes themselves available for the detailed analysis we must effect. I don't think I have to remind you of the seriousness of this loss. We've never experienced anything like this; I don't know what has happened or the full impact on our operations.

"Two:..."

Lipton's voice interrupted him as he came out of his office into the conference room. "Two:" Lipton continued for Hernandez as his deputy took his seat. "The white room has been disabled. We do not know what damage, if any, this has done to the lander, which we must have, as you know, to survive the coming winter."

Lipton stood at the lectern at the front of the room. His white sleeves were rolled up and he wore a navy blue sweater vest. His hair was still perfect and he sported a pair of clear reading glasses, perched on the edge of his nose. From his appearance and tone of voice, there was no indication that anything extraordinary had happened at all. It was Lipton at his best, back in full control.

"Three: there are five criminals lose in the compound who must be rounded up, incarcerated and shipped off planet at the earliest launch opportunity. We can only assume that they plot further insurrection as we speak.

"Finally, four: there's a general state of moral malaise at BC1 which must be dealt with at all cost. It will be our responsibility to correct the problem as soon as possible. Now, let's have your ideas, beginning with the first problem," Lipton directed without emotion.

The administrators felt better hearing Lipton's calm, intelligent voice, assuring themselves that the Director was firmly back in command. Now they began to plot their course.

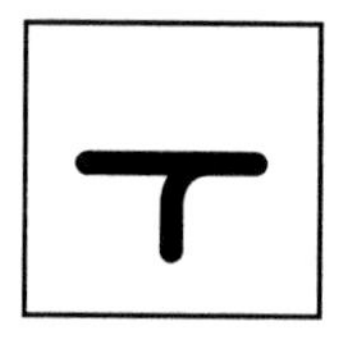
he colonists were not as calm and attentive. Nearly all of them were scientists or engineers, and each considered themself on the same professional level as any other. So in a meeting, especially one as emotionally charged as this one, control was difficult to come by.

"Please! Be quiet!" Gorteau finally shouted above the din, standing on his chair. "Now we do not have much time to chart our own destiny. Lipton and his group could be sending armed Marines into our camp at any minute. We *must* determine our strategy as quickly as possible!"

The group became hushed as Gorteau took his seat and continued speaking in the crowded dining hall. "The list of problems we face is long. First, armed Marines are on their way to take five of us into custody, myself included."

"How are we going to defend ourselves if we don't have any weapons?" a voice asked from the crowd.

"By using our brains," Gorteau replied. "I think we can safely assume Lipton does not want any bloodshed, so he is more than likely to order his Marines not to shoot unless their own lives are in danger. Therefore, we can probably simply refuse to go along."

"What about that crazy jarhead lieutenant?" Mark Teiner asked.

"Problem number two," Gorteau continued, ignoring the question, "is the lander. What is its condition?"

"She'll fly tomorrow if we get our earth links back," said the chief engineer for the colony. "There'll be a load of trash and dirt floating around, but, she *will* fly."

"No significant structural or heat tile damage, then?"

"A few scratches. My techs are fixing it up right now."

"Next problem," Gorteau pressed on. "Dealing with Lipton and company."

"Screw Lipton," someone shouted which jacked the noise level back up again. Regaining control by pounding on the table, Gorteau settled the crowd back to hushed whispers.

"The man may be a despot, but we must find a way to rationally deal with him until our case can be presented to the proper authorities on earth." No one liked what Gorteau had said, but every individual in the room knew it was true. Each person in the colony held a little piece of every other's survival, and, unless they all worked together, they would all die.

Gorteau also knew that in any group of such strong-willed, often stubborn, and highly intelligent individuals, it would probably be impossible to reach a meaningful consensus. They had to elect a leader to speak for them. He suggested this and in about half an hour, the crowd agreed to make nominations. Of course, Gorteau was unanimously suggested.

"No, I cannot accept," he said. "I am but an old man with a closed mind and a rotten predisposition toward all bureaucracies and bureaucrats in general."

"Then why did you lead us down this garden path," one colonist said, her face reflecting the frustration of the group.

"You misunderstood my motives," Gorteau replied. "I think the person we elect should represent the best qualities in all of us; most of all, quiet equanimity, youthful energy and an open, fair mind. I nominate Peter Traynor," Gorteau said suddenly.

Peter was not present, presumably in hiding with Francis, Toon and Ashley, so he could not comment on the fact that he had just been elected leader of the rebellion. Most in the group agreed that the designation was brilliant, even if it meant placing their trust in one of their members who had been named one of the most wanted men.

No sooner had the election results been finalized than Peter, Francis, Toon and Ashley entered the room.

orteau looked around at them with surprise. "You are supposed to be a long way from here."

"Yes sir," Francis replied, "But considering our engineering projects of the last hour and a half, I doubt if the Marines will hit the beach for awhile."

Gorteau stood and approached Peter, talking lightly and gesturing toward the crowd. Peter looked stunned, his eyes shifting over the group as Gorteau spoke. When Gorteau finished, he pulled a chair back, offering Peter to sit down.

As he sat, the room burst into applause and most rose to their feet in the ovation. Peter sat, astonished at what had happened in his absence. Then he stood, embarrassed, and raised his hand for his fellow colonists to stop. Long minutes later, the acclamation dying away, he continued standing and addressed them.

"I don't know whether what I'm about to say will offend any of you here or make you want to change your vote. But let me say that, just as the nation of our birth could not long survive divided, neither can we. In fact, our days are strictly numbered unless we can reach some sort of peace with the administration very quickly.

"The loss of the communications links with earth is serious and unprecedented, and in my absence, I'm wondering whether that situation has been resolved?" he asked, looking out over the sea of faces. Many shook their heads. Without doubt, that repair will be accomplished in just a matter of minutes or hours. Then one crisis will be replaced by yet another. Of course, I'm speaking of my own situation, which has led to all of this. Let me just assure you, that at no time will I act to sell you out. I know how much pulling away from the suffocating bureaucracy has meant to most of you, and now we have committed ourselves to at least ridding BC1 of Lipton and his rule." That sentiment drew another round of applause and cheers.

"I can also assure you, that I will never willingly be taken from this planet, my home, again. If taken, I'll be taken in chains. And I'll never board a ship before Lassiter Lipton!" He couldn't resist this little speech. It somehow fit the occasion and was met with thundering cheers and applause, as he had known it would be.

Ashley stood beside him and reached up her hand to gently touch his back.

"Until this colony is appointed a new, legitimate director, and until this whole situation is straightened out, I would like to appoint Dr. Gorteau as my Chief of Staff. Dr. Gorteau, if you accept, I would ask you to appoint a board of directors of the colony to meet in one hour. Also, contact Lipton and set up a C2-conference call three hours from now. I'll make that call available to the public channels so that everyone can hear our negotiations, and please record it for retransmission to earth.

"Until then, please, friends, go to your places of work to reestablish the communications channels with earth or prepare the lander for liftoff tomorrow. Tonight, we will set about trying to decide who will be on it."

Then Peter considered something, looked to Ashley, then back to the assembled colonists. "I can assure you of two people who will *not* be on the shuttle – neither me nor my wife!"

The crowd paused for a full minute. They all knew of their marriage, but this was the first time it had been acknowledged in public. They began to applaud and cheer yet again as he kissed her ceremoniously, with great relief, having kept the so-called secret for so long.

"Well then, go on back to your quarters and your duties," he said, embracing Ashley. "The excitement must be over for one day."

He was wrong.

nited States Marine Corps Lieutenant Mica Quinton stood at attention in his best dress uniform before his boss, Lipton. They were alone in Lipton's office.

"Lieutenant Quinton, stand at ease."

"Sir!" Quinton barked, snapping to an equally ill-at-ease parade rest.

Lipton loved it. The picture of the perfect Marine in a flawless uniform, ready to respond to his orders, without challenge, would have appealed to Lipton under normal circumstances, but in light of the last few bizarre hours, Lipton was more than ready to slip back into this mode of absolute and total control.

"Lieutenant, I want you to round up these individuals," Lipton ordered, tossing five personnel files on the desk in front of Quinton. They were the files of Peter, Francis, Toon, Ashley and Gorteau. "I want them in your firm custody and ready to board the lander at 0600 tomorrow morning. I don't want any bloodshed or injury to any other personnel, and, for heaven's sake, no more property damage!"

Then he paused for effect, finally adding, "As far as the prisoners are concerned, I don't want them *seriously* injured."

Lipton paused again, and then flashed an almost imperceptible smile at Quinton. Lipton used words with exceptional precision. His delivery and inflections were just as precise and carefully linked. The Marine, however, was trained to communicate on a different, much more subliminally primitive level and missed the significance of Lipton's allegorical expressions altogether. Unknown to Lipton, he had just released any inhibitions Quniton may have had left.

ergeant Irving Brinker, Corporal John Tyler and Corporal Pamela Hiraldo stood at attention before Lieutenant Quinton, dressed in their silver and red pressure suits, chosen to be the prisoner recovery party while the last two Marines remained behind for Lipton's "security." Quinton walked up and down before them several times, dressed in his own suit, a .45 caliber handgun tucked into a makeshift belt at his waist. The officer paced before them several times, hands behind him, and said nothing.

Sergeant Brinker caught a movement out of the corner of his eye, and glanced over to Hiraldo who wiggled her eyebrows and rolled her eyes to the ceiling. The whole ridiculous spectacle made Brinker unable to suppress the first choking cough of a chuckle, but he caught himself just before Quinton would have seen the smirk.

To Brinker, the idea of shipping the best Marines in the country off planet to this frozen hell was insane to begin with. Now, he was about to march off to battle in a tiny colony of plastic tubes to collar five eggheads, led by this school boy whose only knowledge of war was from reading a few books while hiding from the winter snows, somewhere in a Quantico library.

"Sir," Brinker said, "excuse me, sir."

"What is it Brinker?" Quinton asked, irritated at the interruption of his complex cerebral strategy developing on the fly.

"Why don't you let Hiraldo and me go on in and bring these folks out? Not only do we know this facility very well, but we also know these individuals. I can be out in two hours with all five in tow." It was the wrong thing to say to Quinton and as soon as Brinker saw the officer's face, he knew it.

"Who pulled your chain, Marine?"

"No one, sir."

"Then shut up until you're addressed. Don't ever interrupt me again, is that clear?"

"Yes, sir," Brinker replied sharply. This officer was even more naive than Brinker had first thought. Most officers, even ring-knocker academy types, are told long before they reach the real Marines that you never, ever cross your leading enlisted type. Succeeding or not usually depended on the experience he gave you or chose not to give you. It was an unspoken, ugly but irrefutable truth handed down over the centuries. Authority, command and accountability came with the commissioning certificate signed by the President. Such testimonials had nothing whatsoever to do with experience... or survival.

Quinton stepped away from his troops and returned dragging what appeared to be a heavy plastic box. He carefully opened it and withdrew an object from it which he held tenderly in his hands, then held it up to his company. Brinker' eyes widened. Quinton was holding a black, shiny, automatic 12 gauge shotgun with laser sight.

"I brought along several of these weapons, Marines. And you'll each be issued one for this operation."

"Sir, I hardly think...," Brinker began.

"Since when did anyone ask you to think, Sergeant? You've been on independent duty far too long, Marine, and I'll ensure that your evaluation reflects that."

Brinker was tiring of this B-rated movie charade. He relaxed, fished his cigar stub out of his pocket and popped it into his mouth. "Go ahead and write me up, Lieutenant, *sir,* but I think you should know something about use of that weapon here."

"Okay, Sergeant, now that you have our undivided attention, go ahead. But it had better be dammed good!"

"At two meters, the shell from that weapon will blow a hole in the walls of this colony as big as my ass. Whether you actually hit your target or not, it really won't matter. The depressurization will suck the victim, you, me and anything not bolted down through that hole whether it fits or not," Brinker spit out, nearly biting his tongue to keep from mentioning Quinton's recent experience with such environmental effects.

Quinton was so outraged that he dared not reply. Uncontrolled stammering was not conducive to good combat leadership, he reasoned. Instead he grasped a large clip of shells and thrust it at Hiraldo. "See to it that each man has one," he rasped, his voice clearly shaking.

Hiraldo could hardly suppress asking whether she were allowed a clip, too, but she wisely decided against it. She glanced at Brinker, who was nervously looking around the compartment, flexing his legs in quick jerks, bouncing off the balls of his feet. Hiraldo had seen this before; Brinker was furiously considering their options. As Hiraldo handed a clip to Brinker, she slowly moved her ear as close as she dared to his lips, then she nodded.

hile Quinton plotted his next move, Peter and his staff met to discuss the colonists' strategy. There were no surprises in the makeup of his staff. It consisted of Peter and the six highest ranking colonists.

They decided to discharge their plan in two phases. One, Lipton was to be sent a private message, immediately, informing him that the colonists were in possession of his lockers and that a complete analysis had been accomplished, revealing their contents. If he chose to resign and rescind all complaints against them, then they would destroy the lockers upon his return to earth and no one would officially know of their existence. If Lipton refused, then the second phase of the plan would be effected.

The second phase was to keep the colonists' sectors separated from the administrative sectors, allowing exchange of personnel, information and materials relating only to survival. They would wait however long it took for the authorities on earth to send out arbiters to mediate the dispute.

The colonists felt certain that this suggestion would force the immediate resignation of Lipton and his staff. They not only held damming personal evidence against Lipton, but, when faced with the largest talent pool, allocation of space, equipment, and resources firmly in the colonists control, Lipton would have no choice but to talk and eventually acquiesce.

The message to Lipton was transmitted as Quinton and his troops made their first advance.

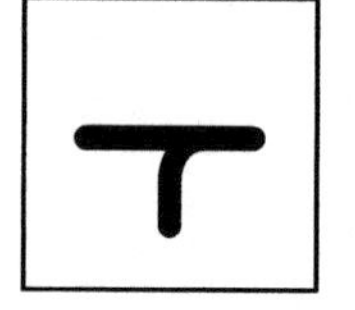

he colonists' quarters and laboratories were separated from the administrative structures by three tunnels. Francis, Peter, Toon and Ashley had not only depressurized the tunnels, but they removed the master pressure cylinders from both sides. The tunnels could not be repressurized without the missing parts. Then they locked the doors from the inside with improvised latches made from wire rope and stainless steel bolts. Next, they disabled the only four airlocks leading directly outside in the same manner and posted guards by them with radio communicators they called PC2's.

No one could gain access to the colony now without ripping the doors off and depressurizing whole domes. Such a move would endanger everyone's lives. Hence, the colonists were counting on the intensity of the fray maintaining itself at a level somewhere less than mass death. Not a single individual thought Lipton was insane enough to think that even he would order that degree of retribution.

Night had fallen over BC1 by the time the four Marines approached the airlock tunnels to the colony. Francis had terminated the power to the tunnels, so the battery powered emergency lights caused the tunnel to glow a dim ruby red.

In the lead, fully suited Quinton approached the door, in a creeping, bent-over stance, weapon raised. Slowly, he raised his head and looked out the glass plate into the empty tunnel. Brinker leaned fully upright against the wall, head back, cigar propped up in his lips inside his helmet. He looked at his leader and shook his head slowly. "They never, ever made a piss ant Lieutenant that was worth a tinker's damn to begin with, but this guy is three, say four bricks shy of a full load," he reflected to himself.

"Tyler, open the door," Quinton ordered the new Marine. Corporal Tyler slipped quietly to the door, also crouched, mimicking the Lieutenant, and grasped the handle, turning it with all his strength. "It's jammed, sir," he said breathlessly.

“Imagine that!” Brinker whispered to himself, but just a little too loudly.

"Brinker, get your black ass over here and help him," Quinton whispered through his lip mounted helmet microC2.

Brinker, who had been laughing quietly at these fools attempting to open a pressurized door against Mars' virtual vacuum, suddenly lost his sense of humor as Quinton made his racial slur. The gullible, ignorant, boyish officer suddenly became something more malevolent. If Brinker had disliked him before, he hated him now.

"... can't open a pressurized hatch, Lieutenant," Brinker replied unmoving, his voice sheathed with obvious contempt, glaring down at the officer.

"And just what makes you think it's pressurized?" Quinton returned with equal contempt.

Brinker said nothing, and simply nodded toward the status panel glowing on the bulkhead beside the door. The status indicators glared bright red, indicating the outer tunnel had been evacuated of air, causing the interior hatch to be pressurized with all the force of the interior domes.

"We can't get to them!" Quinton declared incredulously.

"Not this way," Brinker agreed with cheeky amusement.

"How many other tunnels are there?"

"Two more...," Hiraldo finally replied with contempt.

"Hiraldo, you and Tyler go recon them and report back to me in five minutes," Quinton ordered, his eyes darting.

"Waste of time," Brinker replied.

"What's your problem now, Marine?" Quinton seethed at Brinker.

"If I only had three inner doors to lock, and I was the world's smartest scientist, I doubt seriously if I'd have missed one; how 'bout you?"

"Are you daring to suggest that this operation is impossible?" the officer asked, now clearly hinting for some help.

"You're in charge, Lieutenant," Brinker said, sliding down on the deck. The smart ass could sink on his own, as far as Brinker was concerned.

Quinton's eyes flashed about. His plan to use the bluff of the weapons to root out the prisoners was not working. If he could not get access to the colony, then his big guns were worthless. He stared at the ground for two long minutes. Finally he stammered, his voice barely able to speak the words, "Okay, Brinker, you said you could go in and bring them out in two hours. So let's hear it."

Brinker looked stunned. There was no way he would ever allow this bigoted fool to benefit or take credit for a single fragment of his ideas or knowledge. Let the jerk go it alone. He would just as soon ride along and amuse himself with the little twit's stupid antics. So he said nothing, looking through the half darkness directly at the Lieutenant who was staring down at his gloved hand, reflexively clutching his weapon. It further occurred to Brinker that this arrogant pig had not looked him in the eye or talked to him as a man since he had arrived. But Brinker had seen it before; white faces that couldn't look black faces in the eye, man to man.

Then another thought occurred to him, even caught him off guard: *semper fi . . .*

"Okay," Brinker began, suppressing a sigh, "now listen up." Some principals, he thought to himself, were just worth more than others; but, *damn,* it was a close call.

Tyler and Hiraldo each had portable welders strung across their shoulders, marching through the Martian dust, outside the domes, moving toward the colonists quarters, following Quinton and Brinker.

Their first target was the colony's outermost pressurized zone. There were three and the plan was to depressurize one at a time, sweeping them, driving them all back to the last one, then ordering the prisoners out. There were emergency closets into which the colonists could move if they had to, they could put on their suits or they could die; their choice. Brinker knew that with proper timing and warning, with small, well placed holes, no one would die. It was a classic, professional Marine operation; a well planned surgical strike based on an intimate and personal knowledge of the enemy.

They arrived at the first outer airlock. Brinker walked straight up to and looked through the transparent, plastic window in the door. The guard inside was reading. Brinker tapped on the window, and as the startled guard looked up, Quinton smiled and waved. "Okay troops, do it!" he said with a satisfied grin

One Marine slapped a metal plate over the window while the other tack welded it into place. The frightened guard inside stepped back, clutching his PC2 up to his open mouth, speechless. He could immediately see there was something written on the metal plate. Slowly he stepped up and read,

THIS DOOR WILL BE REMOVED IN 15 MINUTES. ALL OCCUPANTS INSIDE SHOULD EVACUATE FROM THIS ZONE IMMEDIATELY. THE UNITED STATES MARINES ARE PREPARING TO OCCUPY THIS FEDERAL PROPERTY BY FORCE.

"Holy crap!" the guard cried into the open circuit of the PC2 which echoed throughout the colonist's compounds, the administrative quarters and the Marines own circuits. Brinker did not even try to control his convulsive laughter.

Peter and Francis ran as fast as they could through the passageways to airlock 14 where the frightened guard had stammered half an intelligible warning in his PC2. When they arrived, the guard was backed against a wall, pointing to the sign, screaming, "The grunts are going to kill us all!"

"Nobody is going to get killed," Peter assured him, walking over to read the sign. "Well I'll be," he said to himself. "They're actually coming in!"

Then he stood back, trying to assess what they were up to. The first thought was the most obvious; if they wanted the colonists to die, there would have been no warning. So they were trying to control them. After that realization, the rest of the plan became evident.

Toon came rushing into the airlock, followed by a dozen others. Peter motioned to the others, calling out, "Please step outside. There's not enough room in here for everyone." As they stepped out, Peter pushed the door almost completely closed, out of courtesy to those still outside, speaking quietly to Francis and Toon. "Okay, here's the counter attack," he began, his murmuring followed by Francis' loud guffaws.

ive more minutes," Quinton said to no one in particular, eyeing the florescent dial on his watch. "Tyler, Hiraldo, prepare to remove the door," he said with some authority coming back into his voice.

It was a senseless command as they were sitting on the ground by the door anyway. Brinker considered, even savored his comeback, but thought better of it. Quinton had the good judgment to listen and go along with his earlier reasoning. Besides, Hiraldo knew to cut a hole in the door to bleed the pressure first before she cut off the hinges. He had already briefed her on that.

So Brinker sat in silence, under the dark Martian sky. The brilliant stars were the same stars he had seen from earth, only here, under the thin sky, they were much brighter. His favorite, the bright, bluish evening star, appeared earlier and earlier after each sunset for months, then one day didn't rise at all as it went behind the sun. That blue star was home. With any luck, he would be speeding back there tomorrow, this last interesting game and Quinton receding behind him at thousands of kilometers per hour. The BURR would be gone, at last. The real world would be back under his feet. All the rest to Brinker were minor details.

As he contemplated these things, the airlock door suddenly swung slowly open. It caught all of them by surprise. They waited for someone to walk out, but no one did. Quinton and Tyler held their weapons up and to the ready.

Brinker carefully analyzed the strategy. Unfortunately, Quinton simply reacted.

"Okay, let's go!" the Lieutenant cried.

"No!" Brinker replied, having thought through the logic of their actions.

But Tyler had already obeyed the command senior officer and was in the airlock, weapon raised. Quinton followed. Hiraldo looked at Brinker who shook his head and mouthed silently to her, "Fubar." The Lieutenant had just screwed things up beyond all repair.

Brinker was a superb strategist and his plan was based as much on the psychology of his enemy as anything; their intelligence was the only weapon they had. His strategy was laid out three to four steps ahead and he always planned one or two contingencies. In the real world, this was an above-average military talent. Most others in the population did not have this predisposition or emotional substance. Quinton did not; he was basically a reactionist; a single-step strategist. Quinton's intelligence and aptitude were far below Brinker's. Unfortunately for all, his authority was not. The system had bred and sent Brinker a manager to lead, not a fighting man. It was the Sergeant's mistake for not acting on that, and now he knew it. He regretted not having shared with the Lieutenant the most elementary, detailed aspects of his plan. But it was too late now.

e've got Marines in the airlock!" Jack Linde said to Peter and his father, Francis.

"Good! Welcome them into our humble quarters," Peter replied jovially. They had just walked right into his lair.

"I've got four Marines in the airlock, and now I'm closing the hatch," Jack said, moving the appropriate levers. "Pressurizing," he reported.

"I do believe they've got guns; *big* guns," Toon said, eyeing the Marines through the port.

"I'm impressed," Peter responded with scorn. "What I want to know is how they were authorized to bring that much weight in useless equipment to Mars?"

"Pentagon," replied Jack.

"Or NRA," Francis said with a wide grin. "Perhaps they're for duck hunting."

"Special delivery!" Toon said, rushing through the crowded passageway with his box. "Line it up, Jack," he said, thrusting the box to Linde.

Jack took the box, quickly unpacked the instrument, setting it up on a makeshift table. "I need more time," he warned.

"Slow the repressurization," Peter ordered calmly.

"Got it!" Jack finally announced, then sat by his device, leaning back in his chair with his hands behind his head.

"Pressurization complete. Let them in!" Peter said, taking a deep breath.

Quinton stepped into the room, weapon raised. "This facility is being occupied by the United States Marines. I want everyone clear of this room immediately! Follow my orders and do what I say and no one will be hurt."

"Lieutenant, is this a robbery or is this an invasion?" Francis asked, stalling the Marine. Jack's hands worked busily at his small instrument from the far side of the room. With his back to the Marines, he looked carefully down into an eyepiece that resembled a microscope, focused, pressed a series of buttons and repeated his steps again and again.

Quinton pointed his weapon at Peter, "Out, now!" he sneered.

"You realize that if that thing actually goes off, we'll all die, even you."

"Don't screw with me, just move it."

"Well, my work is done," Jack said with a smirk from across the room. "Let me lead the way."

"I'll follow him," Francis replied with a fake smile.

The four Marines were the last to leave the airlock. Brinker could see that the colonists were leading them, so he hung far behind. As they passed room after room, no sweep was made. There was no telling how many waited for them or what kind of plot the colonists had contrived. Brinker knew there was a game afoot. What he didn't know was that the game was already up.

They all walked into the dining hall, where Peter sat down against a wall in front of a table along with Ashley and Gorteau. Francis, Toon and Mark Teiner walked to the table and stood behind them.

"Are these the prisoners, Sergeant Brinker?" Quinton asked.

"Those are the prisoners, indeed," Brinker replied, fighting a more insulting tone of voice. He knew at least part of what would probably happen next.

"Alright; you six, follow me," Quinton ordered, sounding totally preposterous.

"No," Peter replied unmoving, "We will not."

Quinton stood silent, at a total loss for what to say. He held his pointed gun at them and they stared back.

"Brinker, take these people into custody," he ordered, his voice trembling.

"I'd like for you to tell me just exactly how you want me to do that," Brinker replied, his ridiculous weapon hanging uselessly at his side. "I doubt very seriously whether any one of them is going to sit still while I stuff them into pressure suits."

"He's right, of course," Peter added. "Not even United States Marines will risk their own lives by firing on us and chance blowing a hole in the walls of this structure. And, one man is hardly a match for six."

"Alright, but we'll be back," Quinton rasped, now waving his weapon around the room. "Okay..., er, Brinker, you and your squad fall back by twos to the airlock," he said, nervously, claustrophobically eyeing the crowd that had gathered.

Peter saw the man was about to lose it. So did Brinker.

"Ah, yeah... Fall back... now!" Brinker replied, hoping against hope the colonists had enough sense to allow them to retreat.

Peter knew that if Quinton's trigger finger even twitched, everyone in the room would likely perish. He had no idea he would be dealing with a deranged man. His plan of reason was falling apart and it was about to kill them all. Jack, however, did not know this.

"Too bad, jarhead," Jack said from the crowd., "We just fixed your pressure suit. You won't be leaving us at all."

Francis shot Jack a homicidal stare, but it was too late.

"What... huh?" Quinton stuttered, the helmet enclosing his head suddenly became an obstruction as his eyes shot about, looking for the life support gauges on his wrist.

Jack had used a far infrared laser to pepper their suits with a dozen pin sized holes as they walked out of the airlock. The laser's invisible energy completely dissipated on the surface in the red stripes of the Marine's suits so that they never knew they had been punctured. The original plan was to make them their prisoners, but the plan was about to tragically unravel.

Quinton's eyes finally caught sight of his suit pressure gauge, now dipping toward zero. In the pressurized environment of the domes he had not noticed. With horror, he felt trapped and helpless. Peter and Brinker instantly realized the peril of the situation at the same time, their eyes picking up the tiny nuances of insanity in Quinton's face. Peter's body began its motion but far too late. Quinton raised his shotgun to Peter's face and pulled the trigger just as its black barrel was leveled even with his eyes. It snapped closed with an empty click.

Peter more felt than understood in an interminable instant that the Marine's weapon was not loaded, and he froze, looking quickly to Brinker.

"I told you the moron would do it," Hiraldo said to Brinker, the shells she had taken from Quinton's clip unrolling in her hand.

"You traitorous bitch!" Quinton screamed, and then reached for his .45 caliber handgun that no one had been able to unload.

Brinker saw it all coming and, grasping the barrel of his shotgun, was swinging it toward the back of the deranged officer like a bat. He struck Quinton with the butt of the rifle on the helmet behind his head with a loud thump and sent him sprawling across the floor. Quinton fell hands out, slid a meter and lay still.

Brinker removed his helmet and tossed it onto the floor. The colonists were frozen in terror and disbelief. Adjusting the cigar in his mouth with a steady hand, he looked down at the officer and sighed, "I just hope Lipton has more seats left on his prison rocket. I think I'm gonna be sittin in one of 'em."

Quinton lay still, just slightly stunned. His eyes were open, hidden in his face-down position on the deck. His mind was racing. He could feel the weapon still clutched in his right hand. He needed only half a second and a good aim. He had lost all rationality now. His only purpose in life was to use what he knew to kill the turncoat black sergeant and bring his prisoners back to justice.

He spun quickly over to kill Brinker. Peter had already rushed to grab the gun before the Marine could recover and lunged for it even as the Lieutenant was pulling the weapon off the deck. Peter struck Quinton as he fired. The bullet narrowly missed Brinker's suit and struck the wall of the dining hall. Quinton had carved a hollow point out of the lead projectile's head, and as it spun into the wall, it flowered, ripping a jagged, fist-sized hole. Because of the vortex of escaping air and its own spinning energy, as the bullet exited through the wall, it left a ragged metallic edge pointed in all directions. The air of the dining hall began to roar out into the dark Martian night behind the bullet.

The force of Peter's impact knocked Quinton down and they slid together toward the wall, assisted by momentum and the out-rushing column of air. The hole wasn't large enough to pull much along in its wake, but the pressure was dropping far more rapidly than the emergency air banks could resupply. Peter could feel the air being sucked out of his own lungs.

Brinker knew what had to be done. With strength he did not know he had, he pulled himself into the rushing air-stream, jerking Quinton up in front of him, and rode headlong into the wall. Quinton's body stuck, abdomen first, into the gaping hole.

A single sharp fragment of the jagged edge of the hole penetrated the Lieutenant's suit and body. Quinton screamed as the air and fluids were ripped from his lungs, but no one heard. The Martian near-vacuum sucked the fluids out of his body from a pencil-sized wound.

Its powerful force also evacuated his suit, pulling it around his form until the fabric buckled his body over backward.

The colonists pulled themselves off the floor, gasping for air. They all saw the horrible image of Brinker falling and crawling away from the vacuum-packed corpse of Quinton hanging off the wall, the officer's upper torso bent completely backward, his upside-down, contorted face clearly visible through his visor. His body successfully stopped the airflow and the emergency air banks quickly restored the pressure. But Quinton's lifeless eyes stared out over them, a thick red foam dripping from his nose and mouth.

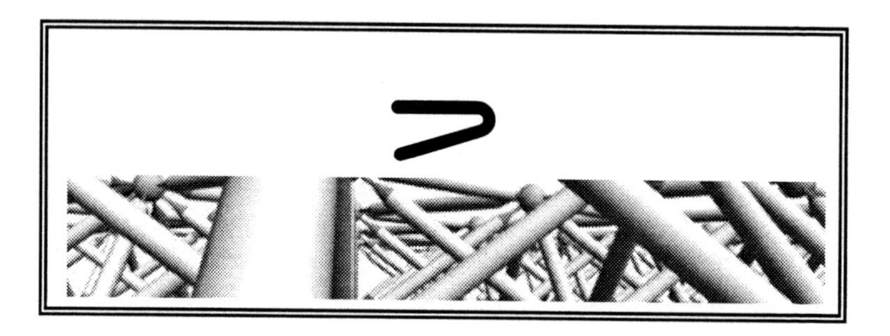

ilitary authority now fell to Brinker. But standing in the dining hall, staring at the body of his former superior officer hanging dead from the wall in the grotesque position into which he had purposefully placed him, did nothing for his own sense of command. Yet there were other lives to consider and none of his troops could handle the job, so he acted. He reached out unaggressively and took a PC2 from one of the colonists. He keyed in Lipton's command channel.

"Director's office, this is Sergeant Brinker here."

After a prolonged silence, a voice replied, "Go ahead, Brinker, this is Hernandez."

"Lieutenant Quinton is dead. Complex 14 dome had been breached but conditions are stable..."

"Are the prisoners under control, Brinker?"

"Yes, but not in my control, sir. Under Marine Corps regulations, this operation falls under the domestic dispute classifications, and I must have orders from higher up to continue these kind of military actions against American citizens. The United States Marines are not permitted to perform domestic police duties with regard to our own people."

There was a prolonged period of silence. Peter waved several individuals over to his side and whispered orders, pointing at Quinton. One immediately grabbed a table cloth and draped it over his body. Several more left to suit up and weld a cofferdam over the outside hole so that Quinton's body could be safely removed from the wall.

Finally, the PC2 crackled to life. "Brinker, this is Lassiter Lipton. Are you refusing to obey my direct orders to apprehend the prisoners and bring them back?"

"I'm just informing you that my commanding officer is dead, Mr. Director, from a civil dispute, and that puts this whole operation into a new category. Until I hear from my command on earth, I'm not allowed by Marine Corps regulations to aggravate this situation."

"What regulation are you quoting, Marine?" Lipton asked, characteristically.

"My actions are constrained by the Posse Comitatus Act of 1878," Brinker replied unhesitantly.

"And just what part of that act are you constrained by, Marine?" Lipton shot back without pause. "Are you aware of the implications of my authority as a Presidential appointee with special ambassadorial status under Title 10, U.S. Code, Section 331 and exactly how that relates to the Posse Comitatus Act?"

"I'll have to wait until I can contact my command and get back with you. I'll need a JAG analysis of that relationship, sir," Brinker replied instantly. He was used to dealing with bureaucratic nit wits. "I'm not permitted to exceed the limitations of my mission without proper authorization, sir."

"If you can offer innocent American citizens no more protection than that, you may as well stay in the enemy camp, Brinker," Lipton said in a fit of anger.

"You heard the man," Brinker replied, tossing the PC2 back to its owner, and directing the comments to Peter. "Looks like I'll be here for a sol or so until we can get this whole mess worked out. But I put you on official notice: I still work for Lipton until directed otherwise."

"Of course," Peter replied. Then to Toon he asked, "Will you assist the Marines with some coveralls and dinner?"

Brinker finally smiled, "Best idea I've heard in two sols."

Jack approached Brinker and slapped his shoulder. "Let me have your suits and I'll patch up those holes."

"You damn well better. Government property, you know."

As the Marines walked out of the dining hall, the other colonists began to speak to one another in hushed tones.

"Brinker, Lipton here," the PC2 echoed. "I want you in my office in ten minutes with a full report. Brinker, acknowledge!"

"Did you hear anything?" Peter asked Francis. "I didn't hear anything." Then he turned the PC2 off.

They removed Quinton's body more quickly than anyone expected. A second plate was hastily welded over the hole in the wall from the inside, and the external cofferdam removed. The plate hung there as an ugly reminder of just how desperate things could get.

Peter asked Gorteau to transmit the details of Quinton's death to Lipton immediately and call off the scheduled teleconference until they could come up with a new strategy.

It was approaching 11PM in the colonist's compound, and Peter asked Communications Chief, Jamie Powers, to prepare an update on the worsening crisis in their inability to communicate with the earth. Then he called another meeting of his staff. This one was considerably more subdued. Now the price of resistance was being measured in lives.

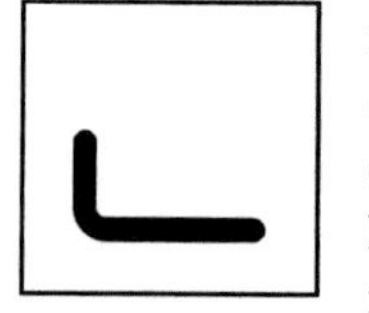

ipton himself had been changed by the affair. He caught himself losing his much regarded self composure in the pressure cooker he now found himself in, and that was unacceptable to his own self image. Yet, as he re-read the report from Gorteau on the death of Quinton, he found his hands shaking. This and the accusations the scientific community were making about his lockers were sure to end his position as Director, regardless of how many others were also ruined in the ensuing political firestorm.

He was losing his ability to think ahead, plan ahead and extract himself from this expanding morass. Or, was it just late? He wasn't sure as the next problem burst into his office.

"What's this crap about launching without the earth links, Lipton?" It was the lander Commander, Ian Cartwright, followed by Pilot Sigourney Michner and his deputy, Hernandez.

"I told you before, it's against NASA regulations to fly out of here without the earth links."

"I have the authority to order you to fly tomorrow morning, Commander, and when the window opens, you *will* fly," Lipton replied, all of the force of his temperament restored. "The count is underway. At T-zero, the lander will lift off."

"Read my lips Mr. Director: forget it - no way!"

"Just in case you've forgotten, there are two serious considerations here that directly affect you, Commander. One, you have a pilot still in orbit. Two, your upcoming rendezvous with the MTSO (Mars Transfer Solar Orbiting vehicle) is exponentially linked to your departure time. Every sol you delay past next week will cost you six sols in intercept time. If you wait until OT (Occultation Terminus - when the earth reappears from behind the sun) you'll be stranded here for a hundred or more sols, perhaps double that. No one has ever missed a cycle, Commander. Are you going to be first?"

"I don't need your lessons on space flight. And, believe me, nobody I know said anything about not leaving, Lipton. In fact, if I thought I could get away with it, I'd be out of this asylum in ten minutes. However, as it is my ship, I'll decide when NASA regulations will be waived and I take the responsibility for the safe conduct of my passengers and my mission.

"And while we're on the subject, I will not take prisoners back on my run without direct authorization from my command. You got that? No revolutionaries on my ship. When I decide to leave this planet, I'll take what is scheduled on the authorized manifest, and that includes people, diplomatic lockers and cargo; no more, no less."

"You realize, Commander, that the communications link is likely to be reestablished momentarily," Lipton said coolly. "And when it is, I will report your refusal to obey a direct order from a superior and your public insolence. Now get out of my office."

"That don't pass the so-what test, Mr. Director," the Commander replied turning toward the door. "Come on, Siggy."

"I hope you enjoy your last run, Commander," Lipton said with a sneer.

"I want the next transmission out of here Lipton," Cartwright replied, pointing his finger at Lipton, and then left the room, slamming the door behind him.

Hernandez looked at Lipton's face and did not like what he saw. He had never seen Lipton lose his composure on so many occasions. As Lipton sighed deeply and sat back in his chair, Hernandez feared for the Director's stability.

"Shall I scrub the launch, Dr. Lipton?" Hernandez asked quietly.

Lipton looked back at him with red, glazed eyes. "No, damn you to hell! The launch will proceed. Now get my staff in here immediately!"

8

IN LOW MARTIAN ORBIT

An ancient Gregorian chant drifted and echoed diffusely throughout the air and joined with the magic of the sunlight's brilliant display out of the spaceship's clear window. The pure soprano voices of the boys' choir were linked to the sun's brilliant golds and silvers, while the deep men's basses carried and caressed the vibrant violets and reds as the sun rose over the Martian horizon.

The *Robert H. Goddard* rounded Mars in its highly elliptical orbit for more than the hundredth time. As the sun rose over the horizon again, as it had every fifty-second minute, Navy Lieutenant and NASA Payload Specialist, Robert Kerry celebrated the magnificent event with his micro-miniature sound system turned up as loud as it would go. As always, nature's most glorious spectacle merged flawlessly with the most consummate cantos fantasia ever composed. It reverberated off the *Goddard*'s thin walls and fused with the light in Kerry's soul. He floated in front of the window facing the sun, chills repeatedly crossing his spine and running down through his legs.

They worried about him alone in space. *They were fools.*

Too soon, the glorious spectacle became too bright to watch and Kerry switched off the music. Better to save it for the next sunrise. But with the silence, the worry returned in force.

The liftoff of the lander and rendezvous were delayed for highly unusual and bizarre reasons. The peculiar happenings on the ground made Kerry as uneasy as he had ever been. BC1 was evidently embroiled in some kind of administrative crisis, they had all lost their earth links, and the normally routine schedule of exchanging people and cargo had been delayed. Such had never happened before in the history of spaceflight.

Any one of these events would have been cause for great concern, but all occurring together was unprecedented. They were already causing a ripple of effects in the *Goddard*. The orbiter continuously collected data about the Mars environment and made a data dump directly to earth every nine hours. Since there was no link, the data was being stored. In one hour, Kerry was going to have to delete one whole data set to make room for the next. No one on earth had planned for this particular anomaly. And that is what concerned Kerry the most. If they had not planned for this little glitch, what else had they overlooked?

Kerry was all too aware of the game of orbital catch-up in store for them. In continuous orbit around the sun was the *Wernher Von Braun II*, one of three unmanned, freely orbiting space platforms perpetually encircling the sun in orbits that periodically intersected the orbit of the Earth and Mars. The *Von Brauns* were thus called MTSO ships, or, Mars Transfer Solar Orbiting Vehicles. They were orbiting life support ships whose only purpose was to provide humans with a large living space and all the equipment necessary to provide life support. This saved the fuel required to accelerate and decelerate great mass every time someone needed to travel to and from Mars.

They had left the *Von Braun II* ten sols earlier for a rendezvous with Mars. If they departed Mars as scheduled, the planned intercept would require eleven sols. However, as orbital mechanics dictated, for every sol they delayed, the amount of time to catch the solar orbiting *Von Braun II* changed exponentially. In other words, it would take longer and longer to catch the ship until, eventually, it could not be caught at all.

The mission of the *Goddard* was to transfer two canisters to and from Mars orbit: one passenger canister and one cargo canister. The canisters were ferried to and from orbit by a launch and landing vehicle simply dubbed "the lander". The canisters ferried up and down by the lander vehicle were identical in shape and power, and fit like twin cocoons, clinging to the *Goddard's* sides. When the ship had first entered orbit, the empty cargo canister from the last run was blasted into orbit from BC1. As the passenger canister departed to land, Kerry rendezvoused with the empty cargo canister and docked it to the sides of the Goddard.

The process would be reversed when the earthbound passengers left the Crippen Spaceport. The fully loaded cargo canister would be released for landing and the passenger canister would rendezvous and dock in its place.

The whole process was essential to the survival of those on the surface. BC1 was unable to provide enough power or find enough water on Mars to continue its existence without regular resupply shipments from earth.

Additional power capacity was provided in the form of new solar panels on each resupply run as the colony grew. A few small nuclear generators were provided with each shipment, but these were political liabilities to the administrative officials and bureaucrats on earth, so not nearly enough were flown. At least one third of each shipment's mass was water. In earth orbit, the cargo canister was spun and the water exposed to the deep cold of space, so that it froze and was delivered as a solid to Mars. Heating elements were built into the canister, so that the ice could be melted on the surface as the water was needed.

Winter was creeping up on BC1. With the additional personnel added, the colony would desperately need the water provided by the cargo canister. Without it, they would have to severely ration their water until the next lander arrived. If, for some reason, the next lander did not arrive, the humans at BC1 would inevitably die.

Of course, items that could not be manufactured, grown or otherwise engineered on Mars were also delivered in both the passenger and cargo runs to the surface.

Winter on Mars did not arrive with a New England vengeance. There were no snows, no blizzards or even brisk winds. Martian winters came on slowly, almost insidiously. The temperature at BC1 dropped from the summer highs of minus 17.2 degrees C (+1 degree F) on a clear sol to winter lows of negative 107 degrees C (-178 degrees F); cold enough so that a morning frost of carbon dioxide ice froze on exposed outside regolith, equipment and shelters.

The use of water and power also slowly increased with the onset of winter. On Mars, water and power defined life.

SHTURMOVOI - REUNIFIED SOVIET EMPIRE

Brett English

Kerry looked through his hand-held Questar telescope at the slowly unfolding Marsscape below. He had aligned his ship so that Shturmovoi, the base built by the Reunified Soviet Empire, also known as the "Little Kremlin", would appear in a few minutes in front of his down-pointed scope. As the planet slowly rotated beneath him, the feature he was looking for rotated before Kerry. It was known as *Solis Planum;* Latin for "Sun Plain". Corrected for historical accuracy, the feature was called "Lake of the Sun" by the colonists, gaining its original name from a classical Mars map drawn by Giovanni Schiaparelli in 1879. Finally, it rotated into view across the planet below. He checked his chart, then the landmarks in his scope.

"Okay, baby, come on now," Kerry prodded, as the planet unrolled before his vision. "Bingo!" he said triumphantly as the first of the obviously human made structures crossed into his vision. The Little Kremlin resembled BC1 in that its structures were interconnected with tunnels, but it had a poorly defined regularity to it. The RSE engineers were forced to add and eliminate design plans at the various whims of political ideologies until Shturmovoi ended up looking like a ramshackle interplanetary mining town with no order and little notice of aesthetic or architectural design.

The Soviets had come to Mars not so much with science on their mind as undisguised planetary conquest. The Russian Commonwealth of Independent States collapsed early in the 21st century following prosecution of the interminable planetary Terrorist Wars in which the chimerical peace dividends of the old Soviet Union's collapse proved to be only wishful thinking. When the 21st century's planetary economic crisis morphed together as an unfortunate constituent of the seemingly endless Terrorist Wars, a new Union of Soviet Socialists Republic emerged from the ashes of the old. It called itself the Reunified Soviet Empire, and it was in historic fact even more of a stiff, totalitarian, ideological juggernaut than the old ever was. In the end, the cold war between east and west that many had declared dead and gone, raged furiously anew.

Yet, more to Kerry's immediate interest, and the single item that made the Little Kremlin unique, was their nuclear power station. Located over a crater wall, distant from the main base was, to Kerry's vision, an asymmetrical, flat black dot which defined the main power kernel.

The power kernel contained the solar system's largest Radioisotope Fueled Thermoelectric Power Generator or RTG. The Soviet built RTG was designed to provide Shturmovoi with constant power while incorporating the least amount of shielding possible. This was accomplished through an ingenious and remarkable engineering technique.

The Soviets first erected the outside of the power kernel, consisting of thin ceramic walls-within-walls to prevent heat loss. Then they installed a layer of thermoelectric generating devices, leaving the center of the core open. Meanwhile, on earth, they launched six, several thousand kilogram unshielded plutonium plugs into earth orbit. It took them 60 days to accomplish this, while the western world nearly self-destructed with protests. The Soviets denied it all, while in orbit, they were attaching long cables to their plugs. Finally, they literally towed them into Mars orbit.

Once there, the Soviets attached the cables to a remotely operated lander which mated to the plugs. The power kernel acted as a lander platform, and the Soviets neatly landed their plugs into the center of the power kernel, detached and went back for the others until the RTG was totally assembled.

This system was totally unshielded or uncontained. They used the crater walls for shielding the base. Inside the crater was literally a no-mans-land. Standing within 15 meters of the RTG for three minutes would be fatal.

The Soviets gambled that the technological wonder of their system and the incredible feat of its construction would far outstrip the temporary flood of criticism, and they took the chance that their launch system was good enough to thwart disaster on launch from Baikonur Cosmodrome. They won the bet that they could pull it off, but they underestimated the degree of world outrage. They ended up with a nearly inexhaustible supply of energy on Mars and a black eye on earth.

"Shturmovoi, this is the United States space vehicle *Goddard*. Please acknowledge."

Kerry turned the volume all the way up and reduced the squelch until all he could hear was a faint background hiss. No response. It had been that way for three orbits.

No one had authorized him to place the call, but that was too bad. Earth wasn't answering their calls of late either.

"Shturmovoi, this is *Goddard;* over."

No response. The Soviets were not answering their incoming messages, either, and Kerry would have almost given up the next sunrise to find out why.

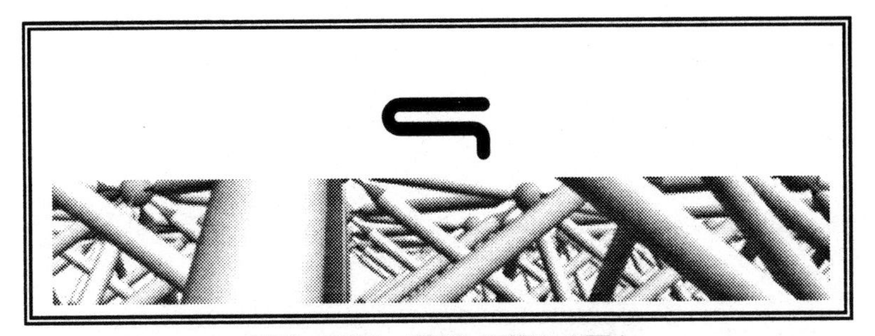

SHTURMOVOI
THE MARS BASE OF THE REUNIFIED SOVIET EMPIRE ON THE LAKE OF THE SUN

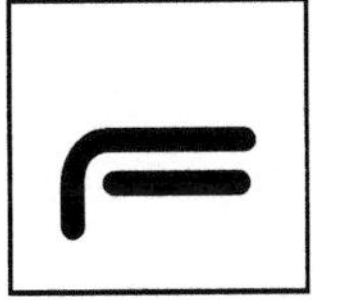

yodor Stepanovich Kirov's feet were always cold. They had been cold since the first minute he landed on Mars. He cursed the pathetic *trutnev* (drones) who had engineered Shturmovoi's living structures. They had either miscalculated the heat transfer characteristics of the floor material or ignored them altogether.

He looked at the clock, nearing midnight, and shivered. The life support system would be automatically lowering the temperatures again in less than an hour.

He pulled a second pair of socks over his feet then he cursed the Shturmovoi's Collegium for prohibiting the use of more than three changes of underwear per week. The most recent lament among the staff at Shturmovoi was that the Collegium had first invaded their minds; now they were dictating what went on in their pants.

As far as Kirov was concerned, the Collegium members (the administrative staff) were "... *pridurkovaty shkurkin!"*, or, self-serving, indulgent imbeciles.

Kirov was the chief scientist and the Energy Systems Chief of the RSE scientific contingent assigned to the Martian base. He sat on the side of his bed, looked longingly at the warm pile of contraband blankets, and exhaled heavily, twice, into the air.

"There! There! The ignorant bastards!" he swore again. This behavior had become a ritual with Kirov. Exhaling into the air of his quarters, watching his breath condense out in the cool air, then cursing the Collegium for not diverting more of their so-called "abundant energy source" for heat. Worse yet, it was Kirov who had designed the plant and was sent to manage it. Still, he could divert no more energy for himself than the rest of his colleagues who froze right along with him.

Kirov was a space systems nuclear engineer - a physicist with the title of engineer; a common and accepted practice in the Reunified Soviet Empire where the prestige of engineer was typically higher than that of a scientist. Prior to his assignment to the Mars base, he had been assigned to serve a sabbatical from Moscow University to the Lyndon B. Johnson Space Center in Houston, Texas. He grew fond of the humid, sweltering weather there and began to hate all forms of cold. Fearing a return to the Baikonur Cosmodrome's bitterly cold weather, he deftly parlayed his assignment into two full years before being ordered unequivocally back to the Soviet manned spaceport.

He cursed the cold and his own stupidity for not considering the consequences of a three year stint on a planet whose warmest equatorial heat made Siberia seem like Miami Beach. Career enhancement notwithstanding, Kirov recently wished he had followed in his brother's path who had married a fat Muscovite, fathered three children and worked in the Leninsky AZLK Moskvich automobile factory. At least he was warm at night.

Kirov pulled a pair of cotton gloves over his hands and flexed them several times to restore circulation as best he could. Then he picked up his folder and turned to leave for the meeting for which he had been summoned from his sleep. He had been ordered out of his bed to meet with Shturmovoi Base Commander, Colonel Zoya Anatolyevna Dimitriov.

He paused to look at the image staring back at him from his mirror. Kirov looked for all the world like a vagrant; his gray hair tumbled wildly across his naked forehead which swept all the way up to the center of his head. His gray eyes seemed to be crowded by his bushy eyebrows and pronounced nose. He wore loose, baggy sweaters that he never changed, although he had purchased half a dozen of them all of the same colors: gray and green. His salt-and-pepper mustache drooped unevenly toward the ends of his mouth. He did not particularly like what he saw, but he had become used to it, in all of its Einstinian moppishness. He wiped a few specks from the shag of tangled hair drooping over his mouth and turned to leave.

Why Dimitiov would call him out of a sound sleep to ask him a question which she specifically labeled "not urgent" was beyond him, but there was little surprise in it. Kirov had worked for an individual like her before. As an enlisted soldier in the infantry, he had served one Lieutenant Fiostich, ostensibly as an adjutant. Fiostich used to like to wake Kirov up to serve him and his fellow officers beer and vodka and then make him shine their boots during their all too frequent poker parties. It became a standard operating procedure that Fiostich should not tell Kirov of his planned festivities so that he could roust him out of bed at bizarre hours. It added something to Fiostich's sick sense of power to see Kirov stumble in half awake and stand at attention, awaiting his orders.

From this experience Kirov came to know and loathe the State, as his father had. Yet, Kirov's experience was inconsequential compared to that of his father, whose hopes and dreams were systematically denied, if not deliberately strangled, from him. Kirov often wondered why his father never spoke to him of those cherished ideas. Later in his life, Kirov concluded it was to protect him. But it did not work. His father died a bitter and unhappy man. If nothing else, they could have shared his dreams together. In the effort to protect him, his father had denied them both what little joy they could have clung to between them. At least they could have shared them together in their hearts.

The Soviet state had not just survived over the decades on its daily feast of self-indulgent paranoia; it had always defined itself thus by its secretive, compartmentalized social dysfunction. The old Soviet Union disappeared amid happy but mostly uninformed Western rumors of self-immolation, but the truth was far more interesting. After their foray into a period of capitalism, state reorganization and secret rearmament, the old Soviet State reformed just as quickly as it had disappeared as the Reunified Soviet Empire - stronger than it had ever been at any time in its history. Just as the Western economies began to disintegrate from excess, the RSE reawakened as a much more powerful, stable reincarnation of what it had been before.

Kirov reflected on these things in a swirl of recollections from far away and long ago. He stumbled, half-awake, down cold and dimly lit passages to Dimitriov's office. He rapped twice on the thin door and waited the customary five seconds before Dimitriov said sharply, "Come in."

Zoya Dimitriov looked up from her desk at him. Kirov knew well that he represented all that his boss and commander loathed in humanity. She had accused him of being sloppy and a chronic complainer, and she had told him he seemed to care about nothing but his science, which he appeared to worship more than the State itself. Dimitriov had told him to his face that she held this low opinion of him. Kirov came from a notorious family of Jewish *refusnik* and his father had repeatedly been denied permission to leave the RSE for Israel because of his intimate knowledge of State nuclear technology. But it could not have escaped her notice that before her stood one of the most brilliant nuclear scientists in the world; perhaps the only distinction that had saved him from the gulags.

"Sit down," Dimitriov said flatly, looking down at her desk. Kirov sat in the cold, plastic seat in front of her. Her office was unlit except for her desk lamp, and had no photos on the wall except for the prescribed black and white photo of the current RSE leader hanging slightly crooked in a cheap plastic frame.

Kirov wound the end of his bare fingers projecting out of his gloves through his mustache and considered the impoverished surroundings. He looked absently at Dimitriov, assuming she was going to inform him that communications had been reestablished with the earth and that he should write up some kind of inconsequential report. Whatever it was, it did not matter; he was cold, tired and wanted only to go back to sleep.

"Dr. Kirov, what do you know of the American base?" she asked him directly. The question stunned him. Was she interrogating him? Did she think he was an agent for the West?

"... ah, nothing, nothing at all. Except, naturally, from what I have read and heard at conferences," he answered truthfully.

She narrowed her eyes at him, holding her head away from the light so that her face was cast in a soft shadow. This muted her sharp features, but Kirov could see that her mordant, stern appearance held up even at this late hour. Her black hair was tied in a thick bun atop her head that seemed to pull her face tight.

"I have information that suggests the American base is tearing itself to pieces," she offered without elaboration. Then she said nothing, obviously waiting for his reaction.

Kirov and the other scientists at Shturmovoi often joked that Dimitriov had been sent to them from the *Lubyanka*, the notorious secret police headquarters and prison in central Moscow. The truth was, none of them had ever seen or heard of her before she was named director of the project. The job of directing a scientific mission with broad political overtones, as with the American base, was a political handoutwhich typically fell to bureaucrats, not scientists.

As for Dimitriov's association with the *Lubyanka,* well, such associations in the Soviet state were hard to differentiate between other party-connected professional assignments. These distinctions were considered to be distrustful of the state. The thought police were sure to root out these types of ideas and expose them; hence they were contemplated only in the recesses of the mind and never expressed by such foolishness as words.

"In what way are they tearing themselves to pieces?" Kirov asked, only mildly curious. Propaganda was typical. He discovered that believing each pronouncement from state sources would be equivalent to Americans believing everything they read on the cover of supermarket tabloids.

Dimitriov paused and lit a dark brown cigarette. While this act did not surprise him, it angered Kirov. Such items were strictly forbidden at Shturmovoi. The life support system was never designed to handle this garbage. The filth from the wretched Soviet tobacco, *makhorka,* would end up infecting them all.

"There has been a revolt there, and at least one is dead because of it," she said, again pausing and watching Kirov carefully while exhaling a putrid, blue cloud over the room. He found the information nearly impossible to believe. Some of the best scientists and engineers from earth had been through the American base, and many were still there. He was a personal friend of Fabian Gorteau whom he had met in Houston.

"What do you make of that?" she asked directly.

"I find it difficult to believe," he responded truthfully, his voice involuntarily catching on the acrid smoke.

"Believe what you will," she replied dully. "Do you have any personal acquaintances there?"

"No," he lied without a pause. Lying quickly and without hesitation was a technique he had learned early on. "Obviously, I have read of many of them and am familiar with a few of their publications." He successfully resisted the urge to carelessly embellish and protect his lie.

"Then you know none of their scientists or staff?" she pressed, causing Kirov's heart to race.

"No, as I told you."

"Very well. We have heard nothing from them since we lost our earth-based communications satellite. Did you know that they have a man still in orbit here from one of their shuttle craft?"

"No, I have no way of knowing that," he replied honestly.

"I would have suspected a communications attempt from them before now, but it is not surprising that we have received none, considering their state of affairs," Dimitriov said disjointedly, perhaps more to herself than Kirov.

Kirov sat still, considering the path down which Dimitriov was leading him. There was always a path. "Have we attempted to contact them?" he finally asked.

"No, of course not," Dimitriov replied, her voice revealing surprise that he should ask such an incredibly witless question.

"Colonel Dimitriov, I would be happy to present several communications scenarios with which we may contact the Americans, if for nothing else, to share information on our communications loss. Perhaps together, we can resolve the enigma. Perhaps we could use their earth-linked satellites to contact our headquarters."

"I forbid it! We both know such a plan cannot be approved at this level," she said, irritated, mashing out the butt of her cigarette and blowing the last cloud of smoke toward Kirov. "There are no acceptable scenarios. A man in your position with your supposed status should know this without discussion," she seemed to threaten him.

"And if they should try to establish communications with us?" Kirov asked without a pause, fully engaging her rebuke with his own logical riposte while anticipating the inevitable.

"Then we shall ignore them until directed otherwise."

"Is there anything else, Colonel?" Kirov asked, looking away from her hard features, his voice betraying his fatigue.

"Yes, there is. Prepare a report on the details of each individual you know or have heard about from the American base. I'd like it immediately. You may transmit it as soon as you are completed. That is all," she said looking back to her desk.

"Colonel Dimitriov," he said quietly.

"Yes?" she asked, continuing to stare at the papers on her desk and shaking another cigarette out of the pack.

"If they did have information on the loss of our satellite, perhaps we could benefit by their knowledge. Perhaps we could borrow transmission time from one of their satellites until ours is repaired," he offered.

She moved her eyes off the desk to his and looked at him with utter contempt, as though she were staring at a cockroach sitting on the edge of her desk.

"I am waiting for your report, Dr. Kirov," she said bluntly.

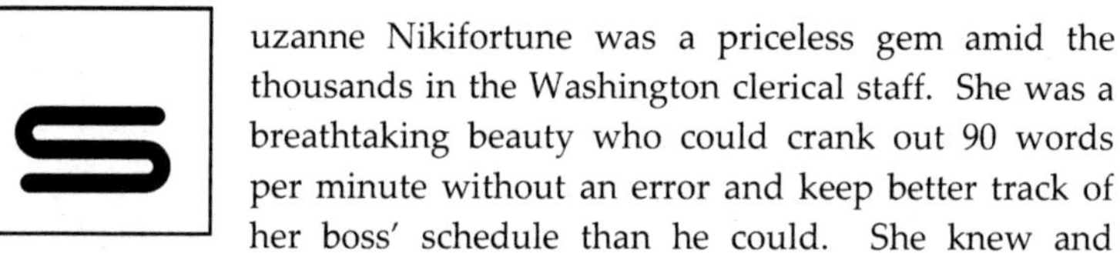

Suzanne Nikifortune was a priceless gem amid the thousands in the Washington clerical staff. She was a breathtaking beauty who could crank out 90 words per minute without an error and keep better track of her boss' schedule than he could. She knew and capitalized on the fact that being a good Administrative Assistant was an innate talent only a gifted few were blessed with. Lassiter Lipton recognized this quickly, and had lured her away from the Gentleman Senator from South Carolina with promises of a quick trip to the top of the Government General Schedule, a junket to Mars, and double her salary. She was worth every taxpayer's nickel of it. She looked her part; her beauty was carefully manicured and appropriately conservative. Yet she was able to package it in a style which served to accent her attractiveness. She had resisted the temptation to allow her appearance to deteriorate while at BC1. She did not show up to work in coveralls nor did she fail to maintain her immaculate wardrobe, even when the BC1 laundry was out of commission.

It was nearing midnight and she was still working. It did not make much difference to her; she had worked longer on occasion and kept careful track of her hours for which she was well paid. It really did not matter whether she had a night life on this planet or not. She was already convinced that any of the people on Mars, squatters or transients, were far from her type and she would save her affections for earthside.

"Suzanne, where is my staff?" Lipton demanded

She had rarely seen him in such a fury. He stalked out of his adjoining office and continued his harangue. "I told Hernandez to have my staff in my office nearly half an hour ago! Now where are they?" Lipton did not aim his barb directly at Suzanne. He would not have done that even if she had just set his desk on fire. Such was the unspoken bond between the professional manager and his closest aide.

"I'll do my best to find them, Dr. Lipton," she responded, with level neutrality, punching in the appropriate numbers on her C2. She was careful not to display frustration, although she had been actively attempting to track them down continuously for nearly an hour.

Suzanne was astonished at how much control Lipton had lost. She had never seen him act so frazzled in her presence before. Five minutes later she stepped into his doorway. Lipton was looking out his wide windows to the dark Martian night, the translucent domes glowing orange in the gloom.

"I'm still unable to locate any of them, Dr. Lipton. Shall I page them?"

Paging after working hours was procedurally limited to full blown emergencies. Each compound and room had a speaker connected to the paging system. To use it late at night was sure to disturb many people.

"Yes. Page them now," Lipton replied quickly. Suzanne returned to her desk and punched in the code just as Lipton's staff entered the office.

"Dr. Lipton has been expecting you," she said to them with all the professional contempt and a look of absolute derision that only a Director's Administrative Assistant could get away with.

Lipton was already at the door of his office. "Where have you been, dammit? Get into my office!" he shouted at Hernandez. As Hernandez hurriedly walked past him, Lipton grabbed his sleeve, pulling him inside and slamming the door. "I've been waiting for you for nearly an hour," Lipton began.

Hernandez pulled his sleeve away from Lipton's pinched fingers with a snap then withdrew from him. But Lipton followed, backing Hernandez into the wall. For barely a second, Hernandez considered Lipton's disheveled appearance. He had never seen him in such a frenzy before. But it didn't really matter. In a few minutes, it was likely to get worse.

"I have the most serious crisis of my career to deal with and you..." Lipton continued, leveling his finger inches from Hernandez's face.

"Back off Lassiter," Hernandez stated flatly. Such an uncharacteristic comment so startled Lipton that he fell quiet. Before Lipton could recover, Hernandez quickly stepped aside, opened the door and waved the other five board members inside. Suzanne Nikifortune followed with her tablet computer. "Wait outside," Hernandez ordered her.

Lipton came to life. "No, Suzanne, come in. I want this meeting on the record. Some heads are going to roll."

"Suzanne, wait outside," Hernandez said to her again, sternly. Lipton acquiesced, and then motioned her to leave with his head and eyes. As she left, she shot Hernandez a killing stare.

"What is this about?" Lipton asked Hernandez as the members took their seats.

"We've been meeting about our situation over the past few minutes..."

"What?" Lipton responded incredulously, slamming his hand down on the table top, seizing Hernandez in his glare.

"It would be better, Lassiter, if you would just allow us to explain our position," Hernandez replied, his voice straining to eliminate a barely audible tremble.

"This had damn well better be good," Lipton replied, his own voice firm and brutal.

"Then I'll get directly to the point, Dr. Lipton," Hernandez revealed. "We have decided to relieve you of your responsibilities for the next few sols, at least until the crisis can be resolved."

Lipton's response startled them all. He smiled and his face relaxed. "You what?" he asked, laughing incredulously. "You have no authority to do that! This is the most ludicrous thing I've heard in my professional career. What...how do you accumulate the aggregate authority to relieve me for any reason for any period of time?"

"Medically... you have been relieved medically," spoke Dr. Julia Friedman, staff Psychiatrist.

"Julia, Julia!" Lipton laughed, this time his voice more strained. "You don't have the authority to..."

"Dr. Lipton, I have the authority under both NASA flight rules as well as the Civil Service Office of Personnel Management guidelines," she replied flatly. Julia Friedman was a no-nonsense, career civil servant. She had been a government psychiatrist for over a quarter century and knew her craft better than anyone. She stared at Lipton over her half-glasses with unhesitant resolve.

"I'll have your career for this, Friedman," Lipton whispered at her across the table. "As for the rest of you, count your sols. You'll be out of here with the other terrorists on the next ship," he said, pointing his finger around the table. "You're all in complicity with mutiny, and that is a capital offense!

"You can never hope to succeed with this plan. No one in this facility is obligated to obey a single one of your directives. If you continue down this path, this community will be in total chaos in two sols, and I will not take the responsibility!" He stared at them for a full minute as his breath hissed lightly through his clenched teeth. Then he started to leave the room.

"Wait...," Hernandez said after him.

Lipton stopped but did not turn around. "What now?"

"I think you should know how difficult this was for all of us," Hernandez began slowly.

"Do you have a point to make, Bob, or is this wasted sentimentality?" Lipton asked his Deputy.

"I have a point, sir," Hernandez replied, slightly above a whisper. "We all decided together that we were concerned for the whole community..."

"Stop being obtuse. I'm tired," Lipton replied sharply.

"Of course. We decided that no one need know of this whole affair. Let the crisis pass, you visit with Dr. Friedman; eventually, it all goes back the way it was. No one need ever know it came to this," Hernandez offered sincerely, "No one." Then he added almost as an afterthought, "This way, we're all protected." But as soon as he spoke the word, he knew it was a poor choice.

"Protected?" Lipton asked, incredulous, spinning around to face them. "You want to be protected from a charge of mutiny? I'll see all of you rot in hell first! But please take this under consideration. I do not accept your findings and I refuse to step aside for sedition of any form, yours or theirs. And, oh by the way, the lander shall lift off from Crippen Spaceport tomorrow morning as scheduled, and you will be on it with the rest. I'll be in my quarters when all of you regain control of your senses." Then he left the room, slamming the door loudly behind him.

"Well, that could have gone better," Friedman said bluntly.

"He didn't accept our findings," Hernandez said in a near trance, a preposterous summary of Lipton's outrage. He stared straight ahead out the windows into the dark Martian sky.

"No he did not, Mr. Hernandez. Nonetheless, by formal direction, you are legitimately in charge," Dr. Friedman said. "This is not an argument. It is not a disagreement. It is a legal finding according to documented procedures."

She looked around the room at the other five faces, all somber, all afraid. They had a right to be, she thought. They would all likely forfeit their positions when they returned to earth. But the gamble was made before entering Lipton's office that the greater risk was allowing Lipton to carry on out of control. One life had already paid the price for his madness, and they were all now at greater continued risk.

Reuniting the community could have no higher priority. Reconnecting communications with the earth, launching the lander with its intended passengers and returning the cargo canister still in orbit were vital and had to be accomplished with as little contention and difficulty as possible. If any part of that scenario failed, they would all likely die. It was much too important to leave in the hands of a man whose emotions had run out of control, ruled by an unrestrained ego.

Friedman looked to Hernandez who appeared completely disoriented. No wonder, she reflected. He was more than likely chosen by Lipton as the consummate follower, not a leader, which would have interfered with Lipton's dominance. So she chose to end the meeting for him. With a leveled, polished voice, she said,

"May I be so bold as to suggest to this cabinet that with proper retrospect, Dr. Lipton will likely agree that our course of action was the most prudent under the circumstances? He is a politician of the first order and, like the rest of us, survival tends to be a priority. May I also remind all of you of the importance of maintaining total confidentiality of these proceedings? If Lassiter decides to go along with our plan, then our own security also depends on restricted access to our administrative agreements. Mr. Hernandez, I suggest we all retire to our quarters for rest. I shall take the liberty of inviting the scientific community to reopen their doors. We must initiate some meaningful dialogue and make decisions pertaining to our safety as soon as possible."

Hernandez nodded, still staring into space.

"Then it's settled. Goodnight all," she stated as the other four members rose to leave.

Lisa McConnel hesitated, and then asked, "Has the count for tomorrow's launch been canceled?" Her eyes had been following the countdown clock on Lipton's office wall: minus six hours seven minutes and counting.

"Yes, it's been scrubbed," Hernandez answered quietly. "I asked them to continue the clock for another hour or two." He clearly implied he was planning to wait until Lipton had retired.

The other members departed, leaving Hernandez and Friedman alone in the room. She looked at him. He appeared utterly defeated. She reached over and placed her hand atop his. "Bob, I know it must be... difficult for you."

"I've been a loyal believer in and assistant to Lassiter Lipton for fourteen years... and now this," he said with a deep sigh.

"You did what was best for all of us; you must believe that," Friedman said quietly.

He nodded his head slowly, and then rose from his seat to leave.

"Goodnight, Julia."

"Get some sleep, Bob. Let me take care of the details," she replied.

Friedman waited a respectful few minutes for Hernandez to leave the outer office before directing, "Suzanne, get Peter Traynor on his PC2 right away."

11

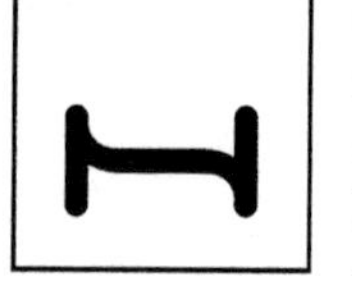

Hernandez got little, if any, sleep anticipating Lipton's rage at discovering the launch had actually been canceled. But it did not happen. Lipton downed a healthy half-liter of contraband scotch and went promptly to bed. He correctly reasoned a rested mind made better decisions. Besides, he also rationalized that a lander without a flight crew was not going into orbit anyway. Lipton had played out almost all his cards and nearly lost it all. Just before he passed out, he accurately assessed he had defeated himself due to his own lack of *judicious foresight*. But he still held one more good card.

At first light on the Elysium desert, the colonists stood on one side of Airlock door 6A, the Administrative staff on the other.

"Lock pressurized," Toon reported.

"Let's do it," Peter said, twisting the wheel that un-dogged the hatch. A slight hiss indicated it was safe to proceed. With only a moment's hesitation, he swung the door wide.

Julia Freedman was already walking down the tunnel with Hernandez in tow. They met near the middle and Freidman held out a small package to Peter. He was accompanied by nearly every colonist, lined all the way back into the main compound.

"If it's not shaped like a horse, it's probably okay," Francis said, winking slyly at Friedman. Peter opened it, a little embarrassed. It was a tiny plant in a small terrarium. To the people from Earth, plants represented life on Mars.

"Thank you, from all of us, Julia," Peter replied, truly touched. Friedman looked rested, although she had managed only a few hours of sleep. Her silver-streaked, blond hair was tied back. She wore a BC1 decal on her green jacket and her black boots were shined so brilliantly that Sergeant Brinker could have signed her up for Marine boot camp duty.

Julia looked at Francis, and then placed her hand on his shoulder and kissed his cheek. "And this guy looks like he needs some warm fuzzy feelings or something," she said laughing, the deep lines around her slate eyes giving way to a natural smile.

"Watch out, people, this woman is a trained shrink. She'll be inside your head before you know it," Francis said, grasping her hand in both of his and returning her smile. "I think she wants to pick our brains or something."

"As a matter of fact...," she replied.

"We have a lot of work to do, people," Hernandez said smiling, obviously feeling better himself in the few minutes they had been in the tunnel than he had for the two sols prior. "Dr. Traynor, will you allow us to accompany you and your staff to the dining hall?"

Peter laughed. "Listen, Bob, since when do you ask permission to the dining hall? I had the impression it belonged to everyone."

Hernandez was appreciative. "Then... we're together on this thing..."

"Of course," Peter replied, "We're a community... all of us, together. It's always been that way and always will be."

The crowd on both sides broke out in spontaneous applause.

Hernandez saw the face of Sergeant Brinker far back in the crowd. "Sergeant Brinker, please ensure that all residents of BC1 are allowed unlimited passage to all areas."

"Aye, sir," Brinker replied, tossing a weak salute and smiling flatly.

There was a good bit of handshaking on both sides as the crowd made its way to the dining hall. The spirit of oneness had never been greater. As they assembled, Peter stood at the front of the room and the buzz of the crowd slowly settled down to a dull mummer. Finally, Peter raised his hand. "Okay folks, let's get started. I've asked Dr. Gorteau to assist me this morning." Gorteau quickly hammered out a few displays on his computer which came to life on a large screen before them.

"Problem number one," Peter began, Gorteau dutifully making entries on his keyboard. "We still have no clues as to why we've lost communications with earth. Number two: we need to discuss the de-orbit of the orbiting cargo canister as soon as it's safe to do so. Number three: as a community, we have to solve our own organizational differences."

"Where's Lipton?" Someone innocently asked from the back of the room.

Without hesitation, Hernandez stood and faced the room. "Dr. Lipton is resting. He's being briefed on these proceedings. Until then, I represent the Director's office."

There was an instant cacophony of voices from the crowd. There were already rumors circulating, many of them coincidentally correct, but no one was sure.

"Let's get back to the problems in order," Peter insisted. "I've asked Jamie Powers to give us a summary."

There was a ripple of mannerly applause as the communications chief made his way to the front of the room. Jamie Powers, a colonist, was in his early thirties, but looked at least ten years younger than his age. His blond, nearly white hair fell across his forehead at an angle and contrasted with the spray of freckles across his nose. He wore a set of well fitted blue coveralls. From his boyish good looks, it was quite difficult to accept that Powers held advanced degrees from Cal Tech and MIT. It was not so difficult when he began to articulate his thoughts as his speech belied his intelligence.

He began immediately and held no notes. "As you know, we lost communications with the earth many hours ago and have not recovered the link. We were linked with the two deep space CERTS satellites in the San Paulo Convergence Protocol..."

Peter cleared his throat loudly. He had already warned Jamie to keep his summary in a reasonably comprehensible format.

"...yes, of course," Jamie said, understanding Peter's unspoken counsel. "Okay, the satellites are positioned, as you know, in orbits around the sun so that the earth can communicate with us at all times through either of them or just one. That method is called the San Paulo Convergence Protocol. In any case, it's a two-way street. Of course, we can also communicate with the earth through one of them or both of them. That kind of redundancy prevents loss of communications if one fails.

"As you also know, the earth slipped behind the sun in reference to us, and that is a condition called occultation, so that direct communications with earth became impossible and we had to rely on the satellites." Jamie paused and shifted uncomfortably on his feet. During this pause, someone asked a question.

"Jamie, is there a way to verify if the CERTS are working properly?"

"Yes, the CERTS have a direct communications capacity and a functional check routine. We've linked with them and both of the satellites appear to be functioning flawlessly. This would, obviously, indicate that the problem is with the earth stations, not the CERTS. There's less than one percent probability that there's a CERTS anomaly."

"How many earth stations are capable of communicating with CERTS?" Jack asked.

"Sixteen. Four primary CERTS stations and a dozen more capable of making the link. All sixteen would have to be malfunctioning to prevent communications with us."

"How about the Soviets?" someone asked. "Have they lost their satellites, too?"

"Yes. We've oriented our antennas to listen for their data stream and it's also stopped. We know that they're no longer receiving data either."

"What theory do they have to explain the loss?" Geoff Hammond asked.

"We don't know. They aren't answering our requests for information."

The silence lasted two full seconds, and the crowd burst into loud discussions with one another.

Gorteau walked over beside Jamie. "May I?" he asked. Jamie nodded as he began. "To keep this manageable, let me add one other bit of pertinent information. Just prior to loss of communications, we received this data burst from earth through the satellites." Gorteau projected a display on which a frequency versus time plot was indicated.

"These frequency spikes represent the last seventeen minutes of communications received from the CERTS. The frequency spikes during the last four minutes relate to pulses of electromagnetic energy within the frequency bands we were monitoring at the time."

"If those are EMP's, I think you'd better go ahead and skip to the end of the story!" Sergeant Brinker said, pushing his way to the front of the room. Brinker was no scientist or technician, but he had been trained in combat, and he knew the buzz words. Most of the rest of the people in the room were not combat trained, but they knew enough about what Gorteau was talking about to worry.

"The Sergeant is right, of course. These are very high energy electromagnetic pulses, otherwise known as EMP's, right across the spectrum. They are typically observed when a very large amount of energy is released all at once."

"Like an atomic weapon," Brinker added. The rest of the crowd knew it was coming. No one but Brinker dared say it. Now they erupted into an even louder exchange. Peter stood and allowed it to continue for several minutes before raising his hand to quiet them again.

"Okay, let's not lose control. Let him continue. Dr. Gorteau, please."

"What Jamie and his team gave us for analysis was these EMP recordings. They were not broadcast by any ground station at all, but received directly by the CERTS from earth. Now, there was a single CERTS station broadcasting all our uplinks through the ground stations to us at the time. The EMP pulses began some four minutes before we lost the signal from the ground, but the CERTS continued to receive the broad spectrum EMPs after the direct link was lost.

"If there were a nuclear war in progress, one would assume there would be a warning of some sort. But there was no warning sounded. Indeed, the news accounts we received indicated there were not even any situations of unusual military build up or tensions anywhere across the globe. The assumption of a nuclear war is just that; an assumption, of which we have no proof at all.

"During the four minutes from the first EMP until loss of the ground station, there was no warning, but there was a sequential loss of data which we have analyzed. The data was lost from stations transmitting to the CERTS before the CERTS ground station itself was lost. The CERTS ground station was located in Omaha. The loss of broadcasting inputs to the CERTS stations were lost sequentially in two patterns from north to south and from the coasts in toward the interior of the United States. There was also a loss of signals from Hawaii and Guam, but they occurred early on. At plus four minutes and three seconds from the first EMP, we lost the CERTS ground station itself. This was the cause of our launch scrub – but the CERTS continued to receive direct EMP for an additional hour thereafter.

"One more analysis was done as well. The loss of ground based CERTS substations is also coordinated with the exact moment of individual EMP pulses." Gorteau paused. The crowd was considerably more subdued.

"So, was there a war or not?" Brinker asked.

"We cannot be sure without additional proof," Gorteau responded thoughtfully, "but the probabilities seem high enough to warrant serious concern."

"Typical egghead response," Brinker replied with complete exasperation. "I want an answer to my question: Was there a war or not?"

"I'm sorry, Sergeant, we cannot be sure. There is no way to be certain. All we have is this data."

"Okay, let's move on," Peter said, directing the conversation. "What else could it be, Dr. Gorteau?"

"If someone wanted to fly out directly to the CERTS satellites and transmit these signals directly to us, to deceive us into thinking there had been a war, they could do so. But I fail to see the point in that."

Brinker's eyes widened and he nodded. "Can you prove they didn't?"

"Not at the present, but perhaps we do have the ability to confirm the theory that the pulses were transmitted from the earth and not artificially originated at the CERTS satellites," Gorteau mused. "We can connect with a deep space probe or two and interrogate their memory. Perhaps one or two of them also recorded the pulses. But they would have to be turned on and receiving and recording data from earth at the time of the pulses. Since there are only twelve active probes, the chance that any were turned on at all is small. Yet, such data would verify the pulses were real. Of course, we are not authorized to interfere with the operation of those probes..."

"Save the thought, Dr. Gorteau," Peter said. "What else? Is there any other sort of proof possible?"

"None that I am aware of at this point," Jamie added. "But we're still looking at ways to analyze the information."

"Of course," Gorteau added, "we can aim our telescopes at the earth in 30 to 60 sols or so when the earth is sufficiently far from the glare of the sun to ascertain whether there is any unusual visual presence..."

"Like the clouds of nuclear winter?" someone asked.

"Exactly."

"What have we done to establish communications with earth?" Ashley asked.

"We've set up a recording that transmits to earth continuously," Jamie replied. "We've received information back from the CERTS acknowledging that it's received the message and that it successfully retransmitted it to earth, but no response has been forthcoming."

"And what about the Singleton?" Peter asked, referring to the next ship scheduled for launch to Mars with its supplies and new passengers.

"The Singleton is docked to the space station and is not scheduled to depart earth orbit for two more weeks," Gorteau responded. "She is neither fully outfitted nor supplied. If there has been a disaster on earth that has disrupted any of the infrastructure to a significant degree, she will not even be able to leave earth orbit at all. Not only would she be inadequately prepared for departure, she would have no command and control and could not leave even if she wanted to."

"Jamie," Peter persisted. "Have you attempted to contact the Singleton directly?"

"Yes," he responded softly. "Nothing. Just like the rest. Nothing."

The conversation continued back and forth. It was revealed that the space stations of the RSE and the United States could not be raised. It was as if the earth had moved behind the sun and disappeared. For those on Mars, so dependent on the mother planet for life itself, the idea that their civilization had self destructed was a horrifying prospect.

The groups discussed their attempts to contact the Soviet base to the south for data corroboration, an attempt made by the colonists without Lipton's knowledge. The failure of the Little Kremlin to respond was not taken lightly by Brinker who suggested they were "up to something."

"It seems real funny that they're also silent in the face of the earth link losses. That makes me think they're a part of it all," Brinker added.

"On to problem number two: get my lander into space," a loud, commanding voice said from the crowd. It was Commander Ian Cartwright walking to the front of the room. Cartwright wore his flight suit with his mirrored pilot's sunglasses strategically propped on his forehead. He was accompanied by pilot, Navy Lieutenant Sigourney Michner.

"We're leaving tomorrow morning when the window opens at 0642, with or without Lipton's blessings."

"Now, see here, Commander," Hernandez said in an indignant tone.

"No, you see here," Cartwright said, driving his finger into Hernandez's chest. "We've had just about enough of all this bad ju-ju about nuclear war. We're fed up with your local domestic disputes, dead Marines and deaf and dumb Soviets. We're out of here tomorrow, got it? Your theories have about as much credibility with me as little green Martians. We link with local launch telemetry and we're gone. You get your manna from heaven and we depart for MTSO in solar orbit. It's just that easy."

"No, that is impossible," Gorteau replied.

"What do you mean, it's impossible?" Cartwright replied, turning his wrath on Gorteau. "I don't remember having to take any crap from civilians."

"In the event your launch into orbit is successful; in the event the untested data link works; in the event you make it back to earth and there was a nuclear exchange, you would still die."

"Wrong, wrong, wrong... You geezer scientist types have a bad habit of chaining way too many events together. In a pilot's world, we like the more simplistic cause-and-effect system. Now, the cause is this: we're falling behind in our solar catch-up game. The effect is spending way too many days in a cramped ship making up for the lost distance which just happens to be growing at a non-linear, ever increasing rate of at least 400,000 klicks per day! Tomorrow morning... 0642... rocket ship lifts off... is that so hard?"

"One question, Commander," Hernandez asked.

"Go ahead; it looks like show and tell started hours ago."

"Why the sudden change in attitude? Just last night, you were refusing to leave without reestablishing the earth links. Now, you want to go immediately. What conditions have changed to so radically alter your judgment?"

Cartwright obviously mused that he was not about to be trapped by these intellectual cretins. He looked at the crowd around him and all were absolutely quiet, awaiting his answer.

"That was two questions, Hernandez. But good ones and deserving of an answer, so you'll get 'em. You let a serviceman die a horrible death here last night, your Director is mysteriously missing, and now you academic types have dreamed up nuclear war to explain a simple communications snafu on two deep space satellites, which just happen to go on the fritz all the time. As far as the Soviet Bloc is concerned, they probably instigated the whole thing anyway.

"Now, my main theory is this: you folks have been here so long you're losing it. Personally, I want out, now. I'd rather take my chances in deep space than in this zoo. At least in deep space it's still cause and effect, which my simple, non-Ph.D. brain can grasp. I also have another theory: if you don't let me fly soon, all of you are going to lose your chance to recover your precious cargo that still orbits over your heads. And no matter how irrational you've become, you'll need those supplies just to live through the winter. Any more questions?"

"No, but I do have a response to your proposal, Commander." It was the polished voice of Lassiter Lipton cutting the air as he pushed his way through the crowd. The assembled colonists and administrative personnel gasped and whispered together as Lipton approached the front of the room. He was back in full form, not a hair out of place, his voice strong and firm.

"You have my permission to leave," he said to the commander, casting an acrimonious look at Hernandez who immediately averted his eyes.

"In case all of you were wondering about the precision of rumors you've heard, they're true. Some have made an attempt to unlawfully relieve me of my duties here, and I'm certain that those responsible will pay for that crime with long prison terms. And since their actions were unlawful, I still have the authority to grant you permission to leave, Commander Cartwright."

Lipton played his final card with an exquisite flourish. His reasoning was impeccable. His hand was a powerful one. The laws concerning the relief of a standing administrator with ambassadorial status were ambiguous, at best. No one but a staff of trained legal experts could have tested the actual act itself and it would probably have ended up entangled in the courts for a decade. The upshot was that no one really knew for absolute certainty who had the authority to act under what circumstances. It was that uncertainty that Lipton seized upon. He could claim to be in charge to manipulate differences in opinion, then declare he had been relieved to side step responsibility if anything went wrong. And the final certainty was that Hernandez was not about to stand against his boss, especially now.

Peter, Francis, Ashley, Toon and Gorteau all looked at one another with confusion. Hernandez and Freidman had assured them this issue had all been taken care of. But they sat in stunned silence, ensnared by their own pact of secrecy.

Lipton was no amateur in these political avocations. Indeed, he was a master and careful student of them and knew how to convolute and confuse the enemy with their own carefully crafted plans.

"I thought they had you hog tied in some closet," Cartwright said truthfully.

"They don't have enough courage for that," Lipton replied provocatively, eyeing each one of his staff individually. What time would you like to lift off, Commander?" Lipton asked.

"Zero six forty two."

"Granted," Lipton replied without a pause.

"Wait...," Gorteau said blinking his eyes several times to quickly formulate his thoughts. "Give us one more sol to reestablish communications with the earth."

"I thought you said the green hills of earth were toasted by now, Dr. Geezer. Change your mind?" Cartwright said accusingly. "Are we going to wake up tomorrow and find out this was some kind of joke?"

"Pray to God in heaven it is," Gorteau replied, then abruptly left the room.

Peter had had enough. "Just in case the rest of you haven't heard," he stated, "Dr. Lipton was relieved by Mr. Hernandez last night in accordance with procedure, for medical reasons. It was by the book. As for you, Commander Cartwright, if you want to go on your way, then so be it. We do need those supplies and I suspect we'll be compelled to go after them sooner or later. You might as well continue on for earth if that fulfills your mission objectives and your own personal desires.

"However, I must warn you that the ascent navigation program you'll be using when you fly has never been employed before. It's an untested, emergency program to be relied upon only as a last result *after* liftoff has already been initiated."

"Don't try to tell me my business," Cartwright glowered.

"You won't be taking passengers, of course." Peter continued.

"Oh, yes I will. I'll be taking the passengers manifested for this flight. I doubt seriously whether any of them want to stay back here any more than I do."

"Whups... hold on," Sergeant Brinker interrupted walking slowly up to the front. "I won't be on your rocket, Commander."

"If you're on orders, Marine, which you are, then you'll be on the ship because I'll ensure your compliance. If you'll look on my collar, you'll notice that I'm a commissioned officer, and you *will* follow my orders."

"With all due respect, sir," Brinker shot back evenly, slurring the "sir", "my seat and the seat of Corporal Hiraldo will be unoccupied. The Marine in command of this unit who came in to take my place is dead. I can't be relieved of duty unless I'm replaced by a commissioned officer or another NCO. In case you need a set of orders to stay here and take my place, *sir*, I'm sure Dr. Lipton will be glad to sign you up." Then he stuck the omnipresent cigar back into his mouth and walked away.

"We're going back, Traynor!" yelled a voice from the crowd. Peter saw Stephan Hicks, who desperately wanted out and had occupied a seat on the outbound lander on the previous launch attempt. He inched his way forward. "I have a ticket out, and I'm using it. The rest of us on the manifest all agree. We're leaving and you can't stop us. We did our time here, and it's over. Lipton's in charge, not you or Hernandez or Friedman. Lipton – he's the boss. He calls the shots. Any more questions from the geek section?"

"Let the moron go, by all means. Good riddance!" a colonist said from the crowd. "Strap him to the outside of the rocket!"

"They're all leaving according to the manifest," Lipton agreed.

Peter whispered to Francis who nodded then said, "Very well, but you fly out at your own risk. I only have one last request, for your safety and that of your passengers," Peter asked of Cartwright.

"What now?" he asked sarcastically.

"Give us one more sol to reestablish communications or determine a cause. Your window will open at 0744 sol after tomorrow."

"Can you give me one good reason? Can you give me any reasonable assurance that this place won't unravel between now and then?" Cartwright asked earnestly.

"The good reason is to ensure the maximum safety for you and your crew. And, no, I can't assure you of anything at this point," Peter replied, looking directly at Lipton who returned his stare. "Surely the aspect of flight safety must mean something to you. If not for yourself, then at least for the innocent passengers you insist on dragging along with you."

Cartwright looked at his pilot, then back to Peter. "I know I'm going to regret this, but you've got one more sol. That's it. Then I'm leaving, come hell, high water, dust storm or flock of little green geese, I'm lifting off that launch pad at 0744 in two sols.

"And another thing. If you and Lipton start chasing one another around the base again, stay away from my ship. Siggy and I are going out there to sleep. The first person that comes near my ship without my permission joins the Marine in the meat locker."

"I'll verify the ascent navigation program," Toon offered.

Cartwright, who had already turned to leave, pivoted sharply to face Toon, barring his teeth, "Don't touch the program... don't touch it!" Then he and the pilot thrust their way through the crowd to leave.

Peter whispered to Toon, "Verify the program, every line of it."

Toon nodded, "I'll do what I can."

It was a toss up as to what killed the spirit of the morning, the appearance of Lipton or the revelations of what may have happened on earth. Lipton left the meeting just behind the lander crew. Several administrators followed closely on his heels. Hernandez convened his group for an urgent meeting which left mostly colonists milling about the dining hall. Instead of a general meeting, Peter sent teams out to investigate the key questions: to interrogate the deep space probes for possible earth links, to attempt to communicate with the Soviet base and to verify the accuracy and adequacy of the emergency ascent navigation program.

Later, Peter and Ashley visited with Gorteau in his office. The senior scientist was busy at his desk, humming quietly to the music of Bach's *Fantasia and Fugue*.

"Ah, yes, my friends, please come in," he acknowledged as soon as he saw Peter's face at his door.

"Now you know why I would not make such a great leader," he said to them as soon as they entered, leaving the impression of some residual embarrassment.

"Oh, please, Dr. Gorteau. No need for...."

"No, I admitted early on that I had no aptitude for the patience required to deal with the simpletons who play the so-called power game. Now it is apparent to all."

"No need to apologize, Dr. Gorteau. I, for one, understand," Ashley offered.

"And I," Peter concurred. "Sometimes I feel like Lipton is so adept at manipulating the process that we'll never be able to solve our problems. Just look at the difference between the way the meeting was going before he showed up and after."

"Don't let that fool you, Peter," Gorteau replied. "The feelings of frustration were there long before he appeared. The others had no advocate before Lipton made his appearance."

"How... who is going to control the community now?" Ashley asked, almost to herself.

"That is it, precisely," the senior scientist replied, "Control is the issue. Control is power. We, the colonists have voted Peter to control in our best interests. Hernandez is in control by administrative default and

Lipton controls by an odd analogy to a physical precept called the Heisenberg Uncertainty Principle. Do you know what that is?"

"Well, if memory serves me correctly, it's an idea in quantum physics that relates to the state of subatomic particles," Peter replied with a curious smile and a glance at Ashley.

"Exactly. Excellent! Lipton's control follows the same rules. Just as it is impossible to know the state of a photon's position and momentum at the same time, Lipton has deftly engineered his status so that one never knows whether he is in charge calling the shots, or just riding on the train to disaster. He is in a position to destroy the colony or dismember it and shift the blame to others. He is more dangerous now than before."

"What do we do?" Ashley asked in a quiet, pensive voice.

Gorteau did not answer. He shook his gray head and looked to the collection of glowing screens arrayed across his desk.

"I'm afraid we're all passengers on the train," Peter finally said. "But I hardly think his terms are going to be acceptable much longer. The thing that troubles me most is that I can't see what lies ahead around the next dark corner and this train is traveling awfully fast for us not to know who sits at the controls."

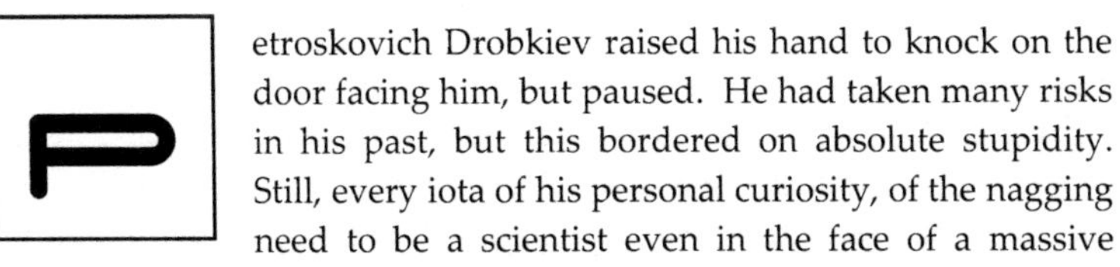

Petroskovich Drobkiev raised his hand to knock on the door facing him, but paused. He had taken many risks in his past, but this bordered on absolute stupidity. Still, every iota of his personal curiosity, of the nagging need to be a scientist even in the face of a massive obstructionist ideology, compelled his hand to knock despite his fears.

The thin door opened to the smiling and friendly face of Fyodor Kirov, his life-long friend.

"Petroskovich, my brother! Enter!"

Petroskovich Drobkiev, Shturmovoi communications manager, and Kirov had attended Moscow University together as young men. Although they had not always had the good fortune of working near each other over the years, they had remained true and trusted friends. They somehow skirted the realities of life and remained in close and frequent touch, even managing a visit or two each year. When they were finally stationed together on the Shturmovoi Mars project, they were ecstatic. For the first time since the university, they could spend substantial time together.

"Petroskovich, what brings you to my door at this hour?" Kirov asked, pointing the way to a seat in his tiny cubicle. As Drobkiev sat, Kirov noticed the deeply worried expression on his face.

Kirov sat down on the edge of his bed, reached over and placed a hand on Drobkiev's shoulder. "I have seen you better, my friend. Are you ill?"

Drobkiev looked over to his friend. Kirov, like he, had lost the youthful face he had grown to love and admire as a boy. Like his own, it had weathered and aged with time. But it was still the friendly face of his trusted companion and he knew every line in it.

Drobkiev reached up and grasped Kirov's wrist. "No, comrade, I'm not ill." The need to talk to Kirov was real and intense. Yet, he wondered whether he dare risk their professional careers or, at the worst, their personal safety, by discussing sensitive matters of state. They had discussed such matters before, but only briefly in absolute privacy; only half seriously and with some apprehension.

Drobkiev's heavy frame and his pronounced paunch pushed his green and blue striped sweater up around his middle. His grayish-blond, bushy beard contrasted oddly with his jet black eyebrows that seemed to lie in patches over his narrow, Slavic eyes. But they were friendly, trusting eyes, and they seemed to invite Fyodor's understanding.

Drobkiev pulled a small black box with a long wire from his pocket and connected the device to the work computer sitting on the desk. Kirov watched in fascinated silence.

"This is a jamming device," Drobkiev said in a virtual whisper. "It amplifies the frequency of the current through the computer and will prevent an electronic device from transmitting our voices."

Kirov knew better than to ask why they would need such a device. But he could feel the hair stand up on the back of his neck anticipating what would motivate his normally timid friend to go to such great lengths and incur such peril. The story he had to tell would have to be magnificent.

"Go on, Petroskovich," he urged. He, too, was aware of the odd events unfolding around them and craved more information from any source.

Drobkiev's eyes brightened with the opportunity. He had been forbidden to speak of it to anyone by Dimitriov.

"It has been sols now since we lost communications with the earth. The loss through our deep space network has not allowed us to analyze our SRK-231D satellite for failure. The SRK is not nearly as sophisticated as are the American CERTS units, and we cannot interrogate it for failure. It's only a transmission repeating device. But the Americans have indicated by their behavior that the situation is grave."

"What do the American's know of the details?" Kirov asked, somewhat confused.

Drobkiev was surprised at such a irrelevant question, but he respected Kirov too much to allow that emotion to show.

"Elementary logic, my friend," he replied evenly. "They have been asking us for information all along, which is how we discovered they, too, lost their links. If they have lost their two deep space satellites and we have lost ours at the same time, then the odds of simultaneous equipment failure are astronomically high."

Kirov's face mirrored his astonishment. "You mean they have also lost their communications satellites?" he asked with a gasp.

"Why, yes, of course. I thought you knew!"

"No," Kirov whispered, shaking his head. "What do you mean they have been asking us for information all along?" he questioned, the level of his surprise mounting.

"The American astronaut in orbit attempted to contact us as did the American base. Finally, they established a continuous recording, requesting our urgent response. Dimitriov has specifically forbidden any response to them, even to acknowledge their transmission."

"At least *this* does not surprise me," Kirov replied, "But go on."

"They are also apparently embroiled in some kind of civil dispute. One American soldier has apparently died in what curiously appears to be a revolt. The events are extraordinary. They must know far more than we."

"Then it is true," Kirov whispered to himself, recalling the meeting with his superior.

"And, I...uh, well, I know something which you must not share with anyone, Fyodor," Drobkiev said in a nearly inaudible whisper. "Our recorders indicate there were a series of very powerful electromagnetic pulses broadcast from earth and picked up by their satellites in a wide frequency band just before we lost our communications."

"What kind of pulses? Be more specific."

"I examined them on the monitor, separated them from the ongoing transmissions at the time, but did not dare reproduce them on paper. They are high amplitude spikes of 500 to 750 millisecond duration all over the band simultaneously."

Kirov gasped, "You do not think..."

"Yes, they match those one would expect from a nuclear exchange."

"I had no idea it was this serious," Kirov said, "I thought we had simply lost our satellite and would recover when the occultation had ended. I had no idea... How much of this have you shared with Dimitriov?" Kirov asked, a shiver running the length of his spine.

"I have not told her of the electromagnetic pulses. But I think she knows much more than she is sharing with the scientific branch. Her behavior is much too deliberate and she is demanding extraordinary security. She has compartmentalized the scientific branch to the point that there can be no sharing of information about the crisis. We cannot hope to solve this until we can exchange information among ourselves and with the Americans."

"You do not suspect Dimitriov thinks we are in a state of war with the Americans?"

"It must be so."

"This is insanity," Kirov muttered, his mind wheeling with the unthinkable scenario. "It is difficult enough to even imagine civilization on earth should have destroyed itself, but to extend that madness to this planet, too..."

"Perhaps we are wrong, Fyodor," Drobkiev interrupted, his voice rising in a hoarse whisper as his hand motions became excessively animated. "It is quite an outrageous hypothesis based on such little information. It is possible that we are just two bored old men dreaming up a pretentious *novella* to entertain ourselves."

"No, no, Drobkiev. We must not dismiss this with such docility. It is possible that we have stumbled on an awful truth. If so, my friend, we must be in a position to salvage what little sanity there may be left in humanity."

"What are you suggesting, Fyodor?" Drobkiev whispered.

"We must have more information."

"These are no longer the days of *perestroika*," Drobkiev reminded him, reflecting wistfully on the period of openness that once hinted at the possibility of a lasting peace between cultures.

"Granted. But there are ways in which we can contact the American scientific branch without being detected," Kirov said in a nearly incomprehensible whisper, moving his face to within inches of Drobkiev.

"How, Fyodor?"

Drobkiev was all but reading Kirov's lips now, and could feel his warm breath across his face.

"If it is true, Petroskovich, we must both come to realize that all that we have ever known is forever gone, and we are in a position to realize real *perestroika* anew. The old allegiances we have sworn to no longer exist. We are free to determine our own destiny now."

Drobkiev was stunned and startled. Kirov was speaking high treason against the state for which trials were only a formality. His words alone promised a certain and swift death. With that thought, he broke off his gaze from Kirov and looked away.

"I cannot, Fyodor," he replied.

Drobkiev's mind ached with the implications of such thoughts against the state. He loved his country dearly; there could be no other Russia, no other love greater than the one to which he had committed his allegiance and very life. The snows of Moscow, the boyhood fields of his wonderful farm *kolkhoz,* the sweet springtime rains of the Belorussian prairie were all a part of him and would forever be. Yet Kirov was asking him to betray that love and allegiance. It was impossible and could never be.

"I must leave, now, Fyodor," Drobkiev said, rising hurriedly and walking quickly to the door. He raised his hand to the handle. Kirov sat still and silent. "I am sorry, my friend," Drobkiev said gently.

"Petroskovich."

"Yes."

"Are you not forgetting something?"

Drobkiev paused, remembered, then turned around slowly. He walked over to the desk computer, and folded his fingers around the jamming device. Then he realized it was not his country or his heritage that Kirov was asking him to betray. It was possible that a country that bore the name Russia, on a planet orbiting so far away, no longer even existed.

He released the device, still in place, and then he slowly sat back down in front of Fyodor. Raising his eyes to meet his friend, he asked, "You realize, comrade, what you are asking?"

"I ask nothing. You must commit *yourself.*"

Drobkiev nodded, but in his heart there was much more sadness than resolution.

eter and Francis sat drinking coffee at a table in what was loosely called the "faculty lounge" in the housing compounds. This large room had been "modified" covertly by the colonists months before, after they were run out of the dining hall for the last time by BC1 cook Roman Adkins Thomas, better known by his initials as Rat.

This single act of extemporized engineering had sent Lipton and company into two weeks of meetings and had generated numerous earthside telecons while consuming terabytes of computer memory. Finally the powers agreed to allow the lounge to stay: the engineers had to write briefs proving it posed no danger to the structure; the life scientists had to prove that the life support system would not be affected; the electrical engineers were tasked to support that the power busses would not fail; the custodial experts decided their contract robots would not be affected; and so on. The colonists concluded that the bureaucracy must have been incredibly bored to devote so much time to such minutia.

Peter finally had been able to relax, as far as it was possible. He had taken a shower and his face reflected a few hours sound sleep in Ashley's comforting embrace. The arms of his blue coveralls were tied around his waist. On the upper part of his body he wore the thick, long sleeved white underwear of BC1. Such undergarments were an absolute necessity; the temperature in the compounds never rose above 18.5 degrees C; 65 degrees F.

Francis, also rested, was wearing his coveralls in his characteristic fashion; stiffly starched, the top two buttons undone. He looked at Peter, who was smiling as he talked, and realized what a good choice the colony had made for their spokesman and leader.

"I'm happy you can maintain such an upbeat disposition after the last two sols," Francis said to Peter.

"I'm just delighted to be here instead of in solar orbit. It was very close, you realize."

"Yes," Francis replied, "It was too close for all of us."

Peter nodded, taking the last sip from his coffee that had already lost its warmth. Gorteau came walking into the lounge with obvious purpose.

"You look like you have some news," Peter said. "I hope it's something we can celebrate over."

"I'm afraid not," Gorteau replied as he sat down beside them. He looked ragged and drained, as though he had not had any rest in a while. His clothing was wrinkled and in disarray and he needed a shave.

"We just finished the analysis of the deep space probe interrogations, and we have received confirmation of several events."

"And?" Francis prodded.

Peter could feel his heart racing.

"There are twelve probes in interplanetary orbits in our line of sight," Gorteau began. "Of that number, seven were oriented so that we could effect a data link. Because of Toon's natural genius in computer driven protocols, we were most fortuitous in being able to connect with six out of the seven. In less than two hours he wrote all the software to make the contacts from what he knew of the NASA commands and directives.

"As you know, the spacecraft had to be actively recording data from earth at the same time we experienced the loss to enable us to verify it. Of the six deep space probes we interrogated, we were again fortunate to discover that two were recording data from earth at the same time we lost contact."

Gorteau paused.

"Go on, Dr. Gorteau," Peter said, as anxious as he had ever been about anything.

"The two spacecraft both recorded a loss of data from earth simultaneously and subsequently went into their fail safe modes."

Peter gave Francis a solemn stare then looked to Gorteau.

"Go on," he said quietly.

"We were able to record the last ten minutes or so of data the spacecraft received from earth. The electromagnetic pulses not only mirror those we received, but they all verify a sequential loss of transmitting stations across the United States and our deep space network around the globe."

"Is that it?" Peter probed.

"I'm afraid so," Gorteau replied wearily. "It was precisely the kind of data we were looking for, although not exactly what we wanted to find. Now we are as certain as we can be that the electromagnetic pulses were real and emanated from the earth. The health of the earth link CERTS satellites appears to be real. We are not being fooled into thinking the CERTS are broadcasting false data. We know for sure and have verification that communications off our home planet were terminated to all known interplanetary sources. I believe that is the extent of what we have learned thus far."

"Do any of the probes we've contacted have the capacity to view the earth and transmit images back to us?" Peter asked.

"None that would be useful," Gorteau replied. "Of the two that we contacted, only one has an imaging system. But it is well beyond the asteroid belt, headed toward a Jovian orbit and earth would only appear as a barely discernible disc to its cameras."

"What about spectral data?" Francis offered. "It could give us some limited information on the earth's atmosphere, even from that distance. At least we may be able to decipher whether there's been some totally radical change."

"You just may be right," Gorteau answered, his tired eyes mirroring his forced train of thought. "I will check into that question immediately. I cannot for the life of me understand why I missed that alternative."

"Dr. Gorteau, when you held the elections, did you vote for me to be your spokesman?" Peter asked abruptly.

Gorteau was taken completely by surprise by such an off-the-wall question. "I nominated you."

"Good. Then you won't argue with me if I order you to get some rest," Peter replied forcefully.

Gorteau looked at him and managed a weak smile. "Let me tackle this one last question..."

"No. It's out of the question, Dr. Gorteau," Francis replied.

"It's off to bed with you, Fabian," Peter added. "You're not a graduate student any longer, and all of our lives may depend on your knowledge in the days to come. We can't afford to have you lose your health. Give yourself six hours rest and I promise to wake you if something important comes up."

Gorteau nodded slowly. "Of course, you are right. Yes, I will get some rest. But may I at least ask Toon to start on the interrogation program so that we can get the spectral data from earth as soon as possible?"

"No," Peter replied bluntly. "I'll take care of that."

"Excellent," Gorteau said, attempting to prevent himself from slouching. As he stood to leave, he remembered something and turned around to face Peter.

"Oh, yes; there was something else," he said. "Curious, really," then he paused as if deep in thought.

Peter looked to Francis then to Gorteau who seemed to be working out a problem in his head. Finally, after politely waiting a few seconds, Peter asked, "Yes?"

"The main computer system has been sluggish. Toon and I both noticed it while we were testing the probe algorithms. I asked Toon to check it out and he said it was busy with an elaborate search program. He examined the identification of the user, and it turned out to be Lipton. Lipton has launched the main computer into some complex routine using the geology files."

"My files?" Peter asked, completely surprised. As head of the geology program at BC1, he was responsible for the computer's geology data files.

"Yes, I thought you would want to know," Gorteau replied.

Peter could almost detect a sly wink from the old scientist.

"He can't alter or damage them, can he?" Francis asked alarmed.

"No." Peter and Gorteau answered simultaneously.

"Pure data is protected from alteration from anyone," Peter continued. "One may make new data, but the master data is always protected."

"Can Toon decipher what program he is using?" Francis asked.

"No. He is using a program on his personal work station. All we know is he is importing geology data in enormous quantities."

"Well, he can't very well abuse anyone with vast amounts of geological data," Francis observed. "But he can keep himself occupied, which is best for all concerned."

"Yes. Quite. That is precisely correct. Let him alone; it is good for all if he is so engaged." Gorteau nodded. "I am off to rest. Please wake me in four hours."

"Of course, six hours," Peter replied with a wink at Francis. Then he lightly scratched his chin, deep in thought. He felt it was probably true that Lipton could keep himself occupied by analyzing large amounts of geology data, but whether or not he could hurt anyone with it was not at all so readily apparent.

he dispassionate evidence was convincing that the earth had suffered a nuclear disaster. They all knew without a single spoken word that if the civilized world had disappeared in such madness that they would probably not hear from their home planet again in decades, perhaps never again in their lifetimes. More urgently to all of them, now even the definition of a lifetime itself was up for reconsideration.

The word of the probe findings spread throughout BC1 quickly. In less than an hour, the dismal report from the deep space satellites had filtered through to everyone: all discernible communications from the earth had ceased, including American and Soviet sources and the probes verified electronic nuclear weapon signatures relayed by the CERTS.

The empty silence of space was eerie. It was the first radio silence the colonists had ever experienced, and the first from earth since the early 20th century.

There were still mysteries aplenty. Why had there been no warning, even over civil or government channels? Why was the U.S. manned space station with the attached Marsship Singleton also silent? Had it been attacked, too? Why was the Reunified Soviet Empire base silent in the face of this unprecedented threat?

There were many different, good, logically consistent answers to those questions and it seemed like everyone had a favorite. From these discussions, there emerged a solitary, deplorable certainty: all the theories were equally dispiriting. Out of them emerged a single irrefutable fact: no one had any hard evidence for anything except for the existence of the electromagnetic pulses. Not a scientist in the group could come up with a single good theory for their origin other than a nuclear exchange.

The colonists and administrative personnel began to mingle as they never had before. Those who before the crisis had made a point of sitting at separate tables were suddenly crowding together as though such camaraderie would somehow ease their plight. If the earth had destroyed itself, it could well take them all with it by default. Their artificial social stratifications had suddenly been rendered meaningless.

On this evening before the launch of the lander, Ashley, who had never openly displayed physical affection toward Peter in public before, walked arm and arm with him down the passageway by the dining hall. Few noticed. Even fewer were surprised or took the time to care. The problems that faced them all were far and away more significant than two "illegally" married colonists who no longer gave a tinkers damn about professional etiquette anymore.

They peeked into the door of the dining hall and saw that the rumors were true. Although dinner was long over, the room was filled nearly to capacity. Rat had given up trying to chase them all away and was now personally serving coffee. Rat himself, like the rest of them, was afraid. Although he held the least of positions among the group, he was still a part of them; a little piece of humanity that now sat facing death on an alien world. Their company and the extra work load were far better than retreating to his empty room and the silence which could offer him only more fear.

Peter waved to several groups, many of whom invited them to join in their animated and lively discussions, but he declined them all. He knew what he wanted and needed, and it was not in the dining hall.

Ashley began to lead him toward his room which he had not even peeked into for the last four sols. "No way. Let's go to your place," Peter said, tugging her back toward her quarters.

"Face it, Peter. You're going to have to return to your quarters eventually," Ashley said with her motherly tone.

"Yeah, and how are we even going to get to the bed, much less in it? If you'll remember, I did a number on the place."

"And who do you think is going to clean it up, wise guy?"

"How about Lipton? He seemed like he was in a good humor."

"He would cut your tongue out if he even knew you were thinking such things," Ashley replied, the laughter mirrored in her eyes.

"And serve it in tomorrow's soup," Peter countered. "No. Your place."

"Then have a nice evening," Ashley answered, turning lose of his hand and walking toward his quarters.

"Okay. You win!" he quipped knowing that the sedative he needed would not be found in an empty room.

Minutes later, Ashley walked to his door, keyed in his personal security code on the lock and opened the door for him. The room was spotless. His mouth opened with surprise. "Ashley! Thank you, sweetheart. It's beautiful." He had never seen his room so orderly. Not only was everything put away and in its place, but it was spotless, dustless and ordered. He grasped her shoulders and embraced her gently.

"Before you get carried away, I didn't do it," she admitted.

He stepped away from her. "Who then?"

"Rat. Rat did it," she said sincerely but with a smile.

"Right," he said skeptically.

"I'm not joking, Peter. He asked me for your lock number today and said he had heard your quarters needed some attention. So I let him in."

"Are you serious?" Peter asked. Rat was the cook. Of course, BC1 had no custodial help. Sixteen domestic robots kept the dust off of passageways. The residents were responsible for their own quarters.

"Yes, Peter. I'm serious. Rat did it."

"Why, that wonderful old coot," Peter said with honesty. "You think maybe he would want to sleep with me tonight?"

"Go right ahead and ask him, Peter. Be my guest. But unless he decides to shave, you're going to get whisker burn."

"Better that than a six inch pile of junk on the floor," Peter said, embracing her again and ending the banter. There was a long moment of silence as the reality of their circumstance flooded back to them.

"Peter, I need you tonight. Please hold me; always hold me," Ashley said tenderly. Then she took a deep breath and admitted, "I'm afraid."

"Of what?" he whispered softly into her ear, not so much to illicit the response, but as a caring, compassionate presence.

"Of the end of the world. Of never seeing family and friends again. Of our own deaths, Peter. Oh, God, I'm so afraid!" she said, her fingers clutching him tightly.

"I love you, Ashley. Don't be afraid."

"Peter, I read a passage from Yeats today, terrible, and fitting. I read it so many times, I memorized it. He said,

Turning and turning in the widening gyre
The falcon cannot hear the falconer;
Things fall apart; the centre cannot hold;
Mere anarchy is loosed upon the world,

The blood dimmed tide is loosed, and everywhere
The ceremony of innocence is drowned;
The best lack all conviction, while the worst
Are full of passionate intensity.

"Peter, who are we in this anarchy? Are we the best who lack all conviction? Or are we, as I fear most, the worst full of passionate intensity? He said, *'The blood dimmed tide is loosed...the ceremony of innocence is drowned.'* Are we... were we... that ceremony of innocence, Peter?"

"Ashley, please..." he said, holding her at arms length from him. Her face was clouded with worry and deeply cast with trouble. "If it's real, isn't it better to think of it as a transition; a passage into another epoch of humankind? As a high school student I memorized a phrase from Thomas Wolfe. I always think back on it when things change in my life. But I don't remember a more fitting occasion than now. He said,

Man's youth is a wonderful thing:
It is so full of anguish and of magic
And he never comes to know it as it is,
Until it has gone from him forever.

"If there's a time of man's innocence, Ashley, let it begin now. If there was a blood dimmed tide, then we've survived it. The youth of mankind may have passed, and if it has, then it's gone from us forever. If we look back, we may lose everything. If it turns out that the earth is really gone, and all we have is ourselves, then we owe it to our species, we owe it to one another, to survive. We must be the best and, whatever else, we must, at best, have the passionate intensity just to survive – just to make it to tomorrow and to the next tomorrow."

She laid her head on his shoulder curling her fingers through his hair, thought of her family, and sobbed quietly. Though she had wept for them before, left them forever on another occasion long ago and far away, this was a parting more final and bitter than any she could ever have imagined.

ieutenant Commander Robert Kerry had been orbiting Mars for seven sols. Seven sols were counted as a single week both on Earth and on Mars. Just to enforce the point, Kerry counted off the sols and tried to remember what he had accomplished on each of them as he floated upside down in reference to the control console.

"... seven sols."

He was bored. Better yet, he was *drastically* bored. For two hours the sol before, he had scanned every dictionary, encyclopedia, reference work and thesaurus the *Goddard* had in its memory. He decided that *drastically* bored was the best adjective he could possibly find in the English language to describe his condition, and he had painstakingly considered all the choices. He certainly had the time.

But, in a little over 12 hours, the lander would be docking and they would immediately leave for solar orbit to dock with the *Von Braun II*, now some three weeks from rendezvous, accelerating away from them faster each sol. He had calculated and recalculated the orbital parameters. He had the time. After that, he had prepared the ship once more for docking and for passengers. But, then again, he had the time.

As Kerry floated in space, looking out the round port over the plains and mountains of Mars rolling by beneath him, he toweled his hair dry from the pathetically inadequate space bath he had just given himself. His heart still raced from the intense hour of physical training and aerobics he had just engaged in. Kerry spent at least two hours of each sol engaged in the most rigorous physical activity possible in such a space – one in the morning and one hour just before sleep. He doubled the space doc's recommended time and effort, and was still concerned that this additional, unscheduled time in orbit was going to be too physiologically costly. Not only was he spending extra time in orbital microgravity, their catch-up time to the MTSO ships was increasing dramatically each passing sol, which would mean even more time in a weightless state.

The MTSO ships, however, were spun and thereby created artificial gravity for the passengers and crew. This little engineering countermeasure helped to undo the drastic effects of microgravity on the human body over extended periods of time. It was discovered early in manned spaceflight that the human body was not designed to live in a state of perpetual microgravity and further, long periods in the condition resulted in changes to the human body that were manifestly difficult to correct, and some of them could never be corrected when the human returned to a gravitational field. Such permanent changes included loss of bone density, the tone and density of major skeletal muscles and even loss of cardiac muscle and tone.

As Kerry floated and looked out his windows, the loss of communications with earth troubled him, yet apparently not nearly as much as it troubled the people on the ground. He had heard of bizarre events in his professional life as an astronaut, but never like the convulsions happening just a few hundred kilometers below him. Commander Cartwright had kept him informed, and now he and Siggy were sleeping in the lander... to protect it; unheard of in the history of United States space flight.

As far as Kerry and the rest of the flight crew were concerned, the loss of communications was best explained as a rare simultaneous loss of two satellites, most likely an event planned and enacted by the Soviets. The commies were not about to come clean about their data links, and were probably using a new satellite with secret coordinates. *Big deal, Cartwright had told him. We can launch with our own software. It was all written by the same twidgets anyway. The Soviets were going to laugh loud and hard when the Americans woke up and saw what fools they had been.*

Kerry had attempted to contact the Soviets anyway, continuously, on every over-flight just to satisfy the desk jockeys back home that they had tried in good faith. Such planning was to performance as premonition was to promotion in the astronaut ranks. With each failure to raise Shturmovoi, Kerry was convinced more than ever that they were involved.

In one of his frequent "flashes of genius," Kerry had decided he could prove the flight crew's theory and communicate directly with the earth through the gravitational lens of the sun. For eight hours he conducted an in depth analysis of the sun-earth occultation parameters, integrated the principals of General Relativity and looked for the fine edge of the lens. While he fine tuned the servo motors of the deep space antenna, he imagined himself at Stockholm accepting the Nobel Prize in physics while his personal entertainment system integrated the music of Prokofiev in his mind. He never found the effect and the fantasy faded away; another flurry of active genius that came to naught, blending again with the quiet monotony and hiss of the cabin ventilators.

The ruddy disk of Mars unreeled below him, orbit after orbit. Conditions on the planet were calm, so that the surface appeared crystal clear to him, even though he flew hundreds of kilometers above it.

The panorama of Mars from orbit was different than viewing earth from orbit. The atmosphere of earth was so dense that it tended to diffuse the landscape. The thin atmosphere of Mars, in stark contrast, lent sharpness to the Marsscape that allowed the red, yellow and brown colors to vibrate together in distinct and penetrating hues.

The vast Mariner Canyon, cutting across over 3,000 kilometers of the Martian crust, stretched the length of the United States across her surface. It was distinct; absolutely three dimensional from space. The huge eye of the largest volcano in the solar system, Olympus Mons, rose three times higher than Mount Everest over the Martian Amazon Plain and seemed to stare malevolently into space, as would the empty socket on the skull of a Cyclops.

There were quiet, diffuse fogs of frozen carbon dioxide, colored a light pink from the desert sands below, that nestled and flowed gently along ancient riverbeds of mysterious origin. These formations represented the greatest enigma of the planet, recalling antediluvian mornings and a time of wild activity on Mars; of huge floods that swept across a hundred thousand square kilometers at once, gouging deep channels and delicate runoff branches before disappearing without a trace.

These geological dilemmas seemed to be frozen in time, traced across shifting fields and deserts of enormous size that defined the planet as a vast and desiccated wasteland. Yet Mars also bore the scars of crater fields, so obviously saturated, that it was clear that some very large areas had been little disturbed over the entire course of its history. It remained a puzzling mystery how just adjacent to these vast crater fields there could exist such clear evidences of enormous geologic and meteorological scarring and upheaval that implied often violent and rapid change. Mars seemed to have painted a spectacularly colorful facade, and then retreated below the surface with her secrets to lie in a dreadfully cold slumber. There she appeared to lie dreamless, awaiting the tiny organisms from earth to awaken her and finally reveal an astonishing past.

Kerry chose another music program and spun around to watch the next sunset: upside down. For the last sol and a half he had given up Gregorian chant and Prokofiev for the timeless *Dark Side of the Moon* and the classic rock of The Green Goblyn Project featuring Travis T. Goblyn's extraordinary guitar. On a previous orbit, the composition "Time" and an upside down Martian sunset nearly made him nauseated. Never having been space-sick a single time in his life, he wanted to see if he could repeat the effect, and then dutifully, painstakingly and thoroughly describe its every nuance in his lengthy journal.

eter sat half asleep on a small sofa he had managed to build out of packing crates and squeeze into his quarters. Ashley lay in his arms, sleeping fitfully. The strains of soft, wordless music drifted quietly around them in the dim light. As Peter was drifting into and out of a fitful sleep, the beeper on his C2 cut through the silence.

"...go ahead," he replied, touching the response button.

"Peter, this is Francis," the voice on the speaker announced. "Better get down here to the Control Center. Lipton just filed the flight manifest for tomorrow morning and it doesn't agree with any previous conversations. He's got all the seats full including one of Brinker's Marines and Brinker is about ready to strangle him..."

"Okay, okay, I got the message. I'm on my way," Peter replied.

"What's up?" Ashley asked in a husky, sleepy voice.

"I can take care of it, babe. You need to get some sleep," Peter said, picking her up and gently placing her in his bed. He covered her with a thick blanket and kissed her gently on her cheek. She snuggled into it to return to her comfortable sleep, flashing a sweet, sleepy smile at Peter as he left his quarters.

Peter entered the Launch Control Center, its door sliding quietly closed behind him. He could hear the raised voice of Brinker over a row of consoles. As Peter had feared, Lipton had made an entrance into the LCC and Brinker had him backed up against a wall.

"You can take your rocket ship, your launch pad and your Courts Martial and stick 'em in your bureaucratic backside!" Brinker screamed at Lipton in a textbook-perfect rendition of everyone's idea of a drill instructor on a really bad day.

Francis was standing within inches of the two, letting Brinker have a good piece of Lipton but ready to pull them apart if it came to blows. The other console operators were standing quietly by their consoles, watching the show.

"Okay, Brinker, back off," Peter ordered.

"He ain't getting my best Marine. *No way!*" Brinker said loudly to Peter, walking over to him, pointing with his cigar.

About this time, Hernandez and Julia Friedman came walking briskly around the corner. Lipton stood stoically, arms folded over his chest, greeting Hernandez and Friedman with an incinerating stare. Peter allowed the group to stop in their positions, assume their fighting ground and let a minute of silence steady the hostility. It also gave him a moment to size up the apparent conflict. Francis understood his method and walked over to him.

"Figure it out yet?" he asked Peter in a whisper.

Peter nodded slightly. "Lassiter, who's on your manifest?" Peter asked, probably a little more harshly than he intended.

"I don't owe you an explanation, Traynor. As far as the law is concerned, you're an accused felon awaiting trial. How that involves you in the affairs of the community isn't at all clear to me," Lipton replied coolly, striking his first blow early on.

"Have it your way, Lassiter," Peter replied, physically turning away from him. "Francis, who's on the list?" Peter repeated.

"It's quite a list. It looks like we're competing with Chicago O'Hare, actually. There're more people on it than seats in the lander and Lipton even has a standby list; go figure."

Peter resisted the immediate urge to laugh, taking a copy of the flight manifest from Francis' hand and reading the names:

1.	P. Traynor	NASA	UNDER ARREST
2.	F. Linde	NASA	UNDER ARREST
3.	T. See	ESA	UNDER ARREST
4.	A. Alcyone	NASA	UNDER ARREST

The list continued, with some other names annotated as UNDER ARREST, and eight names highlighted as "standby".

"Okay, I give up. How is Lipton planning to fly more passengers than seats?" Peter asked. "And what is a *standby*?"

"From what I can gather from His Majesty," Francis replied, "it appears he's building a paper case for gross insubordination. This official manifest is some kind of proof that all of the hooligans on the list whose comment reads "UNDER ARREST" refused to board the lander as he so ordered, so that qualifies them for a special lower floor in hell."

"I presume then that the last eight names on this list, labeled "standby" are the most likely actual passengers?"

"It appears so," Francis replied with an over exaggerated sigh.

"Then why is this list so radically different from the original manifest?"

"I've decided that those are the official passengers for this expedition to earth," Lipton replied.

"I thought you weren't talking to me today, Lassiter," Peter replied, slowly fixing his eyes on Lipton.

Lipton seemed to bite his tongue to keep from snapping back. He apparently thought himself much too polished to engage in a verbal dual with a subordinate.

"That list is final," he continued. "If none of the lawfully accused will board the lander as so ordered, and my assigned Marine guard is in complicity with mutiny, then I have taken the prerogative to assign those eight other individuals as reflected by the manifest on a standby basis to return to earth. They're the individuals who have been here the longest and who are next in line to fly home."

"I see," Peter replied evenly, finally understanding the hidden strategy.

Notably agitated, Brinker walked over to Peter. "Hiraldo ain't going; that's it," he whispered. "She's my best troop, and I'm not going to allow her to fly out of here where she serves the requirements of the military contingent. As the HMFIC I'm authorized to make that decision! It's my call and I'm the one who hangs for it, not Lipton!"

Peter reviewed the list. Hiraldo's name was one of the eight on the bottom of the list, labeled, "standby".

"Tell her to refuse to fly. Order her not to go! What's the problem here, Brinker?" Peter asked, somewhat agitated at such a simple problem.

"It ain't that easy. She still thinks Lipton's in charge. She won't risk her career by refusing to obey his orders. If her name is on the list, then she thinks she has to leave. The joke of it is, she doesn't even want to go, while the new man, Tyler, wants out, and he ain't worth a dime to me."

"Okay," Peter replied, understanding. "How about exchanging Hiraldo's seat with Tyler?"

"Fine, if you can do it," Brinker replied, casting a doubtful look at Lipton.

"We're exchanging two names on your list, Lassiter," Peter said bluntly, making his notes on the manifest. "Marine Tyler is swapping seats with Marine Hiraldo. Brinker is lawfully in military command here and he has declared an emergency replacement, position for position. It's his call," Peter said quickly to prevent Lipton from interrupting.

To Peter's initial surprise, Lipton instantly agreed. "Very well," he said briskly. Too late, Peter realized, his mistake. He had just acquiesced in spirit to Lipton's manifest.

"But I do want to add, Lipton, that regardless of who is on this list, committing anyone but the flight crew to this manifest represents a gross lack of judgment," Peter added in a weak and altogether useless attempt to recover.

"Then why do you add names to the list?" Lipton shot back, playing it out expertly.

Francis was fed up with Lipton's diversion. "You know as well as we do, Lipton, the chance of any of those people surviving when they reach earth is slim to none. If there has been a nuclear exchange, they can't possibly make it. There'll be no place to land. They may even be stranded in space, for God's sake!"

"You've even started to believe your own treachery," Lipton spat back. "And why don't you drop the word "IF"? Your convoluted stories are beginning to sound more bizarre by the hour."

"Then manifest yourself," Francis demanded. "If you're convinced that things are so grand, go back and see for yourself. Fly on a ship that is controlled by an untested protocol in direct violation of every procedure in the book. Let's all see if you have enough guts to prove your theory with your own life!"

Lipton sighed heavily and closed his eyes as if making a colossal attempt at self control. Then he began to walk slowly away. Francis swung around to face Lipton's form retreating through the door.

"You're a coward, Lipton! You don't have enough guts to get on the ship yourself!" Francis yelled after him. "Now it's clear enough that everyone can see it!"

Peter put his hand on his shoulder. "That's enough, Francis. I think he heard you," Peter said.

"What are we going to do to stop him?" Francis asked, facing Peter directly. "We can't let these people fly out to their deaths!"

Peter reached for the C2 and pressed Toon's locater.

"Toon? Peter here. Did you check the flight protocol?"

"Yes," Toon's sleepy voice answered. "I couldn't find anything."

"Can you be more specific?" Peter asked, a feeble question that reflected his complete lack of knowledge about any combination of the debugging process, the flight protocol or the aerodynamic equations that comprised it.

"I was able to spot the ascent equations and they looked good to me... the data set looked in order... But, Peter, I'm a programmer, not a flight dynamics specialist..." Toon warned weakly. "I couldn't even run it all the way through without a simulation routine, which we don't have."

"I understand. Goodnight." Switching off the C2, Peter looked to Brinker. "Tell Hiraldo she's off the hook, and have Tyler pack his bags. Francis, draw up a disclaimer statement for the passengers signatures. Have it reflect the explicit conditions they could find on earth and say something about the untested flight protocol. If they sign it, let 'em go. We can't stop them."

"What good is a disclaimer going to do?" Brinker asked.

"It'll ease our conscience just in case they auger in," Peter answered truthfully, then left to resume what remained of a short and fitful night's rest.

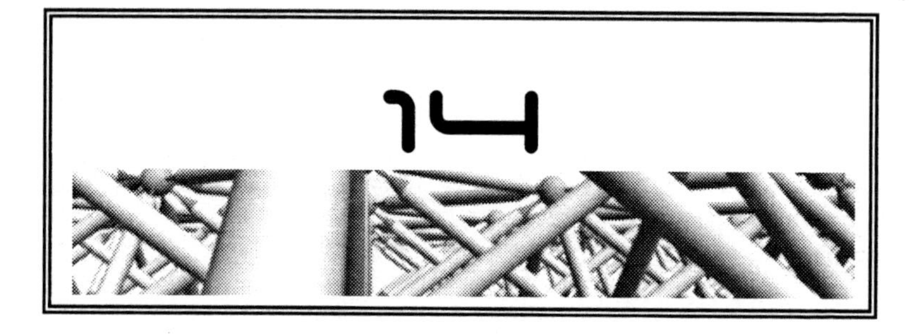

BC1 passed from the night watch to full blown launch preparations exactly at 0500. Although the physical tasks had been initiated a sol and a half before, the psychological pitch did not gear up until the breakfast line started serving at five. The launch window would open on schedule and Commander Cartwright let it be known that his main engines were going to be firing at that moment and not a single millisecond later.

The flight crew had spent the night onboard their ship. By 0500, Rat had sent breakfast out to them. The white room had been repaired and the close out crew was preparing the lander for boarding. The ship had been fully fueled overnight and there were no mechanical problems. It appeared increasingly evident that Cartwright was going to get his wish.

Every evening prior to a departure flight off Mars, a ceremony was held in the dining hall to remember the work accomplished by those leaving and to pass out awards. The awards consisted of certificates and plaques made from fused Martian sand. Since there was no ceremony the evening before, Hernandez stood ready at the departure gate with the plaques and certificates. Lipton had declined to be present, but had dutifully signed each certificate.

Also present at the departure gate was Julia Freidman, who accompanied Hernandez. Peter, Francis and Brinker stood apart from the milling crowd.

The eight departing personnel lined up along the tight passageway leading to the airlock. Hernandez, never one for speeches, simply handed each their plaque and certificate with a weak handshake. It was congenial enough, with smiles from and for everyone.

"Did they sign their disclaimer statements?" Peter asked Brinker.

"Yes, sir. They wouldn't be standing here if they didn't," he replied. "Hicks said he wasn't going to sign anything and slammed the door in my face; nearly crushed my cigar. Hiraldo proceeded to remove the door so that I could inform Hicks that his seat was going to the first person who signed on the electronic line."

"And?" Peter asked.

"He signed. But that boy's not what I'd call a happy camper."

Peter looked at Hicks, standing in line with his seven other fellow passengers. Hicks had signed on as a colonist, but just never fit in and had decided to leave early on. The fact that not everyone would be happy as a colonist was a calculated reality. Indeed, there had been a 19% drop-out rate among those who came to stay permanently. The colonists accepted this reality and never held it against those who changed their minds. They had never had any significant problems with anyone until Hicks.

Hicks' attitude was acutely critical toward the other colonists and he had personally been responsible for many of the hard feelings of recent months. Peter was more than glad to see him go.

As Hernandez reached the end of the line, the passengers turned to enter the air lock for boarding the MATs to the Crippen launch complex. Brinker stepped over to shake U.S. Marine Tyler's hand and wish him the best of luck.

Hicks, standing behind Tyler, became agitated at the delay. "You wanna to step out of my way, people?" he said.

Brinker's eyes moved slowly over to him and gave him a look that would just precede quadruple dismemberment. "I'm talking to one of the nation's finest fighting men, son. Now if you can't offer us the respect of a few parting moments, I may just have to break your limp wrist. Your choice."

Hicks became red in the face and quickly looked away from Brinker. He said nothing.

Brinker handed Tyler a small data wafer. "This is a complete report on what has happened here over the last week. As soon as you regain contact with any higher military authority, please pass it along. Make them sign a hand receipt for it. It's classified, so don't let it out of your sight."

Tyler nodded, taking the wafer and sliding it into his wide breast pocket. "Sarge, I'm sorry I let you down," he said in a near whisper.

"You didn't let me down, Tyler. This whole thing was my decision. Go on back. We need you to deliver that message. Hiraldo needs to stay here; she knows the ropes. You're a good man, Tyler. I'm sorry I didn't have time to teach you how to be the best. But it'll come." Brinker was virtually stuttering. He had no experience or competence at good-byes or anything resembling sentimentality.

Tyler managed a weak smile, and then turned to cast a murderous glare at Hicks.

"If this man gives anyone a hard time, you have my permission to stuff him in the airlock and blow his wise-ass out into space," Brinker said, looking purposefully at Hicks.

"Yes, sir," Tyler replied, popping Brinker a smart salute.

"Knock that off, Marine. I'm not a commissioned officer; I work for a living," Brinker replied with a half smile, not returning the salute. "Now get out of here and take care of yourself."

Tyler stepped into the airlock, slamming the door in Hick's face. "It looks like you're going to have to wait, Hicks," Brinker said, turning away and laughing loudly.

Fifteen minutes later, three MAT's departed for the lander. Peter, Brinker, Hernandez, Francis and Friedman watched the MAT's grow smaller in the distance, all quietly wondering the same thing. *Would these be the last humans to depart Mars for earth in their generation?* It could well be so, but no one spoke it out loud. In just 90 minutes, the lander would be launching.

Every eye at BC1 watched the proceedings with rapt fascination. Lift-offs and landings at Crippen had not yet become passé, even though this was the way each one of them had arrived. Yet, this launch was different; somehow intensely interesting and more important than any other. The rumors of the minute had been based on other rumors and no one wanted to miss a single second of this launch.

Hernandez took his place in the Control Center beside Lipton. Peter, Francis, Ashley and Brinker joined the other colonists in the dining hall where several monitors had been set up to view the procedures on the pad, in the white room and in the Control Center. Of those not watching the affair, the rest were actively involved in the launch effort itself.

The close out crew buckled the eight passengers into the lander, right on schedule, exactly one hour prior to scheduled lift off. The count down continued to proceed smoothly.

Lipton sat at the director's control console passively. His appearance was standard Liptonesque: polished and flawless. But he was not acting out his ordinarily presumptuous and imperious control of the launch proceedings. He sat quietly, allowing Hernandez to answer for the director when required.

The colonists in the dining hall were also subdued. Few comments were made during the final hour of the count, the pressure obviously building toward the final minutes.

"Minus five minutes and counting," came the voice of the launch director.

"Auxiliary Power Units one through four are up and running," came the voice of Pilot Sigourney Michner.

The tension rose another notch. Lipton sat all the way back in his chair, arms folded, facing four monitors. Beside him, Hernandez wiped a bead of sweat from his forehead. They had not exchanged a single word.

"Minus three minutes. All APU's at 105 percent. Aero surfaces powered... verified."

"You're go for launch," relayed the launch director.

From space, Bob Kerry could just see BC1 and Crippen space port through his hand held telescope as a bright, fuzzy dot. The lander would pass ahead of him in orbit. He would eventually catch them in less than three orbits by negotiating both orbital parameters until rendezvous and docking. In just under three and a half hours, they would be speeding away from Mars to solar orbit and a now protracted catch up to the Von Braun.

"Minus one minute and counting. All fuel tanks pressurized. LOX inner tank, pressurized. We are go for liftoff," Cartwright certified.

Peter was virtually holding his breath. There had never been a U.S. launch failure of a manned vehicle from another body other than earth. One reason for that was the strict controls over the launch conditions. This lander was about to intentionally violate one of the more basic of those regulations: a secure data link with the massive and powerful earth based computers. Even though there was a significant time lag between the two machines, they were in a state of continual purge and cross checking of data sent ahead, in advance, that the smaller computer on the lander could not handle with as much efficiency. Such coordinated data streaming, albeit long distance and time delayed, ensured that the astronauts received the best computing power of both systems as each cross-checked the other. The multi-channeled earth base information stream was so powerfully robust, that it operated on hundreds of spaced frequencies all at once so that it could automatically handle launch delays, holds and thousands of other contingencies even while up to 20 light minutes behind.

"Minus ten seconds..... minus five, four, three, ignition, one, liftoff!"

The lander spewed red dust over the desert as the vehicle began an immediate ascent. The three main engines flared and blossomed into a clear, blindingly white flower as the ungainly, barely aerodynamic lander rose above the launch structure, making an immediate upside down roll to its left and heading just slightly south. Its mushroom shaped heat shield, fitted like a saddle over its underbelly, seemed to pull it down for a moment, until its guidance computer straightened the ship, per the flight plan. Within minutes, it was but a mere streaking dot in the dark dome of blue-black sky.

"Plus one minute, Commander," the Flight Director announced. "17 klicks altitude, 19 klicks down range, on the flight path."

Peter found himself biting his lower lip; something that he had never done before. He and the others were now glued to the image on their monitors provided by the powerful downrange telescopic cameras.

"Plus one minute, thirty seconds. 22 klicks altitude, 39 klicks downrange."

The nominal trajectory would carry them into a near circular orbit of 48 kilometers after an engine burn time of six minutes.

"Plus two minutes. All systems are nominal. Negative return Crippen."

This meant that the lander could not return in an emergency on its available fuel to the Crippen landing site.

"Plus three minutes. Negative return."

The lander had just entered the most dangerous portion of its flight. It now did not have enough fuel to return under power to any point on the planet. If the ship lost its power, it would crash. If anything significant went wrong for the next three minutes, they could not land safely on Mars or make it into orbit.

Another half minute passed. The collective pulse rates and blood pressures of everyone present raised several notches. Then the unthinkable began.

"Critical divergence from flight path!" the range officer reported.

"Concur. Critical divergence from flight path," the flight dynamics officer reported.

The ascent program was failing as Peter had feared. The computer was pulling the spacecraft out of the necessary flight path it needed to achieve orbit.

"Status... procedure romeo seventeen...," Lipton ordered instantly, sitting bolt-upright in his seat, rigidly following his procedure at once.

"I've got it!" Cartwright reported over the net. In the lander, he grabbed the flight control stick between his legs. He could see the same divergence from the flight path as the monitors at the control center. The display on the computer screen in front of him showed the flight path as a three dimensional corridor in which the lander was depicted, and the lander was falling below the corridor.

Cartwright's wrist twisted decisively and instinctively on the control stick to bring the tiny craft back into the flight corridor. The lander began to buck and vibrate. Beads of sweat materialized instantly on his lip and forehead. His eyes focused quickly on the time remaining. He had two minutes and fifteen seconds to correct the divergence with the fuel remaining. There could be no second chances.

"Lander, BC1, report status," the flight director asked impatiently.

"I said I've got it!" Cartwright replied sharply.

He could see the display responding to the movements of his wrist. This was clearly different from simulations of similar situations. The control was much more difficult. The vibration was too excessive. Something else was going wrong.

Sigourney Michner, sitting in the opposite seat, scanned the instruments quickly with her eyes. She saw the time ticking away and realized the response was too sluggish. Then she saw why. The autopilot had not been disabled from the control console.

"Autopilot disabled!" she said, flipping the switch on the panel in front of them. Suddenly the wild vibration and bucking stopped.

The mistake had been costly. For nearly a minute, the computer and Cartwright had been battling for two different trajectories. The ship was attempting to fly in one direction, Cartwright in another As soon as the autopilot was disabled, the ship began to respond just as it had in the simulators. But Cartwright's reflexes had been fixed by the effort of the seconds just preceding. Suddenly the image representing the ship's trajectory climbed steeply, too high and too quickly above the flight corridor.

"Out of range high!" Michner warned unnecessarily.

Cartwright responded reflexively, again overcompensating and sending the ship out of the corridor too low. The final seconds were ticking away.

"15 seconds to MECO," the flight dynamics officer reported, referring to main engine cut off, when the main engine fuel tanks literally ran dry.

Cartwright struggled to bring the ship back into the corridor. This time his wrist moved slowly, inching the ship back into the correct flight path. He could see the image apparently responding in the proper degree.

Michner was the first to recognize disaster was inevitable. Her trained eyes scanned the instruments. Too much fuel had been used fighting the autopilot. The vehicle did not have enough inertia to stay in orbit.

"Main engine cutoff!" Cartwright replied proudly, watching the projection of the lander finally drift into the corridor.

The feeling of freefall and weightlessness released the eight passengers and two crewmembers. The passengers began to cheer and remove their helmets. Cartwright's smiling eyes met Michner's profoundly troubled visage. In a single second he could read the reality in her face. His eyes shot back to the display of orbital parameters. The flight dynamics officer on the ground voiced it aloud just as he saw it glowing on the screen before him.

"Suborbital parameters: 191 kilometers by zero. Velocity: 4.87 KMS." He could not bring himself to complete the statistics on the impact. They were some 0.16 kilometers per second short of achieving any kind of stable orbit. The orbit's lower parameter of zero kilometers implied inevitable impact.

Cartwright could see his computer display reflect the facts. The image representing the lander had already risen above the line. The ship was destined to arc high over its intended orbital altitude, then fall back to crash on the other side of the planet. They were out of fuel and out of options. He realized, as Michner had, they were all dead. Awaiting their final seconds was only a formality dictated by the rigid laws of physics and flight dynamics. "TIME TO IMPACT" flashed across his screen, counting relentlessly down: minus 22 minutes 33 seconds.

Lipton sat back in his seat, completely dazed and ineffectual. He watched as his career was following the exact same trajectory as the lander. It was now absolutely over. As soon as communications with earth were reestablished, he would be recalled in disgrace on the next ship out. Above him, due largely to his relentless, even imperious demands, ten people were about to die a horrible death.

The reality of the situation took a little longer to catch on in the dining hall. There was considerable applause and cheering when the main engines cut off and not everyone understood the full implications of "suborbital parameters of 191 by zero". Yet, within short minutes, the reassurance was supplanted by the impending certainty of mass death.

In space, Cartwright was not giving up so easily. He and Michner were busily scheming possible ways to survive. All they needed was to boost their velocity by 0.16 meters per second. But they had to act quickly. Once they reached the high point of their orbit, or perigee, the mechanics would change and even more velocity would be required to recover.

"Interrogate the OMS energy boundaries," he ordered Michner, but she had already pulled them up on the computer screen. With a few deft strokes of her fingers over the keyboard the answer arose: there was not sufficient fuel remaining in the orbital maneuvering engines to give them enough velocity.

"That's it, unless you can dream up another miracle," Cartwright stated to her flatly. He was a fighter, but knew his ship well. There just was not enough energy on board to raise the velocity. Using up the orbital maneuvering fuel would only serve to delay the inevitable; perhaps boost them around the planet a few hundred more kilometers. But the end would be the same.

The passengers were completely unaware of their predicament. None of them could hear the flight dynamics officer report on the orbital parameters, and had they heard, none of them on this flight would have fully understood. Hicks and several others had unfastened their seat belts and were floating about the already crowded compartment. Their lighthearted noise had risen to the point where hearing was difficult.

Michner unbuckled herself, stood up on her seat and turned to face them. "Okay, okay, listen up!" she shouted. The passengers all stopped to listen. She resisted the urge to be nasty. "Please take your seats immediately," she said as pleasantly as she could. "Please fasten your harnesses tightly around you, place your helmets back on and pressurize your suits. Do it immediately!"

"Is there a problem?" Hicks asked, floating just below her.

"Do it now!" Cartwright exploded. Hicks quickly complied.

Michner returned to her own seat, now trembling, wondering if she had made a mistake by ending the last sounds she would ever hear of other human beings enjoying themselves. Cartwright looked at her and placed his hand on hers giving it a reassuring squeeze.

The activity on the ground was frantic. The flight director shouted orders at the flight dynamics officer who was both tracking the ship and doing energy exchange calculations as fast as his fingers could move.

"Approaching apogee, minus 43 seconds," the flight dynamics officer reported, watching the last moments of possible solutions tick by, waiting powerlessly while ten souls counted their final minutes of life as they approached the highest point of their orbit. "Cartwright, invert and fire your OMS immediately!" he ordered as a last resort.

"Negative," Cartwright replied.

"Then what's your plan, Commander?" he asked briskly. There was no response.

In orbit two hundred kilometers behind and below the lander, Kerry could hear and clearly understand their predicament. But he had an idea.

"Twenty two seconds to apogee," the ground intoned, counting off the seconds till the lander reached the top of the orbital hill.

"Ian, listen up," Kerry said to Cartwright. "Use your reaction and control system to keep your nose pointed at an angle to the atmosphere. We're going to skip you back into space like a rock. Raise your altitude... give it all you've got!"

Cartwright felt a surge of energy. Yes, this was their only chance. If he could gain enough speed to impact the edge of the atmosphere at just the right angle, they could use the heat shield to absorb the energy from the atmosphere and bounce back off into orbit. They might be able to gain enough energy from the long fall back toward the planet to pull it off. It was the longest of long shots, but it represented their only hope. The question was one of whether they would have enough altitude and initial velocity to get the boost they needed at the bottom of the gravitational hill.

"Ten seconds to apogee."

"Siggy, fire the OMS engines now!"

Michner did not fully understand why she should fire the engines, but she did as she was told, instantly. She knew by training and discipline that her life often depended on instant obedience. Her fist smashed against the firing plunger.

The lander lurched forward. They had enough fuel remaining to boost them some 0.08 kilometers per second faster. The firing ended all too quickly, just nine seconds later.

The flight director was temporarily disoriented. He had not listened to Kerry's broadcast. The flight director's plan was to invert the orbiter and fire the engines to round out the orbit, giving them a slower reentry profile and a better chance at surviving the reentry heat, never mind the crash landing. Cartwright had just fired the engines with the lander aimed in the direction of flight, which would have the opposite effect. The lander would now achieve a higher apogee, a longer fall to the planet and a higher reentry velocity.

The new orbital figures flashed on the screen: "Suborbital: apogee 223 kilometers by zero. Apogee minus 2 minutes 06 seconds." They had bought themselves a few more minutes.

"What's your plan Commander?" the flight director inquired once more.

"Standby," Siggy replied briskly. They were too busy to offer narratives. That could come later if they were successful.

Kerry was busy calculating orbital limits. The plan was painfully simple and relied on the ability of the lander to preserve enough of its initial velocity, plus that added by the planet's gravitational tug downward, minus the energy lost by the glancing blow with the upper atmosphere when they skipped off; provided they could skip off at all.

It was an exceptionally crude variation of the slingshot effect used by planetary probes. But unless everything was just right, they would burn up on reentry instead of skipping. Being the crew of a manned meteor was not Cartwright's idea of a good flight.

"Ian, I've got some good stuff," Kerry reported. "Adjust your attitude to minus 32 degrees and hold it there. Report your altitude and I'll give you a signal to raise the nose. Prepare to recover at plus seven degrees on my mark. Whatever you do, maintain your azimuth!"

Kerry's voice was now being broadcast throughout BC1. Every individual crowded around a screen, eyes glued to the drama unfolding around them. Lipton sat catatonically, not daring to move or speak.

Peter had removed enough skin from his lower lip that it was beginning to bleed.

"Ian, have you got any fuel left in the OMS?" Kerry asked.

"No."

"Then use your RCS, sparingly, to recover your angle of approach. I want you to arc over apogee. Don't crest or you'll lose momentum. We're going to need all we can get."

"Roger," Cartwright said and swung the ship to change his trajectory just slightly. Now he was aimed toward the horizon.

"Good; now we wait," Kerry said forthrightly.

"Thank you Commander," Cartwright replied.

"I'm just a lowly Lieutenant, remember?"

"Not if this works," Cartwright replied drolly.

The minutes to apogee dragged by. The flight dynamics officer calculated Kerry's plan out to the third decimal. He found it barely had a chance to work, but every maneuver would have to be executed perfectly.

"Now at apogee," the Flight Dynamics Officer confirmed sharply.

Siggy gave Cartwright a hopeful look and a weak smile. They had crested the hill and were now accelerating toward Mars. The finesse with which they now flew their ship would determine whether they would live to see another hour. Cartwright reflected on the only positive side he could envision from such a death: *it would come quickly.*

"Time to interface: 8 minutes 49 seconds," the flight dynamics officer reported. In that time the spacecraft would encounter the Martian atmosphere where, with any luck, they would bounce off with added gravitational energy and glide with all the grace of a wounded goose back into space.

While the minutes drifted by, Cartwright and Michner discussed and struggled with the piloting techniques they would use when encountering the atmosphere. Meanwhile, Kerry slaved over new and radically different rendezvous equations. He was beginning to understand that even if they achieved some kind of bizarre orbit with this technique, it may put them out of range of an eventual rendezvous. He discovered that their angle of skip was most important.

He explained this to Cartwright who appreciated not only the realities of space and aerodynamic flight, but was astonished at the instant creativity and gushing but controlled energy of Kerry. He had always thought of Kerry as quite an oddball.

"Two minutes to interface."

Those on the ground and in the two spacecraft literally held their breaths as the seconds ticked away to the inevitable resolution.

"Minus one minute."

The first encounter with an atmosphere for space travelers is a pink glow around the nose of the spacecraft as it ionizes the thin atmospheric gasses. This particular reentry was far and again faster than the craft was designed for, so the glow began immediately. For the first time in their careers, pilot and commander felt the lander bump against the thickening layers of the high atmosphere, alarming Cartwright.

"We've already got turbulence!" he reported.

"It's too early," the flight dynamics officer reported. "You're half a minute from interface."

Kerry responded instantly. "Start your skip profile early. Start it now!" He understood that the atmospheric limit calculations varied from sol to sol and that with the increased speed, the effect from a radical density change came sooner than predicted by the nominal approach calculations. Together they were working against the calculated limits and eating up the energy of the spacecraft.

Cartwright's sweaty hands gripped the stick and gently eased it back to a positive inclination. They could feel the rising G-forces pull them back and down into their seats. This distressed Cartwright who correctly interpreted these forces as deceleration forces, pulling them toward the surface of Mars.

"I've got a rising G-load," Cartwright warned, his voice obviously alarmed.

"Stay with it, Ian; this is the most critical time. Keep your nose at 12 'till I order otherwise," Kerry said. He, too, was afraid. He was flying the lander by intuition from hundreds of kilometers away, feeling the G-load by instinct, moving his hand on the stick by sympathetic emotions alone. It was not by-the-book flying or even sane flying, but it was all they had.

"Move it to 17.5 now, Ian. 17.5; stay with it pal," he said evenly. "And for God's sake, mind your azimuth!"

The brilliant radiance of the lander had increased. They were glowing even brighter than under normal reentries. This was to be expected. Yet, the temperature was rising in the vehicle and now both Cartwright and Michner were sweating profusely.

Cartwright kept an eye on the glow. Nothing else mattered. If they were going to survive, the glow would start to decrease, and that would have to happen in the next 45 seconds or less.

The flight dynamics officer on the ground had quit trying to figure it all out and just sat in silence in his seat watching the show. The orbital data was appearing and revising itself so quickly on his screen that it was an unintelligible blur.

"Ian, you still with me?" Kerry asked.

"Still alive, Commander Kerry. And I'm happy to report the glow is diminishing."

"Stay with it, buddy. Ease your angle up to parabolic at 24 and hold it steady. You're on your way back into orbit!"

The cheers in the control center and BC1 were deafening. It was hard to find anyone not hugging or slapping someone's back. Lipton was the sole exception. He sat stoically, still staring at his monitor.

Finally the flight dynamics officer had a good number. "Elliptical orbit: 55 by 117 kilometers!" The orbit was stable. The low end was very low, but could last another few sols. The applause and back slapping began anew.

But Kerry began feverishly working out a new set of calculations: rendezvous. The flight dynamics officer began with the same calculations instantly. The answer came quickly.

"Are you certain of your tracking data?" Kerry asked the ground.

"Plus or minus half a klick," flight dynamics answered confidently.

There was a protracted silence.

"What solution do you have, flight?" Kerry asked worriedly.

"No nominal solutions," responded a quiet voice.

"Would somebody please tell me what the hell...," Cartwright asked, his voice rough and agitated.

"We don't have a solution for the rendezvous, yet," Kerry replied, knowing the chances were very good there would not be one at all.

Orbital rendezvous depends on several conditions including the same angle of motion relative to the ground. Changing such orbital angles, called inclination, determined entirely by the three dimensional plot of not just altitude but flight angle or azimuth, was extremely difficult and energy intensive when attempted from orbit. After a given degree of separation, none were even possible at all. The flight computers both in space and on the ground had already cranked through all the possible calculations and found "no nominal solution", which was so much technical jargon for "impossible".

When the lander skipped off the atmosphere, it approached and jumped off at a slight angle, magnified by the ship's velocity so that its inclination was now significantly different than the orbiting vehicle. No rendezvous was possible at the competing angles. Both Cartwright and Michner knew the rules of spaceflight very well. And, although they had not yet been told, they suspected the worst.

The temperature in the lander was still building from the short period of atmospheric contact. The heat exchanger units were working overtime to stem the heat, but never in the designers worst case scenarios had they ever calculated for such extremes. Sweat was pouring off Cartwright, Michner and the other passengers, raising even further the tension in the lander. Hicks finally unbuttoned his harness and floated to the front.

"I demand to know what the hell is going on here!" he screamed in Michner's ear. Instantly she backhanded him, putting all her strength into the swing of her balled up fist. She did not even turn around to see his body fly off in a flat spin and strike the rear bulkhead.

Cartwright held out his right hand. "Thanks, Siggy, I needed that," he said without looking away from his monitor. She slapped the open palm of his gloved hand and continued working.

"Got that solution yet, Bob?" Cartwright asked finally, his voice cracking with fatigue and the heat.

"Negative," Kerry answered, feverishly working several practically impossible scenarios.

"Let us know," he replied as patiently as he could.

Kerry slapped his palms against the sides of the *Goddard* repeatedly, nearly moaning with absolute frustration, "No, God, no, not after all they've been through; not this!"

The flight dynamics officer had already given up and shook his head slowly. There was no way a rendezvous could be effected according to his calculations.

"Ian, how much fuel have you got?" Kerry asked, his voice as straight as he could make it sound.

"Not enough to fill up a piss ant's tea kettle. We're dry. Maybe a little maneuvering juice, that's all."

"How about OMS?"

"Dry."

“RCS?”

“Dry.”

There was a protracted period of silence. They all felt it, every human on Mars and the eleven in orbit around her. The final chapter had been written for ten souls.

"Okay," Cartwright finally said, "how much time till we reenter?"

"Three sols, give or take seven hours," Kerry said, so softly not everyone heard him clearly.

"We won't last three sols," Siggy said to Cartwright, then realized the obvious contradiction. That their life support would run out long before they reentered had nothing whatsoever to do with their chances in reentry. They were out of range and out of fuel and would soon be out of air. They were beyond hope.

"Do we have any chance at all, any that you are aware of, Kerry?" Cartwright asked courageously. It was better that they all knew the full truth up front.

"I'm going to figure it out, Ian. Just give me a little more time," Kerry responded.

"Control, I want an assessment, now!" Cartwright ordered.

The flight director looked at Lipton who did not dare look away from his monitor. He glanced at the flight dynamics officer who shook his head slowly.

"Lander, Control. We honestly haven't been able to work out an option yet, but we're still trying. Hang tight." He spoke of an unwritten NASA legacy: *Failure is not an option… even when failure is inevitable.*

Cartwright looked at Siggy. "This is the big one... no way out. The question we have to ask ourselves at this point is how do we want it; fast or slow?" He was playing out the part of space commander to the bitter end. No emotions, no slack.

"What if they come up with something?" she asked, tears welling in her eyes. Michner was weeping, but had more control over her emotions than did Cartwright who had blocked his out completely.

"You know the realities as well as I do. The computers would have had a solution long before now if there was one."

"Ian, I just don't have enough guts to...," she whispered, not able to continue with the thought.

He did not say anything, just stared back at her. She knew clearly what he was thinking. He turned away from her and relaxed. He had accepted the inevitable. It would not come as easily for the others.

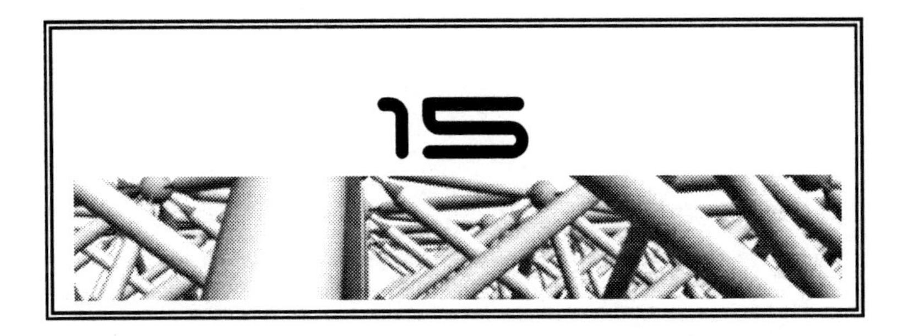

he colonists observing the launch process in the dining hall were paralyzed. They wanted desperately to do something, anything, to help the ten humans stranded in a useless orbit. But they were absolutely powerless. The only other vehicle capable of effecting a rescue was the RSE lander at Shturmovoi.

The colonists had crowded around the table where Peter, Ashley, Francis, Gorteau and Brinker sat.

"Has anyone been able to contact Little Kremlin?" Peter questioned.

No one answered.

"Are they even capable of effecting a rescue?" Peter asked, somewhat aggravated at the lack of response. "Who's our expert on the RSE launch system?"

"I am," said a voice from far back in the gathering. It came from a relatively thin, demure individual; an administrative type who had hardly spoken a word to anyone in the months he had been at BC1. Very few of the colonists even knew his name.

The crowd around the table moved aside and let him approach the table. He was a short, thin man who wore large, round glasses that, coupled with the part down the middle of his chestnut hair, made his moonish eyes look large and innocent. He was, perhaps, in his early thirties, but because of his overall demeanor, he appeared to be in his mid-twenties.

"I'm sorry, sir, but many of us may not know your name," Peter said, embarrassed that he had to count himself among those. He had seen the quiet individual around many times, but as the man kept entirely to himself, Peter had never been introduced.

"I am Julian Covenant of Cambridge University," he said in a polished, British accent.

"And how did you come to be an expert in the RSE launch system?" Peter asked directly, not wasting time on formalities, which reflected his deteriorating mood.

"I am a student of the Soviet and RSE space effort. I came to be here for that specific purpose, as a matter of fact."

"What do you mean, you are here for 'that specific purpose?'" Peter asked with some surprise. He had heard rumors that there were quasi-military intelligence types among them, but no one had ever been able to put a finger on such far fetched hearsay.

"No. We don't have time for that, Peter," Francis interrupted quickly. "Let's get on with the details on the launch system." Then he looked at Covenant and asked bluntly, "Can they effect a rescue or not?"

"I doubt it. Their launch system is completely dissimilar from ours. A little less than half their fuel is supplied by the replenishment ships. The other half is provided by miniature processing systems at Shturmovoi itself."

"You mean they have enough excess energy to process hydrogen and oxygen from the atmosphere?" someone asked, reflecting nearly everyone's surprise at such an abundance of energy.

"Well, excess is a relative term. Rumors have it that the residents themselves are quite cold most of the time. Let's put it this way; the RSE has priorities which are somewhat different than ours. What they do with their energy is not always related to what we do with ours."

"So you're saying that they may not have enough fuel in storage to effect a rescue," Peter interjected.

"That's quite probable. It requires some months to build up a sufficient reserve."

"I want you to find out, Covenant," Peter ordered.

"I'm afraid that's impossible," he replied with little hesitation.

"Why?" Francis snarled.

"Well, for several reasons, actually, not the least of which is that this station has been unsuccessful in the attempt to reach them, as you know. What leads you to believe they will respond to me if they have ignored all previous requests? And secondly, we have not been given the go ahead for such information exchanges. Any such act would be strictly prohibited by diplomatic protocol."

Peter leapt to his feet, knocking his chair to the floor, and faced Covenant. "There are ten lives hanging by a thread right over your head. *I'm* giving you permission. Now go for it. Stand on top of the chow hall and wave your skivvies at them if you have to, I really don't care..."

"Wait," Gorteau said, standing between them. "Covenant, why would you be afraid of contacting Shturmovoi to organize a rescue mission? If you know more about them than we do, don't you think you owe it to all of us to help?"

"Frankly, gentlemen," Covenant replied, "I don't share your contempt for the regulatory system. Similarly, I cannot violate procedure until I am authorized by Dr. Lipton."

Francis exploded with rage. "What? After all you've seen go down here, you're still waiting for that sonofabitch to lead you around by your silk tie? Don't forget who's responsible for the condition of those people up there in the first place!"

Peter spun around to face Francis. "I'm going to end this, right now!" he said angrily, then stalked out of the room.

Francis let a full second pass, caught Gorteau's and Brinker's eyes, then they raced out together after him. Ashley rushed to keep up with the group, followed by most of the others assembled in the dining hall. They caught up to him as Peter neared the control center.

"Peter, there must be a better way. For God's sake, think this through first," Gorteau warned.

"Wringing Lipton's pencil neck requires minimal forethought," Peter shot back. "If I had done this an hour ago, maybe those people would be safe right now." Then he physically kicked open the door to control.

Lipton sat silently at his console. As Peter kicked open the door, the room became silent, and all eyes looked at the assembled group. Peter stalked over to Lipton's console. "Lipton, look at me!" he shouted.

Lipton did not respond.

"Lipton, I'm talking to you... look at me!"

Still no response.

This so angered Peter that he leapt at Lipton before anyone could respond. He grasped Lipton about the collar and lifted him into the air; not difficult in Mars' light gravity.

"You're dog meat, Lipton. I'm not going to see anyone else die around here because of your petty little administrator games. Now you're going to sign your resignation or I'm going to waste you right here..."

"Peter, let him go, now!" Gorteau ordered.

Peter looked at Francis and Gorteau with a uncontrolled rage in his eyes.

"Put him down," Brinker warned slowly.

Peter slammed him to the floor hard. Lipton lay face down, quietly.

"Lipton, get up!" Peter said loudly. "Stand up and face me like a man!"

Lipton lay still and Peter seized the moment.

"Very well. Lay there, but listen. All of you... listen!" Peter said, moving his eyes across the breadth of the control center, meeting each person's eyes as he swept the center. He paused so that everyone there could focus on him.

"I'm in charge here at BC1. I've been elected by the majority of people on this base and in this colony. This man has been declared mentally incompetent to run this facility, and now he may be responsible for the deaths of ten people. Until this can be sorted out, I'm assuming command. Are there any questions from anyone?"

No one uttered a word. The silence in the control center was penetrating.

"Very well. Pass the word. I've accepted responsibility for whatever may happen from here forward. But I also warn you. We exist by the virtue of each individual's cooperation. Without it, we'll all die. If there is anyone here that questions my authority to lead this community, then call a vote of confidence, majority rules. Otherwise, a refusal to cooperate will be dealt with most severely."

He looked to Brinker who immediately shifted his eyes away. It was obvious that Brinker was still slowly, and with some difficulty, digesting this latest assault to his sense of good order and discipline. He looked to Francis who winked slyly. Gorteau was fighting to conceal overt approval. Toon looked at the floor, scraping his toe almost absent mindedly. Ashley could not take her eyes off his. Lipton still lay silently on the floor.

"Brinker, escort Dr. Lipton to his quarters and call in Dr. Friedman to look him over," Peter ordered. "Sedate him if necessary."

Brinker finally looked at him, long and hard. After several seconds of stagnant silence, Brinker replied, "Yes sir!"

"Get up, Lipton. It's bed time," Brinker commanded.

Lipton's head rose off the floor, his nose bleeding, blood dripping off his chin where he had struck the floor. He smiled a toothy, blood stained smile as he stood. "You'll hang. All of you will hang together. And you, Sergeant Brinker, will also hang," he said, moving slowly and pointing toward Brinker's face, spraying him with a fine mist of blood and saliva as he spoke.

Brinker grabbed his hand and pulled Lipton's finger away from his face. "Maybe, Doc. But until I do, I'm not going to take any crap from you. You cost me one of my Marines today, Lipton, and that more than just pisses me off. So don't mess with me or I may just have to drop kick you out the air lock."

"Murderous terrorists...just listen to yourselves. Death, terror, threats. There is no order here... *the truth will come to light; murder cannot be hid long*."

The words came as an abrupt, unexpected slap in the face to Peter. He immediately recognized them from Shakespeare's Merchant of Venice. And with this little, exquisitely placed slice of civilization, his raw anger was replaced with doubt. Ashley's own reminder of the last evening came rushing back, *"...turning and turning in the widening gyre... things fall apart... mere anarchy is loosed upon the world... the worst are full of passionate intensity."*

Lipton saw it in his face; he saw that he had struck home. "Ah! Yes, my boy, Peter, yes...," Lipton said, working his last weapon in deeper and deeper, physically turning on him. "The truth will come to light, and you know it so well..."

"If you don't jam a sock in it, Brinker, I'm going to," Francis warned. "I think we've all had just about enough of his pontifications."

"Don't push me, Lipton," Brinker advised.

Lipton looked at Brinker with the crazed, bloody smile. Then he spit in Brinker's face. Peter caught Brinker's right fist just before the fatal, explosive blow that would have crushed Lipton's throat.

"Brinker, control yourself," Peter warned. "We still operate by the rule of law here, and you're still a United States Marine. Act like it!"

"The rule of law! How dare you....," Lipton sneered.

"Brinker, gag this man and get him out of here," Peter directed.

In seconds, Brinker had a gag over Lipton's mouth and was rushing him out of the control center, his fist pressed firmly into Lipton's back.

"Tell Covenant to get started on contacting Shturmovoi, now," Peter said to Francis. "If he refuses, throw him in with Lipton. Let him see first hand who he trusts his life to."

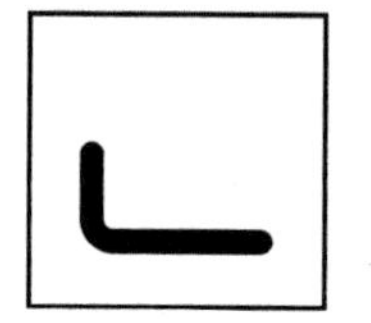

ipton refused to see Friedman. The flight crew marooned in orbit became silent as it was obvious their plight was hopeless. Covenant chose to attempt to contact Shturmovoi rather than spend the sol locked up in the same tiny room with Lipton. Peter named Hernandez and three of his administrative group as part of the colony's governing body. There was no resistance on the part of Hernandez; indeed he felt an unspoken relief that someone other than he was in charge and had accepted total responsibility. There were others in the transient crowd who were grumbling, but those individuals kept to themselves for the most part. There were no overt challenges to the new authority at BC1.

Peter's most ardent hope was that the transients and colonists could achieve some sort of common government, if even just for the short period until help arrived from earth, if any were ever forthcoming at all. He held few illusions. Even if communications were suddenly restored, even if a local settlement was reached and BC1 returned to some kind of productive stability, the predicament they had maneuvered themselves into would probably spell sure and complete disaster for his own future and almost certainly that of BC1 as they knew it. After word and extent of the revolt reached home, the idea of colonizing Mars would almost certainly be abandoned. Regardless of Lipton's state of or lack of competency, the colonists had already pushed the system well beyond the bounds of acceptable controversy.

But the emerging, moment-by-moment situation was far more grave. It appeared that the lander was irrevocably lost, along with ten lives. Of more substance to the living, their winter supplies were stranded in high orbit. A state of rationing would have to begin immediately. Worse still, if there truly had been a world nuclear exchange on earth, rationing would represent only a stop-gap before an inevitable, final disaster. Without further assistance and re-supply from earth, their advanced controlled ecological life support system (known as the ALS or, interchangeably, CELSS) would ultimately run down and they would die. It was only a matter of counting the sols and weeks until the last breath of oxygen, the last drop of water, the last watt of power, was gone.

The sol wore on interminably, an endless succession of whispered meetings, hushed conversations and depressed glances at the Mission Elapsed Time clocks, still ticking away the last hours and minutes of the ten lives from their number circling beyond hope in space. Their fate seemed to be a miniature reflection of those on the planet, stranded in some state of indefinite waiting for the inevitable certainty of death. Those in space could feel their fate closing in on them; they could actually smell and feel the cool shadow of death hover about them. Those on the ground knew only that it was lurking, not so close perhaps, but certainly within range and waiting, always waiting, the final tally of life-giving elements ticked off with each breath, with each passing sol.

Soon the sun settled behind the desert horizon. Those at BC1 who had not already closed themselves into their rooms together began to disappear behind shut doors to be alone or with those closest to them, huddling against the relentless odds stacking against the fledgling colony with cold indifference.

Ashley retired early. She, like everyone else, grew tired of the deteriorating conditions, constant conflicts and unbearable stresses building around them.

Peter sat at the computer console in his office trying to coordinate several ideas that had been offered for rescue of the people in orbit. He had assigned different working groups to coordinate rationing and aspects of long term survival. Just before eleven o'clock in the evening, the ping of his C2 interrupted a calming baroque melody and startled him.

"This is Peter, go ahead."

"Peter, Francis. Get down to Lipton's quarters, and hurry up."

"What's the problem now?" he asked, but the line was already dead.

He ran through the dimly lit and convoluted passageways as quickly as he could to Lipton's apartment. As he approached, he could see several people standing around the open, brightly lit doorway. Francis met him outside.

"Lipton's dead," he said flatly. "Suicide."

"What?" Peter asked, still out of breath. "How?"

"It's easier if you just come on in and see for yourself," Francis replied, his face lined with fatigue and stress. He turned and entered the brilliantly illuminated apartment. Peter hesitated, then followed.

Lipton had not only turned on every light in his apartment, but had somehow gathered ten or so other dazzling florescent light banks and set them up all around the room. Peter squinted in the brilliance.

"Why don't you turn some of these off?" he asked, raising his hand to his eyes.

"Because I wanted you to see it exactly how we found it," Francis replied.

Then Peter saw Lipton. The astonishing image unnerved him. Lipton's body sat on a tall bar stool in front of a tiny sink attached to his illegal wet bar, his feet and ankles locked around the legs of the stool. He was dressed in a white bathrobe, his head slumped deeply into his shoulders and hanging down, chin on his chest, facing the sink. His skin was unnaturally ashen, but in typical Lipton style, his black hair was combed back neatly. His arms lay in the sink, palms upturned. The sink was full of blood, mingled with the warm water he had apparently run to deaden the sensations of death. The crimson water filled the sink to the top drain ports. Except for the bizarre pasty color of his skin, he could have been deep in meditation or sleeping. An empty bottle of Scotch lay overturned beside the sink.

"He slit his wrists to the bone. Apparently he got drunk and killed himself, just as you see it," Francis said plainly.

Peter looked back at Lipton. The image was pathetic. He felt an unexpected surge of sympathy for him. Peter suddenly saw him as another victim of a social structure that demanded too much of an individual trained to protect the status quo when survival on an alien world often demanded extreme and radical change.

He tore his gaze away from Lipton to look at who was gathered about the room. To his embarrassment, all eyes were on him: Brinker, Hiraldo, Hernandez and Friedman, all there, looking at him.

Ashley's words abruptly came back to him again, "*...the best lack all conviction, while the worst are full of passionate intensity...*"

Friedman walked over to him. She looked at Lipton for long seconds, then back to Peter. "I have to accept much of the responsibility for this," she said, her voice weak and trembling. "I should have seen it coming this morning in the control center. I should have come here earlier..."

"Then you found him...?" Peter asked quietly.

"Yes. I came to check on him, saw the bright lights under the door, and when he didn't answer, I let myself in."

"You knew Lipton's door-lock combination?" Peter asked, surprised, in an attempt to piece the events together. When he looked at her, she said nothing, but returned his stare, with harsh and gravely critical eyes. Then Peter realized he had invaded her own privacy at the worst possible moment, and he looked away. Where he felt mild compassion for a man who had been suffering enough to kill himself, it obviously went much deeper than that for Friedman.

But it had been Lipton's decision to kill himself. Peter would be dammed if he would allow Lipton's decision to opt out worsen the chances they all had for survival by deepening a rapidly developing community despondency.

"Julia, get over it," Peter said with more force than he would have liked. "Lassiter made his own personal choices which were not our business to try and change. By the same token, he should not pull us down with him. You're a psychiatrist, for God's sake. You should know that better than any of us."

She slapped him hard. It was carefully aimed and executed. "Such rationality isn't so easy to come by for those of us who knew and respected him; for those of us who loved him."

The reality of his own insensitivity stung him harder than Friedman's flat palm, still burning on his face.

"I'm sorry, Julia, I truly am," Peter said.

"May I offer you some advice, since you've been so quick to assume absolute control here?" she asked, her voice still sharp and caustic.

Peter looked at her and said nothing.

"When the rest find out about this, if those people in space die, as it looks like they will, and if we fail to contact earth, this may became a more common incident than you care to imagine," she said, pointing her finger at Lipton's corpse. "While you work on the engineering realities, keep the human realities in mind as well. It appears that we're all facing some rather difficult tests. If we're not prepared, fully prepared, for what faces us, this is the end result."

"We'll need your help, Julia. We'll need your knowledge and your compassion and your experience," Peter said softly. "I am sorry."

"Spoken like a politician. Lassiter would be proud," she said bluntly.

Peter was sure he didn't know how to take such a compliment standing beside Lipton's lifeless body. But if Peter was turning out to be a politician, Friedman was craftily engineering her own web, created from her expertise as a psychiatrist.

Francis had politely stepped aside to allow Peter and Friedman to discuss their business in private, but he had his ear tuned in, nonetheless, and could hear every word.

"Francis, please ask the medical staff to remove the body," he said.

"You'll want pictures, first, I presume?" Francis asked.

"Why?"

"I would say they would be required in the ensuing investigation."

Peter bit his tongue. He wanted to ask "what investigation?" but realized Francis was leading him.

"Dr. Friedman," Peter asked, "will you have one of the medical staff conduct the investigation?"

"It would be limited to the obvious," she replied. "It wouldn't be productive to waste our resources or time on a detailed effort that would only end up upsetting the others. But Dr. Lynde is correct. Such a course is imperative for the historical record. It must be done."

"Then I can count on you?" Peter asked.

She nodded.

"I'll leave these lights on till the pictures are taken," Francis offered.

"Sure," Peter replied, looking with great interest at the brilliant banks of florescent tubes. "Why do you think he set these up?"

"It's common for some individuals who are deeply depressed to want light," Friedman began. "Light acts as a stimulus that makes depressed people feel better. Some heart attack victims who lose significant whole body circulation crave fans. It makes them feel like they are getting more oxygen. Light acts in much the same way to victims of depression. It makes them feel like they have more control over their environment. Oddly enough, it will also cause some significant physiological and psychological improvement."

"That explains the lights, then," Peter said, and successfully avoided the temptation to look at her. "Francis, will you assist Dr. Friedman?"

But Francis had begun to stare at the lights and it was obvious he had not heard. "I just don't get this," he finally said with vacant eyes, staring into the empty space before his eyes.

"Don't get what?" Peter replied, his eyes sweeping the room all about him.

"This. All of this," Francis replied wafting his hand in a semi-circle all around. "None of this feels right. I just don't get this."

Peter looked at him for a long second, but the stinging on his face and the urgency of the moment pushed him forward.

"Francis, snap out of it, will you?" Peter demanded in a harsh tone totally out of character.

Francis' eyes refocused and he nodded. "How about that computer program?" he asked, pointing to Lipton's personal computer.

"Is that the same program that Fabian mentioned awhile ago?" Peter asked, surprised.

"One in the same. It's still running; still using the geology files."

"Ask Toon to come down here as soon as possible and interrupt it. There's no telling what it's doing."

On Lipton's computer, just a few feet from his dead body, the program continued on, faithfully following his last instructions, flashing the words: STILL COLLATING.

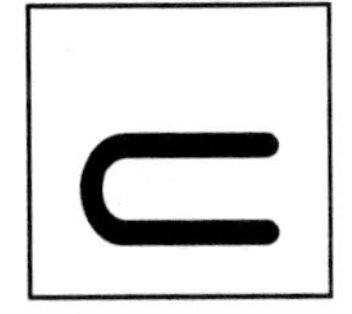

artwright lied to his eight passengers. He told them that the ground was working on their situation and would have it solved by morning. Not one of the admin types knew the difference. They had spent the sol in space quietly reading; no one was interested in challenging the flight crew's plans or nerves after tending to Hicks' bruises. After such a harried sol, they all gladly declared lights out early.

Cartwright aimed his line of sight antenna at Kerry in orbit and put in a PC2 call that could not be monitored from the ground.

"Good evening, Lieutenant Kerry. Got any good news for us?"

"No, guys, I'm sorry," Kerry replied, fighting back overwhelming fatigue and emotions. He had never worked a more exhausting mental day in his life. He had found nothing except the tragic inevitability of their plight.

"Bob, we're going to pull the plug. We wanted you to know."

"No, damn you, - no! Let me work it some more," Kerry screamed back at him. "Give me a chance, at least."

"Bob, you know as well as I do there isn't a snowball's chance in hell. At least admit that and let us go."

At once Kerry's silence betrayed that he understood.

"Let us go."

Yes, it was really that simple. He was just an uncomfortable hindrance in the inevitable. He had worked one miracle, but there could not be another. He had to let them go; to hold on any longer would not be fair.

"Guys, I just want you to know something," Kerry said, his voice choking with emotion. There was a long period of silence while he attempted to recover his paralyzed voice. "I love you guys. I did everything I could."

"Bob, we know that. You gave us these last hours. Thanks," Cartwright replied, his hand gently draped over Michner's shoulder. "Bob, Siggy and I want you to tell our families how much we loved them.

"Ian, Siggy...I...," Kerry tried to begin.

"We know, Bob. We know," Siggy replied. "Now get on about your business, spaceman," she said, then cut the link.

erry had never felt so utterly alone and vulnerable. There was no glory left here in this dark, cold and empty hell. He could not bear to even look out of the window at the angry red planet below. He physically pushed himself away from the console and large windows. Sliding behind his seat, he gripped its back and sobbed openly.

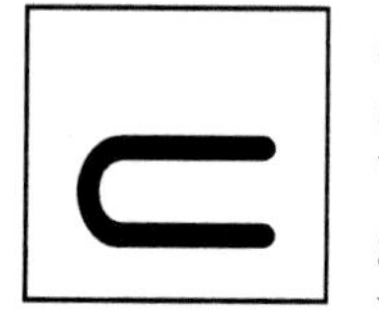

artwright looked over his shoulder at the eight sleeping passengers in the dim lights of the lander. With the multicolored instruments before them, it gently illuminated the cockpit and their faces. And with this image came the altogether surprising memories of childhood Christmas mornings. He then turned and looked to his pilot, Siggy. Her face was no longer strong and determined. It was softer somehow; more sensitive in the dim and multicolored light.

She looked back to him and caught his eyes. The tears began to stream down her face. Cartwright reached up with his fingers and wiped them away. He said nothing.

"Ian, please promise me something," she whispered. "Say something with me. Please say you will."

He nodded.

She gripped his fingers and pulled his hand toward her, squeezing them tightly in hers. "*Now I lay me down to sleep...*", she began in a whisper.

He looked at her and with these words, he heard her sweet voice for the first time. They had worked together for years, but he was so determined to make things equal, that he blocked the fact that she was a woman from his mind. He had successfully removed her body and her voice as irrelevant from their professional lives. *He suddenly realized that before he had heard only her words, never her voice.* And now, as it came to him, he realized how desperately beautiful, how rich and full it really was. The image of her beauty hurried at him, flooding his vision; he could hardly block it away. She was no longer just a female; she was a stunning, vulnerable woman who needed whatever he could give her. He looked deeply into her eyes, surprised at what he found there. He smiled tenderly and with understanding, trying to fathom the full depth of the beauty he had ignored for so long; discovered here, at last, at the very end on the final voyage. And he said,

"*Now I lay me down to sleep...*"

The lander's computers would record that all members were sound asleep before the computer ordered the first change in the atmosphere. The lander's windows were aimed away from Mars, pointing toward the stars. Siggy lay curled tightly in Cartwright's arms. By special order, the life support system slowly replaced all the cabin oxygen with nitrogen, gently reducing the pressure at the same time. The life support system shut down completely after that. None of the occupants awoke from their deep and final slumber.

ieutenant Robert Kerry was not stranded in space. Since the days of the International Space Station in the late 20th century, all permanently orbiting space platforms had been equipped with escape pods. The escape pod attached to the Goddard looked exactly like all its predecessors: a gumdrop shaped capsule whose sole purpose was to evacuate its inhabitants. The capsule fired a single solid rocket to slow down and then droped by parachute until retro rockets finalized its less than glorious landing. The pod's ancestry could be traced in a non-diverging, straight line to the Apollo moon capsule of the previous millennium. With almost no improvements or changes, these life boat pods had been duplicated by the hundreds and used successfully all over the solar system.

Kerry did not necessarily have to use it. He had the clear option of continuing with the original plan, jettisoning the cargo pod into a stable orbit and leaving for earth by himself.

He agonized over the options. He was now completely alone and if he left for earth, he would not see another human for 273 earth-days. He had spent so much time ridiculing the colonist's theory of a planet wide nuclear conflagration on earth, that he had not analyzed it carefully. Now he was not only physically alone, he was one of the few humans in this region of the solar system who clung to the optimistic belief that the earth was unaffected and would be calling at any minute.

Yet time continued to slip by without word of any kind from his home planet.

Soon after the life support systems failed on the lander, and it became obvious to everyone what had happened to the occupants, Kerry asked BC1 for a detailed assessment of the earthside communications anomaly. After a sober appraisal of the information, he began for the first time to entertain grave doubts about his own perilously optimistic hypothesis, but he had still not finally abandoned hope. There was not enough information to understand the full range of probabilities either way. He completed a detailed launch window assessment and figured he had at least four launch opportunities in the next 26 hours. With this assessment, he had time to wait a little longer. Once he decided on an option and pressed the firing button on either craft, it would be too late to turn back and reconsider.

t BC1, Peter had more problems to deal with on the ground than the fate of Lieutenant Kerry. But it was high on his list. Since Kerry's decision would affect the outlook of all of them, he gave it some priority.

Friedman's emotional caveat to consider the morale of the community as a leadership priority was heavy on his mind. Every human at BC1 knew of Lipton's suicide within an hour of its discovery. Not two hours after that, word came from the control center that the life support systems in the lander had failed. Though they all had accepted the reality that the passengers were doomed, the news of their quiet death did not come easily.

As the sun rose over them, the base was like a tomb. So many people had been up all night discussing and worrying about the death of Lipton and ten other fellow human beings that most were sleeping late. Peter himself caught precious few hours rest but was up early nonetheless. This would be a crucial sol.

He poured himself a cup of steaming hot synthetic coffee in the dining hall and sat down alone at the end of a long table. When he had left his quarters, Ashley was still asleep.

He felt a hand on his shoulder and turned to see who it was. The cook, Rat, stood beside him.

"I take it you had a rough night, boss," he said.

"Indeed I did," Peter replied with a weak smile.

"May I offer you some advice?" Rat asked sincerely.

"Please do."

"No offense here, but cool down a little. Lower your blood pressure. You're taking this whole thing too seriously. I remember you before this whole mess started. You were a lot more enjoyable to be around. I mean, if we have you to look up to now, give us someone we can like and respect, no offense."

"None taken," Peter replied and attempted a sincere smile. "Do you really think I'm taking survival too seriously?" he asked.

"You're damn right; excuse my French," Rat began. "You scientist types are either going to figure it all out or you're not. Either way, you're going to give it your best shot, am I right?"

"Yes."

"Then you can give it your best and be miserable and worry or you can go down the same road and let the chips fall where they may. If I'm not mistaken, you're worried about Lipton, worried about those poor dead souls in space, worried about the transients and colonists, worried about the other guy in space, worried about your wife, worried about the earth, worried about the Soviets... hey, look what worry did for Lipton."

Peter smiled and slowly nodded his head. "You called it right on the money, Rat. And you're correct, of course." Then he lifted his cup to Rat. "I dedicate this sol to you. Thanks."

"How's the coffee?" Rat asked.

"Great."

"Good. When I saw you coming, I slipped in a pot of decaffeinated, no offense."

"Now that I DO take offense to, Rat! Go get me some real coffee," Peter barked sternly, looking with revulsion in his cup. "I haven't had any sleep. How do you expect me to function?"

"You don't need all that caffeine, Dr. T."

"Don't call me that, and go get me some real coffee!" Peter shouted, feeling the rush that comes with an uplifted spirit.

Francis walked in as Peter was shouting after Rat.

"What? Rat's coffee no good?" he asked. "How can this be?"

"Rat's coffee is fine. He slipped me a decaffeinated Mickey," Peter explained.

"Other than that, just how are you this morning? For real, I mean..." Francis asked somewhat clumsily, sitting beside him, expecting the worst.

"I'm fine," Peter replied. "After some relevant counseling with the local barkeep, no problems," he said, nodding his head toward Rat.

"Don't tell Freidman the Rat's moving in on her shrinkdom. She'll get upset."

"She's already upset," Peter said, instinctively rubbing his cheek where he still felt a subliminal sting.

"I saw," Francis said with a sly smile. "What do you think brought all that on?" Then he repeated a line from a classic cartoon character: *"Pinky, are you pondering what I'm pondering?"*

"I don't think I want to know," Peter said candidly, then asked, "Did Toon interrupt Lipton's program?"

"No. It actually completed its processing before he arrived. I asked him to verify the integrity of the geology files, and they're intact."

"Good," Peter replied with some relief. "Any word on what Lipton was up to?"

"No. When we can cut Toon loose, I'll ask him to see if he can trace it all down."

"Did Lipton leave any kind of note or a message of any kind regarding his suicide?" Peter asked.

"I couldn't find a thing. It looks like he just pulled the plug, like Cartwright," he said slowly, staring straight ahead at nothing in particular. "It's like a house of cards... tragic beyond belief. And those were just two layers. There must be more…"

"Cut it off, Francis," Peter said in a loud whisper. "It's all behind us. If we expect to make it out of this, we have to force ourselves to look ahead. And somehow, we have to translate that to everybody else. Friedman is right. The morale of the community must take top priority over everything else."

Rat delivered two cups of hot, steaming coffee.

"…this the good stuff?" Peter asked.

"Blow your head off, no offense," Rat said with a wink.

"Good for you, Rat. Take the rest of the sol off," Peter said in jest.

"No thanks. I want to be around here when you drop dead of a triple myocardial infarction. I'll personally spread the word far and wide, *I told him so.*"

"Then you can be boss," Francis offered.

"No way," Rat replied walking away to his kitchen.

"What now?" Francis sputtered after taking in a slug of the searing coffee. His eyes widened as the molten liquid ignited everything in its path on the way down.

"We're going to organize a party, Francis," Peter said without even a hint of a smile.

"Pardon me?"

"A party. A significant distraction. A merry lighthearted event so that a little fun will be had by all."

"Oh, I see," Francis said, nodding his head "That will be some slight of hand. Kind of like a Chinese funeral, no? I suppose we'll take old Lassiter's body, freeze dry it, put a party hat on it and set it outside for all to celebrate? Maybe we can stand outside, wait for the lander to reenter and all kiss and make a wish when it comes flaming over the horizon."

"Right idea, wrong approach," Peter replied, not amused by Francis' misdirected humor.

"Okay, so how are we going to turn this train around, pal? In case you haven't had enough sleep and missed the key events, we're in a runaway locomotive, down a long steep hill and the bridge is out at the bottom. I fail to see a party in all that, although I can think of some fairly clever invitations."

"Cut the crap. We've got to execute a plan today," Peter said, passionately jabbing at the table. "*Today*. Tomorrow will be too late."

"Okay, I'm sorry," Francis answered, setting his coarse humor aside. "What's the plan?"

Peter looked at Francis and pointed over head. "Our orbiting astronaut is going to turn it around, if we can talk him out of running back home."

eter's idea was centered around the spirit of the community. An irrefutable depression had beset BC1 tangible enough to flow down the passageways like the Pharaoh's creeping fog of death. Beyond that lay memorial services for eleven of their number who had perished under less than natural circumstances. Ahead of that lay the uncertainty of a future with barely enough life support to sustain them through winter and only enough to make it another several months beyond. If asked, the computers could give them the numbers to the last hour, totally without any emotion. No one had yet asked, but soon even that would be necessary.

No group of human beings could survive long without some kind of hope for the future. Many of them would not even make it to the Last Desperate Hour if all they had to look forward to was death by suffocation, starvation, freezing or suicide. Perhaps the community would even tear itself apart before then.

Peter planned to feed them hope, above and before all else: some kind of promise that they were not living out their final hours. He was determined that his leadership would be positive, full of promise, vitality, satisfaction and hope, or he would not lead at all. His path to recovery would begin by giving them all a reason to celebrate and minimizing the reasons to focus on a death that seemed more inevitable than not with every passing sol.

Francis and Peter met an hour later in the Meteorology cubicle in one corner of the control center. It was enclosed by transparent plastic partitions that ensured at least some privacy. Peter ordered that Lieutenant Kerry be brought up on a classified circuit.

"Command Center, this is the Goddard, go ahead," Kerry responded without delay.

"Lieutenant Kerry, this is Peter Traynor. We need to discuss your status."

Silence.

Peter took a deep breath and looked at Francis with concern.

"Lieutenant Kerry, what are your intentions?" Peter asked bluntly.

"I want to talk to Lassiter Lipton," Kerry replied.

Peter paused, then said, "Lassiter Lipton is dead."

The silence was total. As the seconds swept by into the first full minute of quiet, Peter began to fear that his plan would not work.

"What happened to the Director?" Kerry asked, his voice permeated with suspicion.

"Dr. Lipton took his own life last night."

More silence.

"I haven't yet decided on my course of action," Kerry said, stunned at the news of even more death, stalling for time. "I'll get back to you."

"Wait!" Peter said before Kerry could disconnect. "Let's discuss it together."

Kerry's voice flashed into anger. "Discuss what, Traynor? It's *my* decision. It's *my* choice, not yours."

"We know that, Lieutenant Kerry," Peter replied calmly, sympathetically. "Just wanted you to understand..."

"Understand what, Traynor? I *understand* that people tend to get dead around there. I *understand* that you want me to come dropping into the local circus after you and your merry band have conveniently disposed of a United States Marine, the Director of the facility, trashed the launch pad and who knows what else? What I can't figure out is, *why*? Why do you all of a sudden need me?"

"Your impressions of what happened here are wrong. If you'd like a more detailed explanation from Robert Hernandez, Lipton's assistant or from our staff psychiatrist, I'd be happy..."

"You can blow that out your rosy cheeks, Traynor," Kerry continued hotly. "I don't know any of those people. Just give me one good, straight answer as to why you want me to drop in."

"Because we need you," Peter replied evenly and truthfully.

There was a long silence as Kerry was obviously entertaining his options.

"I suppose that you're about to tell me why you need me," Kerry finally said very slowly, drawing out the intonation as though he was being fleeced by the local snake oil peddler.

Peter himself was discouraged by the pace and direction of the conversation. He felt and sympathized with Kerry's distrust. His mind hastened to find the words to give Kerry some acceptable reason to understand and believe him.

"Lieutenant Kerry, I understand your suspicions," Peter began carefully. "If I were in your position, I would feel exactly the same way. So I'll give it to you how I would want it, as straight as I can.

"I listened to your handling of the emergency during the launch. I thought it was brilliant and flawless. In short, we're going to need all the genius we can possibly assemble to survive. Your mind may just make the difference between success and failure here.

"Reason number two: everyone heard your effort to save the lander. To be frank, you're something of a hero here.

"Reason number three: the morale here is as about as low as it can get. We need you to 'drop in' so that we'll have cause to celebrate something, anything. We need a new face among us; we need to see a new human added to our population who can offer even the smallest edge to our chances of survival.

"That's all I can offer you, Lieutenant."

Kerry's anger was gone. If Traynor was a snake oil salesman then he had just been fleeced and felt really good about it besides. The belligerence was gone, but the core of his suspicion was still there, clearly embedded in his voice.

"Okay, Traynor, give me the whole story, all of it. Tell me everything as far back as you can remember. And don't lie to me. The very first lie I catch you in, I'll cut the circuit and blow out of here so fast I won't even leave a memory."

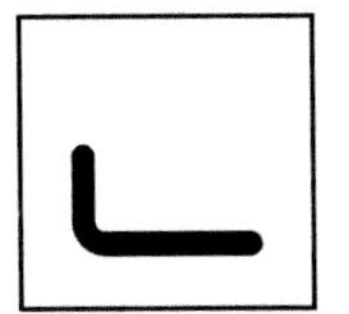

ater that afternoon, they buried Lassiter Lipton and Marine Lieutenant Micah Quinton beneath the sands of Mars, the first humans ever to be interred on the planet. A memorial service was called after the dinner hour in remembrance of the two men. The services were conducted in the dining hall and were presided over by Bryce Gates, a power systems engineer and the community's most devoutly religious member, often called the Chaplain by his friends. That evening, the title was made permanent.

Gates' ceremony was touching and beautiful. Peter had discussed with Gates the necessity of making it as uplifting as he could, and Gates succeeded. Peter risked much in even daring to make a personal appearance, but he insisted that no one should miss except those on watch. And to the surprise of everyone, including Peter, he was asked to read from the Bible by the chaplain in the passages he had marked. Peter stood, clearing his voice, and read,

Lord, how oft shall my brother sin against me, and I forgive him? As many as seven times?
Jesus said to him, "I do not say to you seven times but seventy times seven."
The people that walked in darkness have seen a great light: they that dwell in the shadow of death, upon them hath the light shined.
The voice of him that crieth in the wilderness, Prepare ye the way of the Lord, make straight in the desert a highway for our God.

Peter sat down to a hushed silence as Gates prayed for God to embrace the souls of the departed and deliver from harm the souls of those who lived. But Peter's mind was concentrating on making the highway in the desert. And as he shut his eyes in reverence, he clenched his teeth in determination to make it a highway to survival, and not just straight, but a superhighway to life for the living.

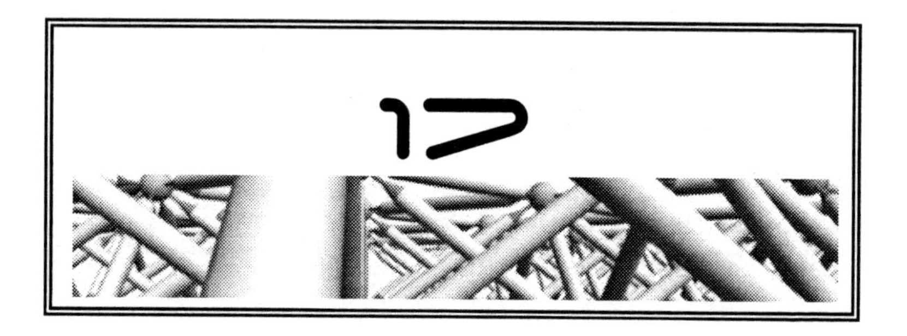

Lieutenant Kerry was fastidious to begin with. But when it came to preparing a spacecraft for dormancy, he was meticulous to a fault, bordering on obsessive-compulsive neuroses. Kerry ran down the NASA checklist, and then his own which was three times as long. He stowed the ship as though it were going into the Smithsonian Institution. He wiped the walls with a damp cloth, then came back with a dry cloth to remove the lint left behind from the first cloth. When they told him at Pensacola's Naval Flight School that the Navy was fanatical about cleanliness, Kerry breathed a sigh of relief. He was probably the only man in the facility, including the drill instructor, who actually fully understood and appreciated the absolute necessity of wiping the barracks floor with the palm of his hand.

He had strong reservations about dropping in at BC1. Like all other human encounters, Kerry did not trust Peter Traynor. Indeed, although he acquired a hint of trust from Peter's voice and the forthright way he related the events at BC1, he had been flimflammed before by real con-artists.

Kerry made his decision to stay on Mars based on a rational evaluation of all the information he had. He was hardly dropping into BC1 to save the community. Indeed, his true motivation was more one of self preservation. To travel back to earth now, to endure the long voyage without the benefit of human company, to risk being stranded in orbit above a radioactively contaminated planet - in short, to run toward the unknown based on the logic of wishful thinking - not only went against the grain of his ordered mind but was also asking for trouble. At least here he had some idea of what he was up against. He also knew that if conditions on his home planet were recoverable, that in time, he would get his ride home. On Mars so far, he knew the names of the players and the story they wanted him to hear. In less than two hours, he would also know the real truth.

eter's decision to hold a double memorial service and get it out of the way as soon as possible was a deliberate effort to turn the corner quickly. Today would be Lieutenant Bob Kerry's day. He was slated for reentry at mid-morning, BC1 time.

The calculations for the landing were already completed. The ability to target the precise landing point of something as simple as an escape pod was almost insignificant compared to most spacecraft trajectories. Indeed, something as elementary as Kerry's "drop" into BC1 was considered primitive. They had his landing position pinpointed, within an accuracy of 10 meters, not far from them.

The anticipation of Kerry's arrival grew at BC1. He had the respect of every person there. They had all witnessed his heroic actions to save the lander and its passengers. Just as Peter had predicted, the collective thought of something positive happening after so many tragic incidents compounded with the wait for Kerry's arrival until the community's response took on an almost festive air.

People were actually smiling, something that seemed to catch on despite the pain of the recent past. An electronic banner welcoming Kerry was scrolled across the displays in the dining hall. On instructions from Peter, Rat was preparing a banquet for everyone in Kerry's honor. After seven sols of near chaos, there was at last something to be happy about. Peter's plan was working.

As they prepared for the Big Event, Peter and Ashley continuously bumped into one another in Peter's crowded quarters.

"When are we going to move up in life?" Ashley asked. "We need a bigger place."

"Agreed," Peter said, tugging a sweater over his head. "NASA never dreamed two people would be sharing these quarters."

"Well, the planners probably discussed it but you can almost hear the bureaucrats addressing cohabitation in red-faced whispers behind double-locked doors," she added.

"You're absolutely right. If they'd ever seriously discussed it in an open forum, Congress would have sent robots."

"So my quarters go unused and we jam everything in here," Ashley said, brushing her hair back in front of the mirror.

"We pay the price of poor planning and naive engineering on their part," he said, kissing the back of her neck. "But some things are just worth the price, don't you think?"

She turned and put her arms around him and smiled. "It may be fine for us now, but as we start to get used to actually living together, I'm definitely going to want a single square meter of space I can call my own to get dressed in." Then she smiled her sweetest smile.

Peter looked at her beautiful hazel eyes, the light spray of freckles across her nose and loved every part of her face. The past week had been excruciatingly painful for all of them. It was wonderful to see things on the upswing again. Already she was talking about tomorrow and better things. He desperately hoped the same kind of reasoning was working its way throughout BC1.

She tenderly kissed him on his lips, but gently pushed him away when his response immediately grew ardent. "Later," she said. "We've got important stuff to attend to."

"Certainly...*mon ami*," he responded with a fake French accent under his breath.

"Huh?" she queried.

He returned his best toothy Garfield smile.

t that same instant in orbit, Kerry stuffed a single small bag into the gaping hatch of the escape pod. He turned around for a last look at his orbiting spacecraft. His trained eyes meticulously covered every square centimeter, instrument by instrument, line by line. All was in order, which was not a trivial condition for an object under Kerry's direct scrutiny and control.

Kerry had put on his cleanest blue flight coveralls. It was required by regulation to wear a full pressure suit, but he decided to waive that requirement. To suit up alone in zero-G was nearly an impossibility anyway. Besides, he reasoned, as far as he knew, there had never been a loss of pressurization in one of these Apollo-legacy capsules in all of their history. And if today was the day for the first anomaly, "*... oh well,*" he reasoned, "*At least I'll die in comfort.*"

Kerry was slender and short, which made him particularly agile in small spacecraft. He had the build of a gymnast and kept his tone by rigorous exercise when in space. His very light blond hair was close cut, a condition he kept by the liberal use of electric "space shears." His eyes were brown and close set, which gave his handsome athletic face the appearance of constant, intense analysis, even though he was about as easy going as the next person when face to face. But his intelligence instinctively commanded his speech and movements. A few minutes with Kerry was all it took to know he was brighter than most.

He turned and floated into the pod feet first. Before closing the hatches, he took a lingering last look around his ship, sighing and sincerely wondering whether he was making the right choice. Soon he would know. If he found himself in an interrogation room, or worse, in an hour or so, then he would be sorry he ever left the serenity and relative security of his floating home.

He closed the ship's hatch, then the pod's hatch behind him, strapped himself into his couch and stuck his music player onto a Velcro patch attached to his leg. As the music rang home between his ears, his eyes and fingers danced over the pod's many switches bringing it to life.

he activity at BC1 had reached a fevered pitch. For some unknown reason, it seemed everyone there had put on their best clothes. It was as though they were forcing themselves into an upbeat mood, or, at the least, that they very much wanted to show a fellow member of their race that they were not uncivilized after all.

Peter insisted that Hernandez occupy Lipton's seat in the Launch Control Center while Peter sat in Hernandez's old seat. He had handed over nearly all of Lipton's administrative tasks to Hernandez who was not only trained to handle them and was good at it, but also actually enjoyed such duties. Peter detested managerial details and had pledged long ago to avoid them whenever possible. It was a pleasure to delegate all these to Hernandez who was truly honored to be given such vast responsibility on his own. Hernandez had been taking care of many of them for Lipton, anyway; a fact he had not shared with Peter or anyone else. Peter's goal was to lead and share, not drag the community along, jealously hording power and credit, as he felt Lipton had done.

Something of a shuffle reordered the Launch Control Center's top row of consoles. Peter and Hernandez now shared seats with Francis, Gorteau and Toon. Peter wanted his own team there if things began to go wrong.

"Goddard, BC1," the launch director said over the net.

"This is Goddard, go ahead," Kerry replied.

"Goddard, are you ready for disconnect?"

"Any time."

"Would you like a short count?" the launch director asked politely.

"I'll give it to you," Kerry replied. There was a several minute pause as he set his switches then checked them for accuracy. The procedure would be to undock the pod from the Goddard, back away a safe distance then set the computer to fire the retro-rockets. The gumdrop shaped vehicle would ride down on its heat shield then the retro rockets would slow him down. Once they slowed the capsule to a satisfactory speed, a giant parachute would unfurl. At 100 meters, the pod would break free from its canopy and retro rockets would slow him to a safe landing speed.

"Okay, BC1, ...all set here. I'll give you a short count and undock," Kerry said conversationally, although he was seriously concerned about who was listening below and under what conditions.

"Three... two... one... breakaway! Undocking successful."

A ripple of applause spread through BC1. Peter sighed and flexed his shoulders. At least things were off to a good start.

"Okay, BC1. Minus seven minutes, fourteen seconds till retrofire," the astronaut reported.

"Roger that, Gumdrop," the Flight Director said smiling.

"Gumdrop?" Kerry asked, slightly amused.

"Roger, Lieutenant Kerry. We just realized your escape pod had no name, so we christened it. Hope you like it."

"I'm not so sure that it's splendid enough for its one and only voyage. But if that's what you guys want, well, okay, we'll be Gumdrop today. Although, I guess you know you're plagiarizing Apollo history," Kerry recounted, referring to the Apollo 9 capsule by the same name.

"No problem, Gumdrop. The old timers are all dead and wouldn't care anyway," the Flight Director mused.

The seven minutes passed quickly both on the ground and in space. Kerry backed slowly away from the massive Goddard with its attached cargo pod. He shivered involuntarily as he viewed the pod, fully loaded with water and consumables - all items vital to the survival of the humans below. With the crash of the lander vehicle, there was now no way to recover these vital materials, attached firmly to the Goddard and stranded in space.

The huge, dark grey hulk reflected the colors from the planet's ruddy surface, the dim red glow making the ship look like an immense live ember. Its cylindrical edges rotated slowly in orbit; the bright, solar powered strobes centered on the docking collar blinking their silent good-byes.

"Minus 45 seconds," the ground reported to him.

"Roger, I'm oriented properly and onboard logic has been enabled to perform the retrofire."

Kerry's mind raced through his options for the last time. There were still enough seconds left on the clock to change his mind and re-dock with Goddard for the trip back to earth. All he had to do was cancel the retrofire command and return to dock. In less than half a minute, he may never be able to return to space again. But Kerry was, to his very core, a being of logic and discipline. He willed his mind back to flying his spacecraft; the decision had been made and there would be no turning back.

"Minus ten seconds," the ground reported, and then counted them down. At zero, Kerry felt the familiar thump of the retrorockets kicking in and he reported a successful firing. Those on the ground responded with another ripple of applause. But the dangerous part of the voyage had just begun, and no one dared display too much excitement yet.

Kerry watched his instruments carefully. The spacecraft was automatically taking care of orientation. All he had to do now was wait for the long fall into the plains of Elysium.

"Ground control, Gumdrop," Kerry said evenly. "I'm in good shape. Touchdown in 29 minutes. Ionization begins in eight. You've got a good data stream. I'm going off line."

The Flight Director looked momentarily confused, then worried, then over to the flight dynamics officer, shrugging his shoulders. Why would Kerry cut himself off from communications? No one on the ground had any answers.

"Gumdrop, BC1. Acknowledge please."

There was no response. The Flight Director checked the stream of telemetry coming in from the spacecraft. Kerry's heart rate was normal, life support normal, all systems operating as designed. Kerry was simply not talking.

In space, Kerry slipped his headphones on. He keyed in *John Williams' American Classics,* turned the volume all the way up and relaxed, his eyes on the instruments. If this may be his last chance to fly in a spacecraft, then he was not about to let any senseless yammering from the ground interfere. *This was his ride.*

The first glimmer of atmospheric contact sent a flickering orange hue across the tiny window just centimeters in front of his face. He narrowed his eyes against the glare and sighed heavily as Aaron Copeland's brassy *Fanfare for the Common Man* seemed to transform the colors and send them rippling along his spine. The G-forces pressed him far back into his seat as Gumdrop slammed into the Martian atmosphere at Mach 18 and was enveloped in a brilliant, white-hot shield of ionized air. At that moment, all data from the capsule was lost.

Zoya Dimitriov touched the tips of her thin fingers together and held them still, inches from her face. Her eyes swept across the surface of the holographically projected chess board in front of her. Her analytical mind evaluated the options of the game with cold precision. From time to time, her eyes shifted to size up the man who sat opposite her, measuring him with the same indifferent standard used toward the chess pieces illuminated on the board before her.

Vladimir Dybenko shifted restlessly in his seat, his eyes darting nervously about the room, while Dimitriov contemplated her next move. He was not a chess player, yet Dimitriov continued inviting him to play frequently. He could hardly refuse; she was his commander. Dybenko was her second in command.

She delighted in toying with him on the board. Like a rat cornered by a barn cat, Dimitriov lured him, pawing him into grievous and embarrassing losses of his assets before she actually moved in for the mauling kill. She allowed the games to drag on endlessly, wordlessly, for hours while she humiliated him in this process of pure logic, strategy and unadulterated intellectual combat for which both knew he was not her equal.

She did it for a reason, of course. She forced him time and time again to submit to her unequivocally superior intelligence so he would never dare challenge her command, to her face or behind her back. He knew it and she knew it. These games served to remind him of the reality of life at Shturmovoi. She took special delight in driving it home.

Dimitriov had seen the checkmate three moves ago, ignored the rules and let it pass, to see if Dybenko would attempt to slither away. He never saw it at all. He had quit competing hours ago – months ago.

"Checkmate," she announced stoically, matter-of-factly. She did not even bother to command the movement of her piece.

Dybenko did not look at the board. He stood up, so restless with pent up anxiety, he was almost ready to explode with an unfortunate display of impertinence. Wisely he held his tongue.

"Another marvelous game, Colonel," Dybenko lied, so clumsily it was laughable. "Well, I must depart; it is late," he said moving quickly toward the door of her office.

"Just a moment, Major," she said slowly.

His hand, already touching the door control, froze. He did not turn around, waiting for Dimitriov to continue. But she did not, taking some pleasure in seeing how long Dybenko would wait for her.

"Yes, Colonel," he finally said, propping his chin up artificially as he turned around to face her.

"Sit," she said, her voice sterile and rigid. "Board off," she commanded and the holographic board dissolved slowly from the tabletop before them.

As Dybenko sat down into his still warm seat, Dimitriov lit up a brown cigarette, blew smoke in his direction and never for a moment looked away from him. Her thin nose seemed to spike out from her black eyes, framed below two narrow, obviously penciled eyebrows. She might have been attractive except for her determined effort not to be. Had she entered a contest for the most sour looking woman in the Reunified Soviet Empire, she would have walked away with the roses. On Mars, she had no peer. To her eternal credit, she deftly coupled her looks with her demeanor. Her personality fit her appearance like nylon spandex on a Muscovite whore.

She looked across the table at this pitiful excuse for a soldier, assigned to her as her deputy in command of Shturmovoi. While she should have received the hand picked senior military officer she had asked for, the Committee had sent her this pathetic cosmonaut. Being a decorated Hero of the Empire was not so difficult, she had said to Dybenko on more than one occasion. When strapped to millions of kilograms of screaming rockets, where does one run? When forced to make life-critical decisions, who decides? The computers decide. When faced with a multitude of options, what process does a soldier quickly use to guarantee life over death? The committee on the ground decides.

Dybenko's handsome face looked like it belonged on a magazine cover; best kept on *Pravada,* not paraded before an ambivalent and disorderly assembly of ground troops.

"Major, what have you heard of the American revolt?" she asked him, then shifted her head slightly to the side, moving her cigarette and its blue smoking trail out of the line of her vision of him. As her eyes cut into his, he looked away.

"The American lander will reenter tomorrow afternoon, between 1600 and 1730. The ten Americans onboard are presumed dead," he said quietly.

"I know that, Dybenko. You briefed me on that information this morning."

"Of course, Colonel; how stupid of me. I lost track of that fact in the heat of our game," he said with a nervous laugh and smile, grasping, in a useless attempt at eliciting a return smile. Dimitriov stared back at him without expression as one would stare at the death throes of a dying insect.

The ensuing silence prompted Dybenko to speak again. "Other than that, we have received no radio intelligence. They are still attempting to contact us by..."

"You are repeating yourself, Major," she said again.

A bead of sweat trickled down his neck onto his collar, just as she had calculated it would.

"Do you know that their director is dead?" she asked, crushing her cigarette out.

"No, I did not," he replied, half wondering whether she was lying to him or really had access to intelligence to which he was not privy.

"He is dead, Dybenko. Murdered by the criminal element who started the rebellion. The American base is tearing itself to pieces." She left the comment to dangle in the air for effect before beginning again.

"The war on earth has left us in a rather precarious position, comrade. Our life support and consumables are limited, do you not agree?" she asked, leading him.

"Yes, Colonel. We have had the scientific branch working in an effort to pinpoint..."

"Please, Dybenko!" she said, cutting him off. "Working to what end?" Then she moved her body forward in her chair toward him till he could smell the foul stench of the tobacco on her breath. "Play the game of our own survival with more zeal than you play this one," she said, pointing at the now empty table top. "Evaluating the inevitable is a waste of our resources. Do you not agree?"

Dybenko felt the same surge of stupidity and ineptness that he always felt when sitting across from her at the game board. Already she was several moves ahead and he was hopelessly lost.

yodore Kirov and Petroskovich Drobkiev found themselves immersed in evaluating the extent of their life support capacity, including detailed calculations of water, food, power and consumables. No official word had been released as to what was going on. Yet the initial suspicions became the obvious. Word had been circulating around Shturmovoi there had been a war on earth which had disrupted communications.

The reality of interrupted communications was obvious to everyone. The pitiful deceptions offered initially for the loss were quickly exposed by the rumor mill as originating in the Director's office. Finally, there circulated a substantial story that there had been a war on earth and most seemed to cling to that as factual within a certain respectable range of probability.

The contingent of the Reunified Soviet Empire on Mars, much like the Americans, consisted of two groups: the scientific branch and the executive branch. The scientific branch was made up of 28 scientists, engineers and researchers. The executive branch was comprised of 29 administrators, consisting of Dimitriov and her staff, including Dybenko. The executives were assembled from a large number of military personnel and a few politicians sent to Mars on a career enhancing junket more than to serve any useful function.

Such was the tendency observed before on earth in nearly every generation of exploration. After the initial voyages of discovery to any new frontier, within the next group were a few individuals who coveted the instant, effortless fame associated with the voyage alone. This kind of waste was made even worse when government funds were involved. Political strings were easily pulled by politically motivated fiscal ploys and soon politicians were involved in the business of exploration. It was true in the exploration and discovery of the "new world" on earth, the Arctic, Antarctic and eventually space; an inauspicious reality of centuries of human exploration.

Kirov and Drobkiev decided that they would no longer tolerate being kept in ignorance of such a critical situation. Between themselves, they formed the "Council of the Informed". Their ultimate plan was to involve as many other RSE scientists as could be safely assimilated into the group and establish a covert, direct communications link with the American scientific branch.

The formation of the Council in itself was a perilous act. Control of information in the Eastern Bloc system of government was a technique that ensured absolute control. To challenge that system of restriction was tantamount to treason

The Council currently had four members other than Kirov and Drobkiev; four other scientists who they felt they could trust absolutely. While they worked to established communications with the Americans, the council also developed strategies to share information freely among themselves.

The Council of the Informed never met together at the same time. They passed information back and forth by computer wafer. The files were encoded so that they could only be deciphered by a password and were read once then obliterated. The password was changed daily. It consisted of the first three words in the Daily Plan, a positively nauseating house organ published by the executive branch.

Kirov and Drobkiev found themselves together in an airlock, following wires to a defective probe. Kirov, following the wire conduit along the floor of the airlock on his hands and knees, looked carefully around him, reached over and pulled the door closed.

"Fyodor, I have heard a rumor that the American Director has been murdered," Drobkiev said breathlessly.

"It is a clumsy ploy, Petroskovich. Dimitriov has planted that rumor to make us believe the American base has been engulfed in civil strife. For what purpose, I do not fully understand."

Petroskovich Drobkiev sighed and sat down on the floor of the airlock. "Everyone now believes that the earth has been cut off from us by war. We have been busily engaged in life support calculations, in figuring out rations, in making detailed assessments of survival, yet not one word has been published about *why* we are doing these things. Does Dimitriov think we are idiots?"

"Not at all, Petroskovich," Kirov replied with a wry smile. "She knows well what she does. I suspect she has carefully monitored the rumors, and, in fact, may be responsible for some of them. I suspect that is the case with the rumor of the American director's death. Dimitriov has been moving all of us along in the direction she has carefully chosen for us."

"What direction? I can sense no direction, only confusion."

"Of course, my friend. If you knew her direction, then she would have no control," Kirov said bluntly.

"When will we attempt to contact the Americans?" Drobkiev asked.

"Soon, Petroskovich."

"How are we to accomplish this feat without being discovered? All communications channels are continuously monitored by people in whom we have no trust."

Kirov laughed. "Petroskovich, did we not earlier agree that we could be successful at this whole affair because we had an advantage over Dimitriov?"

"Yes, we did," Drobkiev agreed, sounding doubtful.

"And what was the advantage?"

"Our superior intelligence," Drobkiev spat. "But there was a wise proverb my father was fond of using on me while I was an indigent graduate student."

Kirov preserved a little smile and respectfully held the seed of silence, waiting for the modest slice of wisdom.

"He said, '*...if you are so smart, then why are you not in charge?*'"

Kirov laughed loudly. "And what did you say to him?"

Not even a hint of a smile stole across Drobkiev's lips. "I said that I was in charge of my own destiny."

Kirov slapped his knee and roared with laughter. As he wiped a tear from his eyes, he looked at his friend, who was just staring at him quietly, obviously thinking him insane.

"Petroskovich, what banal wisdom! Only a graduate student would dare say such to one's own father! A graduate student has about as much control over his destiny as an indentured servant.

"Now let me tell you a story. I visited a colleague's office while in Texas. He was a professor at a university there. For lunch he would take me to a cafe called "Burger King". They had a sign on their wall which said: "Have it your way", because they made sandwiches to your liking. Well, hanging on the office wall of this world acclaimed scientist was an actual Burger King sign he had stolen and defaced. It read, "*Have it my way, or you don't get the son-of-a-bitch at all.*"

Kirov roared with laughter anew, while Drobkiev sighed and looked at his friend with concern. The pressure was obviously pushing Kirov over the fine edge.

Kirov settled down after he saw that his friend was only smiling politely. "I can see that you do not appreciate the American sense of destiny," he said gasping. Then he had a flash of inspiration. "Just for a moment, my friend, just for a single moment, imagine that American hamburger sign hanging over Dimitriov's desk in that little plastic frame behind her seat. Now imagine her looking at you, that sign on the wall behind her, with that despicable cigarette hanging out of her lips."

Drobkiev's eyes flashed away to that scene in his mind. He too began to laugh, slowly at first, then along with Kirov; they both hooted and pounded on the walls of the chamber.

hen Lieutenant Robert Kerry's drogue chute opened, he was back in communications with BC1, barreling in toward the surface of Mars at supersonic velocity. The chute, designed for a Martian reentry, slowed the craft significantly, subjecting Kerry to an uncomfortable G-load. So much so, he took his headphones off and hooked them on a loop attached to his coveralls while he paced his breathing. In two minutes, the automatic reentry computer cut the chute loose and a second, larger drogue opened, slowing the craft even more.

"Gumdrop, BC1, can you read us?"

"Roger that, loud and clear. Second drogue is open. We'll be on the ground in a few minutes." His voice was clear, strong and supremely confident.

Every man and woman at BC1 applauded Kerry's transmission. The most hazardous part of reentry was over. Everyone who was in a position to do so rushed toward an unoccupied window to see if they could catch a glimpse of Kerry dropping in from space.

The second drogue chute cut away and the main chute opened uneventfully. It would slow Kerry's descent to a manageable velocity so that the retro rockets could finally ease him and Gumdrop to the desert sands.

"Main chute nominal," Kerry reported conversationally. "Four minutes to retro-fire."

"Roger, that, Lieutenant Kerry. We've got you on long range camera, now."

Several good pairs of eyes spotted the red dot that slowly enlarged to a discernable disc and finally to a tiny capsule dangling beneath it. The community itself could barely contain their excitement as the capsule neared its destination. Peter looked to Francis who gave him a thumbs up.

"Fifteen seconds to retro-fire," the flight controller said.

If things went well, the main chute would cut lose at the same instant the solid fueled retro rockets ignited. They would fire for twenty seconds, just long enough for the capsule to settle to the ground.

"Four seconds... three... two... one... fire."

All eyes could clearly see the bottom of the capsule erupt in sixteen bright candles of flame pointed at the ground as the huge, red main chute pealed off and dropped in a wad to the ground. The capsule slowed, just as predicted, and plopped down beside the main chute in a very short lived cloud of dust. There was a single second of silence while everyone held their breath and waited to hear Kerry's voice.

"Touchdown!" he said, followed by the chorus of applause and cheers.

"Please allow me to open the hatch," Kerry said. "I have to suit up, first. So please do not approach the hatch until I give you the signal," he said as insurance against an over anxious hand turning the latches before he was ready.

Francis looked over to Peter as they walked quickly out the door of the control center. "The delegation is scheduled to meet together at the airlock. I've slated you, Ashley, me and Gorteau for the welcome wagon."

Peter nodded, then added, "Ask Hernandez to join us."

Even inside the crowded Gumdrop, Kerry was able to slip with ease into his pressure suit. His ability to suit up was considerably improved with gravity to assist him. It was really the best of conditions. In the reduced gravity of Mars, movement and leverage were at once both assisted and unhindered.

Finally, he pulled his helmet over his head and pressurized. As the air hissed into his suit, Kerry lay back for a moment and fully concentrated on relaxing. His heart was racing, his muscles fatigued from this level of effort for the first time in over two months. The last time he had felt gravity was the spinning, artificial field produced in solar orbit.

Kerry sat up and took a deep breath, ready to peer out the window. He hesitated before looking out the hatch and braced himself for the worst. If they were standing in front of the hatch with their weapons, he planned to blow it with the emergency bolts. This way, he could at least take one or two of them out with him before he went down. He looked out the window. This was the moment of truth.

A MAT was parked 10 meters in front of the capsule. On its side, a crudely lettered sign read,

WELCOME TO BC1 ~~LIEUTENANT~~ COMMANDER KERRY!

His face relaxed into a wide smile. "BC1, Kerry here. I'm depressurizing Gumdrop," he reported in a jubilant voice.

He toggled the necessary valves, and then cycled the hatch which indecorously released and plunked onto the sand. Kerry swung out of Gumdrop feet-first, dragging his flight bag with him on the way out. Before he could stand up, two people grasped his arms simultaneously. Reflexively, powerfully, he shook them off, knocking one of them to the ground, which he instantly regretted.

He looked at their faces, laced with half smiles, half surprise. Their mouths moved, but he could hear no sound. His hands raced over the front of his suit, looking for the communications button. One of the suited individuals took a step toward him slowly, his hands raised so as not to alarm Kerry. Kerry put his own hands on top of his helmet and squinted his eyes to indicate he was actually harmless as well as embarrassed. The individual gently touched Kerry's communications switch and it crackled to life.

"Sorry, Commander. We didn't mean to alarm you," said Geoff Hammond.

"I apologize, as well," Kerry said. "I wasn't expecting so much assistance."

"How do you feel? Can we assist you to the MAT?"

Kerry breathed a deep sigh of relief. Things actually looked like they were going to work out.

"Let me have a crack at it. Your gravity actually feels good," Kerry admitted, gingerly testing his first steps on Mars.

Gumdrop had landed within 100 meters of the airlock, just nine meters off target. Several rather industrious individuals had marked the target with a one meter wide bulls-eye. A large "plunk-down" pool had been started and the winner would be the one who was closest to picking the right quadrant and number of meters off target that the Gumdrop had actually landed. The official "plunk-down" pool measurement team passed Kerry's MAT and waved as they headed toward the Gumdrop. Geoff Hammond explained what they were up to. Kerry responded by laughing and complaining at not being allowed to participate in the pool.

The MAT in which they rode pulled into the airlock and he could see through the windows Peter and his company gathered to greet him. The rest of the community had been asked to await Kerry's arrival in the dining hall.

As the MAT pulled to a stop and the airlock began to equalize the pressure, Geoff removed his helmet and looked to Kerry as Kerry slid his off and gripped it under his arm.

"Commander, I don't know what anyone has told you about us, but I want to give it to you straight," he said with a shaky voice.

Kerry looked to him without expression. Was he about to be let in on the secret behind the facade?

Geoff finally began, "Peter Traynor is no criminal. He just did what he had to do. Lipton really did kill himself, and he had already been relieved by the shrink. Nobody here is out to get anybody. We've got no axes to grind; all we want to do is survive, that's all. That's all Peter or me or anyone else here ever wanted. And understand this; we're all glad to have you join us. I mean that. We all mean that."

Kerry smiled, more from relief at the gushing, unexpected confession. He reached his hand out to Geoff. "Thanks...," he said, then paused while looking for a name on the suit.

"Geoff, Geoff Hammond," he replied, accepting Kerry's outstretched hand.

"Geoff, I'd appreciate it if you'd give me a tour of BC1 tomorrow."

"I'd be honored, Commander."

"It's Lieutenant, Geoff. No one has promoted me yet."

"You've been promoted, believe me."

They passed through the air shower and airlock and in minutes stepped out to meet Peter. Kerry faced the colonists, his helmet fitted comfortably under his arm. He was quite attractive, an image that fit the intelligent voice quite well. His wide, Luke Skywalker smile, bright eyes and confident stride declared his poised style and self assured personality.

eter stepped toward him, hand outstretched. Kerry looked uncertain for a nearly imperceptible second, then reached for Peter's extended hand.

"I'm Peter Traynor. And you must be Commander Kerry unless you're a stranger who's been hiding somewhere on the Elysium desert."

"You have my name correct, Dr. Traynor, but everyone around here seems to be a little confused about my rank. I'm a Navy Lieutenant, not a Commander."

"We've promoted you, Commander," Peter said openly.

"*Who* has promoted me?" Kerry shot back briskly, just on the edge of arrogance, betraying his Naval Flight Officer mind-set.

"The community has accorded you that honor, *Commander*. If you don't feel you can accept it, then you'll have to convince them," Peter replied, expertly sidestepping Kerry's opening challenge.

Peter introduced him to Hernandez, Francis and Gorteau. Ashley had been standing behind the group but she stepped out to meet Kerry. "Commander, this is Ashley Alycone," Peter said, his own eyes blinking between them.

Kerry said nothing. His eyes flashed and embraced hers. He grasped her fingertips gently, pulling her a step closer. He put his hand gently atop hers and after a few pregnant seconds said, "The pleasure is absolute. You're an extraordinary woman."

Peter flashed instantly into anger, his face flushed almost as red as Ashley's. Francis stood aside and saw it all in a single sweep, desperately choking back a snicker of laughter.

"Well, let's be on our way, shall we?" he said another acute second later, feeling the slightest touch of guilt.

Ashley tore her eyes away from Kerry's spell-binding gaze and dropped her hand from his, but not before Peter's eyes caught her receiving a momentary squeeze.

She inhaled more deeply than usual and looked coyly away from Peter. If the lover's manual contained chapters on monogamous etiquette, in Peter's view, she had just trashed the whole book in less than one minute standing right in front of him.

"We have quite the gathering for you, Commander," Francis said, quickly adding, "Let's be off," in an attempt to further disarm Kerry's innocent *faux pas*.

Kerry stepped up beside Ashley and flashed her another diamond smile. He offered her his arm. "I'd be honored if you'd accompany me, Ashley."

She finally looked to Peter who's white, granite features and blazing eyes told the whole story. The seconds were painfully ticking away and Kerry's arm was still hanging in the blistering breeze.

Peter released her as he turned away and transferred his murderous look to Francis. "Let's be off, indeed," he said, forcing the words so artificially that Francis finally had to turn away and snort a laugh that he attempted to turn into a sneeze. Hernandez innocently disarmed the whole mess with his naive, "Bless you."

The community at BC1 had only to see the sight of Kerry enter the dining hall before the acclimation began in earnest. If Peter had counted on an exercise in catharsis, he got his wish. BC1 turned all of its fear and frustration into a wild evening of speeches, declarations, and finally, dancing. Where all the bootleg alcohol came from was anybody's guess. But it would be the rare individual who did not feel the dull ache of poorly brewed Martian moonshine the next morning.

Peter still smoldered for hours while Kerry danced with Ashley for many more numbers than his share, which in Peter's opinion was none. Eventually, Francis sat beside him, blinked his red eyes at Peter and focused in with some difficulty. Then he put his arm around him and poured him half a glass of clear liquid.

"You're a genius, Peter," he said.

"Oh?"

"Yep, look all around you. Your plan worked beautifully. Not a sad face in the house," he said, his breath reeking with booze.

"Rat's a genius, too, Peter," Francis continued in an even voice. "Rat is a genius, Peter," he said again.

"You already said that," Peter replied, downing half the glass before he realized he was about to require an emergency tracheotomy just to catch his next gasping breath.

"Rat is a genius, Peter," Francis continued. "While we have been brooding over our own problems, Rat has been busy bottling up medicinal ethanol. Have you ever wondered just where the hell Rat gets his down home wisdom? His grandfather, that's where. Did you know that our own kitchen wastes were not thrown away here in this magnificent kitchen? No, Rat has been saving them, freezing them, working miracles with them..."

Peter's last rational minutes were spent tuning out the babbling Francis, watching Ashley and Kerry talk beside him as they had all evening, sharing what appeared to be a common infatuation for one another. But Peter passed the point of rationality quickly, finally exchanging it for a few fascinating minutes with Francis in an animated discussion of Rat's potential as a degreed alchemist before he could not remember anything more.

ew things are as wretched as an alcohol induced sleep. But at the top of that very short list is waking up from an alcohol induced sleep. A sharp pain emanated from Peter's midbrain and arched over his dry eyes. As he opened them, and turned over, the pain between his eyes became worse. His whole body felt as though it had been run over by something very large with knobby tires. He could clearly remember Francis saying Rat had made the moonshine with kitchen garbage; the taste in his mouth this morning would verify that.

He sat up in bed and looked around him. He was not in his quarters; he was in Francis' bed. He did not have the slightest idea of how he got there. The pulse of adrenalin that surged through his body caused him to leap quickly to his feet and the pain and dizziness that followed forced him to stumble back, moaning.

"Francis, where are you?" he groaned as he looked over the side of the bed. Francis lay unmoving and asleep, curled up in a blanket on the floor. He did not appear to be anywhere near ready to wake up.

Slowly, Peter stood and looked at the clock. It was just shy of five in the morning. He wanted to rush out immediately, back to his quarters. But he realized it would not be a good idea to wander down the hallways in his thermal underwear.

As quickly as he could, Peter dressed and left Francis' quarters for his own. In minutes, he had his door open. His bed was empty and obviously, it had not been slept in all night. He stepped inside his apartment and slammed his fist against the wall. *Where was Ashley? Did he really want to know?* In a fit of rage, he kicked a chair across the floor. Then he sat down and lay his aching head in his hands.

How could this happen? Then it occurred to him that he was actually jealous. The thought so unnerved him, that he forced himself to slowly undress and take a shower.

The warm water washing across his face felt good. But, as with all showers at BC1, it ended much too quickly. Calmly, he attempted to sort through his feelings. He had far too many responsibilities to allow this hostile, resentful feeling to dominate his thinking. It could only lead him down the same path Lipton had followed. But as Lipton had tragically discovered, such *judicious forethought* had little to do with the smooth coupling of emotions with coherent behavior.

Peter dressed and stepped out of his door, intending to go to the dining hall for some strong coffee to clear his slightly spinning head. His heart, however, caused him to hang a left down the passageway and he found himself standing in front of Ashley's door. His rational self screamed at him not to do it but his emotions compelled his knuckles to rap on the door.

A few seconds later, she opened it slowly, peering sleepily outside. "Good morning, love. Are you okay?" she asked with a sleepy voice.

"I'm fine. May I come in?" he asked with too much energy.

She opened the door to let him in and his eyes flashed instantly to her bed, which was empty. He walked in, again torn by what he should say and what he wanted to say.

"How did I end up in Francis' bed?" he demanded, although he had not planned for it to sound so harsh.

"You don't remember?" she asked, sitting on the edge of her bed. He shook his head.

She smiled lightly. "Bob and I managed to carry both of you to Francis' quarters. You were totally out but Francis could point and stumble. We put you to bed and left."

"Just who the hell is Bob?" he asked, though he already knew.

"Bob Kerry, and why are you so angry?" she asked innocently.

"You don't know?"

"No, I don't," she snapped back.

He looked into her eyes which made him even angrier. He loved her desperately and wanted her more than he had ever wanted her before. The confusing web of emotions forced him to think again of the realities of his responsibilities. His headache and dizziness returned. The whole scene was making him literally nauseated. Without another word, he turned and left, slamming the door behind him. He knew it had been a poor scene and an even worse exit. But throwing up on her probably would have made for an even more inauspicious ending.

Ashley walked quickly to the door to call him back, then sighed and lay her head against the frame. Things were clearer to her now. She had honestly not intended to anger him, but she was surprised and hurt that he had distrusted her.

Peter walked straightaway to the dining hall. As soon as he turned the corner he saw Bob Kerry sitting at a table alone, drinking coffee. Just as Peter turned to walk away, Rat spotted him.

"Dr. T! Good morning."

"Good morning, Rat," Peter said, turning around and walking over to Kerry's table. He said nothing as he sat down across from him.

"Quite an early riser for the shape you were in when we put you to bed last night," Kerry said, sipping his cup of coffee.

Rat stepped over and poured Peter a cup of his own. "Just as you like it, Dr. T."

"Thanks, Rat. And don't call me that."

"No offense," Rat replied, walking away.

"Dr. T?" Kerry asked, with a smile on his face.

Peter shrugged and shook his head. He was not in his best form, and hardly knew what to say to Kerry, though he knew he had to try something. Separating his personal life from his leadership role was something he had never anticipated dealing with.

Kerry sat looking at him over the steam of his coffee with a blank expression. If anything, he appeared to be measuring Peter up. Kerry's coveralls appeared to be wrinkle free and he looked fresh and rested which was more than Peter felt, even after a hot shower. He had a pair of small headphones draped around his neck as he stared at Peter with his precise eyes.

Kerry finally broke the ice, aiming straight for the issue that clearly separated them. "Ashley's a beautiful woman," he said first, watching carefully for Peter's expression. "She told me more about you than I wanted to know," Kerry said mercifully. "And I think you're a very lucky man."

At once the internal pressure was relieved. Peter felt instantly liberated, delighted - and like a total ass. He looked at Kerry's face for the first time. "Thank you. I appreciate that," he admitted.

"I knew you would; you had to. Don't get me wrong, my friend; I've never been a chivalrous person. But I have eyes, and know a stupid move when I see one. I don't think I want to start off on the wrong foot around here. It would be witless and selfish for all concerned. Besides, even if I didn't feel that way, Ashley's smarter than that."

Then Kerry smiled and Peter knew he wanted to say more, but was mulling it over. Finally Kerry said what Peter knew he was about to say. "But don't screw up. You've been warned."

Peter laughed under his breath. He appreciated the empathetic honesty and respected it.

"Eros alone has brought down more kingdoms than you have fingers and toes to count," Rat said from behind them. "Let it not bring down this one down, as well."

Peter spun around to see who else had been eavesdropping. Rat stood alone with a coffee pot in his hand. "Need a warmer, boys?" he asked with a sly wink. They tactfully waited for Rat to leave before resuming their discussion, of which Kerry was anxious to begin.

"Now that we're less interested in killing one another, let's get down to business. What exactly is the state of affairs here?"

"How do you mean?" Peter asked. "Politically or what?"

"Let's start with life support."

"As you can clearly see, it's stable now. But in a controlled, bioregenerative hybrid, like our system, stable is a relative term," Peter began, referring to the system that kept them alive on Mars; the Controlled Ecological Life Support System. "The state-of-the-art CELSS system here is the same vintage as the one on your spacecraft, although it's a very different hybrid, obviously. The system's not quite balanced, as you're aware. CELSS requires large amounts of energy which we must constantly supply. And there're losses every time we go out the airlock or spill something outside.

"We've lost the supplies in orbit so we automatically go on rations until the next supply run. If it doesn't arrive, we'll all be dead. We begin rationing after free time tonight. It's going to get cold. And as we reduce the temperature and food, our metabolism will increase to conserve heat and we'll all get hungry."

"What's my job?" Kerry asked straightaway.

"I don't know," Peter said, lowering his coffee to the table and propping his folded hands in front of his face. "What do you do?"

"I fly spaceships," he replied abruptly.

"Sorry; fresh out. We ran out of those just the other day," Peter quipped instantly. "But Rat could use some extra help in the kitchen," he continued with a flat expression, rolling his thumb over his shoulder as he laced his fingers behind his head.

"My daddy always told me it was stupid to mess with the head Kauhuna's woman," Kerry replied, laughing. "Now I see he was right."

Peter smiled widely, then returned the laughter.

"There are some people around here who could party at a death watch," Francis said, slowly walking up to the table. He sat down in a slump beside Peter. "I have this evil taste in my mouth that's vile beyond description," he said, raking his tongue around in his mouth. "I've already brushed the enamel off my teeth and it still won't go away."

"Just a bad taste? That's not so serious...," Peter said.

"Oh, did I forget to mention the headache? Anybody got any elephant tranquilizers? Is there a revolver in the house?" he moaned. "If you'll recall, Rat said his moonshine was made from garbage," Peter reminded him. "He's a certified genius, remember?"

"You boys weren't complaining last night," Rat yelled out from his kitchen.

"That man must have one damn good set of ears," Kerry said. Then he laughed again and looked at Peter and Francis. "I have a confession," he began. "I was actually afraid that you guys, er... this community was going to, ah... confine me when I arrived."

"Then why didn't you go back to earth?" Peter asked.

Kerry smiled, and admitted, "Because I felt like I had a better chance here. And, you know, I'm glad I did. I can see things are going to get tight here, and I feel like I can contribute something useful."

"Well, I have a confession to make," Peter returned. "I came over here this morning and sat in front of you with the clear intention of feeding you a knuckle sandwich. I'm glad I didn't."

"Now that you boys have kissed and made up," Francis said, putting his head down on his folded arms, "would someone please beg the Rat to fetch me an aspirin?"

20

Peter abandoned Kerry to a full blown tour of BC1 under the guiding hand of Geoff Hammond. He sucked in his pride and went off to find Ashley, discovering her in the biology office which sat adjacent to the community's fields of crops. It had wide windows facing the enclosed expanse of food plants growing under both sunlight and artificial lights. The hydroponic system's plant trays were right next to the glass wall adjacent to Ashley's desk, so that her office looked like a huge, brilliantly lit terrarium.

She sat at her desk reading, her white cotton lab coat buttoned nearly all the way up to ward off the creeping cold of the labs. As Peter walked into her office, she passed him that deadly look that only a woman can give a man when something serious is on her mind. She stared at him momentarily over her full, metal framed reading glasses, just enough to stand his hair on end, then back to her document displayed on the projected screen suspended before her eyes.

"Yes?" she asked, her frozen mood hanging like a rotten iceberg ready to calve at any minute, and rain ice shards all over the room.

"Let me get to the point," he said, standing in front of her desk, feeling like a truant ready to catch the paddle across both bare cheeks.

She didn't reply, just flicked her eyes at him again, then back to her document.

"I'm an idiot and a fool and I came to apologize," he said, wanting to get it out and over with as quickly as possible. Unfortunately for Peter, God did not wire the female brain with as much matter-of-factness when it came to matters of the heart.

Without speaking, Ashley turned off the display, folded her glasses up and placed them neatly in their case and walked toward the door. "I'm not interested," she said with a steady, evenly guided delivery.

Peter jammed his palm into the door so she could not leave.

"Okay. What penance do I have to pay? Oh, what price my sins?"

She looked supremely put out that he stood in her way, sighed heavily and sat down in an office chair.

"Peter, it's not so much that you acted like a fool, but that you demonstrated your lack of trust for me. That's what really hurts. I expect more from you - from us!"

"Like what?" he said with a little too much spin on the "t".

"Trust, for one," she said, her voice still plenty angry. *"I love you;* why would I hurt you? Would I be fool enough to hurt you on purpose right in front of you and your friends and the whole community? Give me a little credit, for heaven's sake!"

Peter shook his head and looked away from her penetrating, angry eyes. Every word was true, and he knew it.

"I'm sorry. I was wrong," he admitted as truthfully as possible. "I made an idiot out of myself, and I apologized to all parties this morning. Actually, I came in here looking for some sack cloth and ashes. The Rat gave me the cloth. How about some ashes from your biomass incinerators?"

She smiled despite herself. She stood and walked slowly over to where he leaned against the door.

"Can you give me one good reason why I should forgive you?" she said as sincerely as she knew how. "Just one?"

He looked intensely into her beautiful eyes. Then he grasped her chin with his hand and pressed his lips tightly to hers. With his free hand he locked the door behind him and in his most sincere and candid way, he gave her the one good reason she would accept without reservation.

ationing began at BC1 in phases. The first comfort that felt the pinch was the heat. The plan was to reduce the temperature by a quarter of a degree per sol which would save BC1 several percentage points on daily energy consumption. The community's temperature was to be lowered to a barely acceptable 11 degrees centigrade (52 degrees F). To combat the cold, orders were issued that all personnel were to continuously guard against hypothermia by wearing layered, heavy clothing and doubling blankets on beds. Other energy saving methods were instituted: limiting showers to once every four sols (they had been allowed one every other sol), reducing light levels and severely restricting exits outside from the pressurized compound.

Other ration methods fell under the axe: food, water and air were restricted at once. In order to keep CELSS operational at its maximal efficiency, every resource had to be cut back to its limit.

The Closed Ecological Life Support System on Mars was a wondrous assembly of complex interconnected parts, all of which had to work perfectly together to share the load of life support for the community. As head of BC1 biology, Ashley was in charge of the CELSS system.

One of the major parts of the CELSS system consisted of the BC1 food supply in the form of crops. The CELSS crops supplied an abundant and rich variety of foodstuffs from wheat, soybeans, peanuts, potatoes and tomatoes, as well as a dozen other major crops. The plants in turn absorbed the carbon dioxide from the humans and provided life-giving oxygen in exchange. The inedible part of the plant harvest was directed into a complex set of vats that turned the cellulose into edible sugars. Genetically engineered bacteria thereupon turned the sugars and cellulose products into artificial meats and dairy products of more than a hundred different flavorings.

The final products of the humans and the plants were called "wastes" before the turn of the twenty first century. But because of the pioneering work of Dr. William Knott III and his group of researchers done at the John F. Kennedy Space Center in the late 20th century, these endproducts became identified as "resources". On earth and in space, NASA taught one of the most critical lessons of all space spin-offs; that the human community could not afford to lose anything - all materials and their products were ultimately valuable resources. Hence, when the materials turned the circle in the BC1 system, they all were recovered by what they called the Resource Recovery System. There were no wastes on Mars and therefore, no waste processing subsystem.

The Resource Recovery System fed these resources to bacteria in what were called bioreactors. The 'biological reactors' reduced the products into carbon dioxide for the plants and a sludge which was turned by automated systems into tiny pellets and fed to the fish in the community aquaculture laboratory.

The fish were raised and harvested, while the water from their tanks was continuously circulated through what the colonists lovingly referred to as the "salad fields", consisting of lettuce, radishes, carrots and cucumber vines. To keep the tanks from building up toxins, a part of the system was circulated through to the Resource Recovery System, and periodically, some of the sludge was burned (or combusted) in high temperature incinerators to reduce the level of complex organics that could harm the living systems.

The CELSS system was miraculous, but periodically "ran down". The system continually cycled with just the right amount of materials - water, energy and carbon - but these materials were slowly, daily, lost to the Martian environment. The domes were as tight as human engineering could make them, but there was some seepage through microscopic cracks and leaky door seals. Every time someone went out of the airlocks, air and water vapor were lost. Each trek outside the enclosure in a space suit or a MAT caused some precious resource to be lost.

To maintain its system balance, the CELSS system relied on reserve materials. The most important of the reserves was water. Water was almost nonexistent in the Martian environment. While adequate oxygen could be produced, and some fresh water was available from water that passed through the leaves of the plants, condensed on the sides of the glass CELSS domes and was then purified by high energy radiation beams for drinking and potable use, water also had to be shipped in from earth in enormous quantities to maintain the system balance.

The community produced oxygen in two ways. The system was designed to maintain more photosynthetically (plant) produced oxygen than the human population actually used. If necessary, another system was in place that could produce oxygen by wetting Martian soil, which released a barely significant volume of raw oxygen from natural superoxides bound chemically on their surfaces. These two systems produced enough oxygen so that there was never a problem supplying the human population with these commodities.

The CELSS system was the single most significant energy user at BC1, but such was the price of survival. The energy at BC1 was almost exclusively provided by the Kjellman-Matsudaira Solar Cells (called KMS Cells). These special, micro-thin gallium arsenide cells were invented by the Kinji Matsuhara, Bob Kjellman research team in the early 21st century, for which they earned the Nobel Prize in Physics. They were very high efficiency cells which were sprayed onto a thin film of plastic, making them lightweight enough to be transported to Mars to provide adequate power needs for the community. The BC1 power plant consisted of power regulators for the KMS Cells, batteries for dark period power distribution, and even emergency auxiliary power units (APU's) for use in dire situations.

The decision was made to ration power to conserve the battery life; not because of limited sunlight, but because the batteries only had a given life span and when they were gone, they were gone. It also appeared that the closest supplier, millions of kilometers away, was apparently out of business. During daylight hours, allowances were made to use power above the conservation limits, but only if the regulators could shunt the power directly to the user without having to cycle it through the batteries. This was a special demand that required specific wiring, so each petition was considered based on the warrants of the request and the impact on the community.

There were many different kinds of CELSS systems. BC1 had settled on theirs based on the direction of research and development in NASA since the early 1980's. NASA had chosen to go with the primary life science approach, as opposed to a primary physiochemical approach. In BC1's case, the system relied almost exclusively on living systems to cycle materials. In the physiochemical approach, the systems relied on raw energy and chemical conversion systems to cycle materials. The systems were radically different. The Soviets had chosen the physiochemical method which used slightly more energy.

Peter's approach to leadership was conservative in its foundation but radical in its approach to solving their emergent problems. Foundationally, he based the community's government on a cascading series of assumptions. The first of which was that the community was still an American base and would fall under the United States Constitution until the community found that the United States no longer existed. Secondly, the community was to remain a Democratic Republic and he could be voted out of the leadership position by a majority vote at any time. Thirdly, the existing regulations regarding discipline were still in effect and the authority to lead still rested under the original regulatory charter. The colonists had all come here under this assumption; but if they so desired, the community could change the rules as a majority.

Peter's radical approach began at this point. He spread authority out to the department heads. Hernandez was appointed head of the administrative group; Gorteau headed the scientific. Peter sat in the middle between the two with the authority to direct their activities and the ability to decide the direction of one or the other.

Peter detested meetings with a passionate intensity. He put the word out that if a meeting was called, it had better be essential and if he were invited, his presence had better be truly required. This forced decisions to be made by the department heads, rather than to diffuse responsibility among nameless groups in meetings. This way Peter knew he could get a handle on problems quickly and the department heads were compelled to work harder to keep up with things for which they were personally and directly responsible.

Peter set the priorities of the community:

PRIORITY ONE: Life support, immediate and long term.
PRIORITY TWO: The mental health of the community.
PRIORITY THREE: Rationing plan, life support equipment.
PRIORITY FOUR: Exploration for Martian water sources.
PRIORITY FIVE: Research of possible Martian power resources.
PRIORITY SIX: Continuation of previously scheduled research.

Peter spent the better part of the sol following Kerry's arrival in the dining hall. He set up one of the tables as his desk and began summoning individuals to discuss specific items on his agenda. Francis acted as his chief of staff.

Peter worked with lightning precision, making decisions in minutes that would have taken career bureaucrats sols or weeks. He asked Suzanne Nikifortune to act as his secretary and as fast as she could record the events, he was issuing orders. Before nine in the morning, he had the priorities out on the community bulletin system. Half an hour later, he had developed his governmental agenda and it was posted.

Toward mid-day, Peter summoned Brinker. Francis and Peter were sitting at their table, making personnel assignments and working through the community priorities when he arrived.

"Yes, sir," Brinker said, standing half at attention before Peter. His attitude reflected Brinker's ambivalence at the whole series of events that led him to this point in time. As a career Marine, he had been trained in a life-and-death obedience to the military system. In Brinker's world, change was looked upon with extreme suspicion. Radical change was to be resisted at all costs. But the unique set of circumstances that led Brinker to this juncture was not of his own making, so he endured the neurosis of trying to do his job as best he saw it in a situation he had not been trained to handle or even fully understood.

"Brinker," Peter began, "I'm appointing you the chief law enforcement officer for BC1 effective immediately."

"Can't do it, sir," Brinker replied instantly.

"Why not?" Peter asked, not even looking up from his work.

"Just like I told Lipton a week ago, I'm a United States Marine and I'm not permitted by Marine Corps regulations to engage in or interfere with civilian law enforcement."

Peter was fully prepared for Brinker's answer.

"Brinker, I'm going to give you a series of choices, one of which you must chose. One: resign from the Marines. Two: contact your command in one hour on earth for a special release. Three: accept our "Honorary Community Sheriff" plaque, granted to you by the director of the community for your continued efforts in enforcing the protections guaranteed us by the U.S. Constitution, in accordance with your oath of office. Your choice."

Brinker did not even pause. "I'll accept your plaque, sir."

"And the responsibilities?" Peter asked.

"If it's in my oath, I can't very well refuse, can I?"

"Nope. Congratulations, Marine, on your new assignment. I shall ensure that no one accuses you of involving yourself in "civil law enforcement" duties."

"Thank you, sir."

"That's all, Brinker," Peter said briskly, then remembering a final question, looked up to Brinker. "Do you want a badge?"

"A what?"

"A badge; a shield; a tin star. You know, an insignia?" Peter replied, feeling a little ridiculous.

Brinker laughed loudly. "Now what would I need one of those for when I got these?" he said, flipping his row of expert marksman medals he always wore on his chest.

"Good point," Peter said smiling. "Tell Hiraldo and your other two Marines that I've got deputy plaques for them, too."

The reorganization came together with remarkable smoothness. Peter and Francis quickly passed out the special tasks with relative ease. There were no complaints to speak of; everyone knew of the extent of the straits they were in and that it was going to take a remarkable piece of leadership to pull them out of it. The one exception was Julian Covenant.

Peter learned that Julian Covenant was a full Professor of Business and Management at Cambridge University and, besides being a RSE expert, he was also a widely renowned expert on management styles and systems. He had been asked to come to Mars by the NASA Administrator for Manned Interplanetary Exploration to suggest improvements on the management at BC1.

The convoluted trail that followed Covenant to BC1 would fill a doctoral thesis, but in brief, the White House was looking for a politically expedient way to get rid of Lipton. It put pressure on NASA to find them a way out. NASA Headquarters, in turn, pressured the NASA administrator for Manned Interplanetary Exploration, who turned the screws on the NASA director of Mars Exploration to come up with the wherewithal to pull it off successfully. They hired an outside consultant, Covenant, whom they knew looked critically on the type of managerial style Lipton had imposed at BC1. What they failed to take into account was that Lipton was much more astute than they and smelled the plot before Covenant even boarded a ship at the Kennedy Space Center for the flight out.

When Covenant arrived at BC1, Lipton virtually made a hero out of him from the moment he stepped off the lander. Lipton not only set Covenant up with the most extravagant living arrangements of any individual at BC1, but he personally befriended him. In the course of a month, Covenant was the closest personal friend Lipton had. The outcome of Covenant's 340 sol study was decided within 60.

Covenant was asked to report to Peter for his assignment. Now that Covenant's management study was on hold, Peter was going to interview him to place him in the task best suited to his education and abilities.

Brinker was sent to recover him, but when Covenant arrived, it was clear Brinker's task had not been a pleasant one.

"I am outraged!" Covenant shouted as Brinker ushered him to Peter's table. Peter had been warned that Covenant was going to be a hard egg to crack.

"Outraged over what?" Peter asked in a calm manner.

"The way I have been treated by this, this animal!" Covenant said, looking with a certain abhorrence at Brinker. Covenant meticulously straightened his jacket and tie as he complained, running his hand down his slick-backed hair and evening his glasses over his owl eyes.

"What do you mean?" Peter asked.

"This soldier forced me from my quarters in a roughshod manner befitting a back alley gangster... I am no conscript! I've never been so humiliated."

"Your turn, Brinker," Peter said patiently.

Brinker sighed, put his arms behind his back and said, "I asked him to come along. He said no. I asked him if he had to go to the bathroom. He said no. I told him that all other priorities took second place, I forgot his engraved invitation, and that if he didn't come along I was going to have to hold his hand. He slammed the door in my face so I removed it and..."

"Okay, Brinker, I get the picture," Peter replied, then looked to Covenant. "Dr. Covenant, I apologize for this incident." Brinker looked supremely put out. "But, I instructed this Marine that all former priorities of this community had been rescinded and replaced by the ones I published this morning."

"You mean *your manifesto*?" Covenant spat.

"Call it what you like, Covenant. The game here is survival," Francis replied. He had been sitting beside Peter, and he appeared somewhat absorbed by the whole affair.

Peter raised his hand to prevent Francis from agitating Covenant any further. "In any event, Julian, had I known that you had a problem with coming down here today, perhaps we could have worked out another way," Peter said sincerely, forcing himself to be amiable in the face of this individual who was apparently used to the fast track treatment at BC1.

"Never, never call me by my first name until you have been invited," Covenant began, spitting the "t" at Peter. The veins in his neck protruded as his face reddened.

"Okay, Covenant," Peter shot back, his patience wearing thin.

"It is *Doctor Covenant* to you!"

"I can sec this isn't going anywhere," Peter replied. "Now let me tell you why I asked you down here..."

"You are a traitorous mutineer, Traynor!" Covenant replied, pointing his finger to Peter. "The death of Lassiter Lipton does not change your status as an outlaw..."

"Shut up!" Peter stopped him in an even voice. "The next time you interrupt me I'll have the Marine gag and bag you so that I can finish."

Peter allowed a respectful few seconds of silence to pass to permit Covenant his choice in the matter. Covenant's face grew even redder, his Adam's apple bobbing up and down as his mind and body made their choice. Brinker's muscles flexed and his hands were ready to slap the gag on Covenant from whom he had already taken enough abuse.

"Very well, Covenant," Peter continued. "Now let me lay it all out on the line for you, in words you hopefully can relate to. I called you down here to discuss your future in a professional manner. We were going to discuss your talents and desires and work you into the job that could best benefit the community. Now you obviously don't want to cooperate, so what do we do with you?" Covenant looked like he was about to choke on the answer, so Peter let him have his way. "Go on," he invited.

"You will unhand me this very moment and leave me alone. I will not become your servant or anyone elses. I am contracted to do a job here and that is what I will continue to do. I have no intention of joining in any aspect of your little insurgency!"

"You leave me with an interesting choice here, Covenant," Peter replied, sitting back in his chair, looking closely at the tightly wired professor. "I could let you go on about your merry way, but that wouldn't be fair to the rest of us working for your survival. Now, since there isn't any need for your particular consultation services, I have to find a job for you. As you aren't predisposed to discuss your talents with me, then I have to assign you to a job.

"Henceforth, you will sweep the passageways of BC1, every passageway, a minimum of twice per sol, until you can help us discover some more productive talent within yourself to contribute to the community. I'll not have you lounging around while the rest of us are supporting you."

"You have domestic robots to perform that menial task!" Covenant shouted indignantly.

"Their batteries and mechanical parts are being scavenged and stored for survival purposes," Francis replied with some satisfaction.

"I'll also let you in on another confidential item that may be of some interest to you," Peter said, driving the issue home. "I will not tolerate you going on strike or threatening the other people of this community. If you refuse to work or if you agitate or threaten the community in any way, I'll put you on trial by your peers and recommend they lock you up. When we reestablish communications with earth, you can have one of the first calls out. Until I'm relieved by a vote of the community, I'm in charge, not you. Any questions or comments?"

"I have no peers here." Covenant said flatly, working his mouth into a deep frown.

"You said it, not me," Peter replied. "Brinker, fix this man up with a broom and prop it in front of his door. Covenant, you'll sweep eight hours, seven sols a week. You'll report to Roman Adkins Thomas. He's your immediate supervisor."

"I will never report to a man named Rat!"

"If this man fails to report to Mr. Thomas tomorrow morning, confine him until trial," Peter said to Brinker. "You may go now, Covenant."

"I'll see you hang for this, Traynor. You can't do this to me and get away with it. I'm not the only one who feels like this around here!"

Peter rested his chin on his hand and replied, "Perhaps not. But if you change your mind and decide to join the community, my offer to discuss the best use of your talents is still good."

Covenant looked at Francis and sneered. "You, of all people, should know better than this. Do you have any idea..."

"Oh yes," Francis replied, "Oh yes I know what I am doing. And if you know what's good for you, you'll follow right along with whatever Dr. Traynor wants. *His plan and your plan don't exactly mesh. Don't let them come in conflict if you want to live.*" Francis looked at him long and hard and they exchanged a protracted and bitter look at one another.

"Now get out of my sight, Covenant," Francis warned.

Peter stole a glance at Francis, then back to Covenant who was being led away by Brinker. Covenant was still staring at Francis over his shoulder as he rounded the corner into the hallway.

"Thanks for the help, Dr. T!" Rat yelled from his kitchen.

eter had just retired for his much deserved four and a half hours of sleep. In the darkness, he fitted the curves of his body against Ashley's resting form, already warm under the blankets of his small bed. He draped his arm over her and she squeezed his freezing fingers in her warm palms, just as the C2's pinger sounded.

"Damn!" he swore.

"High cost of being the one in charge," she mumbled from beneath the blankets.

"Where have I heard that before?" he replied acerbically, smashing the speaker with his palm. "Peter here..."

"Peter, Jamie Powers. Better come on down here to radio, right away."

"Earth is back on the line?" Peter asked excitedly. Ashley sat straight up in bed.

"Not exactly... Just come on as quickly as you can," Powers said, then hung up.

"I'm coming with you," Ashley said, tossing the blankets back. "This sounds like it just might be worth the trip."

"Good idea," he replied. "I may need someone to show me the way back to bed."

"I'm your ticket," she replied, shivering in the cold air of the room.

They hurriedly dressed and made their way to the Command Center's tiny Message Center as quickly as they could through the dimly lit passageways. Powers stood in the door when they arrived.

"What do you have, Jamie?" Peter asked, out of breath. Beside him stood Francis.

"This," Powers replied, holding it out to him. "What do you make of it?" Powers handed him a palmtop display unit whose message glared in the darkness:

1 10 11 100 101 110 111 1000 1001 1010 1011 1100 1101 1110 1111 1 0000 10001 10010 10011 10100 10101 10110 10111 11000 11001 11010 10001 10010 11000 1 10 11 100 101 110 111 1000 1001 1010 11100 1001110000111000 0 111010101111110000101100000000 1 10 11 100 10 1 110 111 1000 1001 1010 1011 1100 1101 1110 1111 10000 10001 100 10 10011 10100 10101 10110 10111 11000 11001 11010 10101 1011 1 001 10110 11001 10110 10 10001 10010 1101

(Message signature: 9600 Baud, 101 MS total, 36 MS lead-in tone. Message length: 65 MS)

"What do I make of it?" Peter asked. "Well..." he began with a light laugh, his eyes squinting at the array. "It's binary, of course... a digital transmission." Then he shook his head and laughed lightly again, looking back at Powers. "I guess that's just about all I can tell you."

"Funny. That's the very same in-depth analysis I managed to generate," Powers replied with unconcealed frustration.

"Where did it come from? Was it broadcast from earth?" Peter asked.

"The Little Kremlin."

Peter looked confused. "Shturmovoi! Was it sent to us deliberately in response to our request?"

"We don't know that, Peter," Francis replied, cautiously.

"What do you mean, you don't know?" Peter asked. "Was it or wasn't it?"

"Well, it was broadcast from the Little Kremlin," Powers explained. "It was transmitted from their geostationary satellite on the frequency we've been instructing on our urgent automatic messages. But it's not exactly what we were looking for..."

"What he means," Francis interrupted, "is that this may be a mistake."

"How could it be a mistake?" Peter asked.

"It's a digital transmission over a circuit that just as easily could be used for voice. If they want to talk to us, why not just use Soviet or English or some recognizable computer code?" Francis replied. "Secondly, the entire digital message, including tone was just slightly over a tenth of a second in length. If they're talking, they sure don't have much to say."

"Which leads to our favorite theory," Powers picked up. "We're led to believe it's a misdirected transmission. By the looks of it, it was probably meant as instructions or interrogation of a remote field probe. They apparently broadcast it over the wrong frequency. If it had been a millisecond or two shorter in length, our filters would have ignored it altogether as static."

"How can you be so sure that it's a probe interrogation?" Peter asked.

"Well, its' brevity, for one thing. That and the digital elements in the message appear to be counting sequences which are frequently either used as calibration events or attention pulses," Powers replied.

"Well, I don't know. But I do think we should at least bring in Gorteau for a second opinion before we toss it," Peter replied. "Ashley, what do you think?" he asked.

"I'll buy in with the mistake theory for now," she replied. "But it could also be a code. If it's a code, there're no better brains to pick it apart than Gorteau's. I say we wake Fabian."

A few minutes later, Gorteau arrived, also looking very tired. But, as always, he was as gracious as if he had just enjoyed a restful weekend on the New England beaches.

"What do we have to be so happy about tonight?" he asked, looking at their interested expressions at such a late hour.

"A mystery, Fabian," Ashley replied, then she explained the situation so quickly and thoroughly, no one interrupted.

He let her finish, examining the cryptic note on the palmtop in his hands. Then he replied forthrightly, "It is a code, indeed."

"Well?" Peter finally asked.

"I think I understand its logic," Fabian mused, eyes ablaze with energy and joy, continuously scanning the message.

"Fabian! What does it say?" Peter asked again.

"Ashley, will you permit me this one moment of instruction?" he asked.

"Why not?" she replied with a chuckle, looking back at Gorteau with wonder.

"Look at the message again," Gorteau said to the group as though addressing one of his classes on a field trip as he projected an enlarged display of the palm top screen in front of them. "What do you see right off?"

"It counts from one on up to... whatever," Powers replied looking closely at the display.

"One to twenty nine," Peter replied, guessing at the binary sequence.

"Good guess, but not quite," Gorteau continued. "It counts from one to twenty six, then it leaves a longer pause, indicating a change in logic, followed by three numbers between one to twenty six. Then what happens?"

The three men began to look more closely at the signal.

"Then it counts from one to ten," Francis replied, now understanding.

"Excellent!" Gorteau replied. "The message counts from one to twenty six, gives some numbers, counts from one to ten, gives more numbers, counts again from one to twenty six, etcetera. If it's a code, then what is the meaning of the logic?"

Ashley's face lit up with understanding. "The twenty six numbers represent the twenty six letters in the English alphabet, and, one to ten represents base ten arithmetic."

"Yes! Now if someone will be good enough to lend me another palmtop, I'll translate for you," Gorteau replied. Less than two minutes later, he produced this intermediate translation:

<u>The Base 10 Translation</u>:
01 02 03 04 05 06 07 08 09 10 11 12 13 14 15 16 17 18
19 20 21 22 23 24 25 26 17 18 24 01 02 03 04
05 06 07 08 09 10 3750000 984550130 01 02
03 04 05 06 07 08 09 10 11 12 13 14 15 16 17 18 19 20
21 22 23 24 25 26 21 11 09 22 25 22 02
17 18 13

<u>The Symbolic Translation</u>:
(1-26) QRX (1-10) 3750000 984550130 (1-26) UK IV YVB QRM

"I still don't understand," Ashley admitted, sharing a quizzical glance with the others. "I'm not sure the symbolic translation makes any more sense than the binary."

"Very well, I'll read it to you," Gorteau said. "It reads, and this is a loose translation, mind you:

Dear Fabian Gorteau,
I will contact you again at a frequency of 3.75 megahertz in two days at 0130 local time.
Fyodor Stephanovich Kirov
PS. I am encountering interference."

Peter looked at Gorteau with a wildly skeptical expression. "Dr. Gorteau," he began with an almost patronizing tone of voice, "you know that all of us have the highest of professional and personal opinions of you..."

Gorteau laughed in his deep voice which made them all have to suppress a laugh of their own. "You do not trust my analysis?" Gorteau asked with some amazement.

"Well of course I do," Peter back-stroked. "What I'm trying to say is...well, as a Nobel Laureate you should be able to...," then he fell hopelessly short and knew it. Finally he asked bluntly, pointing to the symbolic translation. "Just how the hell do you get a telegram addressed to you personally out of this:"

(1-26) QRX (1-10) 3750000 984550130 (1-26) UK IV YVB QRM?

Gorteau replied, "Nobel Physics Prize winner Richard Feynman once replied to a similar intimation by saying, quote, 'Hell, if I could explain it to the man on the street, it wouldn't be worth the Nobel prize!'. Fortunately, this explanation is much more simple than Feynman's S integrals of quantum electrodynamics."

"Thank God for small favors," Francis quipped.

Gorteau laughed again, obviously enjoying his edge. "Okay, we translated the binary numbers into base ten numbers. Then from Ashley's suggestion, we translated the base ten numbers into their alphabetical equivalents, just as you see. This is where I learned that the message was addressed to me. You see, Fyodor Stephanovich Kirov, is currently head of the scientific contingent at Shturmovoi, or the Little Kremlin as you call it."

"He was the one who designed their reactor," Ashley noted.

"Yes, exactly; the same individual," Gorteau replied. "Kirov and I became close friends while he was at the Johnson Space Center some years back. We discovered that we had a common interest in shortwave radio. At the time we decided that after he returned to the Soviet Union we would stay in touch through our radio transmitters. His international call sign happens to be UK4YVB. Do you see it in the translation?"

"Yes," Ashley replied, "as UK IV YVB. Now I see how he left spaces to indicate a change in logic between the letters and numbers."

"Precisely. I am almost certainly the only one here who would know his call sign and correctly relate it to a radio code. That's how I knew it was addressed to me."

"What about the rest of the letter?" Jamie Powers asked.

"The message is made up entirely of shortwave codes. QRX is code for 'I will contact you again at a frequency of'. Then he gave us the frequency of his transmission: a shortwave band of 3.75 megahertz and the date and time group of the transmission. He signed out with his call sign and left the postscript at then end of the message: QRM, which means literally, 'I am encountering interference'."

"How do you interpret that?" Francis asked, clearly suspicious.

Gorteau sighed. "It seems clear enough to me that he is not referring to this live radio broadcast. It is obvious that he is referring to the officials at Shturmovoi itself. It believe this reference to be political."

There was little doubt in anyone's mind that Gorteau was correct. The RSE's absolute refusal to communicate with BC1 throughout the crisis had clearly defined their intent to remain disassociated from the American base. The reason for that disassociation was not so clear.

"So we can assume that Kirov will fill us in on what's going on in two days?" Peter asked.

"Most probable," Gorteau mused.

"Isn't he afraid of being caught?" Ashley asked.

"This man is really shrewd," Powers interrupted along the same idea. "Had this message been just two milliseconds shorter, the static filter would have cut it right out. He planned this transmission to be as short as he could make it and still get it past our filters. Look at the signal definition. He had to put a 36 millisecond lead in tone on it just to get it to the right length to pass the filters."

"Exactly," Gorteau replied with full blown admiration for his colleague. "Those filters were designed by an international conference on SETI (Search for Extraterrestrial Intelligence). Kirov was a member of that conference which set the parameters of the equipment. The receivers we use here are third generation SETI equipment. He knew exactly what he was doing."

"But won't he get caught broadcasting messages to us on the shortwave band?" Ashley asked again.

"Not likely," Powers replied. "None of us use shortwave for anything but very limited over-the-horizon probe transceivers. Even those are severely limited due to the poor atmospheric transmission characteristics of the Martian atmosphere."

"If you'll check," Gorteau replied, "I'm sure you'll discover that the time and frequency Gorteau picked for his transmission will be the most ideal conditions for shortwave broadcasts."

"It had better be," Powers responded. "Little Kremlin is over 2,065 kilometers southeast of here."

"The rest of the community will be glad to hear we've made contact, regardless of the circumstances," Gorteau offered. "It should provide quite a morale boost."

"No! We can't allow word of this to leave this room," Francis said immediately, taking everyone by surprise.

"Why not?" Peter asked abruptly.

"Because he said he was encountering interference. We assume it is with the powers that be at Little Kremlin. Until we find out more information, it would be foolish on our part to risk exposing him to danger."

"And how are we going to expose him to any danger from over 2,000 kilometers distance?" Powers asked. "If we all got up on top of the domes and screamed back at him, it wouldn't matter, would it?"

"No, that's not the point," Francis said. "All of us have fairly free access to radio transmissions to and from our own satellites. They almost certainly have the capability of monitoring downlinks with the same ease as we do. They may also have bugs planted in here or even operatives. If we made a mistake of any kind, we would expose him to danger. The fewer people who know about this, the safer he is."

"Oh please, Francis," Ashley replied. "You really don't think there are spies among us, do you? Isn't that bordering on the outer limits of paranoia?"

Gorteau replied, "No. He's right. While I don't subscribe to the bugs and spies theory, if Kirov has gone to such extraordinary lengths to keep his message secure, then we must assume he is in some danger and keep the faith with him. If someone does make an innocent mistake and they find out through our radio transmissions, then Kirov could come to some harm. I agree with Francis. Until we know more, it is best that we keep this to ourselves."

"Well," Peter said, "Fabian, it's your private call and your decision. If you don't want the word out, then we'll keep the lid on it. But I think your idea is way out to lunch, Francis. I personally think this news would do the community a lot of good."

"Thank you, Peter," Gorteau replied. "I'll rest much easier if I know Kirov is safe from harm. Perhaps we can share the news later."

"Okay, folks, you heard it," Peter said. "This is classified until further notice. Nobody else knows till Fabian gives the go ahead to release it. Any problems?" No one had anything else to say.

"Then we're off," Peter said. "Goodnight all. Fabian, work with Jamie. He'll be able to set you up and get ready for Kirov's transmission. And Francis," Peter said almost as an afterthought, "get some rest, will you?"

Two sols later at 0125, Peter, Ashley, Frances, Gorteau, Powers and Toon were assembled in the Command Center. No one else had been told apart from the original team sworn to silence, save Toon. Since it was Toon who would have to establish the complex computer controlled receiving links, Peter felt he had to be informed. Besides, Peter reasoned, Toon was above suspicion.

The attempt to keep the communication from RES Scientist Kirov secret had apparently been successful, since it had not registered on any rumor mill radar, the most sensitive of all human communication venues.

"Three minutes," Powers intoned as they all glanced upward at the master event clock counting down just above their heads. The silence in the room was absolute. Ashley gripped Peter's wrist and involuntarily squeezed it with the building anticipation of the moment.

"Two minutes."

"60 seconds."

"5-4-3-2-1"

Silence.

The room was penetrated only by the sound of the ventilator fans.

"Jamie, did you connect the audio?" Peter whispered.

"Yes, of course," he responded.

All eyes were fixed on the flat, green line that represented data flow from the last transmission of 3.75 megahertz.

Silence.

"Time plus one minute." The green line moved slowly in its flat trace across the data screen. Nothing.

"Toon, did you program the receivers to collect data from all their known transmission frequencies?" Peter asked, but mostly for everyone else's benefit.

"Yes I did," he responded in a whisper, also eying the flat green trace.

"What is the chance that this one was filtered?" Peter asked, desperate to understand the silence.

"Zero," Toon responded quietly. "I disconnected the filters altogether."

"Time plus two minutes."

Silence.

"Time plus three minutes."

"Kirov has missed his transmission," Gorteau finally said in a full voice.

"Perhaps he's just late," Ashley offered, still whispering, as though the data burst would somehow be covered by her voice. "We should certainly give him more time."

"Kirov is never late," Gorteau said in a loud voice, fully challenging the silence. "I'm sorry, my dear," he relied immediately, "but Kirov is a man of exactness, of near supernatural precision. I am very much afraid that he is not going to reply. I fear that the interference he spoke of may be more sinister than we imagine. First, he would never have risked this process unless there were grave limitations placed on their capacity to communicate. And, further, he has often spoken of the repressive nature of his command structure."

"What do you make of it then, Professor?" Francis asked bluntly. "Give us the bottom line."

"Danger," Gorteau responded. "Kirov is in trouble, and so are we. The question that perplexes me is whether or not we are all facing the same dilemma and when or if the parallel disasters will converge."

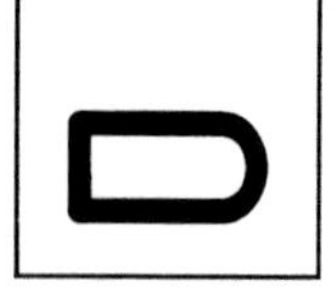

r. Fyodor Stepanovich Kirov sat back in his chair at his scientific console deep in the dark, cold bowels of Shturmovoi. He did not even risk smiling because he was aware that his every expression was probably being monitored by cameras he knew about and a few that he did not. But he felt satisfied that he had successfully sent his detailed message out to BC1 right on time, just as he had promised. True to his character, he had not been even a single millisecond late. Now all he had to do was wait for their answer, and that response would determine whether or not they could all survive the coming winter, and with it the extraordinary disaster that was sweeping upon them.

23

It was fourteen sols and counting until the end of occultation and the moment when BC1 could communicate directly with the earth. Occultation meant that the earth had slipped behind the sun in reference to Mars, and that without relay satellites, no message could be received directly from the earth during that period. Actual occultation - that period when the sun's disk completely blocked the earth - only lasted four sols, but solar interference was so bad that reliable transmission could not occur in a window of 35 sols through the violent, ionized atmosphere of the sun. At the end of that period, the signal would not be crystal clear, but there was a moment in time that the computers had calculated that a minimal, reliable signal could get through the sun's interference.

The whole camp waited; some impatiently, some with hope, some with feigned indifference, but they all waited, nonetheless. It was the waiting that dominated every conversation. In just fourteen sols the earth would swing far enough away from the sun so that direct communications would at long last be possible, and all their questions would be answered. The clock relentlessly and indifferently ticked on; in fourteen sols they would know first hand whether their mother planet would return their calls. In fourteen sols, the life support system at BC1 would be two weeks closer to replenishment or a fortnight closer to final failure. The time-stream rushed on and the small earth-born community rode with it, clinging to a fragile existence on this bitterly cold desert planet. Some clung reluctantly; others boldly rode with a fatalistic rush, and a few with an indomitable sense of quiet destiny.

The rumor-mill had thoroughly ground out all the possible scenarios. A planetary war seemed to be the favorite reason why the communications had been lost, and there were several versions of that rumor, from a simple loss of satellite links to the complete destruction of civilization. Each belief was fueled by an odd mixture of hope or frustration, fused either by bonds left behind on earth or the new ones forged on Mars.

Families and loved ones on their home planet, however distant, bound them all to some belief that catastrophe had been avoided. But to those transients who wanted to leave Mars behind forever, that hope was more like an impassioned necessity. Yet the colonists felt and voiced some sense of independence from the bureaucracy that had smothered them for so long. Such a level of desire and mixture of beliefs led inevitably to conflict.

Brinker and company had their hands full breaking up everything from loud arguments to full blown skirmishes. Just after breakfast, Brinker ran across Julian Covenant reading a report after Rat had ordered the dining room cleared for cleaning. Covenant sat scanning the document reader with his feet on the table, reading glasses pulled down on his nose, dressed in a stiff white shirt and crisp, silk tie.

Brinker unceremoniously kicked Covenant's feet off the table and growled, "Covenant, your boss ordered the place cleared and you don't exactly look like you're ready to go to work. The dishes are stacked high; I hauled most of them back myself. Now I don't want to have to tell you again - get with it!"

Covenant turned the document screen to face Brinker.

"Tell Traynor to check his PC2 screen for this document. I just sent it to him," he said in a controlled voice.

"I don't think he wants to see it, whatever it is," Brinker replied. Covenant simply stared back at him with contempt.

"Marine, that is not exactly your call," Covenant said icily.

Brinker looked at Covenant long and hard, rolling his stogie around in his mouth once. Then he looked at the document screen.

"What is this?" he asked, looking at its glowing face, obviously a computer printing in code.

"You do not want to know what that is, Marine; trust me," Covenant snarled back, his lip curling into a sneer.

"OK, you get what you want Covenant, but I want you in the kitchen, like yesterday. When I get back, those dishes had better be gone."

"Brinker," Covenant replied standing and facing the huge Marine, "I will never go back into that kitchen, ever again. And for the good of the colony, I demand that you contact your fearless leader, now! Minutes count."

Brinker looked as though he was ready to pulverize Covenant. He looked back and forth between the unintelligible code and Covenant's hard stare, not knowing whether to flatten the arrogant twit or search out the boss.

Brinker removed the stogie from his mouth and pointed his finger in Covenant's chest. "This had better be good," he said, boring his eyes into Covenant's unblinking stare, "or you're going to be the first jailbird on this planet doing hard time - starting today."

"Oh, it's good; very good…" Covenant whispered his voice as cold as the Martian air outside.

Minutes later, Peter called up the report on the screen of his PC2 while Brinker stood by. Standing beside Peter was Francis.

"I can't believe this… I cannot believe this…" Peter stammered.

"What?" Francis asked, stepping beside him and looking at the handheld screen. "What is it?" he asked Peter with concern.

"A virus. No worse: a retrovirus."

"What are you talking about?" Francis demanded, his eyes not making any sense out of the display.

"Covenant has downloaded a retrovirus into the mainframe computer," Peter replied, his voice hardening to mirror his face.

"What do you mean retrovirus?" Francis asked sincerely.

"A computer virus, only worse. Covenant has found a way to attack our computer mainframe systems by reprogramming its hardwired PROMS."

"What?" Francis asked.

"You know; the Programmable Read Only Memory chips. The computer's hardwired brains."

"What? How could he do that?" Francis asked incredulously.

"I don't know. But I'm afraid we're all about to find out."

Minutes later, Peter, Francis and Brinker confronted Covenant, sitting with his feet propped back up on the table top, drinking from a steaming cup of coffee.

"I thought that would get your attention, Traynor," Covenant said as they approached his table. "Tyrants always have an Achilles' heel. Typically, the more inferior the tyrant, the easier it is to find."

"What the hell are you talking about?" Peter asked, his face flushed in anger.

"Really, Peter, really," Covenant began, settling his coffee back to the table top slowly. "I thought you, as our intrepid leader should have even rudimentary skills of strategy and foresight. I'm talking about justice for all. About freedom and liberty - all those things you took away from us when you killed Lipton."

"I didn't kill Lipton," Peter shouted, struggling to keep from turning the sneering face of this bureaucrat into Jell-O.

"Control your temper, *mien kapitan*. Of course you killed Lipton - whether by your hand, or by someone else's hand or even by his own - you are fully responsible."

"What about this, Covenant," Peter demanded, producing the PC2 display and shoving it toward his face. "What about this? This means you kill us all? What about this? Who's the murderer now?"

"Ah, but the difference, unlike you gave poor Lassiter, is that you have a choice. A clear choice, to live or die - it's yours today - it's yours to make," Covenant replied coolly.

"What have you done to our systems, Covenant?" Francis demanded with no trace of anger. "How did you do this?"

Covenant smiled broadly. "You should know all about these kinds of things, Francis," he said with a wink. "Isn't this in your little bag of tricks?"

Francis' eyes darted back and forth between Peter and Covenant and he stammered once before quickly regaining control. "Okay, okay, then just tell us the extent of the damage."

"It's called an embedded virus. Very nasty. It lies dormant until ordered to act. Then in just nanoseconds, it's all gone."

"What's all gone?" Brinker asked.

"Everything," Covenant whispered. "Everything."

Brinker turned to Peter with a puzzled look on his face.

"What he means is that he's written a program that somehow has embedded itself into the hardwiring of our computers. It's not software – it's hard wired. It can't be undone without replacing all the computers. You can't change it. It will always be there."

"How did he do that?" Brinker asked.

"You need to be asking me that question, Sergeant," Covenant replied with undisguised contempt.

"How did you do that?" Peter asked sincerely.

"Let us save those minor details until later, Peter. But first, let's discuss the endgame."

"We already know," Francis said in a quiet voice.

"I don't..." Brinker admitted with a puzzled look.

"Total, instantaneous system failure. It's lights off, power off, life support shutdown. We would all be dead in 12 hours or less."

"Less, I suspect," Covenant agreed nodding.

"Well, if I'm not mistaken here, Covenant, that would include you," Brinker said, looking at him with narrowed eyes. "So what's your game?"

"Blackmail," Francis replied bluntly.

"Ah, yes, the ugly 'B' word... it was, after all, inevitable," Covenant replied with a smile.

"Okay. What do you want? What are your demands?" Peter asked with some obvious resignation creeping into his voice.

"I want the lawful government restored to this base, that's all. I want things returned to the way the United States Congress established them. In exchange for lawful government, I will not allow the viral code to be executed," Covenant began.

"Now, I know what you must be thinking," he continued. "'If we take him out, then he can't execute the code.' No, it's actually more clever than that. The code is on a hidden countdown. Some event in normal operational sequence of this base will trigger the code. If I am dead or missing at the critical moment, the code will execute automatically. Without me, the rest of you die. Likewise, if you do not cooperate, I do nothing, and we all die."

"What do you have to gain by your own death?" Francis asked evenly.

"The patriot's dream. Give me liberty, or give me death..."

"You're actually serious..." Peter replied, genuinely surprised.

"Of course..." Covenant agreed.

The room became deadly silent.

"He's right, after all," Peter said.

All eyes turned to face him. They were all surprised, to the man.

"In our zeal, we broke the law and we seized a United States base by force. We've been in a state of anarchy ever since."

Brinker tossed his stogie back into his mouth and looked to the ceiling. It seemed obvious to anyone looking at him that he was going to slip back into the Sarge mode as the officer gentlemen were about to wax philosophical.

"We've not acted any differently than our forefathers either in intent, motive, spirit or in actions. Yet, we've not had their wisdom or held lawful elections or framed documents of intent. Therefore, Covenant is correct and we are in anarchy," Peter said. Then he added without difficulty, "In fact, that makes him the patriot and we are the unlawful criminals." After a long moment, he finally stated, "But I did not kill Lipton."

"I also want to apologize to you," Peter said genuinely to Covenant. "I disgraced you in front of the community, and I had no right to do that. Now this is where it has led. It was poor leadership. I should have found a better way to deal with our disagreement. I see what you mean about freedom and patriotism, and I agree with you. If I were in your shoes, I would act no differently."

Covenant was obviously not prepared for this confession or turn of the argument. He began to speak, but then fell silent.

"Francis," Peter said turning to him, "we need to draw up paperwork to justify our actions. Call it a 'Declaration of Independence', if you please. Then set a time in the next few sols for a Constitutional Convention and an election."

"That will never justify your actions," Covenant said.

"That's correct, but only from your viewpoint." Peter replied. "And even after our process is established, our actions will not be justified from that limited point of view. Just as in 1776, it will only be justified from our narrow circumstances and the precedence of other revolutions. But from the legal process established on this planet, they will be fully established and legal *everywhere on this planet!"*

"You don't even begin to understand the fundamentals of international law…" Covenant argued.

"I only understand the most fundamental issue of international law; that after two governments disagree, force and distance decides the outcome. We don't have the force, but we do have the distance. And, if I'm not mistaken Covenant, this has, in fact, become an issue of *interplanetary law."*

"And what if I kill you first on behalf of the United States government - quell the rebellion personally?" Covenant asked.

"Then we have all died patriots," Peter replied, walking away confidently. "All of us, even you. Rat, release Covenant from kitchen duty. I'm moving him to work in the artificial intelligence team," Peter said over his shoulder. Then he stopped and turned around to look Covenant in the eye.

"Go ahead, and do whatever you have to do, Julian. But I can tell you that we'll all die before we will negotiate with terrorists, and I intend for that sentiment to be clearly stated in our constitution. I have apologized to you man to man, and I intend to do so publicly in front of everyone. Why? Not because you hold all our lives in your hand, but because I was wrong. And may God help me if I ever shrink back to becoming so proud and arrogant that I can't bring myself to apologize when it is my turn.

"If you so desire to pull the plug, I can't stop you. But I have no intention of leaving you in charge, either. The people here will decide their own fate, not me and not you. I'll restore your level of service and expertise to the colony and there won't be any retribution because of your threats. Indeed, I believe you only did what you did because of your own sense of patriotism."

"You're lying," Covenant sneered.

"There's one thing you need to understand about me and about this planet. Here, an individual's word is their bond - better than a signature. Now you have my word. You don't need anything else, I can assure you. On Mars, individual honor is higher than Olympus Mons. I invite you to join us and be a part of this great culture." With that, Peter turned and walked away.

Covenant looked back at the other two men staring down at him. "What are you looking at?" he asked Brinker.

"It looks to me like you're already dressed for your new job," Brinker replied with a shrug as Covenant tugged at the tie gripping his reddening neck.

Two hours later, after some intense scrambling, Toon, as the colony's computer engineering chief, Peter and Francis met behind closed doors.

"Toon, what did you find out?" Peter asked.

"It's in there, all right," he noted with a stern expression. "I found it buried in 13 out of 17 processors I checked at random."

"Can you remove it?" Francis asked.

"No way. I can't even read it. It's not only strongly encrypted, it appears to change its encryption every few seconds or so. Even if we had the thousands of years of computer time it would take to decipher its processes one time, it changes about every time you blink. It's the most rugged bug I've ever even heard of. It's a hacker's dream. Your description of it as a retrovirus is quite accurate."

"How did he get it hardwired into the processors? That's what I can't understand," Peter pointed out with frustration.

"I don't know. But I can tell you it's first rate technology. You can be sure Covenant had a nifty little gadget to make it happen."

"What do you mean?"

"You know - a chip burner that's able to burn a chip in position while operating, one that has already been programmed, or burned in. I've never heard of such a device, but he must have one. There's no way I know of to reprogram an active hard-wired processor without smoking it. It's got to be totally new technology."

"Keep him close to the computers," Peter said.

"What? And risk more mischief from our little anal-retentive friend?" Francis spat with disgust.

"Keep him as close to the machines as you can," Peter repeated. "We sure don't want him behind a set of dishes when his little bug decides to go critical. Besides, I have an idea that he has no more intention of dying a martyr's death than anyone else around here. He talked the line, but if he were going to do it, it would be done by now," he said, his eyes involuntarily looking up at the overhead light.

"What about its cycle?" Francis continued pumping Toon. "Will it only cycle once or does it cycle on some periodic basis? You see…"

"Yes, I know," Toon interrupted. "If it only cycles once, we can nail him one second after the fact. Unfortunately, there's no way to tell."

"Can it be that it's just a ruse? … that the bug is harmless and won't actually do anything?" Peter asked Toon.

"Unknown…" Toon shrugged.

"Can we replace the processors one by one until they're all clean?" Francis continued.

"Not without his notice," Toon replied. "To change so many processors out would take down every system we have. Besides, if he has any brains, he would write a daisy-chain virus that would activate the bug if any individual system in the set were interrupted. There's no way to know that for sure. It may even be reporting back to him in code."

There was a protracted silence before Peter spoke.

"He has us."

"Quite," Francis replied, nodding.

"So now what?" Toon asked.

"This is not what it seems," Peter said, eyes looking at the floor. "He must know that if a system goes down on its own and the virus activates without his direct command, that he'll have killed himself right along with the rest of us. And since I'm convinced he doesn't want to die, he probably wouldn't have written it that way. However, we can't afford to take that chance. We don't have to trust his integrity, just believe he has a will to live. Hence, we stay out of his way, keep him as happy as anyone else, and pray there's not a confrontation."

"What if this gets out?" Francis asked.

"We can't afford to add this stress to that pressure cooker out there," Peter began. "Now, I doubt that Covenant is going to pass the word on his dirty deed. So we need to keep a lid on this, at least until the blackout with earth ends. Francis, you tell Brinker this is a cosmic secret - at least for now."

"Covenant wants your job, doesn't he?" Toon asked Peter honestly, bluntly changing the conversation.

"I'm afraid so. And, he can have it if the rest of the colonists want it that way. But if he wants it by extortion, then we have a problem."

"Were you serious about the constitutional convention and the elections?" Francis asked.

"Very serious. He's quite correct in his assessment of the situation here, and frankly, we're interplanetary criminals at this point. Generations from now, the situation here will either be recounted as a successful revolution like our forefathers held in 1776, or it'll be recorded as an insurrection and we will likely have hung. As for me, I want to at least make an attempt at setting the record straight."

Then Peter looked Francis in the eye. "And I was also serious about my apology to him. I treated him badly and I hurt his pride. If I had done my job as a leader properly, we might not be in this mess right now. Besides, I gave him my word that he faces no retribution, and I mean that."

"Don't be so hard on yourself, Peter," Francis said, slapping him on the back with a loud smack. "You may have screwed up by giving him dish duty with the Rat, but personally, I'd have snapped his little geeky pencil-neck with a smile on my face. So, relatively speaking, you did good!"

hat evening, Peter pubically apologized to Covenant and announced the necessity for forming a Constitutional Convention, and invited every colonist to be a part. He then established a schedule of debate and elections that led right up to the evening before the end of the occultation. The plan was to keep all minds focused on something else besides the impending truth about the fate of the earth. It would require a full two weeks of debate to settle all the issues.

The Constitutional debate began each evening following dinner and raged well past midnight. In the end, the new constitution of Mars, the first founding document of a society outside earth, read almost identically to the constitution of the United States. The argument that finally won out was that it had been the most successful governing document in the history of man, so why change it substantially? The majority chose not to.

Through it all, the "hands off" policy toward Julian Covenant was enforced. Covenant said nothing. He became frighteningly silent, sullen and alone. He spent most of his sols and nights behind a keyboard in Toon's computer center, furiously hammering out something in code. As far as anyone knew, he spoke to no one and counted not one man or woman among his friends.

The election on the eve of the sol contact was to be reestablished surprised no one. Not a single individual challenged Peter or his administration, and few dissenting voices were heard. In the end, Peter was elected President and Francis as his Vice-President. The Cabinet Peter appointed was established in the slots of the already existing department heads. Ironically, as Peter noted in his acceptance speech, they were identical to the positions and individuals Lassiter Lipton had appointed himself.

During his speech, Julian Covenant rose from his seat and walked slowly and dramatically toward the front of the dining hall where Peter was speaking. Peter kept on as though Covenant were not there, but he, like everyone else saw his deliberate approach to the podium. Brinker inched slowly to Peter's side. Finally, when Covenant was even with Peter, he stopped speaking and looked into Covenant's rigid face.

Covenant just stood there for three long seconds until someone shouted, "Sit down, retard!"

As the crowd tittered with laughter, Covenant walked slowly out of the room, casting contemptuous looks at everyone assembled. Throughout the rest of the evening, Peter, Francis and Toon continued to look anxiously toward the lights.

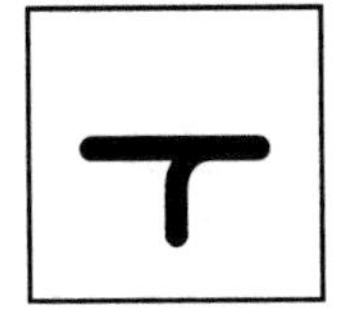

he sol of OT finally arrived.

OT was what the colony referred to in techno-geek slang for "Occultation Terminus": the moment when occultation was to end; the sol contact was to be reestablished with earth. Few people had slept the night before. The broadcast attempt was to begin at 0900 that morning. But hardly any colonists had even left the dining hall after dinner the evening before. They all just sat there watching movies and talking in tight little groups as Rat served up seemingly endless rounds of synthetic coffee. Finally, after breakfast, the Colonists were all assembled in the dining room where a video and audio link to the Command Center was established. They could all see the communicators and Peter seated at the consoles to make the link.

Eventually, the clock ticked down to zero, and Peter made the call,

"Houston, this is BC1; BC1. How do you read, over?"

Static.

No answer.

"Houston, Houston, this is BC1. How do you read? How do you read? Over."

The signals from space crackled and hissed. The screens around the command center depicted the random noise in complex diagrams, each analyzed exhaustively for something other than indiscriminate clatter - but there was nothing.

"Houston, this is BC1, BC1. How do you read, over?"

Nothing. The graphs danced in their colored gyres, illustrated by their complex Fourier transformations, orchestrated to give the illusion of shape and form in a formless, random void, but they gained no useful information from the deathly silence of space.

Five minutes passed with patient calling, calling, calling. But, there was only a deep, chilled silence abetted by the constant hiss and crackle of space noise. The earth was not transmitting anything.

Five more interminable minutes passed. Still nothing. Suddenly, Peter's eyes widened and he sat forward in his chair at the console. He looked over to Jamie Powers, BC1's Communications Chief.

"Jamie, if the Singleton had made it out of earth orbit and were en-route here now, could we establish a link with them?" he asked, referring to the next ship scheduled to depart for Mars from earth. His microphone was still live and the entire colony could hear his question. A hush fell over BC1 as every ear awaited the answer.

Powers looked as if he were taken totally by surprise at the question. "Hmmm, yes, they were scheduled to depart for Mars some sols ago. In that event, they'd be in our line of sight. Wait. Let me check," he replied as his fingers danced over his keyboard.

"Yes, they'd be in range," he finally answered.

"Can you try and establish a voice link?" Peter asked.

"I'm on it," Powers replied, furiously hammering out instructions.

"Singleton, this is Mars Base BC1; Mars Base BC1. Do you read? Over."

Static. Silence. Nothing.

"Is the antenna oriented properly?" Peter asked impatiently.

"Of course," Powers replied with slight annoyance.

"Singleton, Singleton, this is Mars Base BC1; Mars Base BC1. Do you read? Over."

Static. Silence. Nothing.

"Jamie, switch back to the earth's frequency and try Houston again," Peter ordered.

Power's again readjusted the system.

"Houston, this is BC1, BC1. Do you read? Do you read? Over."

Static. Silence. Nothing.

At 0915, his microphone still on and live throughout BC1, Peter stated, "Jamie, give me the low-down." It was agreed before the procedure that fifteen minutes after the window opened a fairly complete analysis of the radio spectrum being transmitted from earth could be performed.

"Sir, I've probed the entire spectrum from television, to radio to radar to random noise, and the earth's not transmitting any frequency that we can detect of any kind."

"What's the probability that the solar environment could block all transmissions?" Peter asked, more to inform the colony than himself.

"Zero, sir," Jamie responded. "The solar environment is quiet."

"What's the probability that under normal earth conditions that we could detect no systematized radio transmissions from earth under these circumstances, at this distance, at this time?"

"Zero, sir."

Peter paused. The fear welled up inside of him. He knew the odds of their own survival had just plummeted to beyond acceptable limits. He felt as if his next words were to be the words of a death sentence to all these people and himself. He prayed for wisdom, then turned to look in the camera broadcasting the Command Center image and said,

"As all of you can plainly see, the earth is not transmitting. We still don't know why. Of course, we'll man the communications station indefinitely, around the clock, looking for a signal, any signal. Until then and until we know more, we must have courage and do what we can to ensure our survival in the coming sols. May God have mercy on us all. But let me not end it there. God will have mercy. We will prevail. We will prevail because we must."

The stress in the dining hall had finally exceeded the breaking point. One woman, Charlene Potempkin, scheduled for the next outbound trip, began to wail, out of control, "My husband! My husband! I want off of this God forsaken rock. I wanna go home to my husband…"

Brinker and several other colonists rushed to her side, and she clung to Brinker, sobbing as he led her gently to her quarters. Others began to weep; some openly, some silently, but there were few dry eyes in the room as the feeling of utter hopelessness began what seemed to be an inevitable slide into the ugliness of open fear.

Word of the depression quickly got back to Peter who ordered that the colonists enjoy a holiday rest. All except essential duties were canceled for the rest of the sol and evening. He ordered that Chaplain Gates conduct a prayer vigil in the dining hall after dinner for as long as anyone wanted to stay. The level of depression was so black, some genuinely worried whether the mood could ever recover.

Peter asked that his staff assemble immediately. Slowly, they filed into the Director's conference room - now President Traynor's Cabinet room - and took their seats. Most would not look into the face of any other individual for fear of revealing their own reddened eyes or seeing someone else's evidence of pain.

Peter began softly, "I know this is a tragedy beyond description. It seems to confirm our worst fears, that something on earth has gone terribly wrong. But we must somehow find the capacity to respond and to survive. We must go on and make our way here. And not just for our sake, but for our children and theirs to come. I don't and I will not accept dying as an option here."

"You're aware, of course, that any response simply delays the inevitable," Robert Hernandez began, tossing a negative but realistic comment onto the table.

"Bob, we don't know what that inevitable means yet," Peter replied.

Hernandez just smiled and continued to look at the tabletop, scraping his thumbnail over its surface in small strokes. "Oh yes, oh yes, we all know what that means..."

"No! We do not!" Peter replied harshly, slamming his fist sharply onto the table and turning to Ashley who looked up at him with a smile of support. "Ashley, how many survival scenarios can you propose out of all the available options?" he asked.

"The scenarios are infinite, of course," she replied, attempting to measure her response truthfully, but optimistically. "The outcome is predictable within a range of options and the life support can be extended if we're creative."

"And Dr. Friedman," he asked of the staff psychiatrist. "Julia, tell me what it takes to be creative."

She recognized his obvious lead and seized it without a moment's hesitation. "A clear head and a spirit of enthusiasm are essential. Peter is right," she continued. "We must do whatever it takes to recover from this malaise and stop focusing on earth and whatever problems they've had. We need to focus on Mars, on the coming winter of Elysium, on our problems, because that's the only way we can possibly survive what we're facing. We're the leadership here, and we need to do our job, which is to lead, not quit - to fight, not to give in. We need to teach them to live - not to give up and die."

"You said it, Julia! You said it. Right on, right on!" Francis replied slamming his palm with a slap on the table.

Hernandez even nodded, and looked up with a resolute stare into Peter's eyes. "We're with you, Peter," he said. "Lead on."

n hour later, Peter sat alone at the conference table reviewing the life support data and various projection scenarios, his white long-john sleeves rolled up and sticking outside his coveralls. There were two soft knocks at the door.

"Come in," he said without looking up.

He saw Ashley enter the room out of the edge of his vision. If it had been anyone else, he would not have even looked up. But out of his deep love and respect for his wife and love of his life, he looked at her as she walked toward him. To his complete surprise, he saw she was suited up in her water-cooled undergarments, used exclusively as underwear only for the space suits. Tucked under both her arms were space helmets.

She smiled and sat on the seat nearest him, laying the helmets onto the desk. "Want to go for a walk?" she asked.

He smiled, not knowing exactly what to say "Have I ever told you that you look sexy in your little tubie underwear?" he quipped, eyeing the white undergarments laced with water tubes.

She just smiled in return and gave him a sly wink.

"I came in to ask you to go for a walk," she replied cagily. "Not to engage you in a discussion of your permanent hormone imbalance."

"Funny you should bring that up," he began, slowly eyeing and following her form, tightly outlined by her undergarment that simply could not hide the bare facts.

"Focus, Peter… focus…" she said, continuing to smile. "Here we are fighting for our lives, and you…"

"…permanent hormone imbalance," he reminded her, his eyes still busy scanning her body.

"How about that walk outside, dear?" she reminded.

He finally looked up to her eyes and engaged them resolutely. He raised both his arms over his head and stretched for a long moment, without saying anything at all. Finally, he spoke.

"Of course," he said, "but then… I mean after we get back…"

She stood up and placed her foot onto his leg as he reached down and began to massage her toes though the thick layers of socks.

"Since when have you *ever* needed to negotiate deals?" she asked sincerely.

"Enough talk!" he replied standing, mimicking the famous line from a classic barbarian movie. Then he swept her into his arms and kissed her deeply. She responded with passion, gripping his hair in her hands. Then suddenly, she pulled away.

"We're going for a walk, Mr. President. And I'll not be detained another moment."

He simply smiled and nodded in return. "At least promise you'll share an air shower with me."

"But of course," she replied, adding, "See you in Airlock 7," as she pointed to his helmet sitting on the desk and walked toward the door.

"A little fresh air might clear my hormone imbalance," he said toward her retreating form.

Just as she ducked out the door, she turned to look at him and said with a wry smile, "I rather doubt it."

Minutes later, he stood in front of his locker in the airlock cluster and, with Ashley's help, slid his own snug-fitting, water-cooled undergarment on over his body. Ashley carefully tugged and arranged the garment so that none of the hoses would be kinked or end up in the wrong place on his body as he slid his space suit on later. Peter stood rigidly still while she did this, his legs spread apart and his arms folded, watching his beautiful wife and feeling her fingers caress his legs and at the same time pull up on the garment and tug it around into all the right places.

Her hands expertly reached behind his legs and smoothed the material up onto his back and down again to his legs. She repeated this motion several times. Finally, Peter said, "I believe we've used up about three times the normal dress-out interval."

Ashley's only reply was a nondescript, "Hmmmm..."

Peter reached down and pulled her up and next to him. He could feel the warmth of her body against his. Passionately they embraced and kissed. Finally, Peter pulled away as she laid her head onto his chest.

"I thought you wanted to go for a walk," he whispered.

"Do we have to?" she replied in her best little-girl voice.

"Depends."

"On what?"

"On the rain check."

"Since when have you ever needed a rain check?" she asked sincerely.

"Figure of speech."

"Not necessary," she replied smiling, pushing away with her fingertips. "Besides, who would be the one to get to hold it?"

Peter laughed loudly and raucously, surprising Ashley with his response.

"What?" she asked. "What did I say?"

"Never mind, dear, let's just suit up. We really need to hurry so we can get back as soon as possible!"

With that, the outer door to the airlock cluster opened. Through it entered Kerry and Suzanne Nikifortune, Lipton's former Administrative Assistant.

For just an instant, it surprised Peter to the point of distraction. His head spun with a near instantaneous evaluation of what this could mean - allies or companions or challenge... His eyes shot to Ashley and hers back to his. He was annoyed with what he saw. It was wordlessly obvious that what she was thinking was not even in the same universe as what he was considering.

This momentary distraction immediately created an embarrassing pause as both couples faced one another. But Kerry, in his typically disarming style, broke the ice by saying, "You guys are having altogether too much fun. Somebody had to come in here and bust this hooliganism and disorderly conduct up, and we decided we were just the team to do it!"

Peter smiled an embarrassed grin and replied, "Busted, but too bad. Somebody needs to be having some fun around here. And we decided that we could maybe start a trend."

Kerry returned the smile and briefly but gently ran his fingers across Suzanne's hand. "Yeah, I would support that sentiment myself."

Peter could peripherally see Ashley bore her eyes into the side of his head. It was not bad enough that her quick instinct had been right about Kerry and Suzanne, but now he was going to hear about it.

Just as Peter was about to turn bright red, Kerry interrupted. "Can we help you suit up?"

Peter chuckled deeply, thankful for the rescue only one man can afford to another. "Please," he said resolutely as he finally turned to fully absorb the 'See-I-Told-You-So' look waiting from Ashley. Venus and Mars had collided - again.

In just 15 minutes, with the help of Kerry and Suzanne, Peter and Ashley pressurized their suits and stepped into the tiny airlock. It was optimally designed for one, but two could squeeze in with enough effort. In fact, it was preferable to go out two at a time to save precious life support gasses.

Peter and Ashley stood in the cramped airlock visor to visor, with no room to move. Peter could have stood facing the door outside, but chose to stand facing his wife. If he had to look at anything, he wanted to look at her.

After the inner door was sealed, Kerry cycled the rapid evacuator pump which recovered as much of the airlock gas as possible. Then he gave them a short count from five to zero. With permission from the command center, Peter cycled the other lock and the door to Mars opened wide as he turned to fully face its red countenance.

Peter was always struck with a consuming wonder at this image. From the first time he had walked on its surface until now, the vista of Mars' red desert was compellingly beautiful and powerfully awesome. While Mars was always visible through the many windows of the colony, seeing the surface through the visor of a space suit was a completely different experience. It was so much more immediate and wild. It was the closest any human could ever come to seeing and experiencing Mars face to face.

He took the first step outside backward, careful not to trip over the inner seal, then he held out his hand to Ashley as she stepped out. He could see her eyes scan the Martian desert as his had moments before, as she, too, experienced the planet for herself in much the same way.

Then, unexpectedly, she reached into her equipment bag and with bulky, pressurized gloved fingers she withdrew a long communication cord and walked over to the window where Kerry and Suzanne were waving at her from inside. She held the plug up so Kerry could see it, then plugged it into the outside receptacle. Kerry withdrew a headset from the wall, put it onto his head and plugged in. Peter could see them talking but could not hear.

After a half minute, Kerry nodded and pulled down a microphone and began speaking. Puzzled, Peter looked to Ashley who unplugged herself from the habitat wall then turned and plugged into his suit. Her voice snapped to life in his headphones.

"We're taking this walk privately. We'll be able to hear from them but they won't hear us. I told them we're going suit to suit."

Peter nodded, then with his gloved hands, turned his outer communications switch to "XMIT OFF". As long as it was in this mode, he could hear the colony, but they had no way of hearing him.

"Peter, I was talking with Francis last night, and he wanted me to bring you out here to be sure and show you something," she said, her breathing also amplified in his ears by the sensitive microphone.

"I'm going to guess if I asked what, you wouldn't tell me, would you?"

"And spoil the surprise? No way!" she said with a smile.

"Lead on," he replied with some curiosity.

Ashley began to walk away from the domes in the general direction of the Crippen Spaceport across the open desert. Peter turned and waved to Kerry and Suzanne who stood at the window and watched. They returned his wave and Peter could see Kerry's hand draped over Suzanne's shoulder as she held his fingers.

"Hmmm..." he said to himself audibly, turning to follow Ashley. Kerry had been a surprise from the beginning and now there were even more surprises from him.

"Hmmm, what?" Ashley asked.

"Forget it," he replied. They would inevitably and certainly discuss it later, as would everyone else.

They walked without speaking for over a kilometer. Peter was just happy to be out of the domes and loved the sheer openness of being outside. He knew this walk was doing him some good. But he was puzzled as he walked. Ashley was in charge of their life support systems and was the most vocal of all the colonists against making unnecessary treks outside which inevitably wasted precious life support gasses. If it were not very important, they would not be here. Ashley would never violate her own life-or-death policy by taking him for a walk, however therapeutic it may have been.

Finally, she stopped. They stood a long distance from the nearest structure on the rock-strewn desert under a clear open sky.

"Well, here we are," she said, turning to look at him, smiling sweetly through her clear visor.

Still puzzled, he looked around him. The colony had receded behind them in the expanse, but they were still a considerable distance from the launch site in the vast open space between the two. It was mid-afternoon, and the sun hung at an angle in the dark rosette colored Martian sky.

"Okay. Here we are..." he replied with a puzzled look, going along with the secret.

"Peter, you need to see this," Ashley said firmly. "It's very important that you see this and understand it."

"Okay," he said, now more puzzled than ever, standing on the empty, rocky Elysium desert, looking at the love of his life through her visor. Her smile was now utterly gone. Her face was rigid - not hard, but intently serious. Then he realized the full severity of the situation she had led him to.

"Tell me," he said in a near whisper.

"I want you to show me the earth," she said.

He stared back at her blankly.

"Show you the earth..." he repeated, still lost.

"Yes, Peter, show me the earth," she said tensely.

"I can't," he replied flatly.

"Why, Peter?"

"Because it's lost in the glare of the sun," he replied, feeling altogether like a schoolboy on a fieldtrip. As he spoke he looked for just an instant at the small yellow orb at the blackened zenith overhead. Instantly the electronic visor darkened to a solid opaque gold, then dissolved in two seconds to transparent clear again as he looked back to her. He could see her face, as if by some magic, in his helmet when the visor cleared.

"No, Peter," she said. "It's not there any more. The earth doesn't exist. It's gone. You can't see it because it isn't there anymore."

He looked back to her as if she had lost her sanity. Then he impulsively looked back to the sun for a longer moment as if to assure himself it, too, was not an illusion. He looked back to Ashley as his visor cleared slowly.

"Peter. Look around you. Where are you now?"

His eyes shot down to the ground under his feet. "Mars," he replied, eyes locking with hers, his mind spinning.

"Peter, what's that over there?" she asked, pointing to the colony.

"BC1."

"Wrong. Wrong! It's no longer just BC1, because it's become everything. It's all there is."

"What's the point?" he asked neutrally.

"Peter, who am I talking to?" she asked with none of the intensity going out of her voice.

"Why do I feel like I'm taking a test for which I've not prepared?" he asked with no humor, staring back at Ashley with a look that could only have been interpreted as demanding an answer.

Ashley withstood the unspoken demand and mirrored his gaze.

"Peter, the earth is gone. Even if it hangs in orbit around the sun, it's gone! It can't help us anymore. We must stop thinking about it. We must focus now on the world that spins under our feet. Over there is our universe," she said, pointing to the colony. "It's tiny, it's frail, and right now it's in critical condition. But it's all we have. And it offers our only hope of making it."

"No... no," he responded. "You know that may not be true. They may fix things or the Singleton may have departed early and may show up later," he said of the re-supply ship that had been scheduled to depart two weeks after the signals were lost.

"Peter, we can't focus there. We have to focus here. It doesn't exist. Please try and understand that!

"And, who are you Peter Traynor? You... you are the single person who decides whether we make it or not. We've all joined together and chosen you as our leader. If you fail, we all fail. If you die, we all die. If you give up, then we all give up with you. But if you can figure something out, then we all live. I hate to say this, my dearest love, but the full weight of the survival of this planet and everyone on it, perhaps all who remain as a part of the human species, rests solely on your shoulders, and yours alone.

"Because of that fact, Frances and I decided you had to see it from this perspective, from this exact angle. Because, baby, if you don't get it, we can't. And if you don't see it, then we all die."

He looked into her eyes through the visors and saw tears welling up in them.

"I don't want to die, Peter. I don't want to die... and none of them do either. We're all counting on you."

Peter looked back and grasped her gloved hand in his.

"No pressure, right?" he replied with a wry, flat smile and an audible sigh. "Okay I get it now. I see it clearly now," he said. Then he touched his visor to hers and looked into her eyes as a tear fell over her lid and slid down her cheek.

"What's the number one rule in a space suit?" he asked.

"Don't throw up or cry," she responded with a half-sob, half-chuckle.

"No hankie..." he said.

"Right," she said laughing and feeling just a little foolish.

"Let's go home, ok?" he asked tenderly. She nodded as they began to walk back, hand in hand. Without saying a single word they made their way back to the airlock cluster where Kerry and Suzanne faithfully awaited them.

As he walked, Peter thought about the importance of the words he had just heard and of the essential truth behind them. Their chances of making it were slim to none - but at least there was a tiny chance nonetheless. And the essential message was correct. The earth was gone; perhaps forever, and all they had was under their feet. It was simply all they had. The earth and the Singleton mission were all pipe dreams... all gone... all part of a history that from their vantage point might as well never had existed at all.

Here on the desert of Elysium, the winter was coming; not with a vengeance, but with a purpose. It was their choice, to live or to die. To mine the deepest parts of their human intellect and creativity was all that separated them from extinction. And now it came down to a single leader, a single man. It was the test of all tests. Based on his capacity and his intelligence - they would all live or they would all die.

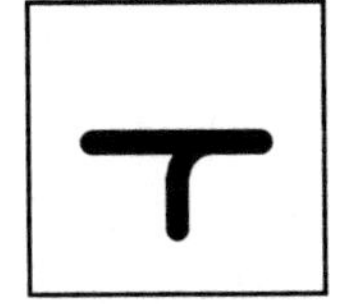

The next sol dawned over a community more emotionally dead than alive. Although the previous sol had been declared a holiday, this was a regularly scheduled workday and yet, hardly any one was actually showing up for duty. The Command Center was manned, but only because the watch on duty had personally rousted his relief. The malaise Julia Freidman had warned them about had set in with a vengeance.

Peter forced himself to rise early, on schedule at 0415, and go to the empty dining hall where only Rat had actually preceded him, starting breakfast.

"Your coffee, o' king," he said to Peter without his usual grin, thrusting a steaming mug toward him.

"Rat, I want to ask you a question," Peter said, leaning against one of the kitchen tables where Rat was beginning to lay out the morning's fare. As he said this, Peter's hand inched toward a piece of bread Rat had just sliced off a hot loaf.

Without altering his expression, Rat slammed his hand in front of the new loaf of bread. "No freebies, Dr. T," Rat said. "We're going on rations soon, I hear."

"And where did you hear that?" Peter asked, involuntarily annoyed at not having a taste of Rat's delicious, fresh baked bread, as was his morning custom.

"It's the word going around," Rat shrugged.

"It's a rumor," Peter replied. "But it's well placed. Rationing is sure to begin. I guess it's just common sense turned common knowledge."

Peter looked at Rat's face. He, like everyone else, was emotionally stretched to his limit.

"Did you lose family?" Peter asked empathetically.

Rat just nodded, trying his best to hide a trembling lip. "My mom is all. She lives in Florida near the Space Center."

"I'm sorry, Roman," Peter said.

Rat's eyes began to moisten. He looked like he wanted to say something, but could not. Peter put his hand on his shoulder and looked into the cook's eyes. "Did I ever tell you that you're one of the best things that ever happened to this colony?"

Rat just looked surprised, and then his expression changed as did his manner of speaking. It was Peter's turn to be surprised.

"Peter, I'm not a cook," he said in a clearly different tone of voice and even an altered accent. His intonation changed from a New Jersey inflection to an unmistakably neutral one. Peter backed away a single step and looked at Rat in silence. Yet another surprise in a whole planet of surprises.

"Let me guess," Peter replied. "...Her Majesty's Secret Service? Bond, James Bond, doing time as a cook on Mars – if you can make it there you can make it anywhere?"

Rat laughed briefly, and then smiled. "No, actually not quite that spectacular. Roman Adkins Thomas is a name I made up, along with my degree and credentials. It was just cosmic irony that someone here discovered my initials were RAT, but in the end, even that worked to my favor. You see, my real name is Raymond Andrew Taylor and I was a launch manager at the Kennedy Space Center. I applied for the astronaut program and was rejected five times before I gave up. Then I decided I was going to go to Mars, no matter what. So I did extensive research into who was getting selected to get into the program and what set of credentials I needed to fit their criteria exactly. Then I bought them. Just to be sure I would be able to do it, I aimed for one of the grunt jobs – and I was selected. Only my mom knows the truth, and she was against it from the beginning. She said cheating and lying wouldn't work and that I would be sorry for it. So now, here I am, a cook named Rat when I could be working in launch control or the command center. I did make it into space and even to Mars, but I pay the price every day and no one even knows who I really am. My mom was right, and now she's gone."

Peter looked into his face, tears now streaming down Rat's cheeks. Peter reached over and pulled the cook to him and embraced him. Then he released him and handed him his personal handkerchief, strictly forbidden in the health protocol. Rat accepted and began to wipe his eyes.

"My first question is what do you want to be called?"

Rat just shrugged. "I don't know. I've been called Rat for so long, I got used to it. And I don't believe very many say it the wrong way."

"Has it ever occurred to you that Raymond Andrew Taylor has the same initials?" Peter asked.

A broad smile came over Rat's face. "No. I guess not," he replied with a subdued chuckle.

"You've sinned against the establishment with your lying and cheating; are you aware of this?" Peter asked flatly.

Rat just nodded in silence and looked away.

"Ok, then. You're pardoned forever. I'm the President and our constitution allows that. Now go your way and sin no more..."

"Are you serious?" Rat asked.

"Deadly. Do you want it in writing or just between you and me?"

Rat smiled, looked to the floor then back to Peter. "Just between you and me is ok."

"Now, is it going to be Rat or Raymond? I'll ensure that you're called by whatever name you like."

"Rat's ok. Besides, there aren't any rats on Mars – except me, that is. And the only one you can locate is in the kitchen every day."

Both men laughed loudly.

"One other thing," Peter said. "I can't afford to keep you in the kitchen when there're more urgent tasks to be done. From here on, you'll stand kitchen duty in a rotation with everyone else and you'll be assigned to the Command Center for training as a watch stander."

"Excuse me, Dr. T.," Rat said. "I've actually come to like my job and people are used to me. How about me doing this job as I have been with the weekend watch at the Command Center? When you said I was one of the best things that ever happened to this colony, I assumed you were talking about my cooking."

Peter laughed aloud and grasped Rat by his shoulder. "You got it, Rat! This is quite a relief, actually! I can't imagine eating something served up by Francis or Brinker, can you?"

Rat laughed with him, then picked up the small loaf of fresh bread and handed it to Peter. "Can I get some fake butter for you, sir?"

"Ok, but you can loose the fake New Jersey accent while you're at it. I always wondered what exit you were from!"

As Peter ate his bread, alone in the darkened dining hall, he reflected on the conversation he had just had with Rat. He had discovered a valuable, even essential, individual in the cook – one with feelings, emotions, energy and talents that, along with the rest, could mean the difference between life and death for them all. And it had been forged in just a few minutes into an unexpected bond between them that led him to an idea.

"Francis, I need to talk to you now," Peter said into his portable communicator.

A full minute later, Francis' sleepy voice replied, "No problem, Chief. You caught me sleeping in to the late hour of 0445. Gee, what was I thinking?"

"Just let the coffee do the thinking for you and hurry up, will you?"

"Any bread left?" Francis' voice asked through the communicator.

"You're a little late," Peter said, mouthing the last piece as he spoke. "It's the sad price of sleeping in."

Brilliant, absolutely brilliant," Francis replied an hour later after fully and carefully hearing Peter out. "Julia Friedman will pin a medal on you," he said of the BC1 psychiatrist.

"That wasn't your first response," Peter replied with a sly smile, still unable to judge his friend's full measure of sincerity.

"Oh, well forgive thee me for not immediately accepting the idea of a spontaneous black tie party as the solution to the most serious problem of survival ever faced by humankind," Francis replied drolly, looking around for Rat's next service of hot bread, as he summarized what he had heard.

"We're to have a formal black tie affair to establish the mood as anything but serious, and then allow each participant, dressed in their best attire, to be interviewed for five minutes in front of the whole colony. Draw out their individual histories and ideas for how to use their position in the colony for a successful resolution. We get bonding, we get touchy-feelie, we get comradeship, we get ideas, we get synergy. Hey, it's a shrink's dream! But, unfortunately, it won't work..."

Peter's smile disappeared instantly. "Why? One second ago you said it was brilliant."

"Cynical license. You know me. Peter, this group of individuals has lost it all – everything - and they don't even know why. Worse yet, they inevitably face their own slow, horrible deaths, tens of millions of kilometers away from all they held dear in life. Now, you really wanna go to these people and suggest a formal party? They might just kill you as a mild form of entertainment for even suggesting such nonsense."

"And that's the key, Francis: nonsense. Nonsense!" Peter said, passionately defending his plan. "Our whole situation makes no sense. We've lost everything because of some bizarre circumstance that's in the end, nonsense. So what better way to counter it than with nonsense? Perhaps we can use it to our advantage.

"Listen to me. We use the party as leverage to pull them out of the pit of despondency, then strike to the heart of their hopelessness by giving them a hope in one another. There's only one way to make that happen – everybody has to stand up and tell their stories to each other. We all have to have a stake in each other's history and in the need to carry one another through this – not just ourselves as individuals. The currency – our only power, our only hope - is one another, with deep friendships forged overnight. And we can't afford to allow our professional facades, our prideful independence and the insane factions between transients and colonists to kill that last hope.

"We all made it here to Mars because we were so great, so perfect and so good as individual stars. But when we leave that party tomorrow night, we had dammed well better leave as family, in this thing together as a unified one, or we can just all go back to our rooms and die strangers. And let's face it Francis, we're indeed the only family there's left in the known universe. The clock is ticking, friend, and we only have a single sol left to jump this train to a new set of tracks.

"Do you know how many of our number committed suicide last night? Neither do I," Peter continued, gesturing in the dark dining hall that should have been filling up at that hour. "We won't know till we go knocking on doors later this morning. But I do know that for every human talent, every valuable person we lose from now on, whether we lose their lives or their energy or their commitment – it doesn't matter, we lose just that much more ground before the train runs off the end of the tracks to extinction."

"Curse your weird brain, Traynor," Francis said after a moment's thought. "I hate it when you sound so right, so logical in the full light of… hell, even defending such a lame plan! Haven't you got anything, anything at all, better to offer than this? I mean, is this… this pathetic excuse for an operational strategy all there really is between the human race and extinction?"

"I think we'll call it the First Annual Mars Coming-Out Party. You have any better ideas?" Peter responded confidently, folding his arms and leaning back in his seat. "Just think of it, pal, in future generations, this will become a planetary holiday! And just by sitting here right now, you are one of its founding fathers."

Francis responded by placing both hands over his face, massaging a newly formed headache, and shaking his head slowly. "Well – it's slightly better than the Debutante Ball. And, hey, I never thought of myself as in the closet – but, under these circumstances, why not? Know where I can rent a white cummerbund?"

rancis was totally correct in his assessment of Juila Friedman's response about Peter's formal party proposal. She thought the idea was not only brilliant, but, "… of historical significance to the survivors and all their ancestry." The word circulated that the party would be held the next evening. There was to be no RSVP because the attendance of everyone was absolutely mandatory except for two watch standers in the Command Center, Toon and Hammonds. Friedman immediately took charge of all party planning and Rat was authorized to double the dessert and coffee portions. A small team of colonists even took off on an incredible hunt for party accoutrements including "electric candles" made from lengths of conduit and panel lights.

The big event finally arrived the following evening as the sun set over the ruddy, cold Marsscape. Black ties had been fashioned out of various lengths of black material that had been found or stolen from anywhere. Some were so well done it was impossible to tell them from the real article while others were little more than black paper cut-outs. But it was refreshingly obvious that every individual took the event seriously and every colonist and administration employee attended. Only Julian Covenant was no where to be seen.

Peter, Ashley, Francis, Dr. Friedman, Chaplain Gates and Hernandez reluctantly assumed their seats at the "head table" where a speakers podium had been set up. Friedman was to be the Master of Ceremonies and Peter would make the keynote speaker introduction The surprise special guest speaker was Rat. After Peter had described his morning's meeting with Rat to Friedman, she looked like she had been spray painted with a fine coat of warm-fuzzy and insisted he tell his story to all. Following the keynote, every colonist would be invited to share with the others. If all went as planned, by the end of the evening, they would unite together as one with no secrets and a special desire to survive this together as a team. At least, that was the plan.

Dinner was served by Rat and a team which consisted of all those at the head table. The lights were dimmed and the "candles" lit with special dinner music appropriately provided. After the last dessert was consumed, Friedman stepped to the podium to make the introduction. She had gone all out for tonight, somehow assembling what appeared to be an incredibly beautiful, formal evening gown out of parachute material.

"I'm honored tonight to proclaim the first annual Mars Coming Out Party where we will begin by giving thanks for all that we have and praying for continued blessings on our new nation."

With that Chaplain Gates prayed his best first petition of thanks. Regardless of the religious affiliation or lack of same from the assembled colonists, no one was about to express any kind of irreverence at a simple prayer during such a harrowing time. Indeed, most would later admit their appreciation of even the smallest comforts and forms of civilized unity.

Friedman rose again to introduce Peter as the young planet's first duly elected leader. As Peter stepped up to speak, the room's applause began, then continued and carried on with a standing ovation. Not one person remained seated.

Finally as the applause died and those assembled resumed their seats, Peter began, red-faced and breathless.

"I guess I never saw any of this coming," he confessed extemporaneously. "I only wanted to settle here, explore my brains out and raise my family on Mars, but I never dreamed that it would come to this. I can tell you I'm not altogether happy with where we are or how we got here, but I can also tell you that we'll play this hand as it's been dealt and do it with all the dignity, grace and integrity we can muster. That is precisely why we're gathered together tonight and that's what our guest speaker represents. You'll all know who he is when he stands up and I'm sure you'll be surprised by what he has to say. And while he made a serious mistake in judgment to get here, I'm certain that not only could none of us do without him and his talents, but that not a single one of us would want to take his place..."

Before he could say another word, the lights went out and the dining hall fell into total darkness. Every person there was trained in emergency procedures, and they all waited for exactly the same thing – for the emergency lights to kick on. The seconds counted up to a full minute, and no one said a word, waiting for the emergency lights to flicker on. But they did not.

With the darkness came total silence: a sound alien to all of them. Not a single machine whirred and not a single ventilation fan processed air around them. No human had ever heard this kind of silence on Mars. BC1 had never experienced a power failure before. According to the design engineers, a power failure was impossible due to the multiple levels of redundancy. They all knew this because it was a part of everyone's training. The silence blended with the darkness, a frightening moment of profound stillness.

Peter could feel a hand grip his arm in the total darkness. "Covenant..." Francis whispered into his ear. "The bastard did it."

The sound and feel of these words in his ear caused Peter to experience an involuntary chill down his spine. They would have less than an hour before the temperature in every part of BC1 dropped below freezing. Another hour after that and the temperature would drop to 20 degrees below zero Celsius. They had to act quickly.

A beam of light shot out from Francis' hand as he toggled his flashlight on. "Stay calm and stay here," he said loudly to the colonists.

A few other lights came on around the room from those who had thought to bring pocket flashlights. Peter reached into his pocket and gave a light to Julia. "You're in charge. We'll be back as soon as we can."

"What's going on?" a voice called from somewhere in the room.

Peter moved back to the podium where Julia held the light under his face. "We don't know," Peter replied, "but we soon will and you'll be the very first to find out; in just minutes after we do. I promise," he said sincerely to the assembled colony as he raced just behind Francis and

Brinker out of the room toward the Command Center. Someone had killed the power in the middle of his speech on purpose and it did not take a savant to figure out who, how or why.

he BC1 Command Center on Mars was the single most incredible electronic control center ever conceived and built by mankind. It had been designed to be the hub of a super-intelligent machine whose wires linked together every aspect of BC1. It was specifically created to maximize and optimize every conceivable aspect of the human-machine interface. It was dreamed into existence by a team of the earth's most advanced engineers and ergonomic specialists. Its' plan was nearly flawless - from its' balanced lighting, open compartmentalization for functional control, and even its' small, glass, soundproof sub-rooms for mini-conferences. It had the appearance of a giant, oblong tube with curved walls and precisely placed, transparent cubes within, all lit by thousands of indicator lights, glowing panels, screens and displays of innumerable form. But when Peter, Francis and Brinker got there, the room was totally silent, black and dead.

The thoughts that swirled through Peter's mind at that instant were many and grave. No one had ever dumped the entire load on such a complex machine all at once before. Not only would the main computer have to be rebooted, but the hundreds of independently functioning machines would have to be as well – from heating to life support. Under normal conditions this would take more than a sol to do safely and without hazarding vital functions. And that is only if all were well with the machines themselves. He shuddered to think what had happened to the machines' logic under Covenant's hand, and their chances of even surviving the night seemed immeasurably low.

"Toon! Toon!" Peter shouted into the quiet, cavernous space as soon as the door was opened.

"Here, Peter. Over here at the Operations Console," Toon replied. Peter could even at that moment hear his fingers madly clicking on a keyboard. As their eyes became accustomed to the darkness, they could see Hammonds standing over Toon's shoulder holding a small pocket light above the keyboard. Peter, Francis and Brinker rushed over to the console.

"What's going down?" Francis asked breathlessly.

Toon just lifted his right index finger into the air for half a second, then he resumed his furious clicking on the computer. Hammonds turned his head to try and make out who had just entered and his light's beam moved off the keyboard. Toon clipped, "Light!" and Hammonds quickly returned to his duty.

Peter looked to Francis and shook his head as the three men standing behind the Command Center watch all exchanged worried glances.

"Bingo!" Toon said after long minutes.

"Bingo what?" Francis asked with exasperation.

"System's restored in 15 seconds." Toon said.

"What's going down, Toon?" Peter asked.

Toon just lifted his right index finger in the air as the numbers on his screen counted down to zero. At that moment, the lights in the Command Center began to flicker on in banks around the room as panel after panel returned one at a time. Then the ventilation fans returned one by one.

Again the three men behind the Command Center watch-standers exchanged looks – this time of clear relief. Suddenly the lights went out again and they were engulfed in total silence and darkness once more.

"Crap!" Toon exclaimed with more than a little frustration, as his fingers began their measured hammering once more as Hammonds returned the tiny pencil beam of light back to the keyboard.

"Toon. Stop. What are you doing?" Peter demanded from behind him.

The clacking on the keys stopped as Toon turned around and faced him. "Look boss, we've got no time for twenty questions. Let me do my job or we all die... tonight," he replied bluntly and uncharacteristically harshly.

Peter just raised both hands and shook his head in surrender as Toon turned and continued his work. About every half minute or so, Toon would say, "Ah" or "Huh" or "Hmmm" and once or twice he said, "Ok – ok – now I see it," as rows and rows of completely unintelligible script scrolled across the screen. Peter also noticed that he could see Hammond's breath condense in the cold air. The temperature was dropping fast.

Again, Toon began a countdown. "Fifteen seconds – count," he said. All of them began a silent count as the numbers raced across the screen. Again, at the end of the count, the lights and panels began to flicker on as they did before, but this time everyone held their breath. No one said a word until the last light flickered on and the fans around them held for two full minutes.

Peter spoke first to Brinker. "Go get Covenant!"

Brinker left quickly and in not what appeared to be a good humor.

"Toon, tell me – now!" Peter commanded.

"Covenant did it," Toon said. "He actually pulled the plug."

"How did you recover?" Peter asked. "I thought we could not recover from his nasty little bug."

"I'm afraid I've been tracking him," Toon confessed. "He's been a busy little creep working against us all along. When he used his ploy to get out of kitchen duty, he only had about half of his virus developed. He'd been working sol and night to finish it, and finally he did – tonight. Then he pulled the plug right in the middle of your speech – good timing."

"How did you recover so quickly?" Francis asked.

"I routed all his files to a dummy server. He thought he was programming his little chips, but he was only programming a cyber fake. I also went behind him and pulled and replaced all his virus laden chips."

"How did you do that without his notice?" Francis asked.

"Easy, actually. He was monitoring a series of fake chips in the dummy server."

"Then how did we lose power tonight if you had a handle on this all along, and why didn't you tell me what was going on?" Peter asked bluntly.

"One question at a time, Mr. President," Toon replied with renewed enthusiasm. "We lost power because we had to let him do his deed in order to catch him and convict him. And secondly, I didn't tell anyone because I didn't want him to hear about it from a third party. He did have the ability to kill us all and himself, as you can plainly see. He's also a near genius that could have easily faked me out if he had known I was cleaning up behind him. As a matter of fact, just a few minutes ago, I thought that was exactly what he'd done."

Peter silently nodded his approval. "Good job, Toon. You're definitely Mars' genuine hero." Then he smiled and extended his hand to Toon who grasped it with a huge grin. "Thanks, Mr. President, or Peter, or whatever."

Peter looked to Francis who was not smiling. Francis' eyes stared out over the room. "This just doesn't make any sense at all," he mused, almost to himself, rubbing a sol's growth on his chin.

"What?" Peter asked. "What doesn't make any sense?"

"I want to talk to Covenant," Francis said flatly. "I find it very hard to believe he's either suicidal or a mass murderer."

"Don't we have all the evidence we need, right here in the files? Didn't we all experience his madness first hand? Didn't he warn us face to face that this was his plan all along? What more evidence do you need?" Peter demanded.

"I want to talk to Covenant," Francis said, turning to walk away.

Peter turned and looked back to Toon, whose eyes were following Francis toward the door.

"Again, thanks Toon, from all of us. Are the power and functions all back on line throughout the colony?" Peter asked.

Toon's smile had faded as he turned back around to the console. "I'll make sure they are. Oh, by the way, can you send me another two operators. I think we're going to need all the boards manned for awhile."

"Sure," Peter said as he turned and quickly followed Francis.

eter had to jog to catch up to Francis making his way quickly to Covenant's quarters. As they rounded a corner in the tubes that connected the living quarters, they met Brinker returning back to the main hub from Covenant's empty room.

Francis stood in his way.

"Brinker, stop," Francis ordered.

"Why?" asked Brinker, his face rigid with rage.

"Because we want Covenant alive," Francis replied. "And by the look on your face, you don't."

Brinker sighed deeply and dropped his shoulders, fished his stogie out of his pocket and leaned against a wall.

"You might actually be right," was all he said.

Peter stepped in. "Ok team, now we know he didn't go back home to wait for us or die. So where is he?"

Both men shook their heads. "No clue," Francis replied.

"Brinker, go collect four men and sweep the colony. Francis and I'll check the command and control sections, but we're going to start with the dining hall. All we need is a lunatic in the party – a gun-slinger or worse in a black-tie."

Just as he said that, his communicator beeped on his belt.

"Traynor," he said quickly raising the unit to his mouth.

"Peter, Toon. You got everyone accounted for in the party?"

"Yep, all except Hammonds."

"Well, I just got a reading from airlock number three. Something has activated a motion sensor," Toon reported.

"We got him," Peter said as he, Brinker and Francis raced toward the airlock.

"Toon, we're going to seal off the tunnel leading to the airlocks on our way in. Lock it from the Command Center behind us," Peter ordered, fearing Covenant might try to kill himself and everyone else by cycling the inner and outer airlock doors open simultaneously. While this was technically impossible, Covenant had shown himself to be quite capable at effecting a certain degree of chaos and destruction. By closing off the tunnels leading to the airlocks, they could at least contain the death and destruction to the immediate area and only they would die along with him.

They ran headlong into the airlock tunnel and found the door locked and sealed.

"Toon, the entry door to AL03 is closed and sealed," Peter reported.

"Not by my console it's not," Toon replied. "According to my data, it's wide open."

Peter looked at Francis. This clearly meant Covenant had changed the programming related to the airlock doors. Now it was anyone's guess at not only the conditions inside the tunnel but whether their operational controls were even reliable. It felt like they were walking right into a trap.

Brinker must have been thinking along the same lines as he said, "Is there any other way into there?"

"Not except from outside," Francis replied.

Suiting up and approaching from the outside could take an hour, Peter mused to himself. It would give Covenant far too long to do whatever he was planning to do.

"Let's suit up in airlock two, seal the adjoining tunnels, come back here and manually open the door to AL03," Peter suggested. "It'll save at least half an hour."

Both other men nodded and they all headed toward airlock two.

"What's the plan?" Toon's voice crackled over the intercom.

Peter picked the unit up to tell him, when Francis snatched it from his hand and winked.

"We're going outside and back into AL03," he reported, and then he handed the unit back to Peter. "We don't need his controls and we don't need to tip off Covenant who probably has his own communicator," Francis explained.

Brinker smiled a contented smile. "You guys might actually make good Marines yet!" he said with a chuckle.

In record time, all three suited up and pressurized, devising their plan while they helped one another into the cumbersome suits. With their helmets on, they walked down the tunnel together to Airlock 3.

Surprisingly, they found the door open. Peter picked up his communicator to ask Toon for a status on doors and motion sensor lights when he stopped and looked to Francis who mouthed what he was thinking.

"Our quarry is into the game," he whispered. "Let's not give away our moves. He's responded to our last known position and is trying to cause us to react to his plan. Brinker, what's he up to?" Francis asked.

Brinker slowly shook his head, his eyes focused on nothing as his mind raced ahead.

"If you were chasing me and I left the door open for you, would you just walk through it?" Peter asked them.

Brinker shook his head vigorously.

"Neither would I," Peter replied. "Covenant is a strategist. He's thinking ahead. So what do we do now? I say we walk through the open door."

Brinker looked back at him through eyes sunken so deep from thought he looked like he was being possessed by his own thought process. He just nodded assent. Francis also nodded as Brinker edged in ahead of them, walking point.

Brinker's eyes carefully assessed every square inch of the long tunnel ahead as he walked toward the opposite end marked in big block letters: AL03.

Francis quietly unplugged the data lines to the Command Center, so their actions could not be monitored, then closed and locked the door behind them by turning its big center mounted wheel.

When they reached the end of the tunnel, Peter ordered Brinker, "Open it carefully."

Brinker disconnected the data lines to the door, then slowly opened it into the Airlock chamber. Inside the red night-vision lights glowed, lending a surreal image to an already unreal chase for an individual who was about as tangible as a ghost at that moment, and one that meant them much harm.

The trio entered the airlock chamber and Brinker closed the door behind them.

"Dump the air in the tunnel," Peter ordered quickly, giving Brinker the instruction to empty the passageway behind them of air so Covenant could not possibly, under any conceivable circumstance exit behind them.

"Wait," Francis said. "Our life support is critical now, and you want to dump 45 cubic meters of fresh, breathable air outside? No. I'll stand guard here. He'll not get past me, even if he manages to make it past you and Brinker."

Peter thought about the truth of the life support picture. 45 cubic meters of almost irreplaceable life support gasses could mean the difference of surviving at some later point. But, if by some means Covenant were trapped in airlock three, which it appeared he was, they could not afford to let him back into the colony. It was better to risk 45 meters of air than lose it all if he escaped back into the main complex.

"Dump the air; all of it. Then disable the replenishment valve," Peter commanded Brinker. He looked to Francis. "It's my call."

Francis just nodded as Brinker cycled the valve and the air began to hiss out of the tunnel into the deep blackness of the Martian night. As the precious, nearly irreplaceable gas rushed out of the tunnel, Peter began to walk forward into the airlock with Francis in tow. They carefully eyed each square centimeter of space around them. There were only a few places to hide here, and by the time Brinker unscrewed the replenishment valve and hammered its threads, they had reconnoitered the entire space with the exception of the main chamber of the airlock itself. By procedure, that space was always closed and locked.

At that moment, Peter realized that the others must have had the same thought as he - that if Covenant were inside, he would be in the chamber behind the locked door. As a group, they approached the door together.

Brinker looked at the door then spread his hands wide and looked at Peter with a question. "No weapon," he mouthed.

Understanding, Peter reached behind him and pulled three stiff geology probe rods from the wall and handed one each to Brinker and Francis. At least they could defend themselves against whatever Covenant had against them.

With a careful, slow motion, Peter peeked into the chamber before him. "It's empty, and the outer door is open. He's gone outside!"

The others looked stunned. Not only did it indicate someone had left the Colony, but they had made a serious and dangerous breach of procedure by leaving the outer airlock door standing open.

"Where could he have gone?" Peter said, voicing aloud the vexing question on all of their minds. He was lost in thought, his mind racing to evaluate all possibilities. There was no where to go in the Martian night. Covenant could never escape outside. Even if he had attempted to steal an MAT, it could only go in the general direction of Shturmovoi - and for what purpose? The MAT would run out of power and supplies long before it reached the RSE base. The only other place he could go was another BC1 structure - and they were all controlled and easily monitored.

"This doesn't make any sense at all," Francis said, voicing Peter's own thoughts.

"Y'all play cards?" Brinker asked.

They stared at him blankly.

"Five card stud. You know - poker?"

"Sure," Francis replied flatly.

"Then you'll understand what I mean when I say this stinks. Somebody has cards they ain't showin'," he said looking at each man through their visors with a steely eye.

eter asked Brinker and Francis to make their way to the adjoining airlock, go outside and shut the outer door on airlock three. He returned as quickly as he could to the dining hall. He was fearful that the power loss and general deteriorating mood would have left the colony in a completely chaotic neurosis.

As he quickly approached the hall through the tunnel, he thought of what to tell the others about what had happened and feared the effect it would have on their already deteriorated psyche. Removing his helmet, he could clearly hear raised voices as he got closer to the dining hall. His greatest fears were reinforced by the din. It sounded as if the colonists had all turned on one another. Taking a deep breath, as his pace moved from a fast trot to a full run, Peter burst through the door and was totally astonished at what he saw.

He was met by a blast of conga music and the colonists dancing around the hall in a rhythmic chain dance. Rat was on a make-shift stage lip-synching the lyrics into a flashlight he was using as a fake microphone. Peter's mouth literally fell open at the sight of the intense, incredibly passionate party with every colonist either joining in the dance or laughing hysterically and clapping their hands with the beat.

As the procession went by, a hand reached out and tugged at Peter's space-suited sleeve, pulling him into the dance line. It was Ashley, who continued to dance but faced him as she pulled him along in the line. The sight of Peter being pulled along, dressed in his space suit, his helmet tucked under his arm, only increased the appreciative noise of the others. His eyes were wide with amazement as he saw the colony in full revelry; the very last thing he thought he would see on his return. He looked quizzically to Ashley.

"When the lights went out and you guys went running out of the room," she shouted into his ear, "everyone started to panic. Then Rat pulled a flashlight out of his pocket, stuck it up under his chin and started a Count Dracula stand-up routine on top of his table. It was so hysterical that we couldn't help but laugh. Then, when then lights came back on, Rat didn't miss a beat. Before you know it, he turned disk jockey and now this!"

Peter's smile turned into a full laugh; a laugh of relief such as he had not felt since Lipton ordered his deportation from Mars. He tossed his helmet to Rat who immediately put it on. Then he spun Ashley around and joined in the wild and raucous dance. President or not, he was going to party. And as far as he was concerned, Mars had two heroes on this evening. One sat at a keyboard in the Command Center and the other stood on top of a table dancing, singing into a flashlight and wearing Peter's space helmet.

eter awoke the next morning to a pounding noise. Someone was hammering on his door, causing his head to ache with each reverberation. His senses returned to him slowly, forced to the front of his mind and overpowering his desire for more rest as he heard the voice shouting, "Peter… Peter, wake up!"

Immediately his C2 began to ping, which forced him to sit straight up in his bed. Ashley awoke and sat up at the same time. They looked at one another, then to the status panel by the bed. The power was still on. It was after seven in the morning.

"Peter… answer the door!"

"Okay! Okay! Hold on for a second!" he said as loudly as he dared for his headache's comfort. He tossed the thick blanket aside and slid his naked body out of bed. Immediately he felt the shock of the cold air against his skin and rushed to pull his cotton long-johns over his bare form. Then he quickly pulled his jumpsuit bottoms on and tied the top around his waist using its sleeves. He watched Ashley disappear into the bathroom as he opened the door to his stateroom to face Geoff Hammond, then he held up a finger before Geoff could speak and reached for the C2.

"Peter here," he said into the mouthpiece. "Wait one."

"What's up?" he asked Geoff in a sleepy voice.

"We lost the Mars orbiting satellites. All of them," he replied in an urgent voice.

Peter spoke into the C2. "If this is the Command Center, I'm on the way. If not, it'll have to wait," he said into the receiver, hanging it up. "Lead," he said to Geoff, and then looked back as he left the stateroom. "Ashley, I'll be in the Command Center," he said with a loud voice while racing to keep up with Hammond. As Peter arrived in the Command Center, he immediately noticed every seat was full. Others were standing behind the consoles watching. His first thought was order.

"Who's the Watch Officer right now?" he asked crisply.

"I have the con," came the voice of Francis. Peter looked to the center Command Console, and saw Francis leaned over the seated form of Toon at the controls.

"Francis, I think we need some room in here," Peter said, not looking at anyone in particular.

"We can't do that, Peter. This is emergency manning for the Command Center. We have no extra bodies in here."

Peter then realized that the colony's Command Center had never been formally manned in an emergency before. The other events that had led up to this moment had all been managed under lesser priority protocols. Now the Command Center was full of people manning specific tasks, and everyone had a job to do.

"Who called the priority emergency?" Peter asked.

"I did," Francis said. "I wanted to wait to see if we were really stumped before waking you."

"Thanks," Peter replied.

"We lost every single orbiting satellite link save one," Francis began. "We still have the navigation set."

"Do you still have ALL of the nav set?" Peter asked in reference to the half dozen navigation satellites that pinpointed their position on Mars and in space.

"Yes. They're all responding normally. All the others are gone."

"Gone?" Peter asked shaking his head. "What do you mean gone?"

"It's as if they never existed at all. No telemetry of any kind is being broadcast."

"Is it our friend?" Peter asked quietly, referring to Covenant. "Can he do this with software; make us think we're blind?"

"No," Toon replied. "I've evaluated every single software avenue. It's real. The satellites are really gone."

"How can that be?" Peter asked. He knew that the probability of a simultaneous loss of all the Martian satellites was less than nil.

"What's the event profile?"

"Simultaneous," Francis replied.

"Give it to me in nanoseconds," Peter requested, knowing events in computer time were measured in billionths of a second and that understanding these very tiny time intervals often told their own story.

"Simultaneous loss. No measurable interval between platforms," Toon replied.

"This isn't an event of probability," Peter replied instantly.

"No. No it's not," Francis agreed. "There's very definitely a human hand behind this event."

"Are we seeing the same profile as the earth links loss? What are the similarities?" Peter asked quickly.

"No and none. That had an event driven profile. Those losses were not simultaneous and they were linked with electromagnetic events. This loss is entirely different. The links just disappeared simultaneously with no profile, no EMP, no link related circumstances."

"Toon, can you be sure that we're not being blocked out of the links with software?"

"Just to test that theory, we sent Jamie outside with a handheld signal locator that's been in my possession from day one," Toon replied. "He dialed in each satellite and there was no response. Then he dialed up the navigation platforms, and they each replied just as they are here in the Command Center. No, it's not software. The platforms are silent."

"Give me the list. What have we lost?" Peter said in a low voice.

"All camera views; weather; earth-links; all communications; and all down-links to Shturmovoi. Except for navigation, we're totally blind," Francis replied in nearly a whisper.

"Can we use the Soviet birds? Can we somehow link to them?" Peter asked.

"No way," Toon replied. "No frequencies. Even if we had them, all traffic is strongly encrypted."

"All this by a human hand and we don't know why…" Peter replied, looking to each of them for an answer which did not come. "No unusual solar activity? No meteor shower?" he asked, almost out of desperation.

"No, Peter, and even if there had been, it wouldn't have been simultaneous and it would have left a clear profile."

Peter pulled Francis aside, as well as he could in the cramped quarters, so only he could hear. "What about Covenant? Could he have done this from a communications node outside the colony – say at the launch complex?"

"First, Peter, we know of no way you can shut down a satellite from the ground. They were created to transmit until destroyed. They're built never to go silent, period; not by mistake and certainly not by design. The military guys put them together just so that this would never happen. As far as I can determine, this can't be done at all," Francis whispered almost shrilly. "Covenant isn't behind this. He can't be!" Francis said too loudly.

"How can you be so sure? Look what he did yesterday!" Peter responded.

"Then what kind of equipment does he have that we don't and what's his motive?" Francis asked bluntly.

"I don't know, Francis," Peter replied. "But I suggest that we form up a search party and comb every square centimeter of this colony and the outlying areas until he or his dead body turns up. And if I find out he's behind this, I strongly hope for the latter!"

shley left the stateroom and headed to the CELSS laboratory. She had decided it would be best to avoid whatever crisis was brewing in the Command Center. She had her own crisis brewing, this one much slower but just as ultimately dramatic. The life support system was slowly running down and it was her job to pin down the times and dates. In the meantime, it was her task to try and suggest ways to slow down the crash and, if there was a miracle to be had, to seize it and turn the clock back or stop it altogether.

The life support system at BC1 was based on a linked set of components. The integrated arrangement consisted of plants that produced oxygen and absorbed carbon dioxide, as well as huge oxygen tanks that absorbed the gas from the superoxides locked in the Martian soil and any excess oxygen produced by the plants. It also removed carbon dioxide by several methods including plant and algae systems. The problem they faced was that the organization was not yet self supporting. They depended on re-supply from earth to cause it to recycle. They needed water, oxygen, food and energy supplements. If any of the elements of the life support equation ran out before the other, the life support game was over, and they would die. While the BC1 organization was complex, efficient and highly advanced, it was still not capable of wringing out enough life from Mars without support from the earth. It was Ashley's job to find out what would end first and when – then find a way to make it last a little longer.

She entered her tiny laboratory office, which was nothing more than a cubical-sized space crammed with a desk and small computer. She sat in front of the screen and watched the computer's projections for life support system failure change after each iteration, each turn of the clock, each moment of time, each movement of the organic colony. As the colonists slept, they gained time. As the colony woke and began to move about, using more oxygen, producing more carbon dioxide, consuming more food and energy, they lost time. Ashley carefully evaluated this diurnal cycle, applying a relatively simple kind of linear regression analysis fused with a complex Fourier transformation, eking a pattern out of the background of mind boggling data. It was a trick developed a generation before by NASA's Jet Propulsion Laboratory for analysis of data in the search for extraterrestrial intelligence.

Ashley sought not only the simple patterns of the colony life cycle, but also the more subtle patterns of chaotic systemic change. She looked relentlessly for the butterfly effect in her data; a statistical concept hinting at broad patterns of change emerging from tiny nuances, buried in the chaotic background, but powerful enough to emerge later as a major, even cataclysmic change. The term 'butterfly effect' was coined when it was suggested that the simple flutter of a butterfly's wings in San Francisco could ultimately lead to a hurricane in the South Pacific. It was these nuances that Ashley labored so diligently to uncover. What had been an interesting research project just a few weeks before, now became on obsession as she worked to project how many sols they had left and perhaps discover a solution, if there was one to be found.

"Any good news to be had?" Peter's voice broke the silence, causing Ashley to jump, startled by his unexpected appearance. She looked over to the doorway of her cubicle and saw Peter leaning on its sill with his hands, peering inside at the dance of figures and lines across her monitor.

"I could ask you the same question," she replied.

"You first," he responded.

"Well, it isn't very good. Rationing must begin today; we're clearly out of options. And we'll have to drop the temperature three more degrees. And, well, I hate to say this, but we're going to have to lower the oxygen to the 2000 meter level." She was referring to the relative percentage of oxygen found at equivalent earth conditions at 2000 meters above early standard sea level conditions.

"Colder temperatures, food rationing and lowering the oxygen..." Peter began. "I realize that isolating each one of these from the other may not be so bad, but all together, their impact may be multiplied. Have you considered that?"

Ashley bit her lip. "Yes. Well – no - not really. I'm just adding up all the little beans here. You're the fearless leader. That's why we pay you the big bucks."

Peter simply sighed without expression. "Yeah, I see what you mean."

s hard as they tried to keep it secure, the secret about Covenant leaked out. Early in the man-hunt, Francis gave up and encouraged the entire colony to join in. As parts of the tale began to leak out, Peter finally called a meeting in the dining hall and told the group everything he knew. Then he made the mandatory apology for keeping secrets. The crowd broke up and began the search in earnest. They searched every room, ventilator shaft, closet, MAT and every centimeter of BC1. They even checked the MAT logs – none of them had been moved since Covenant had disappeared.

The entire manhunt had turned into something of a major entertainment event for the colony. As each corridor and segment of the colony was cleared, it was marked off on a multicolored chart in the dining hall. Ultimately, the entire colony was cleared. The only possible hiding place that remained for Covenant was the Crippen launch complex, which Covenant could have easily reached on foot.

Peter asked Bob Kerry and Suzanne Nikifortune to take a MAT out to the launch complex and check there. They had been working together nearly hand in hand for sols and had obviously developed a well-known professional relationship that had blossomed into something much more. As Peter had looked about for a pair of competent professionals to make the run out to the complex for a look about, they were standing nearby and ready. Everyone else was involved in some other task in the manhunt or on duty.

As the MAT pulled away from the main colony and headed toward the launch complex, the colony search had ended. The colonists then all gathered in the dining hall to watch further progress on the main monitors. It was unfolding like a movie in real time; a drama of life and death, of deep mystery and intrigue flickering on their screens. Unwittingly, Peter had chosen two supremely intriguing characters to carry out the last dramatic moments of the search.

If BC1 had a Most Interesting People magazine, Bob Kerry and Suzanne Nikifortune would have been on the cover. Now they raced across the Martian sands in the gathering desert twilight to corner a desperate man bent on the destruction of them all. Not until it was too late did Peter recognize his mistake. Sending two individuals whose relationship was most accurately defined as "lovers" to trap a desperate killer was the wrong move.

As he watched the MAT recede toward the launch complex on the screen, Peter looked to Brinker and saw it in his eyes. Brinker, in a non-verbal protest from across the room, popped his stogie into his mouth, leaned back against the bulkhead with folded arms and merely shook his head slowly, staring blankly at the monitor. Now it was too late. As Peter considered whether to call them back and reassess, Kerry called in his passage of the final checkpoint on US1 on his way out to the complex. Now Peter would have to watch the events unfold along with everyone else.

The people in the video control center took over the drama's imagery as they began to expertly control the camera feeding the master monitor in the dining hall. As the MAT drew near to the pad, the cameras panned to keep the approaching vehicle in view as it slowly made its way up the incline to the launch structure. At the top, the MAT came to a stop and the doors opened.

The dining hall became deathly quiet as every eye strained to watch the details and hear any voice transmissions from the couple who had just driven into harms way. Not a word was spoken at the colony or from the pad as Kerry and Suzanne stepped slowly out of the MAT onto the complex surface. The cameras zoomed onto Kerry as his helmeted head scanned the pad. The setting sun glinted off the gold visor into the camera lens in a brilliant, four pointed star reflected off of his slowly rotating helmet. It lent an even more surrealistic illusion to the manhunt than before – adding a dramatic, visual flare to the scene at the complex, enacted before them in real time.

Kerry's arm motioned to Suzanne with a sweep and she walked carefully in his direction. They came together slowly. When they met, everyone watched as Kerry gripped her arms gently and pulled her slowly toward him until their visors met. It looked for all the world like a kiss though the visors, but most understood that Kerry was communicating his commands by having her read his lips so as not to tip off their presence by a radio transmission. Still, the image of the forced embraced lent to the incredible excitement of the moment and fed the tension that was building second by second.

Peter realized that mistake or not, he had no choice now but to send in the cavalry. He looked toward Brinker who was already staring at him with laser eyes, and simply lifted two fingers into the air then pointed at the monitor. Brinker needed no more instruction as he collared Hiraldo and thrust her out the door of the dining hall ahead of him. Reinforcements were on the way. But radio silence would prevent Kerry and Suzanne from knowing that until they showed up on the pad.

Everyone watched in lip-biting apprehension as Kerry and Suzanne moved slowly toward the door of the only man-rated, pressurized structure at the complex. If Covenant were hiding out, it would have to be in there.

Incredibly, the front door to the complex was open; yet another serious violation of protocol. Kerry had no way of knowing of the previous wild activity at the complex just prior to the last tragic launch. His movements seemed to assume that the opened door indicated to him that Covenant was probably inside. Just as insane as a screen door on a submarine, no one in space exploration ever left doors swinging wide open, ever. An open door could only mean something most unusual was happening or had happened.

The images on the monitors showed Kerry locate two blunt objects, resembling pipe segments, for self defense, and hand one to Suzanne. They moved to both sides of the open door. Covenant could easily kill them just by puncturing a tiny hole in their pressure suits. As the colonists watched the soundless drama unfold, everyone seemed to hold their collective breaths as they inched forward in their seats.

Kerry stood with his back to the open hatch, then quickly and unexpectedly stepped inside ahead of Suzanne, his pipe held in front of him like a sword. Suzanne slowly and deliberately turned her back to the door as she watched the area behind them. Slowly she backed into the open space and disappeared inside, closing the door behind her.

The monitor shifted to a new camera inside the complex itself. It slowly panned and focused on the pair standing inside. Kerry and Suzanne began to methodically investigate every place a man could hide.

Meanwhile, another image appeared on their screen, imposed at the monitor's bottom right corner. It was the view of Brinker's MAT heading out to the complex, sending up a trail of dust as he raced at top speed toward Kerry and Suzanne. This image caused a stir of voices, but they quickly subsided as every eye returned to the search inside the complex.

As the pair began to eliminate closets and the single toilet, they worked back around to the airlock from which they had entered. Kerry scribbled a note to Suzanne on his wrist pad and she nodded. Slowly she closed the inner door to the airlock as Kerry's fingers raced over the control panel. They were pressurizing the space.

As the air began to rush into the modular room, the colonists could see pieces of paper and other items begin to blow around in the air currents. With this, the colonists began to relax and murmur among themselves. A pressurized space meant security in their minds and it signified that the search for Covenant had ended without unpleasantness.

They watched as Kerry began to scribble more notes to Suzanne and she nodded again. In a minute more, Kerry began to remove his helmet and Suzanne followed. The moment both helmets were off and securely on a table, Kerry ended the radio silence.

"Complex secure," he said tersely. As he said this, Suzanne disappeared from the view of the camera. One second later, the picture was lost and the screen went blank.

Every colonist present gasped together. They stood watching the blank monitor, frozen in time. The smaller image of Brinker approaching the complex showed his vehicle slowing as he reached the pad. The console director saw that he had lost the view from inside the complex and reversed the shots, moving the blank picture to the smaller screen and enlarging the image of Brinker's MAT now stopped just outside the airlock.

The doors popped open the moment the vehicle stopped. It was obvious that Brinker had not even pressurized it for the drive over. He and his Marine leapt out immediately. A voice crackled over the communications circuit, "Video inside lost. Proceed with caution."

Brinker looked directly into the camera on the pad as it zoomed in on his helmet. He simply nodded and made a cutting motion across his throat, which ended any more radio broadcasts.

The camera panned back again, showing Brinker and Hiraldo at the airlock door, repeating the same stance as Kerry and Suzanne had just minutes before, their backs to either side of the now closed door. Hiraldo attached wires to the control panel and then she made a few hand signals to Brinker, who gently opened the outer hatch to the airlock. The camera views showed him disappear inside slowly, Hiraldo backing him up.

The view switched to a camera in the tiny airlock itself, showing Brinker's helmeted head slowly peer inside the pressurized room. Then he turned and looked directly at the camera which panned back as far as it could. Still, the airlock was so small, it only showed his face through his helmet visor.

"It looks to me like we got a man down inside," he said slowly.

"Do you need assistance? Do you need assistance?" the Command Center watch officer asked in a near shout.

"No," Brinker said, shaking his head slowly, blinking into the camera. The entire colony looked on in a stunned hush.

"Can you assist him?" the watch officer pressed.

"No," Brinker replied, turning the valves on high, which immediately re-pressurized the inner vestibule to the airlock.

In the half minute it took to pressurize the vestibule, Brinker began to remove his helmet before the view of every colonist. The sound of the in-rushing air drowned out all possibility of communicating, the tension building to unbearable levels in seconds. The silence of the moment was magnified by the sound of the rushing air; the seconds built into a wave of slow moving time that seemed to go on and on.

As soon as it was safe, Brinker took his helmet off with a hiss, then popped a worn stogie into his mouth and looked into the camera.

"From what I can see from this angle, sir, the man don't need my help. It looks like he's doing just fine for himself."

He moved his head slightly so the camera could see inside the inner room. Suzanne's bare shoulder appeared by the glass, then her smiling face as she draped a black cloth over the window.

"Request permission to light up," Brinker asked briskly.

"Denied," the watch officer replied curtly as the colonists exploded into cheers.

It was as if Kerry and Suzanne's antics had somehow displaced the worry over the lost satellite links and a missing homicidal lunatic. To Peter, their mood was astonishingly upbeat, as though the actions of lovers became the action of heroes. They would live their lives fully regardless of the deadly circumstances that unfolded around them. It was the odd right mix; totally off-beat and nearly bizarre, but it was precisely what everyone needed at exactly the right moment.

That evening after dinner, the rationing and cutbacks were announced. But there was no morose response and absolutely no bickering or complaining. They all knew this was coming and after a few jokes about doubling up on blankets and long johns, a movie re-run was announced and most people hung around to watch it.

Later that evening, when things were back to normal and most had gone off to sleep, Peter and Francis sat alone at the Command Center Watch Officer's station.

"So now what?" Peter asked. "No views, no weather, no communications off planet and no Covenant. I would ask whether it could get worse, but…"

"Don't," Francis immediately replied. "Don't."

"How can a dangerous man just disappear on a planet where there's simply no where to go?" Peter pressed. "And what's he up to? What the hell is going on here? None of this makes sense any more. At least before I understood it…"

"So many questions, so little time." Francis mused, his fingers pointlessly dancing over the controls of his satellite weather station, now lying dead and useless before him.

Fyodor Stepanovich Kirov was in a tight spot – wedged unyieldingly beyond anything his claustrophobic mind wanted to accept. He lay partially on his side in a Shturmovoi ventilation duct just above and outside of Colonel Zoya Dimitriov's quarters. He wanted to scream and thrash about – anything to loosen the shaft's tightening grip on his body – but he bit his lip to prevent even a quiet moan from escaping. He knew that if he were caught, it would be his last hour of life. There were no trials at Shturmovoi. Kirov knew the only hope he had to avoid detection by those in the room below was to relax. To accomplish this when he wanted nothing more than to escape his thin metal prison was monumentally difficult. But he forced his mind elsewhere – to the life support system that was pumping its foul smell all about his body and down into Dimitriov's space below.

The first sense of Shturmovoi was, in fact, its odor. It seemed to attack, then dominate the senses as the single most impressionable sensation as one entered her corridors. Unlike BC1 with its pleasant odor of living plants and the primary thrust of its design centered around human habitability, Shturmovoi was compellingly machinelike. As a visitor removed their helmet upon entering the Soviet base, its thick, dank odor settled around them like a cold, acrid fog. The atmospheric interchange units relied on filters, which had to be exchanged with replacements from earth. They were relatively inefficient to begin with, but with the long periods between re-supply, the filters allowed the collective scents of the community to blend into a composite, distinctly disagreeable redolence that permeated and saturated everything. Like the differences in their composite philosophies, BC1 smelled of life and Shturmovoi of machines.

The difference in design philosophy had distinct labels. BC1 relied on living systems for their life support called a bioregenerative system. The Soviets relied on a process called physiochemical.

The debate between the advocates of bioregenerative and physiochemical life support systems had raged on in both countries for nearly a century before the first human set foot on Mars. The physiochemical ilk was made up of the engineering ranks and carried their philosophy into the contest. They espoused their trained beliefs that any life support system could be engineered by brute force alone; the molecules of creation could be arranged and rearranged by machines to support existence. The life scientists believed and designed their arrangements around living systems. They unabashedly taught that living systems were the very products that had held the earth in eons of elastic balance, hence they were much more adept at providing a malleable, accommodating, balanced environment suitable for life than were their mechanical counterparts.

The winners of the debate in both countries were created out of the prevailing social climate. In the RSE, the engineers, who were already revered, won a clear victory. In the United States, a more cultivated discipline won out; a marriage between the engineering and biological sciences had already occurred, and they called it bioengineering.

The bioengineers had proved their worth early in the design game. Long before the systems were actually required for spaceflight, the bioengineering community had become involved in the planning, building systems that could not only do the job, but also provide a pleasant environment besides. They quickly proved the value of capturing and controlling a system using the entire history of life on earth to reinforce it.

Choosing the right path was a critical decision for both countries. Since collecting all the data necessary to design a particular system required a minimum of 20 years of intensive research. The entire facility was designed around the life support requirements. To change designs in mid stream would be virtually impossible. The battle for advanced life support was, in fact, won with the initial decision and choice, and there could be no turning back.

Yet, one only had to sniff the air in the American and Soviet bases to know who had made the right choice. And most ironically, the primary reason the Soviets had chosen the physiochemical process over the biological was because of its "inherit stability". This so-called stability proved to be grossly exaggerated. In fact, once the biological systems had been properly designed, their stability was built into the genetics of the organisms themselves. While the American system operated virtually without intervention, the Soviet's cumbersome, complex machinery was constantly breaking down and required a vast logistics system just to keep it working.

With these thoughts, Kirov managed to relax and slowly bend his legs and torso enough to break free from his trap, inching another meter and a half forward. Finally, through a vent, he could barely hear Dimitriov's voice and see the back of her head as she spoke. She had convened a special meeting of her General Staff, also known as the Collegium, and rumor had it that she was about to reveal a plan to contact the Americans, at long last.

Although he could not see most of the others in the room with her, Kirov knew their voices well. With Dimitriov was her deputy, the ever-withdrawn Hero of the Motherland, Major Validimir Dybenko who had all the leadership attributes of a lap dog.

From Kirov's precarious perch in the vent, he recognized the more petulant voice of Colonel Sergi Polevikov, the mean-spirited, vicious Captain of the General Staff. Although his rank was equal with Dimitriov, there was never any question of authority. Dimitriov was in control in every sense of the word, both by political and military authority, and Polevikov was not overtly stupid enough to challenger her.

Alongside Polevikov sat his deputy Mikhail Klimov, a certified yes-man who's only stated professional goal was to be more brutal and sadistic than his master. In addition to the General Staff was Leonid Kravchenko, called the Jailer of Shturmovoi, because it was often his task to find places to keep prisoners locked up whenever they crossed Dimitriov. Also in the room was Viktor Nikolayevich, the nasty, perverted, dishonest accountant that the State had seen fit to put in charge of the treasury. Nikolayevich had all the personal morals and hygiene of a gutter rat and did not care who knew it. And finally, just alongside Dimitriov's desk, sat Valentin Anatoliy, a man who was a personal friend of Kirov; a man of great integrity and honesty who had for some unknown reason been hand picked by Dimitriov to be a member of her inner sanctum.

Polevikov's arrogant voice grated on Kirov's nerves, as the man genuflected to Dimitriov with the turn of each sadistic phrase. The Captain of the General Staff could not seem to help but drag some hapless victim into his conversation and slay him before anyone in range of hearing. As the meeting opened, Polevikov began berating the scientific staff, which sent chills down Kirov's spine.

"They are idiots. They are incompetent. They are disloyal. They are conspirators. They will not hear of your plan much less cooperate with it," he sneered.

Dimitriov, ever the master of the pause, waited for the time to assert her leadership, then responded, "How can they know of my plan, Comrade Deputy? How do you even know the subject of this meeting? I have not told any of you. How can you know this in advance?" Dimitriov knew well how to keep her charges at bay, even if their conversations were always wrapped in thinly veiled threats.

There was another moment of silence as Polevikov shifted rigidly in his seat. "All we know are rumors among ourselves, of course," he responded.

"Go on," she pressed.

"Not even really rumors, Colonel Dimitriov," he said obviously feigning confidence, "but we have all speculated together that we would perhaps discuss your plans to make contact with the Americans." It was clear that Polevikov would not hesitate to pull everyone else into Dimitriov's trap if he had to, as he was certain that there was not an individual in the room who was man enough to contradict him.

Dimitriov ignored him as though he were not there. "I have indeed assembled you to tell you of my plans to contact the Americans," she began.

This caused Kirov to lean closer to the vent's opening and strain to hear more. Kirov had himself attempted to contact BC1 twice and had received no response. It seemed his carefully crafted plan had failed altogether.

From his new position he could look over Polevikov's thinning grey brow and see into his pensive, black stare which caused an involuntary shudder to convulse thorough his body. It was at that moment that

Kirov felt at home here, tightly shut up in this vent, safe and enclosed in a metal cocoon away from the sight or knowledge of this brutal man. For a minute, any trace of claustrophobia mercifully fled away.

"And Colonel Polevikov, since you have such a well-developed sense of precognition, I am going to put you in charge of the delegation," Dimitriov said without a trace of flippancy, as she slowly paced back and forth behind her desk.

"I would be honored, Comrade…"

"Shut up, Colonel, until I am finished," she said staring at the wall over his head.

Polevikov's eyes flashed and seethed with anger. This he could not hide, but he said nothing; he dared not speak.

"We will deliver a delegation of death to the Americans," Dimitriov said slowly, with a smirk. "We will draw them into a trap and will destroy them. Otherwise, we will not be able to survive here without re-supply from earth. It is either their deaths or ours. We will capture their base and we will kill them all by stealth and by surprise. It is not a matter of enmity, or of historic, idealistic differences. It is a matter of their survival or ours. We are simply fighting to see who will draw the last breath of life before it is extinguished for us all."

Kirov's body stiffened in the vent. He found himself hyperventilating and dizzy. "Is she insane?" he thought. "Has she lost her mind? What kind of savagery is she plotting? Did she not know that the best way to assure their survival was cooperation together, not by waging war?" Kirov could barley contain his emotions as he shut his eyes tightly against the dizziness engulfing his mind.

Dimitriov lit up another cigarette and turned to face the group. "Our engineers did not have the foresight to construct a life support system that had the capacity to evolve into permanent independence. The American system is so designed and with the proper care and feeding, it does not need a constant resupply from a planet that may or may not exist any longer. Our system was designed to be replenished or it will cease to function. Their system is biologically based and can exist as long as it is supplied simple nutrients - not idiotic filters, not complicated chemicals and not endless bags and parcels of replacement parts.

"We will strike them, we will kill them and we will live. They have created a system which we need to survive and we will seize it by force. The Americans are too naive and stupid to understand what is at stake here. They believe we can share our resources and all live together in harmony. They are such fools."

Dimitriov returned to her seat behind her desk and sat down. She looked to the Collegium as they regarded one another in stony silence. Just above her, Kirov lay trembling, his eyes closed against the vertigo that engulfed him. In the effort to control his emotions and in fighting against the cloud of claustrophobia that began again to close in around him, he began to perspire. Unknown to him, a bead of sweat dropped off his forehead, and in a single, agonizingly slow moment, it fell through the vent and dripped onto a single paper sitting before Dimitriov. The droplet rested on a rare, hand-written paper document drawn in red ink, and it pooled from crystal clear to blood red before Dimitriov's eyes, just as she began to reveal her plans to slaughter the Americans.

It came without notice. The radio receiver in the Command Center sprang to life and a heavily accented voice began calling for BC1's attention.

"This is the RSE Base Shturmovoi, calling the American base BC1; do you read me? Over."

It was with that fateful call that all their lives changed suddenly and without warning. It was as if they knew that a door had slammed shut, another one had opened and nothing would ever be the same again.

Fabian Gorteau sat beside Geoff Hammonds on the console. First, they exchanged horrified glances, then Gorteau's hand shot toward the microphone switch.

"This is BC1. Go ahead, Shturmovoi," he said with a strong voice.

There was a moment of silence on the other end as Hammond's right hand sprang toward another switch as he summoned Peter.

"We are happy to hear that you are alive and well," the heavily accented voice replied from the speaker. "We wish to make contact with your leadership at the earliest opportunity."

Gorteau's eyes shot about, his brain working at its' capacity. Then he replied, "Yes, yes, of course. Please relay your permanent contact frequency and backups," he asked, almost desperately.

The Shturmovoi operator did so after a short pause and left a long string of numbers, which Gorteau dutifully copied to his hand-held terminal. At the end of the Soviet transmission, Gorteau replied with the BC1 frequencies and backups. About that time, Peter came rushing into the control room followed by Francis, Toon and Ashley.

Gorteau saw him enter out of the corner of his eye and held his hand up. "Our leadership is unavailable at the moment," Gorteau said matter-of-factly as Peter stood inches from his chair. "Please give us a time for the transmission later today."

Peter silently nodded, wordlessly understanding Gorteau's motive for the lie. He gave the old physicist an understanding smile.

There was a protracted pause at the other end, then a voice stated, "We are prepared to wait until your leadership can be summoned."

Peter whispered something into Gorteau's ear. He nodded, and then said, "Our leadership is not in the facility at the moment. An immediate exchange is not possible."

There was another long pause, and then they replied, "Very well. We will be prepared to communicate in two hours hence."

Peter shook his head vigorously and held up four fingers at Gorteau.

"Four hours."

Long pause.

"Three hours," the Soviet voice responded.

Peter nodded, unable to suppress a smirk at the nearly instinctual unfolding of such simplistic international negotiations.

"Three hours," Gorteau responded as the carrier signal went immediately to zero.

"How?" Peter asked Hammonds.

"How what?"

"I thought all satellite communications were lost," Peter said.

"This signal is from a Soviet bird, not one of ours."

"Already it's started," Peter said as Gorteau keyed the microphone off.

"Yes," Gorteau replied. "Yes. And I was afraid of that."

"Of what?" Ashley asked. "What's started?"

"The conflict," Peter replied.

Ashley still looked stumped.

"XX and XY," Gorteau responded, smiling at Ashley. "When I was a very young man at the university, there was an old saying – XX and XY. It meant that the male brain and the female brain are wired much differently. The male brain is wired to instinctively understand competition and the female brain is wired to instinctively understand nurturing. Here we are witnessing the underlying and unspoken competition."

"Between leadership?" Francis asked.

"Precisely," Gorteau responded with a nod from Peter.

"Then how do you explain that their leader is a woman?" Francis asked.

"There goes your XX and XY…" Ashley replied smugly.

"I was not referring to the source of the conflict. I was referring to the element of innate understanding," Gorteau began in his best professorial voice, always a prelude to a lecture.

Peter respectfully held his hand up. "Later, Fabian; later." Then he looked at Ashley who was apparently in one of her moods. She simply nodded ascent with her eyes.

"The conflict, Fabian. Why the conflict?" Peter asked.

"You heard it for yourself," Francis said. "Fabian, that was brilliant," he added.

Gorteau just nodded.

"What was brilliant?" Ashley asked looking as confused as Hammonds who sat beside Gorteau.

"Fabian directed the conversation to root out a source of competition and belligerence. They were not prepared for the test and flunked it," Francis replied. "They tipped their hand," he responded as Gorteau nodded.

"And you dreamed all that up in two seconds?" Ashley asked, truly astonished. "Both of you?"

"Let us stay focused," Gorteau said, sidestepping what might have passed for a compliment. "It was very easy, actually. It's not the first direct communication we have had from them and the voice was obviously not Kirov's."

"What conflict, Peter? What do you mean?" Ashley asked again, clearly irritated.

"I don't know," he replied quietly, accompanied by a hard stare.

"Then how do you know there is one?" she asked, now exasperated. "If we dream one up and they dream one up, then we really are going to have one."

"No," Gorteau replied. "Kirov indicated there may be a problem in his message. And I challenged them in my conversation to a conflict and they responded to it with a challenge."

"You mean the schedule for the broadcast?" Ashley asked.

"Yes."

"Forgive my lack of paranoia here," Ashley responded, "but have you ever considered that they may have something else scheduled at that time?"

"No," Peter and Francis replied in the same moment.

"Fabian did the right thing," Peter responded.

"I'm not challenging what Fabian did," Ashley replied, "but I am challenging the conclusion."

"What is the true measure of the probability? That is the question we must accurately assess." Gorteau continued, "Ashley has already labeled her measure of probability. But to all of us, it is still a question of probabilities."

"Can you please restate that clearly for the rest of us, Fabian. I'm sorry but I didn't do so well in my quantum physics class," Ashley said bitingly.

Gorteau's smile disarmed her. "But of course," he replied. "We saw what appeared to be a developing contest that I deliberately set up at the beginning of the broadcast. I did so to investigate their motives as best I could over such distances. There were but a few possible outcomes, and theirs measured high on the conflict probability scale."

Francis nodded, "Yeah. What he just said."

Ashley could not avoid a smirk. "XX and XY, indeed…"

"Ok, so what is your assessment?" Peter asked Gorteau.

"Inevitable conflict, it would seem," Gorteau replied bluntly.

"Oh, come on, Fabian, please," Ashley replied, truly beyond her patience. "You deliberately prompt a Soviet to haggle over time and you interpret that as a conflict between nations?"

"With all the evidence I have at my fingertips, it remains at the highest measure of probability," he replied staring into space. "Of course, there are other probabilities, but they do not rank as high."

"Fabian, please, you can't quantify a hunch like that," Ashley

"*Au contraire,*" he replied. "All science is the systematic enumeration of hunches. It is the ensuing investigations that support or deny the argument."

"So now we engage in conflict based on our hunches?" she asked.

"No. But we must protect our survival based on them," Francis replied. "Look, Ashley, we're only suspicious. That doesn't mean we're prepared to do anything about it."

Peter had remained thoughtful while listening to the exchange, then added, "And I would bet all my Martian sand dunes that they're going to have a conflict over resources."

The rest of them just looked on in silence as Peter left the statement hang in the air.

"From what we know of Shturmovoi, they have less of a chance of surviving the coming winter than we do. They may have the power issue licked, but their life support and consumables are much more dependent on resupply. Our schedule had a Soviet resupply craft departing a week and a half after the blackout, which can only mean they can't make it much beyond the coming winter."

"But don't you see? That's precisely why they want a meeting; to see if we all can share resources," Ashley nearly pleaded. "So why can't we all just share what we have so that we all can live? They have abundant energy and we have better life support."

Francis looked down at his feet. "I wish to God it were that easy," he said quietly.

"Let us caucus on our strategy," Gorteau replied. "We have less than three hours remaining."

In the ensuing three hours, there was much argument and debate. The time passed quickly, and finally, the call came, four minutes early.

"BC1, this is Shturmovoi. Do you read?" said the voice from the radio speaker.

"Go ahead, Shturmovoi," Gorteau replied.

"I am putting our Chief of Staff on the line for your Director," the voice said. Peter nodded and sat beside Gorteau.

"Dr. Lipton, this is Colonel Dimitriov."

Peter looked to Gorteau silently, then back to the microphone. "Dr. Lipton has died," he said evenly. "I'm Peter Traynor, the Colony's new Director."

Without pause, Dimitriov replied. "We must do business, Dr. Traynor. Our survival depends on it, and every minute counts."

"Why have you been in radio silence since the crisis began?" Peter asked bluntly and without hesitation.

"We have been assessing our situation, as you have been," she replied with barely a pause. "And now we must come together to survive."

"What do you suggest?" he asked.

"A meeting."

Peter looked genuinely surprised. This he did not expect.

Meeting over such a distance would be nearly impossible. It was 2065 kilometers away across some of the most perilous Martian regions and the RSE vehicle was barely capable of making but half the distance in even the best of circumstances. She could not possibly have meant a physical meeting, he reasoned, but must be referring to a videoconference.

"A virtual meeting can be arranged if your satellites can handle the frequency and bandwidth," he replied logically.

"I do not mean a meeting by video, but one on one. You must send an emissary with the credentials and authority to negotiate," she said in a voice that sent chills down his spine.

Peter looked to Gorteau with astonishment. "We don't have the means to send an emissary," he replied truthfully. In his mind, he seriously pondered the deepest meaning of the term 'negotiate'.

"We have worked the plan carefully," she replied instantly. "It is imminently possible."

"What would a personal meeting solve that a virtual meeting cannot, Ms. Dimitriov?"

"It is Colonel, Dr. Traynor. And I can assure you that since the dawn of civilization, a personal meeting of national ambassadors has been essential."

Peter paused. "I'll have to consult my professional staff before I can commit to this," he said guardedly. "I do not take risks like this lightly."

"There is little risk," Dimitriov pressed. "We plan to meet your emissary on the southern plains of *Amazonis* at a predetermined coordinate. You will be able to leave your vehicle and return to Shturmovoi in ours. We will return your ambassador to your vehicle after the discussions with enough fuel for the return trip back to your base. You see, it is easy. It is safe. It is, in fact, essential that we meet face to face."

Peter did not reply as he thought about the plan, a growing uneasiness building inside of him.

"We have no time for delay," she snapped, as if to her own subordinates, breaking the silence.

Peter instantly caught her tone and his anger flared. But he checked his voice just as he spoke and did not betray his feelings. The he said, "I understand, Colonel. That is why you must send an emissary to BC1. If your vehicles are more capable, it just makes mores sense," Peter responded, thinking on the fly.

Silence followed his question. The thin sound of interplanetary static cut through the air as they waited.

Finally Dimitriov's voice returned. "Dr. Traynor, please understand the safety of this journey is best assured by your emissary making the trip to meet our vehicle. Safety is paramount for your personnel and ours. If you will evaluate the life support and loading you will see that two persons cannot possibly return to BC1 in your smaller vehicle from anywhere near the halfway point. Therefore, only the trip to Shturmovoi is possible under the circumstances. We have already evaluated that contingency. Indeed it was our first option to come and meet you at your base."

"I'll get back to you tomorrow morning at 8:00 AM. Good evening, Colonel," he replied as Gorteau pulled the switch and cut the transmission.

"Excellent, Peter, excellent!" Gorteau said.

"I've dealt with used car salesmen before," he replied. "Now I need time to think."

he deliberations over whether BC1 would send someone were fierce and filled with strong emotions. In the end, it was decided in a very close debate. Francis argued furiously that no one should be sent as it was obviously a trap. He reasoned that since they were setting up for war, any damage inflicted to BC1 or Shturmovoi would doom that colony and probably the other as well. Ashley argued that unless someone was sent, every human on Mars would surely perish. The argument was so close, in fact, it was agreed on the weight of Gorteau's logic that to avoid dangerous colony schisms, the decision would be left up to Peter as the final authority and one who was ultimately responsible for the welfare of the colony.

Peter weighed the arguments carefully one against another. Then he decided. Someone would have to go. Even if they were lost during the mission, the risk of survival was too great and the possibility of war was ultimately weighed on too many hunches. In the final analysis, the known factors would have to outweigh the unknowns. They knew they were probably all going to die without help, however, and they only suspected a trap. The reality of mass death won over the illusive fear of conflict and war and the risk to a single individual.

Peter announced that the emissary would be selected the next sol and preparations for the journey began immediately.

It was Leonid Kravchenko who personally pulled Kirov from the vent, and he did so with such violence that the edge of the metal vent sliced deeply into Kirov's arm. As Kravchenko roughly tossed Kirov across the conference table, his wounded arm smeared blood over the desktop. Kirov was in near shock from fear at being discovered, but upon being slammed down onto his back across the tabletop, he felt the pain in his arm for the first time. As soon as his fingers touched the warm, sticky blood he knew that the crimson swath on the tabletop came from him. As he attempted to sit up, Kravehenok struck him with the back of his balled fist across his face and Kirov fell back again.

"Enough," Colonel Dimitrov barked to Kravehenok, as if to a dog. Then with slow deliberation, she approached Kirov.

His fingers still grasped the deep wound, instinctively, to stop the bleeding, even though he was about to loose consciousness. He fought the darkness and struggled to focus on the dreadful face of Dimitrov staring down at him. He witnessed her visage, her thin lips and derisive expression.

"Just as I suspected," she said. "I knew you were a traitor all along, you and your staff. My worst concerns are justified. Now, all of you must pay the most severe penalty for your actions, in a most deliberate way..."

These were the last words Kirov heard before the merciful blackness shielded his mind and consumed his fear altogether.

fter an immeasurable passage of time, Kirov's first thought was that he had died and slipped into a silent, dark and frozen hell. There was not a cell in his body that did not ache. The cold was so deep and overwhelming, he was beyond even shivering. He was afraid to open his eyes for fear that he would see the snarling face of Kravchenko peering down over his broken and bleeding form, ready again to crush his face and body with repeated blows. But there was complete silence here in this cold, and quiet anguish covered him like a smothering blanket.

He tried to open a swollen eye. Only blackness. He attempted to open the other. Utter darkness. Then he forcefully tried to open both eyes into the ocean of empty night. His frostbitten fingers reached up to his face and he felt a sheen of semi-dried blood caked over swollen eyes and matted in his hair.

In horror he suspected the brutal Kravchenko had blinded him. Reflexively he sat up in an onrushing wave of panic and vertigo. As he did, his head struck a barrier just above him and he fell back, consumed by even more pain. With both arms he painfully reached his hands to his right and left and his pulsing fingers were met with a cold metal barrier.

They had buried him alive in a metal box, he concluded. They had buried him alive! He was overcome by a wave of terror and crushing claustrophobia whose net effect was whole, systemic shock. Just as he marshaled enough strength to scream, Kirov's barely functioning mind was sucked back into a vortex of absolute unconsciousness, surrounded by the hideous laugh of Kravchenko from the darkness just outside his box.

Peter and Francis met alone in a tiny laboratory adjacent to the MAT hangar. They literally stuffed themselves between equipment and carts as Francis closed the door.

"So who is it you have in mind for the trip?" Peter asked, with some unreserved skepticism, reacting to Francis' urgent request for a meeting. After all, he had led the furious debate against the plan to begin with.

"There is only one resume' in this colony that fits the bill for this assignment," Francis replied confidently.

Peter allowed the moment of dramatic silence to close without interrupting. He just blinked to show his impatience.

"Suzanne Nikifortune," Francis said flatly.

"Forget it!" Peter replied abruptly, his voice hardened with obvious skepticism, his eyes shifting to those outside the MAT hangar who were wondering about the purpose of this private meeting and information lockout.

"She's the only colonist who speaks fluent Russian. Her family is Slavic; it's her second language if not her first," Francis persisted.

"How do you know this?"

"I ran a detailed profile of every colonist last night," Francis confessed.

"Why?"

Francis eyed him back. His eyes shifted to those looking in from outside, then back to Peter. "I was trying to understand the Covenant problem and whether there may be a link," he said.

"And who are your suspects?" Peter asked with contempt in an uncharacteristically hard voice.

"Everyone, anyone...." Francis replied, not shifting his eyes away from Peter, matching his tone.

"Why Suzanne?" Peter continued. "We both know Gorteau has a working knowledge of the language. And if she's so genetically connected, then why does the problem not extend deeper? Why isn't she a prime suspect?"

"At least three good reasons... First: Suzanne has a deep knowledge of the language and will hear things anyone but an accomplished linguist would never hear. Two: they won't know this and may let information slip as they talk between one another. And three: frankly, we can afford to lose an Administrative Assistant, however capable, but NOT our best physicist!"

Peter's eyes flashed into an instant, unhidden anger.

"Wait," Francis said. "Before you speak, think about it. We – all of us – are in a contest for our lives. We can't afford to make a mistake about even the smallest of issues, this one included. If you're willing to give up your own life for the others, then as our leader, you must make judgments for the good of all, even if those judgments are sacrificial. Besides, once you decided someone had to go, you offered up a possible sacrifice for us all. And since no one person is more or less important than the other, ANY name I would suggest should be of equal value to the rest."

"Everyone has value," Peter said sharply, uncertain of his next response.

"Yes. Everyone has infinite value," Francis agreed. "But not everyone carries around the same bag of tools. Peter, this isn't about what Suzanne doesn't have, but what she does have; and that would be counted as a great deal more than Gorteau's insufficient abilities on this point. We need Suzanne's keen ear and keen eyes there. Likewise, we need Gorteau's brains working overtime right here at BC1."

Peter squinted his eyes and turned away from Francis to think. He knew that Francis was right about it all. There was no flaw to his reasoning. "I guess you're right," he replied, feeling the awesome, crushing weight of leadership.

But he would have to face her lover alone. Peter was never concerned about Suzanne's reaction to the plan, but Kerry would be a different matter. Strategically, in order to hold the whole fragile mess together, he would have to be told first.

inutes later, Peter invited Kerry into his office and closed the door while Francis waited outside. He explained the plan as forthrightly and as quickly as he could to prevent Kerry from interrupting. Kerry allowed a full two seconds of dead time to elapse after Peter had finished, his eyes boring into Peter's. Neither of the men backed down. Finally Kerry spoke in that steady, strong voice each man knows from all others.

This was going to be the hill to die on.

"Over my dead body, Traynor! Now you come up with another idea, then we'll see. But NOT this one! You're totally insane if you think for one minute I'm going to stand by while you send her alone over two thousand kilometers across uncharted deserts no human has ever crossed before in a vehicle that's not even designed for the trip. If ANYTHING at all happens to that vehicle, she's DEAD! No! Forget it! You've completely lost your mind."

Peter allowed another two seconds to pass, then replied into Kerry's unblinking stare.

"I know the risks, Bob. But I also know the effort will…"

"Effort? You think of this as an "effort"? No, it's not an effort, or an experiment, or a research study – it's suicide. I'll go; send me! But not her!"

Peter looked away with compassion as Kerry's face reddened.

"Bob. You're not qualified for this…" Peter began.

"The hell I'm not!" he more spat than responded.

"Do NOT interrupt me again, Bob," Peter ordered, looking back in anger. "Unless you're prepared to take my position by force, this is the way it's going to be. Now I appreciate your love for her and what that means here, but unless we're especially creative and take big risks, we're all going to die on this desert. If this were the Donner party on the slopes of the Sierras, that would be one thing. There would come a time when another group of humans would come along and discover the bodies of the unfortunate explorers. But as far as anyone knows, we're the only surviving humans remaining anywhere. That places our acceptable risk-taking at somewhere near the top of the charts.

"Now, I'm ordering you to back off. Don't try to talk her out of this. Don't get in the way. Don't make trouble in the colony. Get a grip on your anger by directing it toward survival scenarios. If you make trouble for us on this venture, I swear I'll toss your arrogant pilot's butt out the airlock in your skivvies."

Kerry responded with force. "I'll just bet we wouldn't be considering this option if it were Ashley we were talking about," he said, scoring a definitive blow.

Peter turned his back on him and looked at the wall. It was more of an act to keep Kerry from seeing the real pain in his eyes than an unspoken power-play.

"Screw you..." Kerry said, walking out and slamming the door behind him.

A moment later a voice spoke behind Peter. "I guess that could've gone better," Francis said softly.

"Leave me alone for a minute, please" Peter responded, touching his forehead against the wall in silence and closing his eyes.

Bob Kerry disappeared somewhere in the colony. Three hours after the confrontation with him, Peter and Francis called Suzanne to the conference room and explained the issue as clearly as they could, ultimately giving her the option to make the trip or not. She instantly agreed in an extraordinarily even manner, which surprised Peter.

"Don't you even want to think this over?" Peter asked. "Why don't you sleep on it and we can discuss it first thing tomorrow."

"No need. I've already have given it a lot of thought."

"How?" Francis asked.

"Bob and I discussed it at length. He wasn't too keen on it, but I wouldn't be either if it were him going. Yet, we also agreed that I could decide. And we also agreed that it was quite important to all of us. So I'll do it."

Peter nodded slowly, feeling a surge of emotions he found hard to place. In the end, if they survived at all, the real heroes were to be Suzanne, Bob and the rest of the colony who viewed personal sacrifice for one another as a routine event. It was a stunning, overwhelming and powerful force.

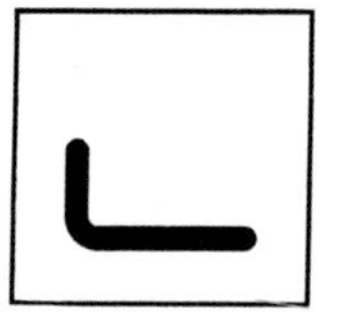

ate that night, somewhere in the deeper, less traveled steel paths of the colony, far back in the silver-lined, dark corridors, Bob Kerry and Suzanne Nikifortune met all alone. They closed themselves into a storage closet simply titled, "AKA 432". By the light of a single luminescent strip, they stood and faced one another in the quiet, near darkness.

After long minutes of silence, as their cold breath curled around them in the unnatural light of the green strip, Suzanne spoke first, looking down and away from the man who she knew loved her more than his own life.

"Bob, I'm sorry," she spoke softly. "I hope you'll forgive me for this."

"No need… I know you feel you have to go and do this. I just don't want to lose you. Ever," he said truthfully. "That's all. I just still can't believe it's you who has to do this. Why not me? Why not one of the others?"

She looked into his eyes, framed by his golden hair, and brows knit together in worry. With a confident smile, she pushed his boyish locks out of his eyes with her gloved fingers. She then began to speak in fluent, unaccented, flawless Russian.

"What did you just say?" he asked, both surprised and amazed.

"You'll never lose me, ever. You can't! Because I love you more deeply than I ever thought possible. You're a part of my very soul," she replied.

"Then marry me! Now!" he said bluntly in a deep, commanding whisper… compellingly. "Be my wife – tonight – now!"

Her dark eyes betrayed the instant shock of the moment. "What?" she asked with surprise and incredulity.

"You are supposed to say, 'Why, of course I will!'" he replied, now smiling. "My darling Suzanne, when you ride over that red horizon, I want you to take part of me with you. No matter what happens, I want that more than anything else," he replied, his lower lip trembling and betraying a wave of emotion.

She smiled and looked at his lips, full and soft, then she said softly, "Of course I'll marry you…"

Kerry held her tightly as if he would never let go. Then he kissed her; passionately – then softly – then deeply - then softly again. As he pulled away from her, he smiled his best catbird grin.

"Let me guess," she responded, knowing her husband-to-be all too well. "I get proposed to in a broom closet and you have a plan bigger than interplanetary space..."

"You're astonishing," he replied, hammering on the door with three sharp knocks.

When he did, the latch turned from the outside, and there stood Chaplain Gates, Peter and Ashley, all smiling. Gates was holding his Bible between his hands and Ashley was holding three artificial roses she had made. Peter looked at Kerry's smiling face and said, "Well then, I guess we have a wedding!"

With one glance at the roses, Suzanne burst into tears and began to hug a weeping Ashley while the men stood by completely mystified.

The wedding took place an hour later - after midnight, in the dining hall. It was announced only by word of mouth, but not a single colonist failed to attend, save the still missing Covenant and the Command Center watch, who viewed it remotely.

Peter was asked by Bob to be his best man and Ashley gave Kerry her mother's ring as a wedding present to give to his bride. It was a simple affair, with the bride and groom repeating the traditional vows. But by the time the ceremony was over, there was not a single dry eye in the entire colony. The ensuing party began just as the bride and groom retired.

Yet, the workday commenced at 8:00 AM that morning without a pause. Peter ordered that, party or not, every life was on the line and there would be no excuses from anyone. And so, as the sun rose over the red skyline, no one was late for duty, least of all Suzanne and Kerry. They ate their breakfast alone and silent, holding hands, staring at one another with red eyes in silent pride, love and the look reserved just for newlyweds on their first morning together.

All the rest saw a newly emerging reality through the eyes of the newlyweds. The gauntlet had been laid down. Now, because of them, there was no sacrifice too great, no payment too large to ensure the survival of all the rest. It was now no longer a duty to survive, it was a sacred pledge, every one to another – the bond had been made absolute by a profoundly powerful expression of sacrificial love.

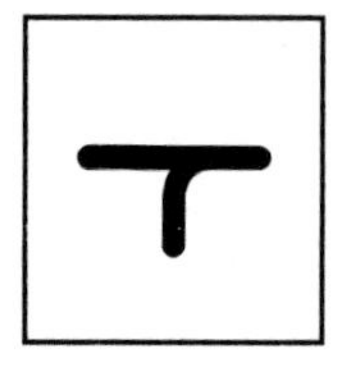

he operation immediately focused on training Suzanne and making the MAT ready for the trip. Francis all but demanded the opportunity to train her personally. Peter permitted this just to get him off his back and allow Francis to focus his nearly out-of-control emotions on something useful. Gorteau asked to be put in charge of readying the MAT for the trip, centering his genius on making the vehicle reliable and covering the huge and growing contingency list.

Francis and Gorteau picked their team members and set to work immediately. Gorteau's team met inside the cramped MAT hangar.

"The exact distance from the MAT hangar here on the plains of Elysium to the front door of Shturmovoi on the Lake of the Sun is 2,065.278 kilometers in a straight line, give or take a few centimeters," Gorteau began lecturing his crew. "Now this vehicle's range under the very best of conditions is less than half that, by some 600 kilometers. Obviously, it's not a straight line to the actual meeting which will likely be near 1,200 kilometers, give or take an unknown or two."

The physicist walked over to the MAT and tapped on its' power system hatch, now open for service.

"Right here is our problem," he said, continuing to tap the open hatch, "...power. Never in the designers' wildest dreams did they count on this proposed expedition across the Martian desert up to and even beyond its designed limits. But now we have to do whatever it takes to make it to the agreed upon rendezvous across the Martian equator on the southern fringe of the Amazon Plain, halfway to Shturmovoi, at the crater Nicholson. There the Soviets will meet our ambassador and transport her to their base.

"Our challenge, meanwhile, is this: We must not only provide enough energy for the MAT to reach some 25 percent beyond its rated capacity, but to make it safely back home as well."

"How is it that their vehicle is so much better than ours?" a MAT technician asked.

"I am not certain how you would define 'better', young man, but I would qualify that by stating that their SAR Craft has a considerably longer range than ours. When properly outfitted it can attain some 2100 kilometers, just barely enough to reach BC1. SAR is a Russian acronym, by the way, which unless you spoke fluent Russian would not make any sense even if I spelled it out to you. So we'll just call them SARs."

"How do they have so much range?" the technician asked.

"The size of the SAR is roughly 45% larger than our MAT," Gorteau replied, snapping a photograph and schematics of the SAR onto the large computer display before them. Inside the vehicle, the available room is well over twice our own vehicle but much less comfortable than our MAT. The extra room of the SAR also went into the power pod storage, which requires that it be considerably larger. In addition, their power source is not nearly as sophisticated as ours and requires roughly twice the size and mass as one of ours. They actually power the SARs with an old variant of hydrox fuel cells while we power ours, as you know, with Lithium Argon Palladium, or LAP pods. But the SAR carries three power pods while the MATs carry only one. Given all of that, the SAR is a lumbering beast with a somewhat slower pace and over twice the total mass as our more sophisticated MAT."

One of the technician's eyes were staring off into space as he was obviously thinking things over with some intensity. Gorteau caught his gaze immediately and fell silent, respectfully waiting for him to complete the thought. Finally, the tech's eyes relaxed and focused on Gorteau.

"I'm sorry," he said shaking his head. "Just thinking."

"That's precisely why you were invited to this planet, young man," Gorteau responded. "Now, unless your mental diversion involves women or taxes, will you please share your silent deliberations with us?"

"Well, I was just thinking, sir, why can't we carry more than one pod strapped to the sides – perhaps two or three?" he began.

"Yes, yes..." Gorteau replied, but was interrupted by a young female technician.

"And why can't we send along a few solar panels to charge the LAPs while Suzanne is gone?"

Gorteau smiled widely and opened his arms to the assembled technicians. "I just want you people to know that you are fantastic! With your minds, your deepest creativity, we can do this!"

Then his face returned to the introspective instructor at the core of his being. "Now, let us calculate. I need detailed numbers and projections. I need a probable route and backups from the satellite photos. I'll need projections on power usage under the worst of conditions and the best and I'll need an average as well." He looked at the tech who suggested the strap-on LAPs. "From you I'll need a design and structural calculations on strapping the power pods on the MAT." Then he looked to the tech who suggested the solar panels. "And from you I'll need a complete set of best and worst case calculations on solar recharge – rates, atmospheric dust anomalies and variations as well as suggested placement angles for ideal solar incidence. I also need volunteers to engineer the charging system including inverters between the LAPs and a variable rate charge controller with automated backup."

He then looked at his assembled technicians. "Now, who will volunteer to handle life support calculations for this mission?" As soon as the first hand went up, Gorteau nodded and replied, "Report immediately with your MAT life support files to Ashley's office. She's waiting for you."

The mission developed by combining the best ideas from the assembled colony. It was determined that Suzanne would depart in the MAT re-engineered to make the run south across the Elysium desert, crossing the Martian equator into the Amazon Desert where it would rendezvous with a Soviet SAR. At the rendezvous point the solar panels would be unrolled to help recharge the power pods in Suzanne's absence. With luck, she would then have enough energy to make it back to BC1. But even in the worst case, Kerry had an agreement that if she were anywhere within range of a standard MAT he would be permitted to lead a rescue party if necessary.

As careful as the plan was, no one had any illusions of the true nature of its risk. Suzanne would be traversing territory totally unseen by human eyes, mapped only by satellites, through deserts and terrain that was constantly shifting and changing in the ceaseless Martian winds. While the charts and maps were good, they were by no means perfect and the argument over the best route and the contingency routes was long and bitter. But in the end, the mapping task was accomplished, the vehicle was made ready and the mission clock ticked down to its final hours before departure.

While the engineering and technical tasks were being developed, Francis briefed and trained Suzanne as best he could on the diplomatic and political mission that lay ahead of her after her perilous drive across the Martian plains. She expressed openly that, to her, it was intimidating, confusing and seemed deceptive, at best. Yet Francis was able to warn her of the full range of possible outcomes, from the disastrous to the best. Meanwhile, against her objections, Brinker handed her a .32 caliber handgun for personal protection. Kerry insisted that she take it and keep it close. While neither one actually fired the weapon, Brinker and Kerry showed her what to do if the time came to use it. The whole 'diplomatic' scenario was so abhorrent to Ashley, that as soon as she discovered the approach of Francis and Brinker, she refused to have any part of it. Peter, after considerable discussions with Francis, finally, but reluctantly, agreed that it should be developed that way, if only to prepare and train Suzanne for all possibilities. He did, however, let them know how embarrassed they were going to be at the incredible level of paranoia they had cultivated between themselves when it was all over.

irov's nightmare seemed destined to last throughout all eternity. He awoke often in his black coffin for periods of time he could not judge. His injuries seemed to him to be severe, and he was in incredible pain while the cold itself sapped the life from him. Between the pain and the cold, Kirov wished only for death and its merciful release.

Then, the light assaulted him – intense, bitter light that streamed down through the open lid of his box. And with the cutting brilliance of the harsh light, the horrific, repulsive face of Kravchenko peered down at him with a sneering scorn.

"Ah, Dr. Kirov. We must talk!" he said, his voice mired in sarcasm. With that, he and an accomplice lifted Kirov roughly out of the box and wrapped him in a blanket. "Warm yourself, comrade! We shall talk," Kravchenko said, cruelly tossing him onto the floor. Then he pulled up a metal chair and sat in it backwards, peering down at Kirov who lay on the floor, barely able even to shiver from the cold. Intense pain radiated from every cell in his body. Through his swollen eyes, Kirov could hardly see his torturers' faces staring down at him.

"I know what you are thinking, comrade. You are wishing to die. But I cannot allow that. Then with whom would I entertain myself? Our great leader Dimitriov has agreed that I can decide when it is that you should die. Oh, yes, I know; you think we need your great genius to run the power plant. Well, my friend, your own intelligence has deceived you. It seems that you have designed the plant to be so easy to run and maintain that even I, a mere bureaucrat, can do it! What a fool you are, Kirov. You have made yourself expendable, and I have been the one chosen to do the expending." Then Kravchenko laughed loudly, pressing the sharp heel of his boot onto one of Kirov's eyes, causing fresh blood to run down his cheek.

"But you have great uses to us, still Comrade Kirov," he said. "For example, I am to be the cat and you are to be the mouse. I shall toy with you until I am ready to feast on your flesh, then I shall, you know! But until then, I will keep you just warm enough to keep you alive. I must say, I have not had such a good time since arriving in this boring red hell."

"What do you want from me?" Kirov whispered through clenched teeth. He meant to convey anger, but it would not come from his mouth; just chattering, whispered half-speech through his crusted and beaten lips.

"Ah, yes," Kravchenko responded, "the motive! I just love geniuses like you, my dear Kirov. Never a dull moment! Now, what do I want? I want to know about transmissions to the American base. You know about any? Microsecond bursts? Sent in code? I can give you a date or dates, if you wish. I can detail the text of the decoded messages, if you wish. It matters not. I can keep you alive for as long as you wish to remain in this state. Or, you can get it all off your chest, and then I can let you die. It's really your choice."

Kirov closed his eyes to block the harsh light; to block out even the shadow of Kravchenko. He wished to die. Indeed, it would be glorious just to die and end this pain and horror. He could not bear another beating, another broken bone and certainly not another moment in his cold black coffin designed for the near-dead. He could feel Kravchenko's foot grinding once more against his eyelid, but mercifully, it was just enough pain to slip him yet again into unconsciousness.

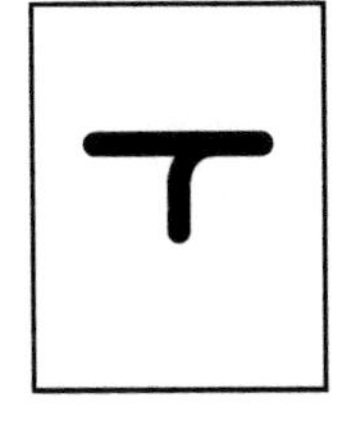

heir sol began well before sunrise. To many at BC1, sunset and sunrise happened on the same watch. On the sol of Suzanne's departure south across the Elysium plains toward the equator, and the meeting with the enigmatic Soviets at the crater Nicholson on the Amazon Plain, the lights at BC1 had burned all through the night. Suzanne was the only one sleeping – ordered to get eight hours of uninterrupted sleep.

The MAT itself was now fully prepared. It was weighed down with the two additional power pods, over 300 square meters of solar cells rolled into four tight bundles, oxygen bottles, carbon dioxide absorbent, food, water and backups of all computer and communications gear.

Toon had rigged up the only available satellites – the navigation systems - to decode written text from the onboard computers for direct communications with the MAT. Without it, BC1 and Suzanne would have been completely out of touch once the MAT disappeared over the horizon. But with it, she could communicate with BC1 all the way, even while at Shturmovoi.

The Soviets would not permit use of their satellites to communicate or even relay signals for reasons they said were "classified", a decision which almost caused the mission to be cancelled altogether. But Toon responded immediately and his work-around system was deemed to be satisfactory.

At 0600 the Soviets were notified through their satellite constellation that the journey was about to begin and the rendezvous point was verified. Without a successful rendezvous, there would not be enough life support to recharge the batteries by solar power and return to BC1. In other words, her life was completely dependent on the success of the meeting with the Soviet SAR at the appointed time and place.

The Soviet SAR and one man crew was also equally dependent on a timely meeting, for their own life support system had just enough capacity to wait there six hours, no more. If there was a slip in schedule for any reason, Suzanne would die.

Peter stood by Francis as they made a final close inspection and walk around the MAT. "This old buggy was never designed for this," Peter whispered quietly to Francis. "And she's going to be traversing 1200 kilometers of terra incognito. We can call this off right now, you know."

Peter could feel Francis' red, sleep-deprived eyes boring into his. "Your decision," Francis replied mercilessly.

"That's all I get for reassurance from you?" Peter asked, near exhaustion.

Francis stopped his inspection and turned to face Peter. "I know what you're after, Peter. So I'll give it to you. This trip is going to be dangerous and is not without its significant risks, which may well result in Suzanne's death. You know this, I know this and she knows this. But without some kind of teaming arrangement with the Soviets, we're probably all going to die. So we take the risk, and Suzanne assumes the burden. Your decision was a good one, my friend, and under the circumstances, the only viable one," he concluded with a sharp nod of his head and a prolonged blink.

Peter looked down and thought for a moment. "But you don't trust the Soviets..."

"Look, Peter, we've already been through this," Francis began. "No, I don't trust the Soviets. But here, trust and logic are incompatible. We have to take this chance to see if I'm wrong or not. If they're not here to kill us and take our food and air, then we desperately need to team up with them. If they're really our enemies, then maybe Suzanne can pick that up while she's there and we can mount some kind of defense against them. We need to know this before we just open our doors and give away our lives to whoever walks in. Our back is against the wall - their back is against the wall. Now what do we do? This uncertain plan, is unfortunately, the only way to find out."

Peter stood listening with his arms folded. He nodded and looked away and took a deep breath. "Then we roll in an hour."

Francis put his right arm on Peter's shoulder. "Yes, my friend; we roll in an hour. And you are doing the right thing."

"What about Covenant?" Peter asked unexpectedly.

Francis looked as though he were taken off guard by the question. "Huh? What about Covenant?"

"What do you think happened to Covenant? Is he in on this?" Peter mused.

"Peter, your lack of sleep has caused your brain to go into overload," Francis replied reassuringly. "First, Covenant is probably dead on the desert somewhere. If the Soviets are after our goods and they had him, then they wouldn't need Suzanne. And even if he wanted to go to Shturmovoi, there is no way he could get there. Even the SAR just barely has that kind of range. And even if it got all the way here, how could it return without resupply?. No matter what the scenario, there's still some available logic here. Peter, the probabilities are endless. Don't torture yourself with them. Let's stay focused on the knowns, which are overwhelming enough."

Peter looked back at him and shook his head slowly, "You're right, of course. I just hate big puzzles with too many pieces. They make me crazy."

"I know what you mean," Francis replied in all sincerity.

Fifty minutes later, Suzanne climbed into the MAT which was packed so tightly that there was barely room for her to fit. Kerry gently strapped her in and kissed her through the open visor on her helmet. Then he lowered the transparent faceplate and latched it into its closed position. She looked back at him and managed a weak smile.

"No crying in the helmet. Not allowed," he warned, since once sealed, '...no tissue can be applied to the affected areas...' as the NASA manual stated clearly.

Suzanne nodded and continued to smile, looking back into her husband's eyes. "I love you," she mouthed silently to Kerry as he returned the same.

Allowing a respectful two seconds to pass, Brinker said, "Com check," into his microphone to Suzanne.

"Clear. I read you loud and clear," she replied. Kerry closed the door to the MAT with a pop, allowing her to tend to business. Then he walked briskly out of the hangar.

Peter watched Kerry walk away, then looked at Brinker and winked, nodding slowly. His list of worries matched Peter's nearly exactly and they had coordinated Suzanne's departure from BC1 carefully. If Covenant was alive and did plan a surprise, they would be ready for him.

"All personnel out of the Hangar," Peter ordered. Once clear, they could begin the process of depressurizing it so they could safely open the doors to the outside.

Peter walked up to the door of the MAT and pointed to the instruments inside. The green lights indicated the MAT was safely sealed. Peter offered his best smile and a thumbs up which Suzanne returned. He then walked out and sealed the inner hatch just as the air began to bleed out of the hangar.

Three minutes later, the big hatch opened, exposing the Martian landscape before Suzanne. As she gently engaged the electric drive motor, the MAT began its long journey south into the unknown.

It moved sluggishly at first, then, as if it had found its legs, it began to move outside the airlock dome. It pulled onto the desert illuminated a ruby red by the dim Martian sunrise.

To nearly everyone's surprise, Kerry walked up to the side of the MAT in his space suit and rapped on the window. It seemed to surprise Suzanne as much as anyone and as she saw the figure rapping on the window, she jumped. "Bob!" she said. "What are you doing here?"

"Just wanted to walk you out the gate," he replied, holding one of Brinker's shotguns in the air.

Suzanne laughed loudly. "Ok, partner. I'll ride and you can walk."

The assembled colonists inside heard the exchange through the speakers and cheered.

"Going offline now," she said as she switched to direct communications with Kerry, which was followed by a collective moan from the crowd.

Peter looked at Brinker and gave a thumbs up. If Covenant were going to ambush her on the way out of BC1, he was going to have a nasty surprise.

Kerry walked alongside the MAT until he reached the outskirts of the camp. There he stopped and the colonists watched as the suited figure tenderly touch the window of the MAT. The overloaded vehicle slowly pulled away as Kerry waved. He stood there, slowly waving his arm until the MAT disappeared over a nearby ridge.

Inside the MAT, Suzanne watched Kerry recede through her side mirror, while keeping a careful eye on the older MAT track ahead of her, radiating away from the camp. She would try and remain on the worn path for as long as she could, making the best possible speed as she departed BC1. But the well-worn trail disappeared just 20 minutes after departure. Taking advantage of BC1's tall antenna sitting atop the launch tower at the Crippen Spaceport, Suzanne stopped and radioed back to base.

"BC1, MAT1, over."

"Go ahead."

"I've reached the end of our last trail south now. I'm going to begin the transit phase."

"Godspeed, MAT1."

Suzanne sighed deeply. In less than an hour, BC1 would have disappeared not only from her view, but from her radio range as well. Having only a line-of-sight transmitter, BC1 was about to fade into the distance for real. From then on, they would have to communicate by the difficult, arduous method Toon had worked out through the remaining navigational satellites. In order to do so, Suzanne would have to stop the MAT, rig the navigation receiver and burst transmitter, and then decode its reply through the onboard computer. They would have only sketchy communications at best.

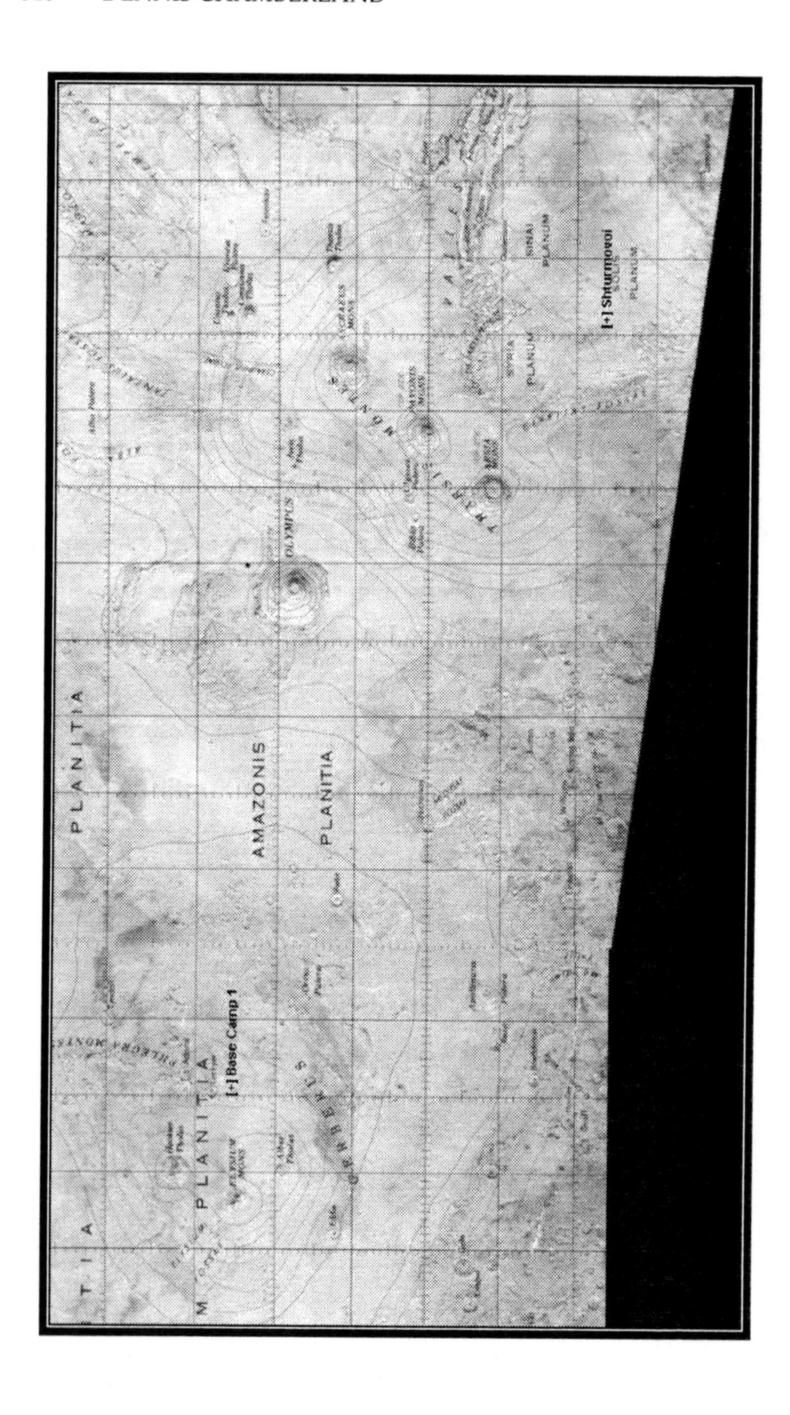
PLANITIA
AMAZONIS
PLANITIA
OLYMPUS
[+] Base Camp 1
[+] Shturmovoi
PLANUM

Suzanne looked ahead of her into the unforgiving and hard Martian desert called Elysium. As the red dot of a sun rose over the horizon to her left, she eased the MAT's electric drive engine ahead and onto untrodden sand. From this point on, she knew her eyes would see things no other human eyes had ever seen directly.

The trick to navigating the deserts of Mars was straightforward – avoid the rocks. The navigation routine was to try and avoid as many as you could. Since it was impossible to miss the rocks altogether, the plan was to run over as few as possible and only the smallest ones. Yet, since the MAT had four rather large tires, the idea was to do the best you could with the rocks you had no choice but to roll over. The MAT was designed for this kind of abuse, and while it was not an unforeseen hazard, certainly the extent and incredible duration of this task was never in the designer's wildest dreams.

Inside the squat, fat MAT, the seats were designed as suspended web affairs built for day trips – not for long, relatively endless, straight-line jaunts across the continental expanse. Nor was it designed for long term comfort. The MAT's suspension system worked very well at protecting the vehicle from damage by repeated encounters with rocks, but the human was jolted with each one.

Not only was Suzanne tossed, rattled and jerked continuously, but she had to maintain extreme vigilance as the MAT rolled along the desert to avoid any rock passing beneath or even nearby that could snag or cut the fragile, thin skin of the vehicle. Any cut, gash or tear would be instantly fatal to the mission and ruin the gas and energy balance, making it impossible to repressurize it at a later date. It could also cut or tear wiring bundles, optical cables or hydraulic lines.

If the MAT lost pressure permanently from a puncture that could not be repaired, Suzanne could not then remove her pressure suit helmet. Without that ability, she would not be able to refill her suit's water reservoir or change out her carbon dioxide scrubber canister on a daily basis. Within 30 hours of latching her helmet, she would die.

In light of the gas and energy balance, the BC1 engineers had worked out a series of concentric circles radiating away from BC1. The inner circle was labeled, "TRANSIT PHASE", or the beginning of the non-surveyed and unmapped regions. The next circle was drawn and it was called "ASSISTED RETURN", when the energy of the MAT was low enough that a safe return was not possible without another standard MAT ready to meet it somewhere in the middle. If beyond this circle the MAT was disabled, not even a rescue vehicle could reach her. Another ring further out was labeled "NO RETURN" when no safe return was possible at all, even if the MAT turned around and made the run back in the direction of BC1. Beyond that was the distance to the meeting point with the Soviet SAR. If anything happened to the MAT beyond that point, any rescue by either Shturmovoi or BC1 was out of the question.

By mid-sol, Suzanne had reached a set of small canyons that were well marked on her map. She began to thread her way through them, first driving down into the canyon and between the walls, rising hundreds of feet over her head. As far as Martian canyons were concerned, these were definitely small fry, but to her, they were very impressive, dwarfing her and the MAT and casting cold, frightening shadows before her.

As the sol wore on, and she threaded and turned her way through the canyon walls like a huge maze, Suzanne becameg intensely uncomfortable. The seat was nothing more than a nylon-webbed affair draped and fastened around an aluminum tube frame. She was strapped in while dressed in her pressurized spacesuit, gear jammed in all around her so that she could barely move. While the Martian gravity was just a third that of earth, she had become accustomed to it and the constant jolting about was becoming increasingly uncomfortable. Even worse, she had a problem with an ingenious system the engineers had devised just before the trip. They had come up with a system where she could use the bathroom in her suit for five sols, if necessary, without changing. It was not working as they advertised, and it was starting to become annoying to the point that all the danger around her seemed inconsequential. Finally, between a cut in a very large canyon wall, she stopped the MAT.

In the full light of the Martian sun, she unstrapped herself from the vehicle, turned the drive motor to idle, unlatched the door and stepped outside. Since the mission called for full, continuous pressurization of her spacesuit for safety, the MAT itself was not pressurized during the drive.

As she stepped out of the MAT, Suzanne looked around her, supremely self-conscious about what she needed to do. Then she laughed at her own sense of paranoia, standing in this canyon where she assured herself that no human eyes had ever gazed. She gripped the crotch of her suit with both hands and straightened the equipment out that had been pinching her for so many kilometers. Finally she breathed a long sigh of relief. Comfort at last! While it was not exactly the most lady-like movement, it sure made all the difference.

No one had ever discussed stopping and getting out of the vehicle at any point in the mission planning. But it felt so incredibly, deliciously good, Suzanne decided to risk it every two to three hours. Then she climbed back in and resumed her traverse.

Just before the first sunset, she pulled away from the canyon and onto another expanse of desert. Here on the broad and empty plain, she would be forced to stop for the night. She planned to pressurize the MAT for 11 hours to enjoy dinner, the first scheduled communications with BC1, a movie on a portable entertainment system Ashley had given her and hopefully get some much needed sleep. Her entire body felt like a bowl of gelatin.

As she finally stopped, the sky darkened perceptibly and quickly. With little atmosphere to scatter the light, night fell suddenly on Mars.

Inside the MAT, Suzanne was dead tired. She allowed herself the opportunity to step outside one more time to stretch her legs. As she did so, the darkness was nearly complete. There was no moonlight as on earth – tiny Phobos was like a brilliant satellite, at best, streaking unceremoniously across the deep blackness of space over the desert. All she could see outside was illuminated by the interior lights of the MAT and some nearly ineffectual starlight. As Suzanne adjusted her suit around her again, she did a few deep knee bends.

As she turned her faceplate to the ground while stretching her neck muscles, she could see a faint pattern in the sand. Stunned, she looked back carefully, moving her faceplate as close to the ground as she dared. And there it was – what appeared to be an unmistakable vehicle track left in the sand. It seemed to have been weathered over time, but it was faintly visible nonetheless. And it was at least as wide as the MAT's track, so it was not left by a passing probe from decades earlier.

Suzanne bent over and moved the sand with her fingers. It was a light track, and certainly could not have been there for very long, as the winds of Mars constantly move the sand around. With what she knew about Mars, it could have been there for sols, weeks or even months, but certainly not years.

She stood up suddenly and looked around her in the pitch darkness of the southern Elysium plain. Everything was quiet, black and very dark.

So, she was not the first intelligent eyes that had seen this terrain after all. And with this certain knowledge, she could not suppress an involuntary shiver that ran down her entire body. Was she now alone on the deserts of Mars? She had no way of knowing as she retreated to the relative security of the MAT and latched the hatch tightly down. The next thing she had to determine was what to tell BC1.

She decided to tell them nothing. Peter had assured her that she had total command autonomy on the mission, and so she made her decision. If she changed her mind later, they would be there. She reasoned that the tracks could have been from an earlier Soviet mission years before that had somehow been sheltered from the wind. What she knew for sure was that she did not want Bob or anyone else to worry over inconsequential things that no one would be able to do anything about anyway. Besides, she reasoned, ultimately the mission was more important than her own life and nothing would cause her to turn back.

So Suzanne settled down to pressurizing the MAT and eating. Since she had not eaten for nearly 12 hours, she was totally ravenous. After dinner she set up the communications gear and, right on schedule, she typed in her first report, just a dozen pre-decided words that required over an hour to upload. Her message ended in a sequence of numbers: b1219X5oo. When the message was returned from BC1, it ended in the same sequence: b1219X5oo. It was a code just between her and Bob. As she saw it come across her screen, she sighed and smiled the secret smile known only to lovers. All was well, at least for the moment.

Suzanne skipped the movie and turned the lights out in the MAT. She was totally exhausted and needed the extra two hours. She thought about Bob in the darkness for the first few minutes, then about the tracks just outside. Before she fell asleep, she squinted outside the window once more. Out there in the darkness, where the canopy of bright, steady-state starlight met the black horizon, all was not right. She just knew it. She felt and feared the disorder of it. She hated its uncertainty and she faced it through the thin plastic window, one on one. Whatever it was, she had no control over it anyway, she decided, just as she dropped off into a fitful sleep. Her dreams were full of endless, bouncing motion and sand creatures that left strange tracks wherever they went.

The next morning, the computer awoke her with a shrill alarm. Suzanne could see the sunlight approaching as the Martian horizon glowed in a thin, red line. She immediately sat as upright as she could, her muscles aching and complaining with the cramped sleeping quarters. She ate a quick breakfast, then filled her suit water bottle up with fresh water all the way to the top. After that task was done, she refilled her suit's odor filtering canister with fresh chemicals. With the rigged bathroom system installed in her suit, the odor canister was a must.

She then reconnected the insanely difficult communications gear once again and broadcast a short message back to BC1 through the navigation satellite that she was about to get underway for the sol. Afterwards she turned on the MAT's compressor and sucked the vehicle's atmosphere back into a storage bottle. At 98% vacuum, she popped the hatch and stepped out onto the Martian desert to stretch her legs one last time before starting again. As she did, she noticed the tracks she thought she had seen the evening before were gone.

Suzanne breathed a deep sight of relief, then laughed at herself for being so paranoid as to actually see tracks deep in the Martian desert where no human had even been before. But as she looked closer, she saw that their disappearance was only an illusion. She realized that in the light of the morning, they only appeared to have gone away, but were, in fact, still there. By looking from an exact angle, she could see they were indeed still present – a very, exceedingly light, nearly non-existent trace of a track. If she had not stood last evening with the MAT's lights at the precise angle they were, she would have missed them altogether.

In the gathering light, Suzanne attempted to see where they led or where they came from. But it was impossible. Without a careful, patient, study of the sand at just the right angle, they could not be seen at all.

She looked all around her again... nothing but sand, rocks, desert and dunes. She was alone on a vast desert, the nearest humans hundreds of kilometers distant. At least, that was the story her well-ordered mind tried to tell her. Her eyes, on the other hand, were telling her quite another story.

Shaking it off, she stepped inside the MAT, latched the hatch and powered it up for the sol. The electric motor whined as it came up to speed. As soon as the tachometer's light turned green, Suzanne shifted it into forward motion, starting a full 15 minutes before her scheduled time of departure. She had stopped only because it was unsafe in the darkness to navigate the Martian plains in the MAT. But now she had plenty of light and would need all the kilometers she could get. This morning she would cross the "ASSISTED RETURN" line and this evening, just before sunset, she was scheduled to cross the "NO RETURN" line. By nightfall, she would be beyond anyone's rescue.

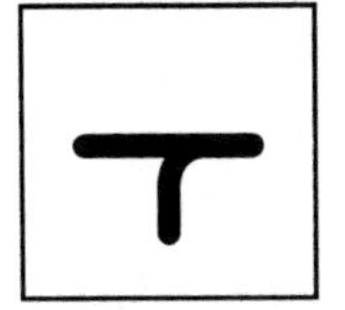

The second sol's traverse was much easier than the first's. Suzanne's eyes traced her path for safe passage, but at the same time she continuously looked for more tracks. She saw nothing and soon got a headache for her efforts. The navigation satellite had her well ahead of schedule by noon when she stopped to rest for 20 minutes and stretch. The size and number of rocks had dropped off until the MAT hardly lurched at all and she made much higher speeds than any of the mission planners had anticipated.

In the afternoon, she continued to make good progress and by her evening stretch, Suzanne had gained an astonishing 20 percent on her trip schedule. She smiled and slapped the skin of the MAT with her gloved hand. Bob and Fabian would be very pleased. As for her, she could think of nothing better than waiting for the Soviet SAR for four hours while watching the movies that Ashley had sent along. The road had been smooth the entire sol; Mars had been kind.

By nightfall, the small sun dipped below the western horizon and Suzanne could make out a rolling line of hills due south of her position. It was a ripple in the Elysium plain called Cerberus. It was not a mountain range, but a geological wrinkle that passed directly across her path. Cerberus appeared as but a smudge on the southern Elysium plain from orbit, but from the ground it was an elevated, chaotic,

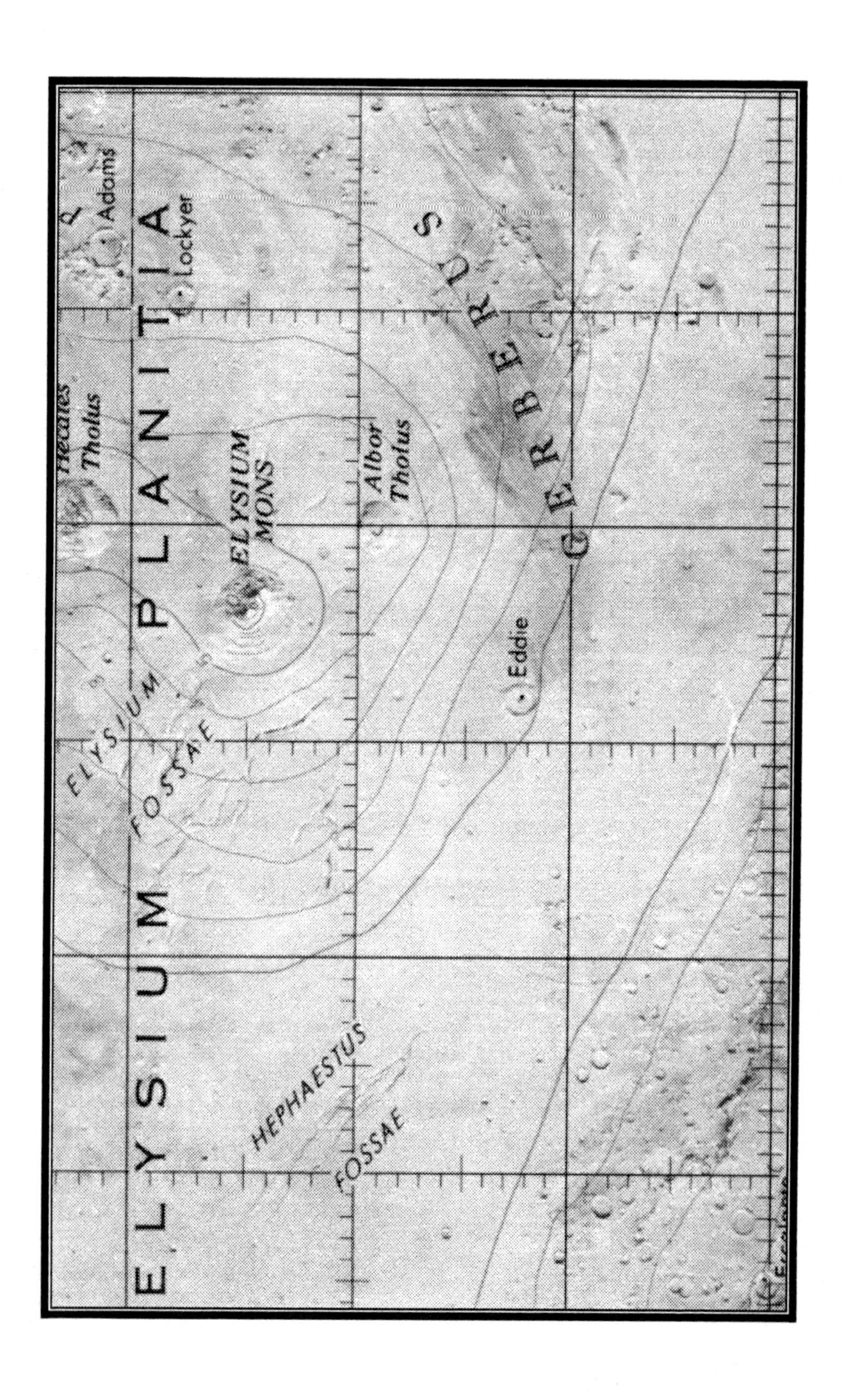

ELYSIUM PLANITIA
Adams
Lockyer
Hecates Tholus
ELYSIUM MONS
Albor Tholus
CERBERUS
Eddie
ELYSIUM FOSSAE
HEPHAESTUS FOSSAE

boulder strewn mess and there was no way around it. She had a satellite-view plan for getting through the individual geologic formations that made up the Cerebus, but as the earliest lunar and planetary explorers had discovered, the view from the surface was much different than the view from orbit. It was everyone's prayer that Cerberus would not be as bad as it could be, and the mission planners had calculated a 35 percent reduction in forward speed as she passed through the various chaotic formations of the Cerberus labeled the *Tartarus Montes* and the *Tartarus Colles.* But on the other side, following her fourth night, the Soviet SAR was scheduled to rendezvous with her there.

Suzanne repeated her stretch of the night before and looked for more tracks outside the window of the MAT. There were none to be seen. She was so elated at her progress that she ate slowly, savoring her food, and then actually watched a movie after the communications procedure. But just as she turned off the interior lights of the MAT and began to drift off to sleep, the apprehensive feelings returned. Suzanne stared out the window of the bulbous MAT at the brilliant stars studding the velvet and absolute darkness. Sleep escaped her. The uneasiness revisited and invaded her mind. She lay there, knowing sleep was essential and watched as tiny Phobos sailed, as it had before, quickly across the Martian sky. She forced her eyelids to shut. Tomorrow was going to be the test, and she had to be ready for it. In the dark Martian night, the same dreams returned with an unending, continuous motion and peopled with beasts and their funny feet that marred the red desert as they left strange, indelible tracks in her uneasy mind.

Suzanne awoke early the next morning, determined to begin as soon as time and light would allow. She planned to proceed a full hour ahead of schedule and get the earliest start possible. She wanted most of all to be the first to arrive at her rendezvous point and planned a great feast with a movie while she waited for the Soviet to meet her. At first possible light, the MAT lurched forward in its initial motion of the sol.

Within two hours of the start, the small sun had risen high over the horizon to her left, illuminating the desert with a clear, bright sky. As she moved cautiously, but rapidly for the MAT, on her southerly route, Suzanne began to see the terrain was becoming more and more rocky.

She could also see that just ahead of her lay a row of hummocks and short hills. But it was not until she struck a large rock at high speed that she realized that this sol was going to be far different than any of the ones before.

The rock was clearly in her path, but she was pre-occupied, staring at the short hills some kilometers in the distance. It was so large, that it caused the MAT to bounce, arching its nose into the air, then actually go airborne. The MAT seemed to soar interminably, then arc over toward the desert at a steep angle. Suzanne braced herself for impact.

When it came, it slammed her forward against her restraints and her helmet crashed into the MAT's forward windshield. The MAT itself then dug its forward wheels into the sand and began an arc forward. It seemed that the MAT was about to roll end over end. But, at the last microsecond, it balanced in the air on its two front wheels, paused, and then slammed backward to come to a rest on all four wheels. One fraction of a moment later, one shred of energy more and it would have rolled over.

Suzanne's eyes darted around in her helmet, stunned by the impact against the windshield. She desperately looked about the cabin's panels to see if her suit had lost pressure. It had not. All systems were normal. Then she sighed and burst into tears, slamming her fists against the hatch beside her. It was a close call, way too close.

Minutes later, she composed herself, pressurized the cabin once again, then removed her helmet and wiped her face with a cloth. She pulled out the transmitter and sent an unscheduled message back to BC1.

"BOB, I LOVE YOU. ALL IS WELL. CONTINUING ON NOW." She then signed it with her position.

Securing her helmet and evacuating the MAT's air back into storage, Suzanne felt much better. She really needed that cry, she mused. It had been awhile.

She now understood more clearly than ever before the razor thin margin that separated her from disaster and death. It was but one moment of inattention or one glance in the wrong direction. There would be, there could be, no second chances. Out here, no one could be counted on to save her. No one. The smallest breakdown would mean certain death.

The MAT proceeded more slowly and cautiously now. Whenever she needed to look far ahead, Suzanne either slowed to a crawl or she stopped altogether. But she kept her eyes mostly on the desert just ahead of her vision - the sand on which her wheels were about to touch was paramount.

Eventually, Suzanne came to the hummocks. They were the raised, chaotic ridges that marked the beginning of Cerberus – Tartarus features. It was far worse than anything they had planned for. Rocks and boulders were strewn everywhere - many larger than the MAT itself. As she tentatively rolled to the top of the first rise, she could see the image repeated all the way to the horizon - kilometer after of kilometer of absolute chaos.

The Cerberus seemed to be the resting place of universal entropy. From mythology, the Cerberus was the horrible three-headed dog who guarded the entrance to the underworld. As she surveyed the chaotic scene, Suzanne mused that somehow the ancients must have dreamed of this place in their darkest nightmares. Here on Mars, the Cerberus was a great primeval, alluvium ghost-land of house sized boulders and rills, tossed by the hand of God into an ultimately chaotic scene of endless disarray and geologic turmoil. She had never seen anything like this. The ancient flood that deposited this must have been planetary in scope and awesome on a scale she could hardly imagine.

The satellite photos had not hinted at this degree of disarray. With their limited resolution, they could not. But now Suzanne would have to somehow navigate this rolling sea of wave after wave of barriers safely and in time to make the rendezvous window. Yesterday it looked like she was going to arrive early. Now it looked as though her odds for survival were not good at all. But she knew she had to make it through this. She had long since passed the point of no return.

Suzanne sighed deeply and looked at the path ahead. From this position at the top of the ridge, it appeared totally impassible. Worse yet, numerous boulders on both the right and left blocked her view of the paths on either side. The only solution would be to back down the ridge, sidetrack and drive back up until she found a safe, navigable path down the ridge. It was going to be extremely slow going.

She managed to back down the ridge and drive laterally along the base, then back up again. This time she found a path down. But at the bottom of the rill and at the rise to the next ridge that rose some seven or eight meters high before her, she was blocked again.

"This is not going to work," she said to herself bitterly. "I'm not going to make it."

Suzanne felt the panic rise inside her. She felt her breathing increase and a tingle in the tips of her fingers. As soon as she recognized the symptoms, she stopped and closed her eyes. If she panicked, she knew for sure she was going to die. So she steeled her nerves, then opened her eyes again. She knew she needed a plan.

She backtracked again and found a clear path to the top of the ridge on a steep, upward climb between huge boulders. At the top, she saw that the ridges rolled on and on to the south, directly in her path. Yet, again, she saw that her path down was blocked. Once more she would have to roll backward down the ridge and drive along its base to try at the top again later.

Painfully, slowly, she backed down the steep incline to the base and threaded her way to another rise to the top. Suzanne then realized that this was an impossible task. At this rate, she would be sols behind schedule and would certainly die, hopelessly lost in the middle of this chaos. She stopped the MAT's motors. The overhead sunlight gave her a degree of confidence she did not have in the shadow of the boulders and inside the deep valley behind her. Here at least she could see the terrain for miles, regardless of how impassible it may have been.

Suzanne pressurized the MAT and removed her helmet. She then called up displays of the charts, maps and satellite photos before her. The onboard computer caused a tiny, lighted "bug" to crawl across the map and stop on her location, blinking. She asked for an enhanced display of the latest satellite imagery on her monitor. It could not show the details of the chaos all around her, but it did clearly show the faint outline of the ridge she was on and her projected path to rendezvous. At her current rate of travel, the computer estimated she would not even come close to making her deadline.

Suzanne's mind then interpreted the lights and shadows of the maps from her past route to her current position to indicate a rough degree of the terrain's irregularity or measure of chaos. She was gratified to know she seemed to be in the worst of it, but it was still far too rough to try and thread her way deeper into the Cerberus. She looked at the chart carefully to see if there was a clearer path through. By the chart she viewed, it seemed to be mostly chaotic.

It was then that she realized she would have to try and go around the Cerberus entirely. This option had been discussed in great detail before the mission as one of the possible scenarios. Since no person or probe had explored here before, there was no way of knowing that the region was virtually impassible. But in the event that it was, an alternate route was devised around it. Unfortunately, even under the best of projections, going around required far too much time and energy. The MAT simply had to go through it, period.

Suzanne's mind began to work at a frantic pace. She began to calculate how much time it would require backing out and re-routing. She compared her former route and the satellite photos of an alternate route. She then spotted a faint trace of what appeared to be a less chaotic route on the far eastern side of Cerberus, just to the edge of a formation called *Orcus Patera*. The entire region was rough except for what looked like a clear thread. And it led very near, or possibly even directly, to the rendezvous position.

It was almost noon. Suzanne calculated the time required to backtrack and the time it would take to go around. No combination of calculations showed that she could make it at all.

Then she realized if she could find a mostly clear path, she could drive at night, using her lights. Suzanne recalculated again and discovered that, by driving all night at some reasonably safe speed, she could barely make it at the end of the rendezvous window.

"Yes!" she said, and topped off her suit water reservoir and swapped the carbon dioxide canister for a new one. She ate a few high-energy "cruise bars" and popped her helmet back into position. After depressurizing the MAT, she then began to thread her way backward, slowly, out of the chaos of the Cerberus.

By mid-afternoon, Suzanne was free of the worst of the boulder field and tracking nearly due east along the nearest ridges. The terrain was nowhere near as clear and clean as the sol before, but at least she was on the move. Remembering the near tumble she had endured that morning, she was cautions. As the sun began to dip closer to the western horizon, she began a long, slow arc southeast toward *Orcus Patera*. And as she did so, her eyes looked for the trace she had seen on the map of a clear route south. But the road ahead of her was still rough and getting rougher. Suzanne was continuously jolted and bounced and grew weary of the beating. But she knew there would be no rest if she were going to live.

She debated stopping once before nightfall to swap carbon dioxide canisters and eat a bite, but she decided to rest later. BC1 was going to miss a regularly scheduled transmission, but now minutes counted and they would have to wait. She felt sorry for Bob who would worry, but she would have to put it off until mid-evening.

As night fell, Suzanne realized that although the route was rough, it was passable and she was tracking right down the center of what the chart had shown to be the clear path through. As the sun neared the horizon, she realized that she had no choice but to slow down. She sighed, knowing that she was very tired and overly stressed, probably suffering from high carbon dioxide levels but that this route would require an even slower speed and greater attention to detail.

Realizing this, Suzanne forced her eyes to focus on the sand in front of her. And it was at that moment that she discovered she was riding in the tracks made by another vehicle.

Illuminated clearly by the setting sun, this time the tracks were obvious and distinct and ran out before her. She stopped the MAT, checked her suit pressure and stepped outside the vehicle. She bent down and looked at the deeply set tracks closely. They appeared to be somewhat wind blown, but they were distinctive. They were also deep, which indicated they had been made by a relatively heavy vehicle, and wide, indicating a manned vehicle. Suzanne had never heard of any nation launching a probe with this large of a track base. It did not take much deductive reasoning to understand that the vehicle that had made these tracks was almost certainly Soviet. With that thought, she sighed intensely. If the tracks continued, she could probably follow them safely around the Cerberus.

By this time, it was almost totally dark. Suzanne slid back into the MAT, pressurized it and immediately set up her communications gear. She carefully considered her transmission and sent it. She relayed the scarce details of her re-routing, her decision to drive at night and added, "AM FOLLOWING TRACKS. BELIEVE THEM TO BE SAR."

She had no way of knowing that her transmission would never be received.

Suzanne then quickly ate a few more cruise bars, replaced her helmet and started again. If driving the MAT during the sol was torturous, it was positively inhuman at night. Suzanne soon discovered it to be a near impossible task. She could not see the tracks at all from an upright position, so she had to lean her body as far as she could to the right and peer out a tiny window at the base of the egg shaped MAT where she could barely see the tracks. That required that she drive to the left of the tracks themselves so she could see them in the lower window. Then she had to sit upright and watch out for boulders. She discovered that the tracks often led her between boulders so that driving to the left was a hazardous proposal. After about an hour of this and two near misses with large boulders, she was near exhaustion and realized that something was going to have to change.

Suzanne stopped the MAT, repressurized it and took off her helmet. She then took a small screwdriver from the MAT's toolbox and pried the interior camera off the upper instrument panel. She bit through its wires with her teeth and spliced into a two meter length of wire she had ripped out of a rear light panel. Using a sticky label from a fuse panel, she insulated the splices. Then she put her helmet back on, depressurized the MAT, popped the door open and attached the camera with silver tape to the front of the Mars vehicle. She would not be able to latch or pressurize the door with the wire running through it, but it did not matter; her suit was pressurized anyway.

She got back inside, tied the door shut with a length of wire and switched her large front-facing monitor to the camera. Now she could clearly see the tracks illuminated by the MAT's external lights!

This process had cost her an hour, but it was worth it. Suzanne was able to more than double her speed. She could clearly see the tracks before her and boldly pushed ahead in the darkness. At this rate, she would make it to the rendezvous even before the deadline! Over an hour later, Suzanne was alarmed when she noticed the tracks veered sharply east. She stopped and looked at her displayed chart. This would definitely lead her away from the rendezvous point. If she continued following the tracks at this pace and in that direction, she could not possibly make her deadline. Yet, there was no hope of making it by trying to blaze a totally new trail at night. Stopping until daylight would be fatal as well. There was always the distinct possibility that this path led around some obstacle and would turn south again soon.

Suzanne then prayed out loud, "Oh, God, please let this lead me to the right place." Then she started up again and faithfully, blindly began to follow the tracks in the darkness. Soon, the tracks began to turn south. Within another hour, they pointed directly at the rendezvous point. Realizing this, Suzanne sighed and relaxed against her seat. The tracks were so well defined that they seemed to miss most rocks and the ride became gentle. So gentle, in fact, she soon fell asleep.

Less than a minute later, the MAT crashed head on into a house sized boulder.

t BC1, the last transmission from Suzanne had been received in the mid morning of the second day: an unscheduled, cryptic broadcast routed through the clumsy patch-through from the navigation satellites. While she was on schedule, they felt it was very unusual that it was sent out of sequence and with few details. Three hours and twenty minutes after receipt of that report, Toon informed them that the navigation satellites themselves had also failed. They would not be able to receive any messages at all from Suzanne. Now, they were totally cut off from the entire planet as well as the rest of the solar system.

Peter immediately arranged an emergency meeting in the Command Center. He called Francis, Toon, Gorteau, Kerry and Brinker. Hammonds was manning the controls.

"Toon: analysis," he commanded with some great degree of frustration, noting Bob Kerry fuming silently to himself.

"I have no clue, boss," Toon replied. "It's not software. It's not uplink equipment or downlink equipment. They're just not there anymore as far as we can tell."

Peter's mind raced for ideas - something.

"Okay," he finally stated. "Contact the Soviets on their birds and tell them we have a situation."

"I already did that," Toon replied. "They're not home."

"What do you mean, they're not home?" Kerry asked in undisguised anger.

"I've had Hammonds on this from the beginning. It's like they're just not home."

"Give me the damn microphone," Kerry said, bursting with anger, grabbing Hammonds by the shoulder and pulling him around in his seat.

"Back off, sir," Brinker replied stepping forward.

Kerry stared back at Brinker in fury.

"I said, *back off*," Brinker said evenly, locking his eyes onto Kerry's.

Kerry released Hammonds and turned away. "This isn't happening," he said with resignation, facing the wall.

"Fabian, what's your assessment?" Peter asked firmly.

"None of this adds up, Peter. The raw probabilities of losing all our satellite links in the manner in which we have are staggeringly small. In the absence of data, I would suggest human fault is at play here."

"Define," Peter replied, pursing his lips in tension.

"Since very little of this can be controlled by the Soviets, I would suggest our processes here are either in error, which is causing us to lose control, or there is deliberate human intervention."

"Toon, you control these processes, what about it?"

Toon smiled his best fake smile and replied, "Ok, blame the operator. But if you feel you can do any better, have at it!" he remarked, dramatically sweeping his hand over the consoles in the Command Center.

"It's got to be Covenant; that's the only explanation," Francis replied quickly.

"Then where is he?" Peter replied. "How can he hide out here where there is absolutely no place to hide? How is it that he could somehow sabotage our equipment without the operator catching something amiss? And if he has system interface, then from where? Toon, have you checked this?" Peter demanded.

"Top to bottom, Boss. The system is clean."

"Geoff, have you gone behind him? Checked every line of code, every piece of equipment?"

"As best I can, Peter," Hammonds replied with an obviously limited confidence.

"If Covenant were up to something, don't you think we would have seen *something*?" Peter asked Francis.

"Then it leaves no other explanation. The birds are just dead," Toon replied. "There's just no other possible reason for what we are seeing."

"Covenant. It's Covenant, I can assure you," Francis replied. "I don't know how, but he's up to something here, and you can bet your life on it."

"Just one problem with all these theories, my egghead friends," Brinker responded.

All eyes turned to him. "You folks got all these pieces of the puzzle all laid out on your table, and one piece still don't fit."

"Ok," Peter said impatiently, "Go ahead..."

"The Soviets," he replied. "I can smell rotten cabbage all the way over here."

"Evidence?" Peter pressed.

"Plenty. They called this little risky cross-country meeting and demanded we come to the party. Even a grunt like me can see it would have been easier and probably safer for them to make the trip in their SAR, but they demanded that we show up. Why wasn't a teleconference good enough? They have the birds that are all working and in good order. We didn't even bother to ask the question."

"Why?" Kerry asked, turning to rejoin the group.

"In the history of warfare, messengers were often used for purposes of interrogation - to ferret out information about the opposing camp. They don't want to talk to us anymore because they got what they want. They simply don't need to talk to us anymore. Easy enough for you? The pieces all fit together very nicely on my table," explained Brinker.

"Why didn't you warn us?" Kerry asked with a seething resentment.

"Excuse me, but may I interject something here?" Gorteau interrupted. "There was no need for a warning because this possibility was never discussed and it was clearly not necessary. This scenario is still pure conjecture, Sergeant, and, frankly, out of place. Your comments only serve to heighten anxiety and are not based on any fact or evidence whatsoever. The joint plan we put together was very workable and quite safe."

"Listen, Gorteau, you pay me to run security around here, and that's my job," Brinker replied, pointing his cigar at Gorteau. "Now, I didn't go to Harvard or Princeton, but I did go to some of the finest military schools in the Marine Corps, and I do believe that between you and me, that makes me the real brains on this topic."

"Stop it, right now!" Peter interrupted, his mind processing furiously, his eyes darting about the room, focusing on nothing in particular.

"Fabian, you've mistrusted their intentions from the beginning - from the first transmission. Why the sudden change?" Peter inquired.

"Nothing has changed. And I don't believe I've ever used the term 'mistrust'. I only initially suggested a process of diplomatic positioning. My caveat to Sergeant Brinker is a simple prudence against starting rumors which may lead to panic and improper decisions, further reducing our life support capacity. I believe all our lives are dependent on making decisions based on fact and not wild conjecture. We must… *we must* deal with the situation based on quiet reason and not baseless, emotional inferences.""

Without even a moment's hesitation, Peter responded strongly. "I believe you're wrong here, Professor."

Gorteau responded with an upraised eyebrow. He was, after all Peter's chief mentor and advocate.

"Given these circumstances we must invest a great deal of resources to security issues. While it would be nice to believe that we've left our savagery behind, I rather think it's packaged in our genome. Therefore, I've decided to rely heavily on Brinker's instinct and security training. While we don't have all the answers, or even a few answers, it's obvious that something is going down. As you said, the probabilities that all these things could be the result of chance are vanishingly small. Therefore, we'll assess together the various scenarios and prepare for what we can. I only ask you to shift your great mind into a fair assessment of possible outcomes and team with Brinker to give me a list in one hour. Bob Kerry, you're also on their team. Brinker's in charge of this. And don't hold anything back from me - I want to see it all."

Gorteau just nodded in resignation at Peter and glanced at Brinker who looked away, closing his eyes and sighing deeply.

34

Suzanne knew she was dreaming.

It was a cold dream - deeply, bitterly cold. But she also knew somewhere in her mind, that she had to be awake. There was some background understanding that she had to be alert at all times to prevent disaster and to keep herself from dying all alone. It was a powerful, forceful fear; almost a command. It consumed her mind; but she was cold - way down deep in her mind and her body and her bones. And she was profoundly sleepy. The urge to sleep was powerful, and it drew her into her inner self. She knew that she could forget about the cold and forget about the urgency if she just gave into the sleep that so seductively beckoned her. But this urge to sleep forcefully conflicted with a quiet but persistent call to urgency and vigilance.

In the end, she could not, would not, give into sleep. There was a part of her mind more powerful than that which urged her to sleep - to give up to the cold and to the urgency and to the pain.

It was the recollection of pain that finally forced her eyes to open. Suzanne regained consciousness with a start. Her eyes could not focus. She was trapped and could not move. She could see dim, diffused lights flashing through a haze and fog, but she could not focus. And she could not move.

Her body was pressed forward, head down, trapped by her seat restraints. She thought she could hear a cacophony of alarms and buzzers dimly in some distant background. And she was as cold as she had ever been.

Suzanne's first effort was to move - move something, move anything. She could feel the strength of her muscles try to move, but she was tightly trapped in her seat. As she breathed, she could see her breath curl inside her helmet. This kept her from total panic; just being able to focus on something - anything. She realized that she could not see outside her helmet because her breath had condensed on the cold faceplate of her pressurized suit. She clearly knew her suit was intact and still pressurized or she would have been dead long ago.

Her mind began to awaken and work more quickly with each passing moment. Suzanne understood that she must have nodded off and rammed the MAT into something. She also realized she must have been unconscious for some unknown period of time and that her suit heater was turned off. She had been relying totally on the MAT's heaters when underway, so the MAT's hull must have been breached by the impact.

She needed heat, fast and urgently. She could not feel her feet or toes and her fingers screamed with the pain of frostbite. Suzanne raised her right hand and moved it in an arc toward her suit front. There she found the toggle for the suit heater and turned it on. Immediately she could feel the warm liquid begin to flow through her cotton skin-wear across her body, down her legs and to her feet, arms and hands. She could feel the warm air blow across her faceplate as she toggled the helmet defogger fan. In less than a minute, the faceplate had cleared and she could see again.

The MAT was a wreck. Most of the gear behind her was now piled on top of her or pressed her forward. With as much strength as she could muster, Suzanne pushed backward and moved enough of the weight pressing onto her to have a few inches of space to leverage her body.

She then realized that she could see clearly out of her right eye, but the left was blurred. She switched her helmet light on from her arm controls and looked at the image staring back at her reflected in her helmet faceplate. Suzanne was horrified when she saw herself. Her face was caked and streaked with blood from a cut just above her left eye. The blood had run down her face, cheek and neck and into her suit. Fortunately for her, when the impact shoved her body forward, the helmet itself, which had caused the cut, also held pressure on it while she was unconscious. Otherwise, she felt certain she would have bled to death.

The problem with any injury inside a pressurized helmet was that it could not be attended to until the occupant could be taken to a pressurized compartment and removed from the suit. Suzanne understood that such a break would not be forthcoming soon. She silently prayed that between the pressure of her body and the cold that the cut was sealed and the blood would not flow again.

Her next order of business was to get out of the MAT. She attempted to move sideways to her left toward the door. To her surprise, the seat restraint unlatched on the first try and she slid easily toward the hatch. Not able to turn her head, she reached for its latch. It was not there. Suzanne then realized that the door was not in place, so she slid all the way outside and onto the ground.

Her legs would not hold up under the weight of her body, so she fell to the sand, face first. She then felt a wave of fear. It was still night and darkness surrounded her. She was alive, but for how long? There would not be, could not be, any rescue for her here.

Suzanne turned over on the sand and began moving her legs, arms and feet to see if she had any broken members. Then she looked back at the MAT. The vehicle was totally destroyed beyond all repair. It had run headlong into a huge boulder, rising some seven or eight meters above her. Its shell had literally imploded on impact and both hatches lay in the sand. The solar panels lay in an unfolded heap around it and the area was strewn with bits and pieces of the MAT and the equipment that had been strapped to it. The panel lights inside glowed and flashed uselessly.

Suzanne realized at that moment that her life was over. Her clock was simply ticking down for the final count. Her only fear was that Bob would be so upset that he would try something stupid like mounting a party to find her body and risk his own life in the process.

She summoned all of the willpower inside her and sat up in the sand. She began to feel tingling in her feet as she moved them; one good sign, at least for the moment. Suzanne stood upright and a wave of dizziness engulfed her mind, but it passed in a few seconds. Her fingers and toes screamed with pain as circulation began to return.

She was determined to send a message to BC1 to let them know what had happened and where they could find the precious MAT equipment much later on, if they survived the coming winter. She turned and began to pull equipment away from her seat so she could get in and cycle the transmitter, which still appeared to be operational. She sent a short message back giving the details, the position, and a brief encrypted message to Bob. Once again, she did not know that they would never receive it.

She looked at the time. It would be sunrise in less than an hour, and she would be long overdue at the rendezvous. She determined that she would not die sitting there on an empty desert waiting for a ride from a passing UFO. At that thought, she laughed. And upon laughing, decided she was going to die with some dignity, after all. At the collective thoughts of meeting her destiny, Suzanne was surprised how well she was able to accept it.

Her mind began to operate normally now with the heaters in the suit providing all the warmth she needed. She decided to back track on foot to wherever the MAT had veered off from following the tracks, then start following the tracks south. She would carry as much oxygen and power packs as she could and still be able to walk. She realized that the limiting agent was her carbon dioxide scrubber which she could not change without removing her helmet, which of course she could not do. When it ran out in 14 hours, she would die of carbon dioxide asphyxiation. But she did have at least 14 good hours.

Suzanne understood clearly that the Soviet SAR would not come to her aid or even spend any time looking for her. They could never be expected to take such a risk, even if it did have the range. Her friends at BC1 could not come, of course. It was to be her last 14 hours of life, and she accepted it fully.

Gathering up her bottles and power packs, Suzanne strapped them onto her body as best she could with tape, Velcro and a makeshift backpack. As the sun rose across the bitterly cold desert, she began to follow the MAT path backward. In just a few minutes, she found where the MAT had left following the first set of tracks.

Immediately, she began to follow the other vehicle's track prints south into the gathering, pink morning light of Mars. As she did so, Suzanne felt an unusual peace about her decision to walk for the few remaining hours of her life. She would have a lot to think about, even to pray about, as she trekked along this most bizarre of all places. As she dwelt on these things, she remembered a poem her mother used to have hanging on her wall called, "Footprints". After considering its verses and its meaning to her now, she had to forcefully will herself not to cry. No matter how poignant her thoughts and reminiscing turned out to be, Suzanne determined that she would not cry. Not only was weeping not a good idea in a space helmet, but when, or if, they ever found her, she wanted Bob to see that she died with a peaceful smile on her face, thinking only of him.

Nearly two weeks had passed since the loss of communications with Suzanne. All hope that she would ever be seen again seemed absolutely lost. Brinker worked like a man demon-possessed on security arrangements and perimeter defenses, convinced that an attack on the base was imminent and would come without warning. With Peter's blessings he posted remote security sensors at locations surrounding BC1, watching the colony's flanks sol and night.

Surprisingly, Brinker's greatest support came from Ashley. As the sols wore on, she seemed to sense that her friend Suzanne was dead or captive. For the first time in her life, she began to express thoughts of effecting personal defense against an enemy. She confided in Peter that she had never considered this before in a civilization spanning two planets that seemed to struggle toward and actually attain freedom from war, one small victory at a time. And after having settled Mars, it seemed that it was entirely possible that war could actually be left behind forever; millions of miles behind. Yet now it seemed to her that war had become inevitable and that she would have to participate in their common defense or become spoil to another ideology. She stated bluntly that regardless of how much she despised war, she despised the thought of slavery and death worse. Furthermore, she fought and was losing an emotional battle of mounting anger over the disappearance of Suzanne.

This idea quickly permeated BC1. With the passing hours and sols since Suzanne had vanished without a trace on a mission of peace, the entire colony was fully engaged in preparations for the first war of the planet aptly named for the ancient god of conflict.

At sunset on the twelfth sol after Suzanne's last transmission, one of the remote sensors signaled the Command Center of an incoming vehicle. The Command Center watch immediately sounded the general alarm, which blared throughout BC1. Alongside the alarm, his voice rang out over the public system, cutting the air like a knife, "This is not a drill. This is not a drill. Incoming vehicle headed our way!"

Every colonist paused for just a half second. While Brinker had drilled them on this alarm, they had prayed they would never hear it for real. Then they sprang for their assigned defensive stations and shelters.

Brinker and Peter shot into the Command Center at once. On the monitor above their heads, they could see the vehicle making a slow approach to BC1, just northwest of the launch tower, some three kilometers out.

"It's not one of ours," Brinker stated bluntly, getting as close to the screen as he could.

"It's Soviet – a SAR," Peter replied confidently. "It's definitely one of theirs."

"Radio contact?" Peter fired at the Command Center watch officer.

"Negative," he replied. "Dead on all channels."

The vehicle continued to advance.

"It could be loaded with explosives," Brinker said. "We've got to stop it before it gets within range."

"A remotely guided vehicle? A suicide pilot?" Peter asked to no one in particular.

"Either way, it won't matter much if we let it get any closer," Brinker snapped.

"But what if it's Suzanne returning?" Ashley asked over their shoulders.

"Two and a quarter klicks and closing," the Watch Officer noted.

"What's your plan, Brinker?" Peter asked, eying the Marine.

"I'm on it," he replied, racing out of the Command Center.

Brinker raced to the MAT airlock, and without benefit of a suit, leapt inside the MAT nearest the door and closed the hatch. Sensing the urgency, a technician burst into the MAT/ Airlock control room and began to sidestep every procedure in the book, his fingers racing over switches and dials, trying to get the airlock depressurized and the door open as quickly as possible. He dumped the raw air of the hangar outside, a grievous violation of procedure. Brinker meanwhile started the electric drive of the MAT and inched it toward the door, impatiently slamming his right palm against the wheel while his left hand wildly gestured the technician to open the hatch. But the door was held shut by the laws of physics; pressure and the inability of the hatch to open until the safety interlocks were satisfied.

Finally the door began its slow swing open into the darkening Martian desert.

The whole colony watched the action unfolding from their emergency stations; every eye glued to the monitors controlled by the Command Center.

"Open the damn door!" Brinker roared over the MAT's radio.

"Going as fast as I can," the technician replied. "Don't hit the door, whatever you do…" he added, which everyone correctly interpreted as, "There's no replacement if you wreck it."

Finally, Brinker successfully inched past the barely open door of the airlock and accelerated as fast as the MAT would go into the red desert. But this had cost them precious minutes.

"Your target is 1100 meters ahead of you," the Watch Officer reported. "Constant bearing; decreasing range. It hasn't deviated or slowed its approach since first sighting."

Brinker could see the vehicle approaching. It was definitely a Soviet SAR, with no lights showing, headed straight toward the MAT airlock. As he neared the vehicle, he cursed not having his spacesuit, which severely limited his options of whatever he was going to do when they met. But it was too bad, he reasoned. The minutes were just not there to work this by any reasonable semblance of a procedure.

The two vehicles closed quickly on one another as the colony watched things unfolding in abject horror. Brinker and the oncoming vehicle were obviously engaged in a game of interplanetary chicken. Neither craft appeared to be backing down. If they collided, even in a side-swipe, Brinker would die instantly. But a second or two before one craft would have had to turn, the Soviet vehicle slid to a sudden stop. Brinker's MAT also braked as they faced one another head-on in the frozen Martian desert.

For long minutes they faced one another, unmoving. No one in the colony spoke – or breathed. Finally, Brinker's MAT slowly pulled alongside the Soviet vehicle, their sides nearly touching.

"Let us both back into the Hangar," Brinker commanded over his radio. "And hurry up!"

Brinker's MAT circled the Soviet SAR vehicle, then turned to lead the way back to the MAT airlock hangar.

"Brinker, what do you have?" Peter asked.

"Wait and see for yourself," Brinker replied. "Just have plenty of manpower waiting. I want my Marines there, first in line. And I'm gonna need a medical team, stat!"

Brinker entered the hanger first followed by the oddly shaped Soviet vehicle. Just as the SAR entered, the door swung slowly shut as the technician re-pressurized the hangar.

Peter, Ashley, Bob and the rest of the colony's leadership were just behind two Marines, armed to the teeth, waiting as the airlock pressurized. As usual, the pressurization process caused a certain amount of dust and fog to obscure the view, further heightening the tension while they waited. But, eventually the access light blinked green.

The Marines popped the hanger's access door opened and stood with weapons raised on both sides of the Soviet vehicle. Brinker's hatch raised and he stepped out of his MAT, cigar in his mouth.

"Open it up, Covenant," he ordered, tapping on the hatch door with his knuckles.

The SAR hatch released and Julian Covenant looked out at Brinker with his typically confident sneer. "No need for the weapons, Marine, I can assure you."

"I'll make that decision. Now get out and I want to see your hands up and open," Brinker snarled. "Take this man into custody," he ordered his men. Covenant looked agitated, but complying fully, stepped out of the vehicle with his hands up and spread.

While everyone else was occupied with the sight of Covenant, Bob Kerry gasped, "Oh, my dear God!" and ran toward the vehicle. He yanked the opposite side hatch open and there, in the other seat, lay two unconscious forms; one of them Suzanne.

He grasped her face gently in his hands to see if she were still breathing. As he did so, she opened her eyes and smiled weakly. "Trust him…." she said softly as she drifted back into unconsciousness once more, her fingers tugging weakly against his arms.

ob Kerry personally rescued Julian Covenant from Brinker's grasp as the medical technicians unwound Suzanne and Fyodor Stepanovich Kirov's intertwined and broken bodies from the front of the Soviet SAR. Suzanne had been beaten and her limbs showed signs of advanced frostbite. But Kirov was in a much worse state – a deep coma, half frozen and battered nearly to death. Covenant did not show even a scratch.

Covenant convinced Peter that he required an immediate but private conference with him in a room whose security was guaranteed. He also demanded that only Peter and Francis be in attendance. On the urging of Bob Kerry alone, Peter agreed to the private conference but also heeded the insistent warnings of Brinker not to trust him or anything he said.

Peter, Francis and Covenant met behind closed doors.

Peter started the meeting out bluntly. "Let me start this by saying, up front, that I don't trust you Covenant."

Unfazed, Covenant replied, "This colony has but a few sols to prepare for war. They Soviets should have left Shturmovoi already, hell bent on destroying you."

"How do you know this?" Peter asked, still untrusting.

"Have you ever heard of Hernando Cortez?" Covenant asked.

"The Spanish conquistador?" Peter asked neutrally.

"Yes," Covenant replied. "One and the same. You see, he left Spain bent on conquest of the New World. His idea of conquest included mostly booty – the gold of the Central American Aztecs. But he left Spain for one thing – utter and total conquest. Gold was his reward, but his goal was the annihilation of a whole civilization. In short, he wanted the resources and he did not care about anything else; it was all trivial to him, especially resistance, or peace or mercy. The interesting thing about Cortez was that he was very anal, very single minded, very directed, and very goal oriented."

"Why do we have to suffer through this history lesson, Covenant?" Francis snarled.

Covenant ignored him as though he were not even in the room. "When Cortez arrived in the new world, he unloaded his ships, his army and his animals, and then burned the ships in the harbor, not even leaving himself an avenue of escape. They were to conquer or die, and there was no other option, not even for himself."

"And your point is?" Francis asked with premeditated insolence.

"You're about to witness the madness of Cortez repeated on this planet. You see, my friend, the SARs fully loaded with people as they are, well, they're only capable of a one-way trip. Once they arrive, they will be critically low on life support and they'll have no way back. Their mission here is to kill all of you, leave no one alive, and finish the Martian winter in your quarters, breathing your air and feeding off your consumables. They know that all of them and all of you cannot possibly survive what's to come. If any of us are left alive, it'll be as expendable slaves, nothing more."

"How do you know this?" Francis asked, fully skeptical, looking toward Peter. "I, frankly, don't trust you, Covenant, any more than he does."

"Well, obviously, I just came from there and witnessed it with my own eyes," Covenant replied, looking to Peter. "You know, my ex-mother-in-law never trusted me either. So you're in relatively good company."

Peter took the cue and stood between them. "Francis, we need to back off a little here," he said bluntly. "Logic seems to be on his side. He appears to have saved two lives and has a good story so far. We need to cut him some slack and let him talk."

Then Peter looked squarely at Covenant as he walked a slow circle around him. "I'm not saying that I actually trust you, Covenant, but I'm dying to hear the rest of the story – all of it."

"Very well," Covenant replied, nodding his head and looking down at his feet. "And so you shall. I am a British agent, who was requested for assignment to this base by the late Lassiter Lipton."

"A British Agent?" Peter asked with all incredulosity, laughing aloud. "Why would Lipton assign a British ..."

"Because he knew you were infiltrated with RSE Agents – at least one and perhaps two."

"And why would it matter, Covenant? Who would give a tinker's damn if there were a spy here? Everything we do, everything we think, is published in international journals! We've no secrets here worth hiding! And why a British Agent? What about the CIA or the FBI? Don't we have plenty of our own spies to go around?"

Covenant replied slowly. "I realize this is very difficult to explain in such a brief time, but please allow me to continue."

"Peter, I want to hear this," Francis responded, now surprisingly taking the position of the cooler head between them.

"I have credible scientific credentials, which would have hidden my identity better than one of your own agents. Furthermore, I've been an operative in the specific area of RSE intelligence for most of my career, which also made me the best choice. And finally, Lassiter Lipton was informed that the Soviets had seriously developed plans for sabotage of our efforts here at BC1. Of course, it didn't hurt that Lipton has a famous British heritage."

"Why? Why would they want to harm or even interfere with our effort here?" Peter asked with an amazed look on his face.

"We didn't know. But we felt like it was worth the effort to understand the situation and be in a position to block their efforts if it were true. Furthermore, we had no idea if BC1 had been infiltrated for purposes of sabotage and, if so, who it would be. It was my job to find these things out before it was too late. As a MI5 agent, I'm trained to accomplish these tasks."

"If that's so, then why didn't you tell me when I was elected leader of this colony?" Peter asked angrily. "Didn't you think I had a right to know this subterfuge was occurring right under my nose? If Lipton knew, then why was I left out?"

"Frankly, Peter, you've always been one of our suspects." Covenant replied bluntly. "And after the death of Lipton and the rather extraordinary change of command around here, you actually moved up on the list."

"Oh yeah, and who would the rest of 'our' be?" Peter replied instantly, facing Covenant. "Who else around here works for your little undercover spy-versus-spy team?"

Covenant stared back coldly. "'Our' is merely a reference to MI5 headquarters."

"Liar," Peter snapped. "You're a cold blooded liar, and probably a murderer; and even more probably, you just moved up on my list of chief suspects as a double agent for the Soviets."

Covenant smiled. "Touché. Well done," he replied softly. "Your point is well taken and understood. I fully recognize your sovereignty here, Peter and even if I don't agree with how it was achieved, I would be a fool to disregard it, and I shall not. Understand that it is difficult to lose contact with base and not have any other recourse left except continuous self motivation based on endlessly shifting realities."

"Continue," Peter responded neutrally.

"My primary task here has always been to ferret out the infiltrator, or infiltrators. That's the sole reason for my being here. When Lassiter died and there was no more connection with base, I began to work alone on the case, and it was obviously becoming more urgent. I noticed that as the community now operated in a completely open mode, where there were no secrets, my job became infinitely more difficult. The Soviet agent was obviously capable of freely sharing everything with Shturmovoi and no one would be the wiser. You see, they've had a briefing transmitted from here to them each sol since this base opened, including every sol since the crisis began."

"How do you know this?" Francis asked.

"I have intercepted three of them in code. But the agent is brilliant and continuously changes his mode of operations. And I haven't been able to decipher the messages."

"Then how do you know what they are; that they're secret messages sent to the Soviets?" Peter pressed.

"Because they are precise and directional; aimed in each case directly toward Shturmovoi."

"Why didn't you share this with Gorteau? He would've been able to decipher them for sure!" Peter asked, exasperated.

Covenant stared back at him in silence. The unspoken answer was obvious; Gorteau was also a suspect.

"Go on," Peter said in disgust.

"At first, my strategy was to take on the role of a traitor to your little government, to try and draw the agent to me and make a contact. That failed miserably. The next attempt to identify him – or her - was to plant a dummy virus in the computer system to see if the agent would be curious and try and activate it himself. I had it all wired to determine exactly who it was. The virus was a clever fake, of course, and would never have damaged your systems, but it certainly would have found my suspect. Unfortunately, that did not work either. I realized at that point that you had compartmentalized the information and he either did not know about it or the infiltrator was one of your inside people. Finally, I knew that I would have to go to the Soviets and find out directly, one way or another. I knew that time was running out."

"And how did you manage to make the trip across 2065 kilometers of desert to Shturmovoi?" Peter asked, astonished.

"Easy. I just called and ask for a pickup, and they obliged. You see, I put it to them in a way that they couldn't refuse. After my request, their local plant advised them I was for real since I had made such a jerk out of myself around here, and I now wanted to sell you out. So they had nothing to lose and everything to gain by a pickup. They sent a SAR with one driver, and had supplies cached along the route, for a round trip. It was very easy. All I had to do was stage a walk-out and hoof it to hide behind the nearest big rock over yonder hill until they arrived."

"I thought you said they couldn't make a round trip." Francis noted.

"The SARS are very capable vehicles. It all depends on how they're rigged. This particular rigging could not have been made with two people; but only a single passenger one way and two the other made it possible."

"Then why did they want or need Suzanne? And why did they demand she meet them halfway?" Peter demanded.

"Because they didn't trust me and they needed verification of my story before they could proceed with their invasion plans. Their whole idea was to bring an American in and torture them until they spilled the truth, the whole truth and nothing but. They understood that you never even dreamed they were nuts enough to start a war and thought they could glean enough information out of an unwitting witness to stage their war plans properly. As far as the SARs capabilities, they lied to you, plain and simple. Furthermore, they needed a real live MAT to see if you had lied to them about its capabilities. After all, it would be rather embarrassing to pass each other in the desert on the way to conquer one another, now wouldn't it?"

"But why didn't they just ask their spy – why did they need a live body?" Peter pressed.

"In the world of intelligence, one never trusts any single source. You see, if they had three separate data sources – their plant, me and Suzanne - they would have a three point fix on the truth and proceed with certainty. Basically, they're so deviant, they expect everyone else to be the same and they don't trust anybody, period. It's always been a sad reality that in the wide, wide world of spies, everyone is suspected of lying to everyone else, because they usually are."

"Then why didn't they torture you?" Peter asked, still full of suspicion.

"They were always uncertain as to whether I was for real or not. If you take on a willing defector, treating them nicely gains far, far more useful ground than torturing them."

"He's right, of course," Francis added, then looked to Covenant. "I believe you; go on."

"They kept almost everything away from me while I was there. But they did not know that I understand Russian fluently even though I speak it very badly. I was able to glean enough random bits and pieces to verify they were planning action against BC1 and that they were expecting a visitor."

"I was standing on the airlock dock when Suzanne arrived, half frozen and unconscious. She had apparently crashed her MAT before the rendezvous point and was actually walking toward the pickup when the Soviet SAR saw her and snagged her at the very last moment. She was down to her last breaths of oxygen and her CO2 filter had all but burnt out. They actually saved her life and brought her in. Later that sol she regained consciousness but found herself in more of a torture chamber than a hospital. Fortunately for her, she was so weak that it took only a relatively light beating before she slipped under."

"And what were you doing while all this was going on?" Peter demanded.

"Planning the escape, of course. I knew I would have only one shot."

"I'm dying to hear the rest of the story," Francis said without betraying whether he was being sarcastic or not.

"The escape was actually fantastically easy," Covenant began. "The security structure there was never designed to keep people in. So it was a simple matter of poking a hole in the walls of the infirmary and the SAR hangar and letting the computers sense the pressure loss. Their system then began to seal off the infirmary and the route between by automatically closing doors. But I had wedged the doors leading out of the infirmary to the SAR airlock. The drop in pressure between these points kept anyone from being able to enter anywhere in between.

"As pure fate would have it, they moved Kirov into the same room as Suzanne on the sol of the escape. It seems they were keeping him barely alive so they could continue to torture him for whatever weird reasons they had. So once the alarms began going off, I taped fire escape bags over their heads so they wouldn't suffocate as the air pressure dropped and dragged them both out to the SAR hangar. I then stuffed them into the SAR closest to the door and blew the outer door open with a packet of explosives to let myself out quickly. They had already rigged the unit I selected to make the trip to BC1, so it was a relatively simple matter of snag and drag."

"So why didn't they come after you?" Peter asked.

"Easy. I slashed all their tires and as many of their hydraulic lines as I dared before leaving in a bit of a rush!" Covenant replied with a visible smirk.

Peter looked disappointed. "Do you mind explaining how you slashed the tires of the most puncture and tear resistant material known to man?" he asked in reference to the material of all tires used in Martian exploration. "Don't you think that story is just a little hard to believe? Doesn't the slashing tires part of your story make the rest of it very doubtful? Isn't it impossible, in fact, to slash over 40 tires in just a few minutes?"

"Not with one of these," Covenant replied confidently, pulling what appeared to be an ink pen from his pocket. With a twist, a bright red beam appeared and Covenant sliced a 4 inch thick glass paperweight in half with the sweep of his wrist.

For the first time in his memory, Peter smiled at Covenant.

"Only one more question, Julian."

"Shoot."

"How do you know they're just getting started on their invasion?"

"Just a matter of guesswork on my part, actually," he replied. "Two sols to fix the airlock door and regain access to the SAR fleet. Another two to fix and change the tires and hoses; and one more to finish their attack preparations at an accelerated rate. I left them six sols ago which means they probably left yesterday morning at first light. I could be wrong, of course, but I can assure you that there's someone here in this colony who knows for sure. We just need to find out exactly who it is before more damage is done and they find out what we're up to. If we can find their mole, then our chances improve considerably. If we cannot, then we may not survive beyond another week."

With that, Peter walked to the door and opened it. Brinker was standing there facing him, arms folded, looking at Covenant with murderous eyes.

"Brinker," Peter said, and waited untill the Marine had made eye contact. "Trust him."

Brinker's eyes burned into Covenant's, then back to Peter. "You don't pay me enough for this," he hissed.

Peter did not hesitate, as he replied confidently, "You don't work for pay around here, Marine. Just the honor of serving the Corps for yet another glorious day."

Brinker's expression eased slightly, as though his contemplation of simultaneous dismemberment had somehow miraculously morphed into simple homicide before their eyes. "Oh, you think so, do you boss? Well, maybe you're right about that. But I don't work for the likes of him," he said pointing his middle finger at Covenant, "... and I never will."

"Of course you don't. You're actually partners now – equals. And both of you need to come up with a strategy for defending this colony ASAP. You can save your differences for later, if you have any left after the bloodletting."

"Look at it this way, Sarge," Covenant added in his best clipped British accent, folding his arms across his white shirt. "We're actually pals now."

"Now you listen to me, you Limey punk," Brinker replied with an acidic edge. "We ain't pals till I say we're pals. I nearly tore this place apart looking for your sorry ass."

"Well, hey, let's just say you're now more ready than ever for the next command inspection," Covenant added, then stepped over to Brinker and slid his arm over his shoulder. "No harm, no foul; what do you say?"

Brinker tossed Covenant's arm off his shoulder with obvious contempt. "You touch me like that again, you slack jawed pommie faggot and I'll rip your arm off and stick it up your..."

"No touching on the playground, boys," Peter interrupted. "You know the rules. Now why don't you two run along, finish up your bonding and get to work."

Brinker looked tired and totally exasperated. He sighed deeply, looked to Peter and said again, "You don't pay me enough for this."

ovenant and Brinker worked into the night without rest, even though Covenant had had little sleep in the past few sols. In less than an hour, Brinker appeared to have decided that Covenant was one of the most impressive and best trained individuals he had ever met. He was eyewitness to a fleet of seven SARs sitting ready in the Soviet hangar, not counting the one he had hijacked. The seven SARs were being prepared for the attack; every Martian vehicle the Soviets could piece together for the long trip. Covenant's sharp and focused mind remembered even minute details about their preparations, such as how many bottles of gas were laid out, packs of supplies and even piles of navigational gear. It also helped considerably that he had stolen a fully readied SAR sitting at the head of the line, and much could be interpreted from its configuration. It was also apparent that Covenant saved all their lives by giving them a few essential sols to prepare for the attack.

It appeared that if the Soviets were able to successfully repair all of their vehicles, the attack would come in the form of seven SARs, which could carry six individuals each. They would be jammed in but able to make the one-way trip alive. Therefore, it was assumed that the attack would be carried out by at least 42 individuals. By midnight, Brinker and Covenant had lost all pretense of any combativeness and appeared to be solid, trusting cohorts.

Suzanne was resting comfortably and in stable condition in the infirmary with Bob Kerry never leaving her side. Kirov, however, was in a deep coma and on a respirator. No one expected him to live through the night or even regain consciousness. The extent of his beating was beyond belief, and there was no part of his body larger than a few inches that did not have a cut or contusion.

As Peter summed up all these things, he took stock of the situation. He sat in the dining hall with a hot cup of Rat's best java, deep in thought. There was an attack coming in just a few sols; of this he was certain. For all practical purposes, it was to be either a wave of suicide fighters or the BC1 colonists would die in the ensuing battle; probably it would be some of both. Even if they surrendered peacefully and even if they were not killed outright, the life support system would be exceptionally overloaded and they would all die horrible deaths in just a matter of weeks. No matter how it went down, many people were inevitably going to die. Their colony, structures and systems were so fragile, that one committed individual alone could kill them all, much less 42 people bent on their destruction.

"You look tired, sport," said Ashley sitting across from him at the table.

"I am, actually," Peter confessed to his wife. In his deliberations, he had not noticed that she had been sitting there. As he looked back at her, he realized that she, he or both of them could be dead in a few sols, and he had not even noticed her presence.

She stared back at him wordlessly, with the look that only lovers can give to one another in grave times. His mind caught her look and immediately tried to reason against it. "This is just not the time, not now," he thought to himself. But the other part of his mind struggled against the first thought. "There may never be another time again for the most important person in your life," it said. "She needs you now, right now."

His thoughts were primal; they ran deep, scouring his reasoning and tossing aside all pretense of rationality. For how could there be rationality here, now? It could not coexist with this madness. His mind was caught in a whirlpool of emotions, racked by fear that he dared not show, slammed by conflicts that were too powerful to argue against, by love too deep to say no.

Her warm hand circled tenderly around his. He closed his eyes and could feel her warm breath fall gently around his hand. Soon, he could feel her lips brush against his hand as she raised it to her lips.

He opened his eyes and smiled at her beautiful face; so warm, so open and so full of love reserved for just him, for all of his lifetime. It was a bond and a trust he never wanted to ever question again. "I love you," he mouthed silently.

"I love you better," she replied in a hoarse whisper.

Without speaking, she led him back to their quarters. He did not remember seeing anyone or anything else as they walked slowly, just the picture of her face highlighted against the corridor's red night lights. His hand moved the handle on the door, but he could only see her face, her smile and the fire in her eyes as they shut themselves into the darkened space.

In the dim light, he fell to his knees before her, moving his hands across her clothing which he pulled gently away. As she kissed his hair, he felt the warmth of flesh against flesh and the slow, deliberate assault of obsession, of fear and pain overwhelmed by the love that engulfed it all. In the end they were both consumed and carried away to that special place where lovers go, in a brilliant rush of time and space and passion, both erotic and childlike in its simplicity, which finally, merely, dissolved away into the quiet abyss of merciful sleep.

Zoya Anatolyevna Dimitriov's black spacesuit clung to her 38 kilogram frame like the get-up of a cheap motorcycle whore. The invasion fleet was ready and had moved outside the airlocks into position. Dimitriov stood beside the lead SAR outside the main airlock, on the desert of Mars pointed northwest. Five other SARs lined up behind hers were filled with 30 heavily armed combatants. Counting the three in her vehicle and herself, she was able to muster 34 attackers. In the Shturmovoi domes behind her, she had left the rest who could not fit into the vehicles, or those who she did not trust - all of them scientists. Counting those whom she had executed in the past five sols for treason, subversion, dereliction of duty, disrespect, hooliganism and loitering, only eight scientists remained behind. She had clearly deemed them useless members of the new society and told them repeatedly how she regretted they would be left to consume priceless oxygen and food while she was away.

With her bulbous helmet, Dimitriov looked ridiculously like she was suited in sprayed-on leather and just about to climb into a cannon to be shot into a net. Yet those who faced her trembled in abject fear. She had successfully made herself into the most ruthless human imaginable, and she dispensed life and death with premeditated horror. No one knew who was going to be next. She stood on the Martian desert, the malevolent empress of all she surveyed. She was determined with her life, and everyone else's, to plant the New Soviet Empire on this planet. Whether it destroyed them all or not, it obviously made little difference to her.

Only six SARs were able to make the week long trip northwest to BC1because Covenant had done such a through job at trashing as much equipment as he could on his way out of the airlock. By the time they had gone through their entire replacement parts inventory, and cannibalized to make the necessary repairs, they were only able to utilize six vehicles. Many of them were repaired with borderline fixes. Six people were literally stuffed into each of the five SARs behind her, sitting atop one another and rotating positions to allow their blood to circulate. Dimitriov limited the number of passengers in her command vehicle to the number of available seats in order to preserve her level of personal comfort. Thirty-four Soviets had thus assembled to depart Shturmovoi.

Each SAR was loaded with just enough consumables to make the trip. There was no margin for error. If their mission did not proceed exactly as planned, they would all die. The assignment was simple: arrive as quickly as possible; in a surprise attack, puncture the walls of the colony and kill the Americans; capture BC1, patch the holes, execute most of the survivors and live at BC1 until spring. If BC1 was found to be a superior base, as everyone suspected it was, then Shturmovoi was to be cannibalized and the equipment moved to BC1. The main thrust of the plan was to kill everyone except for those who are absolutely necessary in order to conserve enough oxygen, food and water to survive the coming winter.

Leonid Kravchenko unfolded his ungainly and slightly pudgy form from the SAR and walked to stand beside Dimitriov who was silently staring north. "It is sunrise, Colonel Dimitriov; we must be going now," he said through his helmet communicator. "There lies a great victory ahead of us!"

She turned to look at him with the same contempt with which she looked at everyone. "Shut up and get back into the vehicle," she spat. "I'll decide when it is time to leave. You decide nothing." Kravchenko was used to her stare and knew what it meant. He knew she would just as soon kill him as one of the scientists or a cockroach. But he also understood, as did she, that this wretched woman had no friends and less than a few she could trust, and he happened to be one of them. Such loyalties equated to one of life's few guarantees here or back in the Soviet society on earth.

Kravchenko shrugged almost imperceptibly and walked slowly back to the SAR. Meanwhile Dimitriov turned around and faced the domes of Shturmovoi. She felt no kinship toward this place, the genius of its construction or even of what it meant for the human species. She pulled a remote control device out of a pocket on her suit and, with no remorse, she pointed it at the Shturmovoi domes. Then she pressed a button on the remote with no forethought at all, and tossed it out onto the sand as she turned toward her SAR. She had rigged a small canister of carbon monoxide secretly in one of the ventilation ducts to expel its deadly fumes at the touch of her button and she had also programmed the computers to simultaneously shut down the life support system. She would simply fumigate the scientists like the disloyal vermin that they were, and then freeze their bodies before they could rot. When she returned to Shturmovoi, she wanted to find a full load of life support consumables. Their solidified bodies would be no trouble at all to remove. How dare they assume they had any right at all to breathe her air?

rom inside the Shturmovoi domes, Petroskovich Drobkiev watched as Dimitriov slid quickly into her seat, closed the hatch on her SAR, and began the long trek northwest. He continued to watch as the other five vehicles followed hers, kicking up a thin veil of short-lived dust in the vacuous air and light of the dim Martian sunrise. Then he withdrew a small canister with a severed hose from his coveralls and laughed aloud as its useless control box light blinked on and off. While he had never considered himself a genius like his friend Kirov, he was not stupid either. He had detected the canister of carbon monoxide and easily removed it. He then just as easily overrode Dimitriov's shutdown of the life support system.

He turned and looked at the other seven scientists standing behind him and smiled.

"Comrades, when we have assured ourselves that Dimitriov and her useless interplanetary band of idiot outlaws can not possibly return, open up every communications channel and satellite link we have and get me Peter Traynor on the circuit. He needs to know a few things." Then his eyes scanned the dome above him. "Let us also pray that there is yet enough time and Dimitriov did not leave any more surprises for us of which we are not aware."

C1 was now being run as a full scale military base, preparing for an imminent fight to the death with as many as 42 invaders just sols away. Brinker and Covenant had been appointed military commanders who answered exclusively to Peter. They were given total autonomy to make whatever decisions they deemed best to save the colony. No resources or information were withheld.

With Covenant's disclosure that there was, in all probability, a cunning and accomplished spy among them, they began to carefully compartmentalize information. In the end, only Peter, Brinker and Covenant knew the whole plan.

The base began to run at full tilt around the clock. But because of the increased activity, the energy requirements doubled and the life support system began to strain, pumping out unprecedented amounts of life giving oxygen, pure water and heat. The colony literally watched as their life support system lost sols and weeks of vital, life-giving capacity in a matter of hours. Not only was oxygen being consumed in larger than planned for quantities, the carbon dioxide was beginning to build up beyond the capacity to remove it, and the air became uncomfortable. The system was never designed to handle so many people working around the clock and sacrificing sleep to get so much accomplished.

Peter and Ashley worked tirelessly, with Peter directing every move personally and Ashley struggling to keep the life support system as balanced as she could under the strained circumstances.

Brinker and Covenant split their duties. Covenant was responsible for the close-in defenses and Brinker for the external defenses and organizing the ultimate conflict itself.

Two sols before the expected attack, Peter, Brinker and Covenant met privately.

"The biggest problem, as I see it, is suits. We only have 12 suits that we can spare for outside defenses," Peter said, referring to the number of available, operational space suits.

"So that leaves us outnumbered outside over three to one," Brinker replied, stating the obvious.

"And it leaves only four suits for defense inside the structure," Covenant finished the thought. "And twenty five colonists inside with no pressure protection except the walls, which may be punctured at any time during the attack. They only need to get a single projectile in here and the ones who are not suited will die at a distance and in quite a hurry."

"I can't see them penetrating the walls in too many places, or they won't be able to crawl out of their own suits," Brinker noted.

"They need just one hole, Bupkis. One single, well-placed hole," Covenant responded.

"I told you not to call me that," Brinker said, annoyed and tired.

"We can assume that depressurizing the structures during the attack is a part of their plan," Peter said. "So we must be prepared for that, no matter what."

"Where are we going to protect 25 bodies?" Covenant asked.

"In the shelter, of course," Brinker responded, referring to the life boat shelter common to every off-planet habitat. These shelters protected the crews during solar eruptions, fires, or other calamities that could destroy large sections of the life support systems.

"No," Covenant responded. "That's the first place they'll attack, knowing we're short on suits."

Peter and Brinker sighed together, wordlessly acknowledging the truth of the statement.

"I propose a secondary shelter that no one but us knows about in advance," Covenant continued. "It will be a duplicate of the life boat shelter in a very inconspicuous place."

"Big enough to shelter 25 people for many hours, hidden from our own people until the last minute, totally unobtrusive and one that can be constructed in two sols or less?" Peter asked disdainfully.

"Yes, we have to do this. It's suicide to assume the life boat shelter will not be attacked immediately," Covenant replied as Brinker nodded.

"Okay, make it happen," Peter replied. "Now, Bupkis, tell me about the defense plan."

"You're going to love this," Covenant interrupted with a stiff British grin, eying Peter directly.

Brinker raised his eyebrow and returned a hard stare back to Peter. "Bupkis?" he asked with contempt.

"Sorry; go ahead," Peter replied with a grin.

"Three rail guns outside the perimeter of the domes," Brinker began. "Each strategically placed to intercept the enemy from any direction that they come at us. We monitor their advance with a camera mounted on a weather balloon tethered out at 4,000 meters. That way, they can't easily sneak up on us."

"Wait," Peter interrupted. "What rail guns?"

"The ones we have under construction right now," Brinker responded. "The rail guns that were planned for a future magnetic rail system to the launch site. We've now cannibalized them and have a plan in place to finish them tomorrow, just in time to mount and deploy in position. All we had to do was separate the pieces they'd already shipped."

"But what're you going to use for rail gun bullets?" Peter asked.

"Rocks, what else?" Brinker responded with a smile. "It's not like we have any lack of rocks around here. We got more rocks than in my grandmama's garden. We load up five-liter canisters with the right size rocks then project the loaded canister down the rail. At the end of the rail, we have a reinforced screen that stops the canisters, but the rocks, well, they keep on going – at mach 1.5, give or take a little! And in the thin air out there, they just keep on going! Professor Gorteau designed it himself! The spread of the projectiles is like a super-gauge sawed-off shotgun filled with quadruple ought shot and a shell as big around as my arm! If anyone is anywhere near the end of that gun, even a full klick out, they're gonna wish they'd stayed home!"

"Unbelievable!" Peter replied.

"We can fire one round every 90 seconds from each rail, with one operator per gun," Brinker continued, beaming. "He'll be busier than a one-legged ballerina, but it can be done. The way we have them positioned, we can even shoot through the spaces between the domes if the attack comes from only one quarter, so that all the guns are useful at some aspect of the battle, and totally overwhelming at defending the outside parameters."

"Excellent!" Peter replied. "What about individual weapons?" he persisted.

Brinker looked away, the fatigue returning to his face. "Well, it's not good. We have no more than five weapons – three 12-gauge shotguns and two .45 caliber handguns. We have a grand total of twenty-two 12-gauge rounds and a box of forty-eight .45 caliber handgun rounds. That's it."

"And who's surprised?" Peter replied. "It's not like anyone expected a war up here... It's a miracle even that much got through! Have you improvised other weapons?"

Brinker shook his head slowly. "We're still working out some weapons. We don't have much time and what time we have had I've been spending on the rail guns. Fabian is working on some lasers now. But if it gets close up and personal, it looks like knives are the weapon of choice for everyone outside."

"Hand to hand combat outside?" Peter asked, incredulously. "These people are scientists and engineers. We don't have time to train anyone for this!"

"It won't matter, anyway," Covenant added. "The enemy is very well armed. I estimate they each have high-powered weapons and plenty of ammunition. I don't believe that it'll come to any knife fighting. If they get close enough to see us, they're going to use their guns."

"That's exactly why we've got to keep the war as far away from us as we can. We have to seize the initiative, anticipate their strategy and meet them outside in front of the big guns," Peter said firmly. "This is a matter of life or death for them. By the time they get here, they're going to need to get out of their suits and get to some fresh air. They know this is a war for survival, to live or die out there, so they're going to be coming at us with a desperate, all-or-nothing attack. We won't have time to give them any quarter at all, or we could easily be overwhelmed. If even one of them gets through and inside here with a single weapon, we could lose it all."

Brinker simply nodded. Covenant looked tired and said nothing.

"I need you two as rested as possible," Peter said firmly. "I need you to be sharp; I need you to be frosty, awake and functioning at your best. Therefore, I'm ordering both of you to take a 4 hour rest period, beginning right now."

"Talked me right into it," Covenant said with a deep sigh.

"Sorry, boss, I can't; not right now," Brinker replied.

"Why not?" Peter asked.

"Because I've laid out our defensive plan in such a way that if certain milestones aren't accomplished, then we won't be ready and we'll all likely die."

"What is it that can't wait four hours?" Peter persisted. "What job is there that you have that can't be delegated to someone else for four hours?"

"I need to plant the camera balloon anchor right now – in fact I'm late. And I need to spot it myself for maximum advantage. No one else can borrow my eyes or brain for the job," Brinker said hoarsely.

"Then I'll do it for you," Peter responded, unwilling to give in. "That way you can follow orders and get some rest."

"With all due respect, sir, I need to do this, personally. As soon as I return, I'll grab a few hours," Brinker replied with a sigh.

Peter rolled his eyes and responded, "Alright then. But, that's the last task, then rest." He looked at Covenant. "You stay up until Brinker is done; I need both of you on the same shift."

"Out of all the mates to land, I had to get a gung-ho Marine. What a bargain!" Covenant said with all good humor.

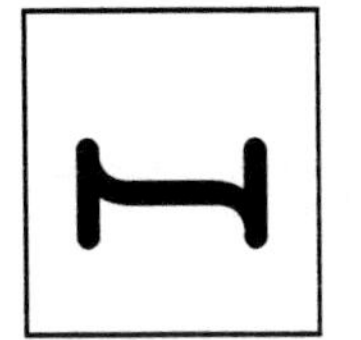

alf an hour later, Brinker and Corporal Pamela Hiraldo shut the hatch in a large, fat MAT dubbed "Cedro," and prepared to disembark the vehicle's airlock bay. The vehicle had been especially outfitted to haul cargo around the base. It consisted of a large, cavernous bay behind the control console. Outside it was chubby with a narrower front that seated the operator, so it had all the external appearance of a pig with wheels. Hence the colonists had named it "Cedro" - Spanish for pig.

Every time a MAT was depressurized, even though the internal air was recovered by directing it back into a holding tank, some of the precious mixture was unretrievable. The use of Cedro was very restricted because each time it was depressurized, a greater amount of unrecoverable life support air was irretrievably lost from its rather large interior than from the smaller MATs. But Cedro was needed on this essential mission to plant the anchor that would fly the camera balloon.

The location Brinker had proposed was halfway between the main colony perimeter and the Crippen Spaceport. The huge MAT rolled outside and onto the sands of Mars. The sun was brilliant and high in the sky. The winter air was still, without dust particles, which made for a crystal clear sky that faded from a dull pink at the horizon to an odd, tinted azure at the zenith.

Cerdo plodded slowly past the domes and toward the exact spot where Brinker had purposed to place the balloon anchor. In the back of Cedro lay a huge Mylar bag, a sand pump, a large length of hose and a spool of super-lightweight wire with which the camera balloon would be anchored. Cedro was pressurized, but Brinker and Hiraldo were both fully suited, except for their helmets, which lay on the floor behind their seats. Soon, the last structure passed behind them and Cedro headed forward on a straight-line path toward their destination. Hiraldo drove, skirting the larger boulders and rocks while Brinker studied a map of the area. In minutes, they arrived.

Wordlessly, Hiraldo shut the MAT's system's down, and donned her helmet, pressurizing her suit. Brinker removed his precious stogie from his mouth and placed it on the lip of Cedro's control panel, then donned his helmet.

"Ready when you are," he nodded to Hiraldo, who slowly depressurized the MAT with the twist of a single dial.

When the gauge read close to zero, Hiraldo and Brinker simultaneously popped their hatches and stepped outside, almost in perfect unison.

They immediately busied themselves to precisely place the bag in position and then to fill it with sand using the sand pump and hoses. When complete, the bag bulged with fine, red sand, which was more than enough to prevent the balloon from blowing away even in a moderate redwind. Then, with hardly any discussion, they loaded their equipment back into the bay for the drive back to BC1.

The moment the pressure gauge read green, Brinker and Hiraldo removed their helmets and placed them behind their seats once again.

"Take your time driving back," Brinker said. "I'm going to grab a quick nap." His eyes were obviously red and he was deeply tired.

Brinker laid his head back against his seat, tugging on his suit's neck ring to keep it from digging into the back of his head. He fell asleep immediately.

Hiraldo slowly and methodically turned Cedro in a wide arc and pointed it back to BC1. Seven minutes later, just 10 meters from the first dome, there was a loud, unexpected clunk followed by a shrill series of alarms as Cedro rolled over onto its top, then back onto its side.

The MATS were never designed to roll, and the weight of its mass immediately caused cracks to appear all along its length. The pressure in the vehicle immediately began to lower as air seeped out along a dozen hairline openings in the hull.

Brinker was wide awake as soon as the MAT inverted itself. Both Marines had followed procedures and were tied into their seats with their harnesses, so they hung sideways in their seats with Brinker down and Hiraldo above him.

Hiraldo immediately retrieved her helmet with her right hand from just above Brinker's seat, then began to fish for his.

Brinker could not move from his position, and he could see Hiraldo was desperately tugging at his helmet that was obviously jammed behind his partially collapsed seat. He could also feel the pressure drop and knew they had but seconds of consciousness remaining.

"Put your helmet on, Marine; now!" Brinker ordered.

She eyed him in panic and continued to try and dislodge his from behind his seat. She knew that only seconds separated them from life and death.

Brinker saw the panic in her eyes, and gripped her helmet with both hands and shoved it with all his energy in front of her face. "Do it now, Marine! Do it now!" he screamed.

Hiraldo looked at him with horror, and then complied. In record time, she had her helmet on and pressurized her suit. With no hesitation at all, she unlatched her belt and fell atop Brinker with a thud. She dug her knee into his forehead as she repositioned herself to wrench his helmet out of its position behind his seat. With one mighty tug, she popped it out, inched away from Brinker and extended his helmet to him.

It was in that moment that Hiraldo saw his eyes; empty and glazed. The pressure had dropped too low and Brinker was on the edge of losing consciousness. If she did not act soon, he would be dead.

In the incredibly tight confines of Cedro, she lifted his head and placed the helmet into position, and swung the latching ring into place. It was jammed. She attempted it again, and again it was jammed. She fought the panic in her mind, and screamed to herself, "...do it Marine; do it now!"

Once again, it was jammed. She ripped the helmet away from Brinker and looked at its ring. To her horror, she saw it was severely bent and would never again fit on properly.

Her mind raced. "He can't die; he can't! He's the only one who can save us!" she thought.

In an instant, she knew what she had to do. She hyperventilated, sucking as much air into her lungs as she could, then depressurized her suit, and, while holding her breath, removed her helmet, and placed it on Brinker, pressurizing his suit as quickly as she could.

The air pressure in the MAT was not at zero, and it was dropping off slower than before, but it was below the pressure required to sustain consciousness and it was below the safe pressure to prevent the nitrogen bubbles from slowly forming in her blood. Hiraldo knew death was but minutes away, and she prayed it would not be painful.

She shook Brinker to awaken him; shaking him and even slamming his helmet into the side of Cedro. But soon, she would be losing consciousness, and even now her thoughts were not fitting together very well...

Brinker awoke completely with Hiraldo's last thrust of his head against the bulkhead. He saw her eyes lock onto his just before she lost consciousness. Instantly, he realized what she had done.

He grabbed the other helmet and started to put it on her when he saw its malformed ring. He thrust it aside and looked desperately around him for anything. Then he saw the backup anchor bag of Mylar. Quickly removing his knife from his side, he cut a large square of the plastic and wrapped it over her head. Grasping a roll of duct tape, he began wrapping it around her suit collar, pulling it tight, as he slammed his fist into her pressure console, starting the flow of air into her suit.

The bag inflated immediately, but not fully. Brinker knew it was leaking. Desperately, he taped all along the edge of the bag to seal it as best he could, until it inflated tightly and the pressure gauge on her suit evened out to a safe pressure. He looked at her form, now lying silently in his lap, and knew that she had stopped breathing.

"No, no, no, Marine; no, no, nooooo!" Brinker screamed at her. "Wake up, Marine; wake up, damn you!" he shouted, as he shook her violently. "Wake up, Marine; that's an order!"

He laid her body on what was now the bottom of the vehicle. Brinker desperately considered his options, which were few. He could not slit the bag and begin mouth-to-mouth resuscitation; that would, of course, be impossible. All he could do was try and restart her heart and force the air in and out of her lungs mechanically.

Immediately, Brinker pumped her chest, on her sternum, five times in rapid succession. Then he placed his fist on her diaphragm and pulled her body toward his chest, lowered her, then pulled her toward him again, three times. Frantically he pumped her chest again, and repeated the mechanical attempt at making her breath.

"Come on, Marine; come on, wake up!" he screamed as he worked. "You don't have my permission to die, Marine! I need you! Wake up!" On the fourth cycle, he could feel her body convulse in a cough.

Desperately, he stood up and forced the door over his head open with unnatural strength. He climbed out of Cedro, and reached back inside and pulled Hiraldo out behind him. He then tossed her over his shoulder and began running back to the nearest pressurized airlock.

The Command Center had been monitoring the accident and had already sent a team to prepare that airlock. When Brinker arrived, the door swung open to receive them.

In the briefest time an airlock had ever been cycled on another planet, the inner door swung open. Brinker laid Hiraldo on the floor among a team of colonists who had gathered around, including a staff physician.

Without a moment's hesitation, Brinker removed his knife from its sheath and cut the plastic away from her face.

Her eyes were open as she looked up at him in an oblivious fog. "Sarge!" she said hoarsely. "I thought I went blind!"

Brinker removed his helmet and placed it on the floor beside her. Then he swept her up in his arms and held her tightly. He did not speak a word.

eter called Brinker into his office as soon as Cedro had been examined by Covenant. Hiraldo's in great shape. Between the partial pressurization of the MAT and your quick thinking, she'll make it," Peter began. "And considering the story you're telling, she's quite the heroine, as well." Then he added bluntly, "It was sabotage. The axle had been partially cut along an axis that virtually guaranteed it would roll the vehicle when it was in motion."

Brinker just nodded. "Then we really do have a spy among us," he said.

Covenant nodded. "I checked all around Cedro's departure position in the airlock, and there were no filings whatsoever. So it's impossible to tell when this was done. I have the technicians inspecting all the other vehicles now."

Brinker's eyes focused on the empty space just before his nose. The stogie rolled around in his mouth in an even, patterned circle. Then he turned and looked at Peter and Covenant.

"When we find this spy, this mole, this plant, this traitor, this conspirator, or whatever he is, whoever he is - he's mine. I want him. It's personal now."

No one argued with the Marine.

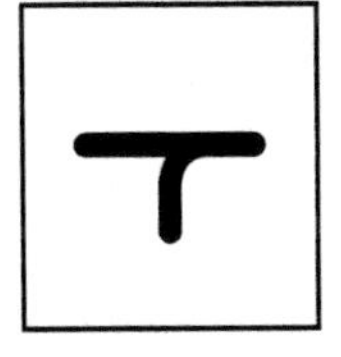

hey had made it halfway; at high noon on the ninth day after Covenant's escape, a caravan of six Soviet SARs sat on the equatorial edge of the Elysium plateau pointed northwest. Dimitriov had ordered them to get out of the vehicles and stretch to celebrate the halfway mark.

The thirty odd passengers looked exactly like they felt; totally repugnant and experiencing painful discomfort. Because the SARS were outfitted for a maximum of four passengers, they literally had to sit atop one another. And because they were commanded to ride with their suits pressurized in case of disaster, they had exceeded the suit's design in every conceivable aspect. The suits were outfitted with emergency urination devices, even had a slim lower compartment for emergency defecation, and each person wore super absorbent diapers in case of leakage. But these systems were not easy to use to begin with and were absolutely impossible to use in the tight confines of the overly packed SARs. In order to use the defecation compartment on the bottom of each suit, the wearers had to position themselves precisely to open the normally closed and narrow orifice leading to the device's pouch. Since this was impossible while sitting still, most passengers had literally missed the mark and filled their lower suit with a mixture of foul body wastes.

Each suit was also designed to filter out personal organic odors before allowing the suit's exit hoses to pass the suit gasses back into the SARs master scrubbers to which they were all attached. But the organic loading was so far beyond the designer's worst nightmares that the filters had failed long ago. They were literally breathing and re-breathing one another's waste organic gasses, and every time a new bodily function took place, it injected yet another round of nauseating gas into the common air system.

To make matters worse, the life support system was not designed to remove as much carbon dioxide as was being produced in the grossly overloaded SARs. Even though they had quickly engineered a second canister, the system was not working as they had hoped. They were all literally suffocating in their waste carbon dioxide – slowly but with certainty.

Between the suits chafing their bodies with each lurch of the SARs, whole limbs asleep from a lack of proper circulation, and a layer of painfully inflamed skin between their legs and armpits, the entire company was functioning at their absolute limits.

After ten minutes outside the vehicles, Dimitriov ordered everyone back in to resume the trip, but she found that not everyone was as motivated as was she to continue.

"Colonel Dimitriov, may I have a word?" said a timid voice over her suit's common communication's circuit. Since everyone could hear the transmission, they froze instantly where they stood.

"Who said that?" she replied harshly.

"It was I, Comrade Leader," said a suited figure raising his hand into the air, near SAR 4, three SARs behind the lead vehicle.

Dimitriov paced quickly to the figure, Leonid Kravchenko following closely on her heels. "What is it?" Dimitriov rasped to the suited individual who stood rigidly before her. His nametag read, "Molosovich".

She could see the man's eyes blinking in desperation behind the bulbous helmet's visor. His mouth twitched but apparently could not form words as he stared back at her in fear.

"Speak!" she commanded sharply, staring holes through Molosovich.

"Comrade Leader, I er, need to inform you of a piece of critical life support system information, if you would please..." Molosovich stammered.

Dimitriov looked back at him with supreme annoyance and flexed the jaw muscles of her firm and hateful face. "What..." she rasped.

"Comrade Leader," he stuttered, "I have made careful calculations and the carbon dioxide scrubbers are failing in each SAR. If we continue at this pace, we will all be dead before we arrive at our destination. Each of us in the rear five vehicles is all suffering from severe hypercapnia, even now."

Dimitriov's expression changed immediately from annoyance to rage and then to deep thought. After ten seconds of silence, she turned and looked at Kravchenko. "Is this true?" she asked him bluntly.

Without hesitation, Kravchenko replied, "No; he is lying!"

Instantly, Dimitriov pulled a Makarov semi-automatic pistol from her suit and pointed it at the visor of Molosovich who shut his eyes tightly.

"Stop, Colonel Dimitriov! He is correct, I can assure you," said a strained voice from the suit's communications circuit.

"Who is now speaking?" Dimitriov demanded, lowering her weapon from Molosovich's face.

"It is I, Colonel; Valentin Anatoliy."

"Come here to me immediately," she demanded.

Anatoliy shuffled as quickly as he could to stand beside her. He had been riding in SAR number three. "Yes, Comrade, he is correct. All of the systems of the rear five SARS are overloaded. None of the occupants can survive the journey. I have personally validated the calculations. All of us are suffering the same symptoms of hypercapnia. Before night falls, there will not be any among us in the five rear vehicles capable of safely piloting for another sol."

"Is this correct?" she barked again at Kravchenko. He looked back at her as their eyes met through their visors.

"Of course, Colonel Dimitriov. I verified his calculations in my head just as he was speaking! I am afraid it is so." They all knew it was a pathetic, undisguised lie, but it was all part of the game called survival in the presence of an insane megalomaniac.

Dimitriov looked contemplative for just a moment, and then ordered, "Everyone stand behind their SARs. Quickly; I do not have all day! Do it now!"

In a few moments there was a cluster of six individuals standing behind each of the five rear SARs. As Dimitriov was closest to SAR four, she walked over to face Molosovich. Still holding her Makarov in her right fist, she looked him in the eye.

"I very much appreciate the courage it took to inform me of our plight, Comrade Molosovich." Then, astonishingly, she smiled at him; a cold, sterile smile. "You have saved us from certain defeat before our enemies."

"I... er, I thank you Comrade Leader..." Molosovich responded with an uncertain stutter in his voice.

"But I hate chronic complainers," she said dropping her smile and raising her weapon to his face. She held it there a full two seconds before pulling the trigger and blowing Molosovich's brains and large pieces of skull through the back of his helmet. His suit instantly evacuated as Molosovich's lifeless body fell onto the sand covered rocks of the Martian desert.

Dimitriov then walked to the next SAR back and stood before the assembled group of six who waited for her, frozen and unmoving.

"Is anyone uncomfortable in this SAR?" she asked flatly.

No one said a word. No one dared to look at her through his or her bubbled visors.

"Very well, then," she said mockingly, and then raised her Makarov to the side of the helmet of the suited figure closest to her. Without warning, she moved the barrel down below the helmet ring and pulled the trigger again, blowing a gaping hole in his neck, killing him instantly.

In the near vacuum of the rarified Martian air, no sound could travel, but they could all feel the strange thump of the vibration passing through their feet as he hit the ground and all watched as the victim's body fluids bubbled and foamed into a ring of ice around his neck.

Dimitriov then walked back to SAR six, at the rear of the convoy. Kravchenko thought better of following her so closely this time and did not move. As she arrived at the rear of the convoy, she stood three meters from the assembled six individuals and asked, "Anyone have any problems here?"

No one moved. Dimitriov lifted her Makarov and pointed it in their general direction, with a slight waver from side to side. "Anyone want to volunteer to stop breathing in SAR 6 for the motherland or do I have to choose?"

It appeared that they had finally figured out Dimitriov's purpose, and the group collectively looked like so many deer in the headlights of an oncoming monster truck. Instantly one of the suited figures stepped out from the pack and leapt at her, a long pipe gripped in his hand. In the Martian gravity, he was able to nearly fly a full two meters in the sky and came down toward her with gritted teeth and makeshift weapon raised.

Dimitriov simply stepped away at the last fraction of a second and allowed him to slide across the sand. The individual sprang into instant action, rolled deftly and expertly end over end then bounced to his feet, facing Dimitriov, rushing back again for the kill. Dimitriov calmly waited until he was just beyond arm's length, raised her weapon and fired directly into the visor. Again, the odd vibration was followed by the instant deformation of a face into a fog of blood and bone which was being sucked out of the gaping hole into the angry, red desert.

Unmoved, Dimitriov turned and paced back toward SAR three as though she were in a great hurry, aimed in the general direction of the suited figures and fired. The bullet struck one of the members in the arm, but the evacuation of the suit was instantaneous and death followed in an explosion of air and fluids from the Soviet's lungs as he fell to the sand. She then walked quickly back past the unmoving Kravchenko to SAR 2. The six suited figures looked at one another in a panic.

"We can take her!" one of them shouted. "We can take her; all of us together. We don't have to die here!" he shouted. He looked at his companions who did not share his commitment. Indeed, it became instantly evident that as far as SAR two was concerned, the victim had just identified himself. As if to signal their unified resolve, they each began to point to the one who had just spoken, backing away from him.

The man suddenly found himself alone and facing a quickly approaching Dimitriov. Seeing the approach of certain death, he turned and broke into a run across the desert. Dimitriov watched him flee for a moment, then turned and walked toward her own vehicle. Once there, she stopped and turned again to face the fleeing form, running away as fast as he could into the Martian desert. Then, with flair, she slid her Makarov away into its hidden holster.

"Shall I pursue and kill him?" Kravchenko asked, more out of begging an eager permission than from duty.

"No," she replied as she watched the figure recede. "Before the sun sets tonight, he will wish he had allowed me to finish him off quickly. Besides," she sneered, "we can collect his suit later and not have to make any repairs to it. And in the process, we save valuable ammunition."

"Brilliant, of course, as always!" Kravchenko gushed with a sickening smile.

She turned and looked at the SARs and their crews standing rigidly in the ruddy sand and rocks. "Let's move one," she said to them all with a terrible resolve. "Now there will be more room and everyone should breathe easier until we arrive."

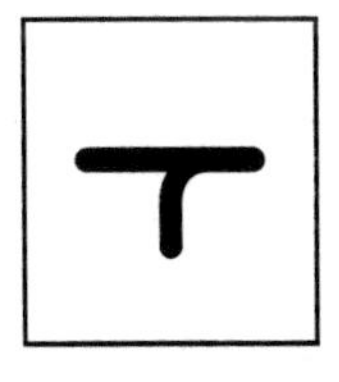

The evening meal at BC1 was served hurriedly – mostly sandwiches and the enormously popular baked potato chips that Rat had invented from the CELSS garden. Many grabbed their allotment and took it directly to work with them. Peter, Ashley, Toon and Francis ate together in the Command Center.

"How's goes the war, boss?" Toon asked Peter, stuffing his face with a huge bite of sandwich.

"We might just be ready for the earliest contact with the enemy any time tomorrow afternoon or later," he noted, glancing up at the master clock glowing down on them with its three inch, bright LED numerals.

"Humph," Francis grunted, his mouth stuffed with chips. But before he could clarify his thoughts, a sudden explosion of static and a voice in broken but distinct English came over the external communications speakers.

"BC1, this is Shturmovoi; do you read, over?"

Their faces and bodies froze for a long second and they looked at one another with wide eyes.

"I've got it," Toon replied instantly, swinging around his chair at the console. "It's a shortwave frequency.

"Shturmovoi, this is BC1; we read you loud and clear."

"Tell them we'll be on the line in one minute," Francis said firmly.

Peter caught the unspoken imperative in his voice.

"Yes, tell him we need one minute," Peter said.

"Why?" Toon asked, looking surprised.

"Toon, you and Ashley need to leave here for a few minutes. I'm sorry," Francis said flatly, eyeing Peter and obviously taking the heat off of him for the social embarrassment.

Peter looked firmly at the clock so that he would not have to look at the others. "I'm sorry, but we've agreed that any significant finding will be held in check until we can evaluate it and announce it to everyone."

"So we're not a part of your inner sanctum?" Toon asked, his voice painted with surprise and hurt. Then, as if to underscore his point, he looked to Ashley. "Ashley, you're not a part of the inner sanctum?"

"Toon, just shut up and get out," Francis responded with pent up fatigue. "We really don't need this right now," he replied directly to Toon, not daring to look at Ashley.

Ashley rose slowly and wordlessly to leave. It was apparent that she did not fully understand what was happening, and that she was obviously somewhat hurt by being so abruptly shut out, but she trusted Peter explicitly and would never publicly challenge him.

"This sucks, you know that?" Toon replied in an uncharacteristic bark, and walked briskly out of the room.

"Do not, repeat, do not mention this outside of this room," Peter said firmly to no one in particular.

As soon as they closed the door, Peter shook his head slowly, squinting his eyes. He was not so sure that he agreed with Francis at this point, and he almost called Ashley back into the room. But realizing that he would explain everything and apologize to her later, he focused on the present.

"Cue up the transmitter," Peter replied in his own terse whisper.

"Shturmovoi, this is BC1; go ahead," Francis said.

"BC1, this is the base Shturmovoi. We are calling to warn you of an imminent attack, repeat, an imminent attack..."

"Shturmovoi, do you have the capability of a link-up on a secure circuit?" Francis said, breaking into his announcement.

"Negative. Negative. But it does not matter. While we fully expect they will intercept this transmission, it does not matter. They do not have the capacity to return to Shturmovoi at this point and we are all hoping you will kill them upon their arrival there. It is our most sincere wish that they do not return here, ever."

Peter and Francis looked at one another with total astonishment. Francis cupped the mike and verified the switch was on "mute".

"They may be lying," he whispered, although they both knew there was no possibility they could hear their conversation.

"Why?" Peter mouthed silently. Francis' eyes darted about, and then he looked at Peter and simply shrugged.

"Shturmovoi, how many are in the convoy?" Francis asked, keying the mike back on.

"Six SARS and a total of 34 armed individuals departed here six sols ago. We did not contact you until now so that we could ensure they did not have enough power or consumables to return without replenishment. According to our satellite tracking, they will arrive there in roughly twenty-four hours from now. You must kill them all. You must show them no mercy. They will destroy you if you do not kill them all."

Peter put his hand over the mike and looked at Francis. He blinked twice, thinking at utmost speed. Then he pulled the mike to himself and nodded for Francis to key the switch. "This is Peter Traynor, leader of the American base at BC1. Shturmovoi, tell me in the greatest detail about your situation and about your reasoning. If I catch you in any lie at all, I'll send them back to arrest you; do you understand?"

Francis looked totally surprised at Peter, and shook his head as though he had been slapped. Then he managed a half-smile. "Well, I guess that's one approach," he said looking neutrally at Peter.

"Go on, Shturmovoi," Peter ordered.

In the next ten minutes, the scientific contingent left behind to die at Shturmovoi unfolded their story of terror and certain death at the hands of Dimitriov and her deadly cluster of yes-men. When they finished, Peter sat silent for a full two minutes. Then he spoke back into the microphone.

"Shturmovoi, can you tell us if you have any knowledge of any of your operatives at work here?"

"Please amplify, BC1. Define 'operatives'."

"Spies," Peter and Francis spoke together in unison.

A long period of silence followed, broken with a short reply, "No, we know of none. But then, we are just scientists and they tell us nothing."

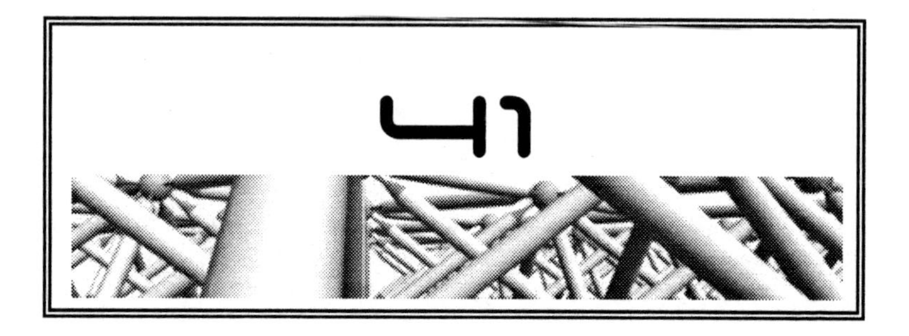

n the expanse of the Elysium desert, six SARs sat parked in a semi-circle facing northwest. An hour after sunset, in the center of the circle, 26 individuals in spacesuits sat about a cluster of bright lights, as though it were a camp fire, but they all sat in silence, daring to say nothing.

Just two hours before this, beginning in the rearmost vehicle, Dimitriov had allowed each member to pressurize the vehicle, remove their space suits and clean up, donning a new absorbent pad, one at a time. She did not allow this act out of mercy or kindness, things she had never felt, but because she, as well as the others, had developed such serious eruptive skin rashes that, had she not allowed this, they might not have been able to walk at all on the next, critical day. Besides, she reasoned, there were now enough life support gasses to waste on the process since five of the consumers were dead.

In the convoy's first vehicle, three individuals sat listening intently to the end of a broadcast between the vermin Dimitriov thought she had exterminated and the quarry she now intended to kill. Moments after the last crewmember had completed his clean-up task, the broadcast ended. Dimitriov and her deputies listened inside the SAR as the scientists back at Shturmovoi related their findings to Peter and Francis at BC1. Kravchenko's expression seemed to indicate he found it odd that she did not utter a single word at the end of the broadcast, but simply slipped her helmet over her spacesuit and without a word, began to pressurize. With no warning, she sharply turned the dial to suck the air from the SAR into its storage container as Kravchenko and her deputy, Major Dybenko just barely managed to don their helmets in the last possible half-second. She then popped the hatch and strode into the darkness of the Martian desert. Dimitriov walked some thirty meters away and stood facing the direction of BC1 alone. No one dared approach her.

A full twenty minutes later, she abruptly turned and walked back to the assembled 26, seated around the light. As she approached, they all stood, totally out of fear. She stopped three meters from them as Kravchenko and Dybenko approached on her right and left, facing the others, but well out of her arm's reach.

Calmly she addressed them. "Here on this planet, failure means a certain expectation of death. Today, I have experienced an enormous disappointment without precedence in the many years of my service to my country. Dybenko, will you please come over and face me," she spoke to her deputy.

He approached her with the same wariness and reluctance that he had for each game of chess she forced him to suffer.

"Dybenko, it was ultimately your responsibility to render the staff at Shturmovoi ineffectual, was it not?" she asked calmly.

The many endless hours of manipulation by Dimitriov finally paid off for Dybenko as he quickly recognized her ploy and answered, "Why no; no it was not, Colonel Dimitriov. You asked me to assign it to a competent party, which was, as a matter of fact and record, Comrade Kravchenko, which I did," he said, pointing at the now completely disheveled deputy on her right. "It is he who has failed you, not I, Colonel Dimitriov."

"You are a lying dog! You are a lying whore dog…" Kravchenko savagely responded.

"Silence!" Dimitriov snapped.

She slowly withdrew her Makarov from her holster and handed it butt first to Dybenko. "You and you alone have failed, Major Dybenko. Now I expect you to do your duty as an example for all those who are assembled here."

"What? …" Dybenko asked incredulously. "I have served my country faithfully, Colonel Dimitriov. You cannot mean this; you cannot…"

"Stop whimpering and just do it, you coward," Kravchenko spat in disgust.

Dybenko swung the muzzle of the pistol around and faced Kravchenko, pointing the barrel of the Makarov at his face. "You are the soulless animal that deserves to die! We have endured your disgusting brutality for too long!" he shouted.

Dimitriov looked supremely annoyed. "Major Dybenko, may I remind you that you have my orders and I expect you to carry them out instantly! Cease blaming others for your failure and carry out your duty. As a senior officer, and 'hero of the motherland', you must show yourself an example to those assembled before you who have not achieved such high office," she continued distainfully.

Through the dim instrument lights in Dybenko's helmet, everyone could see the disbelief in his eyes as he looked at the pistol in his hand with abject horror. His eyes shot between Dimitriov, the pistol, Kravchenko and then back again.

"Carry on, you buffoon. We don't have all night to watch you sweat and whimper like a common coward," Dimitriov urged mercilessly, clearly enjoying her belittlement of the popular Cosmonaut hero.

With that, Dybenko's face contorted with rage. "No! No you bitch; no! It is you who will die tonight," he yelled, leveling the Makarov at her heart.

"You don't have the courage," she said calmly, staring him in the face with icy black eyes.

Dybenko's finger pulled the trigger repeatedly on the Makarov, which lay useless and impotent in his hands. There was no response from the weapon because Dimitriov had emptied the magazine as she stood alone in the desert. "Checkmate," she spat as she took one step toward him, snatched the gun from his hand, and then backhanded its butt against his face shield with all her strength.

The Americans chose to use a nearly indestructible, laminated polycarbonate for space helmet face shields. The Soviets chose a significantly thicker but less durable and less expensive polyethylene product that would not shatter, but it would crack if struck with a well place blow – like this one.

The air began to leak out of Dybenko's suit immediately. He clutched at his face shield with his hands as though he could somehow stop the slow leak. As he did so, he began to spin in slow circles, "No, no, no, oh God no…."

"There is no God," Dimitriov said evenly, as she withdrew a large bladed knife from her pouch and cleanly sliced Dybenko's air hose as he staggered past her. The explosive decompression completed the task in but a few agonizing seconds.

ight was not observed at BC1. Peter ordered that rest intervals not exceed four hours on a rotating basis. Everyone had a wartime duty and at one minute after midnight, a condition of war had been declared. The colony was expecting an imminent attack and the word quickly spread that it was no longer conjecture but a fact. They would have to prepare for the worst. All must be prepared to fight to the death.

The colonists expected the attack would come at late evening, just as the light dimmed or at night. They could not speculate on how it would come or from what direction. Worse yet, the colony would have to be evacuated with only a few minutes notice for those who would not have the protection of a spacesuit and must disappear into the carefully prepared shelter. While Peter had tried his best to keep the new shelter a secret, word inevitably leaked out, and if there was a spy in their midst, it could be assumed that he or she knew everything. So to counter this threat, Peter decided that whichever of the two shelters they would use would not be announced until the time the attack begun. Every colonist was to be ready to go to either shelter on a moment's notice, or possibly split into two groups and use both.

Keeping any secrets under these circumstances was nearly impossible and everyone knew it. The news from Shturmovoi had been shared between only four people: Peter, Francis, Brinker and Covenant, but the inevitable rumor train coalesced with the high intelligence of the populace of BC1, and just about everyone had the entire picture figured out within hours after it was suspected that Shturmovoi had called.

Brinker had his high-flying camera in the air and Toon, appointed Command Center Director by Peter, kept it pointed in the right direction and its monitor continuously manned. With the camera and its super-sensitive infrared lens, they would have at least 45 minutes warning of an attack from any quarter.

The Sarge had also staged his combatant's spacesuits at designated airlocks so that they could be suited, armed and outside in six minutes flat. The rest of the colony practiced life station drills so that it was determined that everyone could be at either of the two designated lifeboat stations within five minutes. If they decided to use both, each colonist had an assigned number, and odd or even determined to which station they would evacuate.

As a rather welcome interlude in the pre-war activities, it was reported just after the normally scheduled breakfast period, that Soviet Scientist Fyodor Stepanovich Kirov had regained consciousness. Although weak, he begged an immediate conference with Peter to relay the full horrors of Shturmovoi and Colonel Dimitriov. Kirov ultimately drifted off to sleep, but not before leaving Peter with a horrific view of what they were to face and, with it, a new resolve to win at any cost.

The clock hurried toward noon, the time when all war preparations at BC1 were to be completed. Not a single individual questioned the inevitable conclusion. If they did not utterly defeat the onrushing enemy, they would all die. None was so foolish as to believe that there would be any negotiations, any last minute peace deals or even any prisoners taken. The reason for the attack was, after all, a capture of the life support system, which was already impossibly overloaded. For the human ace to survive, a lot of people were going to have to die.

At noon, Peter and his team met together in the dining hall. As Peter called roll, every station answered "ready." He then picked up his personal communicator and addressed the entire outpost through every speaker in the colony, including their PC2s:

"It's a sad day for humankind that we should spend our time preparing to fight one another to the death on this, the very first extraterrestrial body we have permanently settled as a species. And yet, let history record that it was ultimately not our decision to fight, but only to spend ourselves in the defense of freedom and to preserve for ourselves and our descendants the opportunity to live to see tomorrow. Today, we struggle to live, to survive and to defend ourselves; not to take, not to deprive and not to hinder another life, but only to preserve our own. Barring a miracle, it's a virtual certainty that some of us, or many of us, will not live to see tomorrow. But let it be recorded that as long as free, decent people live anywhere in the solar system or beyond, we steadfastly choose to live together as one, or die together as one, and that not one life was taken out of selfishness or treachery so that another might survive. In this battle, let there be courage among us all, knowing that we'll all chose willingly to take on one another's burdens and that in so doing, our destiny is defined not by what we took, but by what we gave. May God have mercy on us all."

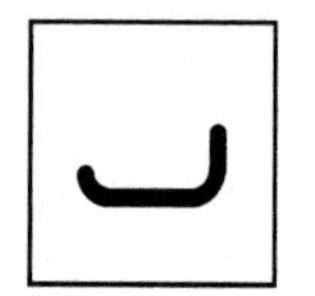

ust as Peter spoke those words, at high noon on the Elysium plain, the six Soviet SARs bore down on BC1 like a train of death. The single most damming piece of evidence Dimitriov and her men had gleaned from their spy was the lack of space suits at BC1. Hence, they would outnumber the untrained American scientists fighting outside by two fighters to one, and the colonists' weapons by an enormous margin. Their SARs had been outfitted with a long barrel strapped to each side, which acted as make-shift missile launchers. Each was armed with two crude missiles equipped with 12-gauge warheads whose single purpose was to puncture the fragile walls of BC1 and evacuate the life-giving air. The vehicles had also been outfitted with a welded frame and ramming rod designed to smash into and puncture targets without affecting the SAR's rugged body.

While Dimitriov knew she had lost the element of surprise after Covenant escaped, she was totally confident that her fire and manpower alone would easily conquer the Americans, whether they knew she was coming or not. The vermin back at Shturmovoi had revealed nothing she did not suspect the Americans already knew from Covenant's testimony, so they, too, would all have to die as soon as spring assured her return. The only reason she had left Kravchenko alive was to carry out the most horrible, slow executions conceivable by the human mind. On earth or on Mars, Kravchenko had no equal at this undertaking. And, he enjoyed his task immeasurably. To Dimitriov, he was a slobbering, barbarian idiot; but he was a useful idiot nonetheless.

It was Dimitriov's decision to strike after nightfall. While she knew that it handed the element of knowledge of the terrain over to the enemy, she also felt as though her strategy of brute strength and massive force would overwhelm whatever defenses the colonists could conjure up in the short time they had after realizing they were going to be attacked. It was not a tactic of finesse, but it was one of historic strategic importance that had long dominated her nation's past military strategy and historic successes. Strike with as much stealth as possible and strike with everything at once. Reloading was a game for losers.

Dimitriov had gained a constant stream of information from BC1 about every conceivable aspect of their preparations from her private ace-in-the-hole spy, including the exact locations of the life boat stations, numbers and names of fighters outside, locations and purposes of the rail guns, their ranges and their blind spots. Given her computer generated diagrams of BC1's total current defensive posture, she fully expected to be in a nice warm American bunk, after a long shower and a full meal, by midnight. She intended to keep only one of their number alive - her informant; the rest were all going to die before the next sunrise. The only possible exception, and one on which she had not fully decided, was Peter Traynor. After she had Kravchenko slowly kill his wife in his presence, she would toy with him for sadistic pleasure.

As Dimitriov downloaded the last of the informant's messages, Kravchenko broke the silence, having not spoken a word since the killing of Dybenko the night before.

"Colonel Dimitriov, what is that, over there?" he asked, pointing at the eastern horizon.

Dimitriov looked up from her console in the lurching SAR to see at what Kravchenko was pointing. Immediately, on the horizon, she recognized the unmistakable serpentine trace of a dust devil rising off the Elysium desert. She was about to lower a verbally abusive volley in Kravchenko's direction for daring to disturb her important thoughts over something as inconsequential as announcing a dust devil, reflecting to herself that dust devils were common on Mars, particularly at the change of seasons. Their telltale traces had been seen cutting across the Martian sands by orbiting satellites even before the turn of the millenium. Most were akin to their earthly counterparts – spectacular, very short-lived, and usually impotent.

Yet the Martian dust devils did have their own unique characteristics. On Mars, any mechanism that tossed dust and small pebbles about at high velocity was a concern, since even the smallest was capable of puncturing a suit or even a SAR with a well placed projectile. And Martian dust devils had the potential to become massive, resembling terrestrial tornadoes. Without the earth's dense atmosphere, higher gravity and water to mediate their potential and kinetic energy, the Martian versions could spin into monsters with core wind velocities of well over 900 kilometers per second. Because of the lack of atmospheric pressure and the low gravity, Martian dust devils were capable of creating multiple vortexes that came and went in a matter of seconds as they spun. The larger ones, especially, resembled malevolent hydras as they grew from the desert sands and rose to thousands of meters in height. And this one was indeed massive - larger than any she had ever seen - and it was bearing down on the convoy.

"Colonel Dimitriov, we have a dust devil at constant bearing and decreasing range approaching from 128 degrees true," came a report over the communications channel from the rear.

"I see it, idiot. Break off immediately," Dimitriov ordered. In her mind she was clearly ordering them all to split off the convoy and go in different directions to reduce the probability of being struck broadside by the oncoming monster. Much too late she would come to recognize that they had interpreted her order to "break off" to mean "stop communications traffic".

Dimitriov's eyes were glued to the oncoming red cloud as it approached them at a velocity that they could never hope to outrun. She saw it gaining momentum as it raced toward them, mutating from deep red to black as it spewed sand out its top into the air and blotted out the sun. She witnessed its tail break into three independent vortexes that rose off the plain, thrashing at supersonic velocity and snapping the desert floor like whips. Then, the hydra merged back again into a single funnel as it dipped once more toward the desert, rushing in their direction with astonishing swiftness.

Too late, Dimitriov managed to unlock her stare from the onrushing dust devil and look behind her. None of her convoy had broken off as she had commanded and they were all following her way too closely, no more than one meter apart. The driver of each SAR was increasing speed in their terror while trying to both drive and observe the oncoming disaster at the same time. Before she could speak and warn them away, the SAR behind them struck the rear of her vehicle and the metal spear mounted on its frame did what it was designed to do: puncture her vehicle and depressurize it instantly. Fortunately,

Dimitriov's standing order had been that they all travel in their fully pressurized suits in the event of any given calamity.

In the moment of depressurization, all the water vapor in the air inside the SAR condensed and froze, rendering every window and helmet visor an opaque sheet of ice. Reflexively, but stupidly, Kravchenko stood on his brake which caused the vehicle following them to ram into them again at full speed. Likewise, every SAR, save the last one, rammed into the rear of the one in front of it. And since they were all outfitted with ramming poles designed to depressurize the BC1 structures, each one depressurized the other.

The last SAR saw the mass collision and miraculously managed to swerve and avoid the rest. Because of the frozen condensate on every window and helmet visor following the mass collision, only the last SAR could see the full extent of the disaster and view the mighty vortex bearing down for the kill.

In a panic, the driver of SAR 6 swerved away frantically and began to drive in what he thought was a safe direction away from the hideous dust devil that had risen like a blood red wall of death before him. He could no longer see the dust devil, and assuming it had passed them safely, quickly ground the SAR to a stop. He immediately popped the hatch on the vehicle and stepped out onto the desert to view the situation. What he did not see, and could not have known, was that the dust devil had risen off the desert floor and was now above him, split into four whipping vortexes right over the top of the SAR. Far too late, he looked up and saw the massive maw of four spinning and lashing claws poised over him like a huge talon hovering over its' prey. Before he could react or move, in the blink of an eye, one vortex descended and, with a single, violent touch, caused the vehicle to explode into thousands of smaller pieces, killing everyone inside instantly. Then the deadly cloud moved on, and, in less than two minutes, dissipated into the atmosphere as quickly as it had formed.

At that moment, in SAR 4, there was absolute silence, save the various alarms echoing through its interior. The occupants in this vehicle had made a secret pact hours before that they were going to remove their helmets and pressurize their SAR so they would not have to ride in constant discomfort. After all, how could Dimitriov ever possibly find out? They had all died in an instant, their faces frozen in total surprise and covered with a thin sheen of ice.

In a rage of inhuman magnitude that surprised even herself, Dimitriov clawed the ice off her visor with her gloved hands, screaming and cursing over the common communications circuit, using creative word combinations that no one had ever heard before. She slammed the door of her SAR open and leapt out onto the Martian sands planning to immediately execute the driver of SAR 2 on the spot.

But she did not expect the full extent of the disaster she saw before her. All around her on the sand lay bits and pieces of SAR 6, its main hulk lying in an unrecognizable pile of debris some 75 meters away. And every other vehicle had impaled itself onto another.

Dimitriov withdrew her Makarov and held it tightly in her fist. She resolved that in the next few minutes, someone was certainly going to die.

The occupants of SARs 2, 3 and 5 piled out of their vehicles dazed and shaken, all of them scratching ice off of their visors. In a rage she walked over to SAR 4 and opened the door. Before her were the frozen faces of the four men and one woman, all without their helmets, staring back through crystalline death masks. Dimitriov was so overcome with wrath that she paced quickly away from the pile-up and walked into the desert. After standing there a full 15 minutes, she turned to walk quickly back.

"Before you return, Colonel Dimitriov, may I have a word?" came a voice through the common communications circuit.

Dimitriov stopped and looked at the assembled group at a distance. "Who is speaking?" she demanded.

"It does not matter who of us it is who speaks, Comrade Leader," the voice of Valentin Anatoliy said with measured control. "But if you insist on carrying out more executions on this desert, I can assure you that we will all die right here, right now."

"Do you dare threaten me with mutiny?" she demanded.

"Colonel Dimitriov, we have all faithfully followed you thus far to destroy the enemies of our country. But if you continue to execute us one at a time, they will soon outnumber us by too great a margin and we will not be able to succeed. Already, our number has been reduced to 18 and I do not believe that mathematically we can afford to risk even one more Comrade and achieve our goals."

Dimitriov stopped, and in an instant, willed her anger away. In a totally uncharacteristic moment, she responded, "You are correct, Comrade, of course. I never meant to return and execute anyone. I was simply here grieving over the loss of our countrymen. Now let us repair our vehicles as quickly as we can and move on. By this time tomorrow, we will have achieved an historic victory!"

The assembled individuals were all ecstatic that none of them was about to be executed and they immediately and enthusiastically began to attempt to pry the SARs apart from one another. It was determined that SAR 4 was in good working order as were SARs 1, 2 and 5. They unceremoniously dumped the bodies out of SAR 4 onto the sand.

The ramming rods on each vehicle were designed to make jagged tears so that they could not be easily or quickly repaired. The design worked so well that they determined that none of the vehicles could be pressurized at all until they could be placed into a pressurized airlock and repaired. Now they were in a tight race to the finish; for without a pressurized compartment, they could not replenish water reservoirs or carbon dioxide scrubbing chemicals, and, of course, they could not eat. After a quick calculation, it was determined that they would all be fighting the BC1 battle breathing elevated carbon dioxide levels and only a few suits would have adequate water. In the end, they understood well that they had to proceed with maximum speed and fight the battle successfully, or die in their own suits just a few meters short of their prize.

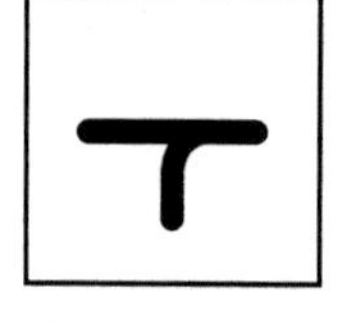

The big red countdown numerals in the dining hall of BC1 and in the Command Center indicated five minutes and thirty-two seconds past six in the evening. All combat posts had been manned continuously for six hours. The small red sun was about to drop behind the distant desert horizon, and already the clear, cold sky was mostly black, emblazoned with stars that never twinkled.

Every colonist had an assigned duty. There were only 16 available space suits in the colony. Twelve suited individuals had been assigned to meet the Soviets as they attacked outside; each designated a specific station. Four suited individuals were tasked to guard the safe room or safe rooms in which everyone else, the remaining 31colonists and Kirov, were to take shelter during the attack. Both safe rooms had been lined with sand bags on every side, and even the doors were shielded with bags of Martian sand, piled in front of the entrance with just enough room to allow it to swing open.

Only Peter knew which safe room he would order to be manned, and he shared this information with no one. At the last moment, he would make the announcement instructing which safe room would be used. The consistent rumor was that both would be used to divide the chances for full disaster in half. It was only logical, and the scientists and engineers quickly deduced the probability of Peter's decision. But no one really knew for sure, so they waited for the inevitable alarm.

Peter, Ashley and Toon were sitting together in the Command Center, musing over better times, when Toon asked, "Do you remember how all this started?" flashing his infectious, toothy smile, his straight black hair falling over his eyebrows.

"It seems like it's been going on forever," Ashley replied with a sigh.

Peter suddenly looked puzzled, which Toon instantly noticed.

"What?" he asked.

"Lipton… I was thinking about Lassiter," Peter replied with a distant look in his eyes.

"What about soup-man?" Toon replied with a smirk.

"I wonder how he would have handled all this?" Peter said wistfully. "Face it, Lipton was no push-over. I just keep wondering how he would have set this whole thing up." As he spoke, Peter's eyes drifted to the monitor that displayed the view from Brinker's high flying balloon. As its cameras rotated around the horizon, the image of the desert depicted before them an empty wasteland from horizon to horizon. His eyes bore into the image, attempting to make out any movement, any speck out of place. "You know, Toon, this image is remarkably bright for sunset. I don't even see any sunset shadows."

"Of course, my friend," Toon responded expertly. "It's a combination of infrared and illumination amplification and false colorization, all managed by the computer so that night is never night. That image will look just the same as it does now, even at midnight."

"Amazing," Peter responded in awe.

"It's also a dammed lie," came Francis' voice from the door to the Command Center as it swung slowly open.

Peter, Toon and Ashley looked away from the monitor to see Francis enter with a raised handgun. It had a laser sight whose bright, red dot reflected off Toon's forehead. Just behind him entered Brinker, Hiraldo and Covenant. Brinker and Hiraldo also held laser sighted pistols and added their bright red dots to dance across Toon's brow. Covenant quietly closed the door behind them.

"What… what is this?" Peter demanded, standing up and waving his hands while shaking his head in bewilderment.

"Your spy, sir," Brinker nodded to Toon as the three laser dots moved in near random circles around his forehead.

"What?" Peter and Toon asked simaltaneously.

"Peter, this man is indeed our spy," Francis responded. "Covenant and I have been working together to catch him since Lipton's death. We both knew Lipton's death was no suicide. He was murdered by Mr. See here on direct orders from Shturmovoi."

"How do you know this?" Peter rasped in astonishment.

"Let's begin with Lipton's diplomatic pouch. It just happened to be our friend Toon here who first tipped us off that it was full of Martian quartz. The x-rays showed it clearly. It was also Toon who first hinted at pulling the lockers off the lander so that they would have to remain behind. But last night I hammered the lock off the box and found balls of gold foil inside that advantageously also have the same x-ray reflectivity of quartz. Lipton was always a first rate ass, but he was also innocent and Toon set him up."

"Why would he do that?" Ashley asked sharply.

"To totally destroy the colonists' position here," Francis replied. "It would have appeared as though we planted the foil to destroy Lipton and kept the evidence here on Mars. Lipton or one of his staff would have ultimately discovered and reported it and every permanent colonist would have been ordered home. The Soviets were sorely threatened by our permanent colony here at BC1 and they wanted it gone.

"But, too bad for our little spy here, the circuits were cut, and the Soviets had to find a new way to get rid of their only competition here. So Toon began by altering the lander's program and in so doing murdered everyone on board, also on orders from Shturmovoi. Remember the virus program? Also his handiwork, except it was never, and has never been, a fake. While he thought he was smarter than the rest of us, he's not. Want to talk about the loss of satellites? His work also. He was in a position to make it all happen and cover his tracks. My son, Jack, has been seeing hints of it here and there and just yesterday discovered its full definition, extent and even its author. After we reviewed his computer deception, it was a simple matter to figure out the rest, including the diplomatic pouch. The virus is real, Peter, and it's in place ready to shut this system down at any minute. And I don't have to tell you what happens to us and our little war if it goes off."

"It is, shall we say, the smoking gun we needed to finally identify our leak," Covenant added in his clipped, precise accent. "Although it's been more like a gush than a leak. Our friendly Toon-meister has even been transmitting constant reports to the enemy even while they approach in the desert. He's been a very busy bloody little devil indeed."

Peter shook his head as though trying to awaken from a bad dream as he looked to Francis. "You… you've been working with Covenant all along? You knew even while we were looking for him? And you didn't even think it worth your while to tell me?"

Francis' gaze shifted between Peter and his carefully placed red dot as he targeted his weapon on Toon's head. He said, "Peter, at first no one knew who was talking to Shturmovoi; no one. It could have been you. In my mind, it could have been Covenant; hell, how was I supposed to know? No one had the big picture. Everyone was a suspect."

"And just who were you to take on the sole responsibility of doing any tracking down alone and outside of official channels?" Peter snapped, leveling his anger at Francis.

Toon's eyes shifted frantically back and forth between Peter and Francis. "This is just so much insanity! You should just take a minute and listen to yourselves," he shouted at Peter. "Tell them to lower their weapons! Do it, now!" he screamed, pointing directly at Brinker.

"We don't have a minute," Brinker replied sharply. "I need someone's permission, anyone's permission, to shoot this man. And if you move your hand one more time, I won't wait for permission," he said with a steely-eyed resolve, pacing two large steps toward Toon.

"Brinker, stand down!" Peter ordered sharply. To Peter, that meant simply to stop advancing directly toward Toon and to stop talking. But to a trained Marine, it meant something else entirely different - lower your weapon.

Uncertain over this nonsensical command, Brinker shifted his eyes away from Toon just for a half-second and looked at Peter, as did Hiraldo. At that moment, Toon seized the opportunity, grabbed Ashley by the arm, pulling her in front of him and using her as a shield. Then he reached behind his belt and withdrew a six inch switchblade knife, flashed it open and held it to her neck. In that instant, Francis's read dot flashed over Ashley's eyes and onto her forehead.

"Lower your weapons!" Peter instantly commanded, not believing that a man he thought to be one of the closest friends he had ever had in his life was actually holding a knife to his wife's throat. "Toon, this can't be," he gasped in horror, shaking his head. "Let's work this out…"

"I would love to lie to you some more, Peter, but I am afraid time's up," Toon responded, raking the razor sharp tip of the knife over Ashley's throat.

"Somebody had better do something in a big hurry, Peter," Brinker warned, eyeing the monitor, "because that image up there is yet another one of Toon's fakes. We're officially blind and they may be making their approach as we speak".

"Anyone moves, and she dies," Toon responded, gripping Ashley tightly and slicing through her skin so that a trickle of blood began to ooze down her neck.

"Ask them how they came to work together," Toon hissed, nodding his head in the direction of Francis and Covenant. His voice was hardly recognizable as he now spoke in a strange accent. "Go ahead, tell him and see who he trusts."

Peter looked at Francis, who averted his eyes for a second in an apparent moment of guilt, and then looked back at Peter. "See, he knew the entire strategic picture here all along. I've been an operative for the Central Intelligence Agency, who also knew we had a mole in here. Lipton knew as well. We don't have time for this, but I am a degreed meteorologist and I just passed along information to them from time to time. Most of the time, I passed it to Covenant who sent it to them."

"Why?" Peter asked, in total shock and disbelief. "You and Covenant, and even Lipton, all working together in this?"

"For the money, I might add," Toon responded with a sneer.

"He's right, Peter; for the money. How do you think a staff meteorologist, twice divorced could afford to send my sons to MIT? Besides, all I did was keep my eyes open and write a few reports; that's it, I swear it. And I've never lied to you, not once, ever."

"No, Peter, he's been lying to you all along," Toon responded, raking his knife deeper into Ashley's throat. Ashley looked to Peter and mouthed, "I love you."

Toon saw her mouth move and gripped her tighter, inching the knife deeper. "Shut up, you self-righteous bitch!" he screamed.

In the micro-second that Toon moved his eyes to Ashley, Covenant expertly withdrew his own handgun from his belt and with a single move placed a bullet directly between Toon's eyes. Toon looked momentarily surprised, and then fell away face down onto the floor.

"Fourteen seconds; move, move people!" Brinker roared lunging at Toon's twitching body. Peter grabbed Ashley and pulled her out of the way. He quickly eyed her neck and saw that the wound was not life threatening.

Brinker and Hiraldo turned Toon's body over with a snap. Hiraldo withdrew her knife from her belt and with a single, exact motion sliced his sweater and shirt away from his torso. On Toon's chest were pasted four electrodes, each with dim but discernable unblinking red LED lights. Meanwhile Covenant was stripping his own shirt away.

"Move it people; hurry up," Francis roared as Covenant lay onto the floor beside Toon. Brinker peeled the first electrode away from Toon's chest and placed it in the nearly exact position on Covenant's chest. He repeated it for the other electrodes as quickly as he could. But the electrodes would not stick and two fell away.

"Crap! Hold them on with your fingers; hold them on!" Brinker shouted at Hiraldo. As she did so, the red lights began to blink with Covenant's own heart beat.

Francis sighed and swept his hands across his hair as he backed away. "That was close; way too close!"

"What was close?" Peter asked as he pressed his handkerchief against Ashley's bleeding throat.

"What you're witnessing is the ultimate dead-man's switch," Francis explained. "Toon wired himself up to his virus trigger. If and when his heart stopped beating, the real virus triggered itself and melted down the computers permanently. He gave it a 14 second delay so if one of his electrodes came off, he could put it back. You see, in the event that he was killed in the war or killed by the invading army for any reason, everyone would die with him. He lived or no one lived. Not a bad insurance policy, if you ask me. Now it's wired to our man Julian, here, who is designated to be in one of the shelters anyway. If I were you, I'd carefully watch over this man."

"Ashley, are you okay?" Peter asked, looking into her eyes. She just nodded, holding the cloth to her neck.

"Hiraldo, grab that first aid kit off the wall over there and tape these electrodes on so they will NEVER come off, then help him put on his sweater... carefully," Brinker ordered. "Now we'd better figure out how to get the real image back from that balloon before it's too late to make any difference," he said, pointing to the monitor.

But it was already too late. An explosion rocked the Command Center as alarms sounded. "Pressure's gone in Dome 6. Damn; it's all the way down to zero! Power gone in 6 and 5!" Francis reported as he looked at the monitors.

"Dear God!" Peter cried. He sprang to the console, triggered the communications circuit and spoke loudly, "We're under attack; all hands to general quarters. Shelters code Charlie; I repeat, shelters code Charlie." In so doing, he instructed the colonists without suits to retreat to both shelters as previously assigned.

"Hiraldo, see to it that Covenant makes it to his shelter, then join me outside," Brinker snapped, lurching out of the room.

"Who's going to man the Command Center?" Peter asked, looking in the direction of Francis. The critical and exceedingly dangerous job of Command Center watch naturally fell to Toon whose lifeless body now lay on the floor beside them.

Francis looked momentarily stunned, and then back to Peter. "The next in line would have to be Geoff Hammods."

"Then get him suited and in place; hurry," Peter ordered, helping Ashley toward the door.

"No, I can't do that," Francis said in a near state of shock. "I can't do that."

"Why not?" Peter asked urgently.

"Because, damn it to hell, my son Jack is the only one who has the knowledge to make this work. He has a handle on Toon's little surprises including the virus program. He's the only one who can keep us out of trouble; not Geoff Hammonds, who Toon specifically trained to stay out of his personal files and routines."

Peter paused and looked to Francis. Jack was scheduled to be inside the safe cocoon of the shelter. But now, he would be sitting in the hottest seat of all; the Command Center which was deemed the primary target.

"It's your call, Francis," Peter said dispassionately, helping Ashley out of the room as Francis just looked back at him in undisguised agony. But Ashley stood firmly in place.

"Peter, I can make it. You must go with Francis," she said to him with a raspy voice. Then she pulled him to her and kissed him passionately. "No mater what happens tonight, know that my love will always be with you," she said in a broken voice.

Their eyes locked together for a long moment. "I love you," he replied as she turned and ran away into the dimly lit passageway.

"We have a job to do," Peter said to Francis who still looked like he was in shock. "Now let's go do it."

As he spoke those words, yet another explosion rocked the Command Center.

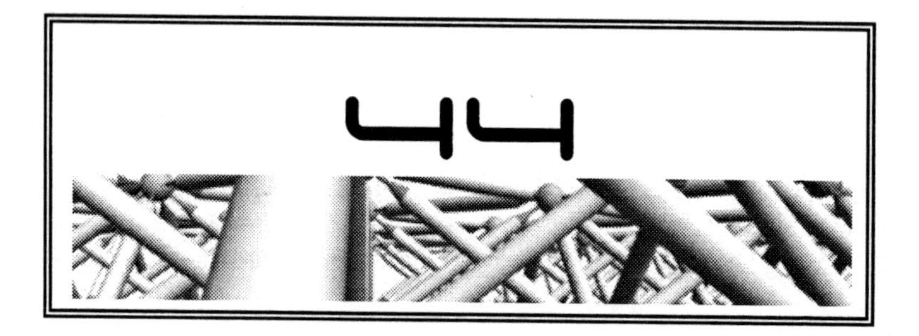

44

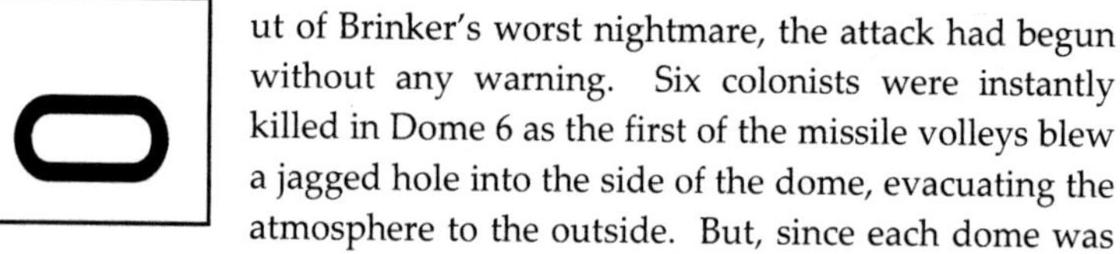

Out of Brinker's worst nightmare, the attack had begun without any warning. Six colonists were instantly killed in Dome 6 as the first of the missile volleys blew a jagged hole into the side of the dome, evacuating the atmosphere to the outside. But, since each dome was sealed from the others, the damage was limited to the single dome. By the time the second missile had struck Dome 4, the colonists were out of harm's way and sealed into, or headed toward, their lifeboat stations. The damage and death would have been far greater, except that the make-shift missiles were nearly impossible to fire with any accuracy and more than half of them either missed their targets or failed to detonate at all.

As Brinker and Hiraldo quickly pressurized their suits and exited the airlock to the outside, they activated the night vision selection on their helmets which projected an enhanced image of their surroundings onto their visors. They immediately saw a single SAR headed directly toward the Command Center intent on ramming it. Hiraldo sprinted to the rear of the SAR and leapt onto its frame. Sliding expertly around to its driver's window, she placed her short-barreled shotgun up to the window and pulled the trigger. The SAR ground to a halt immediately. She opened the door and the body of Nikolayevich fell out onto the sand. She looked inside to find no other occupants.

"Command Center! Command Center, do you read me?" Brinker shouted repeatedly into his mike. He needed their communications and their cameras, or this was going to be a very short war.

"On the line," Jack Linde announced as he stepped over the body of Toon and slid into the command chair.

"I need some eyes and I need them now!" Brinker screamed.

"I'm working on it, Sarge," Jack responded calmly.

"Hiraldo, man your rail gun," Brinker shouted as five other colonists appeared in suited form exiting the nearest airlock.

"I'm on it," she responded, running quickly into the darkness.

"Ok, I got video," Jack reported as he bypassed Toon's fake image.

"Talk to me; talk to me," Brinker commanded.

"Four vehicles in view now. One vehicle near the Command Center!"

"It's out of action," Brinker responded instantly.

"Ok, ok," Jack continued. "Three vehicles in motion. Vectors follow: 48 degrees, range 210 meters; 128 degrees, range 80 meters; and 135 degrees, range 120 meters."

"Damn!" Brinker swore. They were all lining up precisely in the rail gun blind spots.

"How many vehicles do you have, Jack?" Brinker asked. "There should be seven."

"Negative. I only see four, total. Sarge, there're people coming out of the woodwork."

"Spot them for me," Brinker responded.

With that, there was a piercing, shrill whistle over the communications circuit. The enemy had obviously jammed the frequency. The noise was so loud and deafening, every suited figure from BC1, including Brinker, had no choice but to shut the communications receiver down. Now they were not only blind, but deaf as well. There would be no more command and control outside as Jack sat helplessly at the console, able only to watch events unfold. But his helplessness lasted only a few seconds, as he seized upon an idea of his own.

eter and Francis both had to shut off their own communications circuits as they exited the airlock together. In horror and disbelief, they saw two suited figures step from behind an external vent and simultaneously gun down a suited BC1 colonist.

Peter made a quick motion with his hands as Francis nodded an understanding. They split and went around the dome to approach the suited figures from behind. Since there were few guns to go around, Peter was armed with a powerful taser capable of 250,000 volts of raw electromagnetic energy and a razor sharp knife. Francis still held his handgun with laser sight.

As they approached the figures from behind, the two Soviets split up and began to walk in different directions. Peter followed one and Francis the other. Peter stealthy raced up behind the Soviet and with a sweep, cut his primary air supply hose. The figure died immediately and fell to the ground. As he did so, the other figure looked around and Francis shot him in the heart. They hurriedly picked up the Soviet weapons – each held a shotgun and a handgun.

As they rounded a corner, they met another Soviet face to face, separated by only two meters. Francis raised his gun to fire, as the Soviet, Valentin Anatoliy, fell to his knees and placed his hands behind his head. Without any hesitation, Peter pulled a small can from his suit, stepped up to the man as he knelt and sprayed Anatoliy's visor. Instantly it was coated with black foam that totally blinded, and thereby immobilized, him.

Anatoliy began to move his hands in an odd motion that looked like something between praying and outspread palms, as though he was begging for mercy. Then he extended his forefinger slowly and reached to write in the sand. In perfect English, he inscribd: surrender – 1056.78.

Francis took the man's guns from him and looked to Peter as he looked around them again and again, making sure there were no surprises lurking for them in the darkness. Anatoliy then bent over and drew a lambda symbol in the sand. Suddenly Peter understood. The Soviet had just revealed their communications frequency!

Peter pointed to the number and to the Command Center. Together, he and Francis retreated to the window of the Command Center, which was piled over with sandbags. Francis began removing bags while Peter stood guard just as they were rocked with another explosion. Peter fervently prayed it was not either of the shelters.

Francis cleared away a fraction of the window and rapped repeatedly. They could see Jack working feverishly at the control console keyboard. Because the Command Center still held pressure, Jack could faintly hear the rapping, and looked around to see the suited figures staring at him from outside. Jack then held the microphone up and made a twisting motion with his fingers, speaking into the mike. Peter reached down and pressed his communicator to the 'ON' position as Francis turned away from them and fired a shot into the darkness.

"Can you hear me?" Jack's voice asked clearly.

"Loud and clear," Peter replied.

"I filtered the jam," Jack said proudly.

"Jam this," Peter said, repeating the Soviet frequency to Jack. "But give us and Brinker some data first," Peter said. Jack simply nodded as he turned back to his seat and began speaking into the microphone while his fingers raced over the keys.

At Rail Gun 2, Colonist Mark Teiner sat at the controls, his eyes staring through the darkness with the use of his visor's night vision display. He sat still, but ready to leap away from the gun if attacked or ready to fire if anything came into his sights. Suddenly, he saw three figures approach at 50 meters, stop, then face one another as though there were talking. Ever so slowly, Teiner raked his foot along the sand, turning the great gun in their direction without making any sudden movement. He lined them up in his sights over the barrel of rocks that lay on the rail just before him.

Just as he was about the squeeze the trigger, all three looked his way, obviously startled. Not wasting another second, Teiner squeezed the trigger and unleashed 400 megawatts of hellish momentum in their direction at mach 17. Their bodies instantly disintegrated in the onrushing volley of 40,000 tiny stones.

"Yes!" Teiner celebrated, standing up in his seat. But it was a short-lived celebration. He never discovered what had startled his victims and caused them to look in his direction. A pair of Soviets had approached from behind and killed him with two well placed volleys of double-ought buckshot that he never saw coming.

Brinker watched all this in horror. He had been worried about all the missing troops and whether they were laying back for a second and a third strike. But now he saw something even more horrible; two enemy soldiers were mounting the rail gun and aiming it to take out the Command Center.

Brinker motioned frantically for Hiraldo to flank him as he approached the gun on his stomach. As he did, one of the figures hoisted a drum of rock onto the rail and positioned it as the other spun the gun around to face the Command Center. But Brinker had arranged a block on each of the rail guns to prevent them from being pointed, accidentally or otherwise, back at the colony. While it was only a temporary block that could be removed with enough effort, it did buy Brinker enough time to get within striking distance as the suited figures attempted to determine why they could not point the gun at their target.

Hiraldo had disappeared behind the gun from the opposite side. Brinker cursed the lack of communications, and now realized that Hiraldo would have to read his mind.

The two Soviets worked side by side to tug out the layers of sand bags that blocked the guns motion. So it was with some ease that Brinker slid his knife into the kidney of the closest figure, who immediately fell away in an agonizing, yet quick death.

The second figure reacted with lightening speed, and swung his shotgun around to face Brinker head on. With a single reflex, Brinker backhanded the barrel away just as it went off, spraying his face shield and helmet with black debris and smoke. He then lunged at the individual and threw him to the ground in front of the gun. He looked through the face shield and did not know that he was staring directly at Leonid Kravchenko, eye to eye.

Kravchenko smiled his ghastly smile at Brinker. Fights to the death were a common activity for him. And now his ugly face betrayed that he was planning yet another sadistic kill. But Brinker was no stranger to death struggles either as they gripped one another with uncommon strength, each having no intention of giving in to the other. With a precise knowledge of the enemy's weaknesses, Brinker crushed the top of his helmet into Kravchenko face plate with all his strength. It was a gamble, since he knew he might crack his own face plate with such a savage blow, as well as the Soviets. But in the end, no one's face plate cracked and it enraged Kravchenko to the point that he managed to thrust Brinker's grip away and then kick him aside with a savage foot to the Marine's side. Feeling his rib snap, Brinker responded with agony and fell away, his breath knocked out of him and his diaphragm arrested with the excruciating pain raking up his side.

Kravchenko sensed this and lunged at Brinker with all the fury of a killing machine. He withdrew his knife from his sheath and raised it over Brinker, ready to plunge it into his heart. His right hand held the knife and his left hand was raised in a defiant fist, as though he were going to pummel Brinker with it. Brinker's hands shot up and gripped Kravchenko's left arm and held the knife in check. But Kravchenko was now too strong for him, as Brinker's breathing was compromised and his pain was too great to maintain his grip for much longer. His mind grasped the inevitable; that these were his last seconds of life. Looking at Kravchenko, he could see actual enjoyment on the smiling face of the man who was about to kill him. Brinker seethed with rage and he held on for just a single second more, trying to summon some energy deep inside that he desperately hoped was there.

What he could not know was that this extra second was just enough time to allow Hiraldo to line up on Kravchenko's left hand, still poised in a balled fist, just one meter away from the end of the rail gun's barrel. She pulled the trigger and Kravchenko's hand and left arm disappeared in a mist.

Kravchenko stared with horror at his missing arm. He released his grip on the knife and looked at the part of his suit where his arm had once been. In the ensuing maelstrom of energy, the supersonic rocks had miraculously twisted and sealed his suit in an instant. Kravchenko held his mangled arm up as his blood gushed down inside the suit and sprayed into his evil face. He fell in agony and looked over to Brinker, gasping for air on the cold Martian desert sands. Kravchenko's body lay across the gun's forward leg, his head hanging down. The blood from his severed arm ran down his suit and began filling his helmet. Just as their eyes locked for a single instant - as the sinister eyes were covered in the rising pool of his own blood - Kravchenko died.

Hiraldo rushed to Brinker and pressed his communications circuit. "Sarge, we're back on line. Are you okay?"

"Hiraldo, you got a bad habit of pulling my rocks out of the fire, you know that?" he responded.

Hiraldo turned her head sideways and looked down at the hideous sight of Kravchenko's lips quivering; his sardonic mouth still moving, half out of the pool of his own blood. "Look's like this one's gonna need a refill," she said dryly.

"Com center, you still on the line?" Brinker snapped into his com-circuit.

"Yes, Sarge, still here," Jack replied. "I just jammed all their circuits. They're out of contact with one another and they can't hear us. All our people are now back on line."

"Damn good work, son; damn good work!"

Peter heard the communications between the Command Center and Brinker and asked, "Brinker, what's your status?"

"Ok. Fine."

"We need a roll call. Everyone sound off, one at a time. I need a last name and a position." Of the twelve outside fighters, eight replied, including Peter, then Jack at the Command Center and both safe rooms.

"Okay, now I need an enemy damage report," Peter continued. In the ensuing reports, it was determined that eight of the enemy were dead, one had surrendered and two SARS had been knocked out.

"I want to talk to the one who surrendered," Brinker said.

"Meet me there," Peter replied, giving directions to his location that only Brinker would understand. A few moments later, they arrived at the location of the surrendered Anatoliy, who was still lying in the position they had left him; face down on the sand.

Brinker pressed his helmet to the helmet of the Soviet. "How many SARs made it?" he screamed, trusting the vibration of his voice would be heard.

"Four," the faint accented voice replied. "And there were 17 survivors who made it here with Dimitiov."

Peter looked quizzically at Brinker.

"What do you mean, survivors?" Brinker asked.

"Colonel Dimitriov; our leader," came the reply. "She is insane. She killed all but 17 of us along the way."

"That leaves nine wandering about," Peter responded, looking around them, peering into the darkness.

"Correction, there are eight," Francis said over the circuit. "We just took out another one trying to get into the Saferoom 2 passage."

"Eight is one hell of a lot better than 34," Peter responded. "And I think I've figured out their plan. Command Center, do you see any SARs? We're missing one," Peter said as he looked at Brinker who was nodding as though he had just figured it out as well.

"Wait a minute, here comes one now, approaching at full speed, right down Gun 2's blind spot!"

"Anyone in position to take it out?" Brinker asked.

"Negative. Somebody needs to get over there, now. It's going to ram the CELSS laboratories!"

Peter shivered as he leapt up and ran toward the Laboratories alongside Brinker. If they took out the labs, it would be over for everyone, no matter who won the war.

As they rounded the edge of the laboratory, they could see the SAR rapidly approaching. Manned by Colonel Polevikov, his deputy, Klimov, and two soldiers, it was obviously on a collision course with the CELSS domes. It was frighteningly apparent to all that, in view of their suits' depleted life support resources and the inevitable Soviet loss of this conflict, the officer had decided to assure the ultimate destruction of the victors. He was going down but he planned to take them all with him.

Brinker sprinted to face the oncoming SAR and fired repeated volleys at the onrushing vehicle. Although he scored more than one direct hit, it just kept on coming. The suicide driver was apparently well shielded.

"Hiraldo, can you see this?" Brinker shouted into his microphone. "Can you make Gun 2 and get the shot off?" he screamed.

"I'm on it, Sarge," she replied as they could see her running at the rail gun emplacement some 75 meters away.

"There's an open line of sight just in front of the CELSS dome. If you hurry, you can just make it," Brinker screamed.

"Hiraldo," Peter shouted, "you can't afford to miss this shot!" Clearly, if Hiraldo shot too far in front of the racing vehicle, she would destroy the dome that held all their hopes for survival – food, water and air. If too far behind and she missed the SAR, she would destroy Saferoom 1 and kill everyone inside. If she didn't thread the needle just right, it would be an unmitigated disaster.

They all watched Hiraldo sprint to reach the gun as the SAR raced through the darkness toward the very heart of their life support system. Hiraldo reached the gun and, in a single skillful leap, landed firmly in its seat. She then stuck her foot outside down into the sand and expertly stopped its momentum. In a solitary, excruciating second, she took careful aim and pressed the trigger to the gun.

Millions of kilogram-meter-seconds of momentum exploded off the rail and into the night with a shower of sparks as the rocks burst out past the screen at supersonic velocity. Half a second later the SAR vanished in a cloud just 15 meters short of impacting with the dome.

"Yes! Yes!" Brinker shouted as everyone assembled watched and applauded.

Jack broke into the celebration with an urgent appeal. "Folks, we have company outside the front door of Saferoom 2. You'd better get there and get there fast."

Peter bolted toward Saferoom 2 in fear. Ashley was holed up inside that lifeboat. Any puncture, no matter how insignificant, and she, as well as everyone else, would die instantly. Peter, Brinker, Francis and Hiraldo rushed at full speed inside the evacuated and open passageway leading to Saferoom 2. As they approached, Brinker urged them to stop just before rounding the corner to face the room.

"Let me and Hiraldo handle this; please," Brinker whispered into their suit communicators. As he said this, he motioned Hiraldo to stand opposite them so they would round the corner first.

"You are wasting your time, Marine," came the voice of a woman speaking English with a thick accent over their communications circuit.

"Identify yourself," Brinker commanded.

"I am the leader of the Soviet contingent, Colonel Zoya Dimitriov. And if you surrender, I will not waste the lives of everyone in your Saferoom 2, including the dear bride of your leader, Peter Traynor."

"I don't think you're in a position to dictate the terms of surrender, Colonel Dimitriov," Peter replied.

"You are wrong, my American stooge. You have 30 seconds to surrender, or these people will all die."

Peter started to walk past Brinker who stood in his way, but Brinker held him back forcefully. Then Peter showed him a note he had hastily entered on his handheld computer.

"What are the terms of your surrender?" Peter asked, watching Brinker make frantic hand motions to Hiraldo and wildly exaggerated facial expressions so that she would clearly understand. She nodded and left the passageway.

"I have a United States Marine approaching your position from the opposite corridor, Colonel Dimitriov. Please do not fire on her; she does not mean you any harm. She's only approaching to give you a personal note I have written for you."

Hiraldo coughed weakly into the communications circuit as she rounded the corner. This was the signal for Brinker to peer around the corner for a quick reconnoiter of the situation in front of Saferoom 2. He swung back around and formed the number "two" with his fingers and drew their positions with his finger on the wall.

Then Peter spoke as Brinker nodded, "Colonel Dimitriov, I will now walk toward you from the other passageway. Please do not be alarmed.

I want to talk to you face to face about surrender and working out our differences."

With this, Peter rounded the corner slowly, as Dimitriov pointed her shotgun at his midsection, not more than six meters away. He looked at Dimitriov and her guard by the door, who was also turned away from Hiraldo to face Peter.

"And I wish to speak to you about the Rat."

This was the code for Hiraldo to kill the guard. She instantly withdrew her handgun and shot him at point blank range through the side of his lungs. He did not see it coming.

Dimitriov fired her weapon at Peter, who had begun his dive toward her ankles the moment Hiraldo fired. It was a desperate move as the shotgun pellets missed his helmet and suit by scant millimeters. Just as she was backing away and ratcheting another round into the chamber, Hiraldo slugged Dimitriov's chest with her balled fist, throwing all her strength into the punch. The blow was so powerful that it broke Hiraldo's two outside fingers and three of Dimrtriov's ribs with a crack. Dimitriov fell to the floor just as Peter landed on top of her, his body pinning the shotgun between the two of them onto the floor.

Brinker was less than a second behind them as he gripped the shotgun's base and yanked it safely from between them and away from Dimitriov's clutching fingers. Peter immediately rolled from atop Dimitriov, but not before he could see that her breath had been knocked from her and she was wild-eyed and gasping for air. Instinctively, from long years of training, Peter reached over her shoulder and turned her oxygen regulator valve to 100% flow, the proper treatment for a suit-bound injury involving the lungs until first aid could be summoned.

Francis noticed the move as he approached and asked, "You planning for a trial?"

"Of course. She'll stand trial along with any survivors," he replied, turning to look back at her.

"You Americans are such sentimental fools," she gasped at him through her visor. "Did you really think victory was available to you at such a small cost?"

"I'm not sure what you're getting at, Dimitriov," Peter replied, "but your spy is dead and his virus has been disabled. At least one of your men has surrendered and given us the rest of the information we need. And, as you probably already know, Shturmovoi is not exactly putting out the welcome mat for your return engagement. So the only one who will be paying the cost appears to be you. And as far as your scientist, Dr. Kirov, is concerned, he's alive and well and asked me to pass just a single message along to you – checkmate!"

Her face contorted in rage as she whipped out a hidden knife from her pouch and thrust it toward Peter. He blocked it with his right hand as he withdrew his taser with his left hand and shoved it toward her. Dimitriov grabbed it with her other hand as Peter slowly lowered it steadily closer to her, its arcing 10 centimeter bolts of electrical power reaching toward her suit. Her lithe frame was no match for Peter's superior strength and soon the bright blue spark touched her helmet.

It was Peter's desire to simply disable her. But he had forgotten that her suit was now purged with 100% oxygen. The rest happened far too quickly for anyone to be able to react or do anything to save Dimitriov; even Peter, who stared down at her just inches away from her helmet visor.

Her hair caught on fire first. It flared and glowed red, then yellow, then a brilliant white. The skin on her face actually began to burn; first as tiny flamelets exploding through her nose, then as a white hot sheet that covered her head and neck. As she opened her mouth to scream, Dimitriov inhaled a sheet of flame that disappeared down her throat in a twisting, brilliant vortex of deadly fire.

Peter instinctively pushed himself away from the hideous spectacle just as her suit ballooned, then a tongue of flame peeled away from her chest and leapt toward the ceiling before being extinguished by the near vacuum of the passageway.

"Now that's what I call a terminal case of heartburn," came the stoic voice of Hiraldo through the communicators.

Brinker, who had been staring at the incredible sight of the exploding Dimitriov, looked up and over to Hiraldo. He burst into wild laughter, walked over to Hiraldo and slapped her upraised palm with his. "Hiraldo, you are one bad-ass Marine, you know that?" he said with glee.

"Jack, I need a status report," Peter said quickly.

"I've been watching you and everybody else, Peter. The war appears to be over. Three of the enemy have surrendered; all the rest of them are dead."

"What about our people?" Peter asked.

The circuit fell silent for a long moment.

"Jack, I need to know about our people."

"Six are missing from Dome 6 and presumed dead and three were killed in combat outside. Both Safe rooms are holding. Everyone else is online with me now."

"Brinker, take the prisoners into custody and hold them at the Spaceport. I don't want them anywhere near here until we can work this out. I don't want another spy in our group, at any cost. Jack, pull together a damage report after we release the rest of the colony from the Safe rooms. Let's put teams together to patch the holes as fast as we can. Francis, can you work with Jack to make that happen?"

"You don't mind if CIA works on this project?" Francis asked with a weak grin.

"Yeah, like to whom are you going to send your report out? Rat?" Peter responded.

"Hey, I heard that," Rat's voice came back over the communications circuit. "If you guys ever want to see any coffee again, you'd better hurry up and get with the program."

The war had cost them all dearly. Between the precious lives taken in the battle, life support consumables lost in preparations, various irreparable damages to spacesuits and other vital equipment, and the loss of life support air and water when the surprise attack came, they had lost more than one third of their total reserves. The deaths of ten colonists would mediate their life support burden somewhat, even though they had picked up three additional personnel as surrendered prisoners. Ashley was in charge of this most important area. Her neck wound amounted to a deep scratch; one that she covered with a warm, high neck sweater. But she had been given the immediate task of working through the complex calculations it would require to fix their exact survival state. It would be a long and laborious process requiring at least two sols of calculations, summaries and scenario modeling.

The biggest and most welcome surprise was the three captured Soviets: two women and Anatoliy. All three immediately renounced Dimitriov as a diabolically insane megalomaniac - utterly stark raving mad. They recounted their horrific journey across the desert to BC1 in graphic detail, describing the excesses of both Dimitriov and Kravchenko. Peter released transcripts of every interview in full as soon as they could be made available. When it was discovered it was Hiraldo that had killed Kravchenko, there was another round of celebration in the camp and Hiraldo's reputation grew well beyond reasonable limits.

Soviet Scientist Kirov was now up and about with the aid of a walker. After having heard the testimonies, he confirmed that the two females were unwilling conscripts, personally vouching for their previous reputations at Shturmovoi and recommending that they be allowed to join the colony without reservation.

Kirov also noted that the man who had surrendered and gave Peter Dimitrov's communications frequency, was Valentin Anatoliy, a deputy of Dimitriov's. After much furious debate between Kirov and the remaining scientists at Shturmovoi, it was recommended to the Americans that Anatoliy, too, be trusted. It was, after all, Jack and Brinker's sworn testimony that without the frequency revealed to them at that precise moment, the battle probably would have gone the other way. Ironically, it seemed that it was one of Dimitriov's own most trusted few who had helped decide the fate of them all.

Jack immediately set about the task of unraveling Toon's extensive treachery. The first task was to unwire Covenant from the dead-man's switch taped to his chest. He simply and eloquently established an artificial software heartbeat generated by the computer itself. This little software patch was then written into seven different places in the computer's many complex subroutines, so that if any part failed, the other took over automatically. They made the transition between Covenant's harness and the computer smoothly and without incident. Jack also planned to seek out Toon's extensive re-writing and re-programming and undo the damage a little at a time.

Toon had effectively knocked out all BC1 communications satellites around Mars. But, again, Jack discovered the problem was entirely secreted away in strongly encrypted software patches Toon had hidden in the BC1 computers, and he removed them all. In a mater of 36 hours, all satellites were back online again.

In just two sols, the dread of battle had turned into a celebration of victory. But it was quickly turned back into dread again as the outcome of Ashley's findings began to hang over them like a cold blanket. They all knew that much had been lost and none of it was retrievable. The question was, ultimately, could they actually make it up the life support hill toward permanent regeneration of their life support needs? Nearly all of them knew that if they could not make it before, it certainly was not to be any different now. There were a few hold-outs, however, who believed with all their hearts that Ashley would return with findings that would allow them to live; to somehow make it through the dark, cold abyss of the Elysium winter. Yet most knew it was not a matter of "if" but of "when".

On the morning of the third sol following the attack, funerals were held for the ten BC1 victims. It was a somber ceremony. Their bodies were stacked and covered with some of the many sandbags that had been filled in preparation for the attack. That afternoon, a very much abbreviated ceremony was held for the Soviets who had died. Their interment was conducted in a similar fashion. Peter had ordered that the least amount of consumables be expended in the process.

At the end of the dinner hour on the third sol, Peter rose to speak.

"I suppose you all feel like I do; that it's wonderful to be free here on Mars, and that we can all celebrate that freedom that was nearly lost, and cost us many precious lives. But you also know I'm not here to make speeches, but to tell you what Ashley has found in her analysis. Let me just say that it's a complex analysis. I'll release it in its full detail in a few minutes so all of you can pour over it. If you have any findings or suggestions, please send them to Ashley. After a much-deserved rest tonight, she'll be looking at them all tomorrow.

"There are three scenarios, based on the life support consumables we have available. All three scenarios identify the same limiting factor: water. We'll run out of water before anything else, and that'll cause the system to fail first.

"Scenario A defines a very austere posture here at BC1, calling for prolonged bed-rest; 18 hours per person per sol for everyone in a minimal energy position. There will be no outside excursions except for dire emergencies. The temperature would be reduced to the mid 40's Fahrenheit inside and there would be one meal a sol of 1500 calories for men, 1200 calories for women. In this scenario, the life support would diminish to the minimal rate in about 120 sols.

"Scenario B is less rigorous. Required bed rest would be reduced to 12 hours per sol. No outside excursions except for emergencies and inside temperatures reduced to 48 degrees Fahrenheit. There would be one meal served per sol of 1800 and 1500 calories respectively. In this scenario, the life support would diminish to the minimal rate in about 97 sols.

"Scenario C is the least rigorous. It would require only a 10 hour sleep period, the temperatures raised to 50 degrees with two meals and higher caloric intakes. This scenario gives us 76 sols.

"After having reviewed these choices, I've selected Scenario B," Peter ended bluntly. There was a murmur among the group, but it was clear that the idea of sleeping in a frigid bunk until death was not exactly being received as the best of news.

Finally, after an awkward moment of silence, Bob Kerry stood up from his table.

"What if we can find more water?" he asked.

Peter looked to Ashley for the answer to that question. She stood and replied, "Water is a key, but not the only key to topping the hill," in reference to the life support equation. They all knew well that "topping the hill" meant having the capacity to recycle and regenerate everything they would need to live indefinitely without re-supply from earth. "Our immediate need is water. If we could find significant water, we could effectively double the life support capacity. But if we could find enough energy as well as water, we could extend it for years and probably top the hill."

"What if we could bring the supplies down from orbit?" Kerry persisted. "And what if we can go get water and power from Shturmovoi?"

Peter held his hand up to quiet the crowd. "We have no orbiter, no access to space and the orbiter on the pad at Shturmovoi has no fuel and no way to produce any. They were waiting for their own re-supply ship. And Shturmovoi has only enough water for their own needs. In fact, their life support equations are even more grim that ours."

"How much energy do we need? Can't we get it from solar collectors? What if we could make our own solar panels?" Rat asked.

"If we had more water, we would then need enough energy to split the water and even the carbon dioxide in the outside air into breathable oxygen," Ashley replied with patience. "We have the ability to build some of those devices here. But we don't have nearly enough solar collectors or energy storage to create a difference and we don't have the industrial capacity to build solar panels here. Besides, there's no water to make any of that necessary."

After a long pause that seemed to be equally laced with despair and silence, Brinker walked slowly to the front of the room apparently consumed in thought.

"Okay, now I've got a "what-if" question for all you rocket scientists," he said in his swaggering style, pointing his stogie at Peter and Ashley. "What if, let's just say, well, what if, what if I, right here and right now, were to ask Hiraldo to marry me, right here in front of God and everybody?" Then he turned and looked directly at Hiraldo who started a deep blush.

"Well, what if I did that?" he asked her.

"Oh my God! Oh my God!" Hiraldo said in utter astonishment. Then she stood and said, "Yes! Yes, I would!" and rushed into his embrace.

"If I only got 97 sols left," Brinker said, his arm laced over her shoulder, "I can't think of anyone else I'd rather spend it with than the best damn United States Marine in the solar system!"

The crowd erupted in wild applause. One of the technicians, Randall Markley, who had manned Rail Gun 3, stood on top of his table and pointed at the couple.

"Yeeeeeessssss, Sarge! You're the maaaannnnn!" he yelled, pointing his finger at Brinker.

Then the assembled crowd erupted in a chant, "Brinker! Brinker! Brinker! Brinker!" which continued unabated for long minutes.

Brinker interrupted his own tribute with a wave of his hand. "And unless anybody here can give me one good reason why not, I want the wedding put on today's schedule!"

Again the crowd erupted in wild applause and started to chant anew, "Yes! Yes! Yes! Yes!"

In the midst of the cacaphoney, Fabian Gorteau suddenly stood and slowly made his way through the chanting crowd to the front and motioned to Peter for the floor. Gorteau had become silent, sullen and withdrawn after the war. Many speculated it was because he felt personally responsible for so many deaths on both sides.

"Quiet! Quiet, please. Professor Gorteau has a comment," Peter said, quelling the crowd.

Gorteau's whole demeanor had changed and he looked much older and less robust. Yet, even as he walked, his slightly bent frame and totally disheveled hair belied his superior intelligence, and everyone knew of his legendary discoveries. Each colonist became very still, straining to hear his profound statement.

"I have made an important discovery," he said quietly, twisting his shaggy moustache with his fingers and looking down at notes written on his tablet computer. Then he nodded with certainty. "Yes, I believe I am correct. Yes, indeed."

There was a very long pause as he formed his thoughts.

"I have determined that it is entirely possible and well within the range of many of us here today to calculate with some degree of certainty the level of carbon dioxide generated in Sergeant Brinker's honeymoon suite on his wedding night. I propose installing a gas monitor and establishing a CO2 level pool – the closest estimate in any given 10-minute interval wins it all! And for heaven's sake, don't hold out – we only have 97 sols left and I believe this should be the biggest jackpot in this planet's history!"

Randall Markley bounded across two tables and landed at Gorteau's feet. "Professor, you're the maaaannnnn!" he yelled, pointing his finger at Gorteau who began to smile broadly, then winked slyly at Peter. At this point, everyone was on their feet cheering, even the somewhat mystified Soviets.

"Wait a minute! Wait a minute!" Covenant yelled above the noise, standing on a chair. "I had the privilege of working closely with these Marines for what seems like forever, and now I propose the ultimate toast to their betrothal." Withdrawing a miniature acetylene torch from his pocket he said, "I propose 'we light his stogie' once and for all!"

Randall Markley rushed across the floor to stand at Covenant's side. "Covenant, you're the maaaannnnn!" he yelled, in his now well-rehearsed act, pointing his finger again at Covenant who struck a switch and lit the tiny torch in his hand.

Brinker strutted over to Covenant smiling broadly, with Hiraldo in tow, holding the well worn stogie in front of him. But just as Covenant's lighter approached the stogie, Ashley screamed "WAIT!" Then she approached the two with a plastic bag.

"Go ahead and do it," she said with a smirk. "But by all means, exhale into the bag!"

Brinker laughed loudly, as Covenant lit the stogie and Brinker took a long, deep drag and held it for well over a minute in complete silence. Everyone present held their breath as well, savoring every second of the moment with him. Then he exhaled dutifully into the plastic bag and crushed the cigar out on the table-top.

"Just once before I died; just one more time; that's all I wanted," he said with real tears brimming in his eyes. The whole colony roared its approval anew.

Colony psychologist Julia Friedman walked over to a wildly cheering Peter and touched his arm lightly. "You know, Peter," she said with all seriousness, "none of this, none of this fits anyone's previous models of the behavior of social groups in stress. And you know, if we ever do make it and if there ever is an earth to go back to, I seriously don't believe anyone would ever believe this even if I managed to write it up."

As she said this, Markley cleared a table for Gorteau who sat down, opened his tablet computer from his pocket and began collecting bets. Brinker placed the first one.

omehow, they all managed to pull themselves out of the clutches of total despair for nearly a week. Between Gorteau and Psychologist Friedman, they drew out the long awaited announcement over the carbon dioxide pool for almost seven sols. The colonist who won collected $21,345 in now worthless U.S. dollars and another 246.25 in RSE currency notes.

Once the routine set in, when the temperature was lowered and the severe rations instituted, BC1 slipped into a kind of muted silence – somewhere between despondency and a soundless, controlled, but altogether neutral, state of quiet survival. There was no meaningful work assigned to keep treks outside to an absolute minimum. And all activity that raised the carbon dioxide output or required caloric intake was strictly forbidden.

For Peter, the most difficult task of all was the order to stay in bed for 10 hours per sol. For his entire life, his sleep periods rarely lasted longer than six hours. Thus, he typically lay awake in his dark room listening to Ashley's deep breathing beside him and brooding over their plight. It was during one of these times, just before 0500 that he sat straight up, suddenly, wide awake and his heart pounding.

"What is it, Peter?" Ashley asked, also now awake.

"Get Francis on the line. Have him and Jack meet me at the Command Center. You come too," Peter said quickly as he leapt from his bed and pulled his coveralls up around himself in the cold air. Then he burst out the door, only to return three seconds later.

"Forgot my drive," he said, fumbling around his cluttered desk. Then he grasped the portable, thumbail-sized device and headed back out the door again without another word. He paced quickly down the darkened passageways toward the Command Center, his breath condensing in the frigid air, tightly clutching his solid-state mini-drive in his fist. Peter burst into the Command Center, interrupting the watch who was quietly viewing a movie, surrounded by the muted glow of hundreds of console lights, gauges and monitors.

"Nick, you're relieved," Peter said as he entered. "Thanks for letting me have the Command Center for a meeting. I've got the rest of your watch."

Nick looked back at Peter, silently shrugged, and turned his movie off. He then began to call up the different consoles that routinely displayed information that the oncoming watch commanders required in order to turn over the duty to the next watchman. When executed properly, this turnover duty required about fifteen minutes.

"Skip it, Nick, I can review it myself," Peter snapped.

"Well, goodnight then," Nick replied without a smile and headed toward his own quarters.

As he departed, Ashley, Francis and Jack came walking briskly through the door, passing Nick on his way out. Jack was buttoning his shirt as he walked, his shoes untied.

"What?" Francis asked dryly.

"Jack, sit here at the console; you need to drive," Peter ordered briskly. "Call up the main computer access logs for control date 11-12-79-04. Then plug my drive into your console and match the access logs on the monitor here where everyone can see them."

Jack sat down without a word and soon his fingers snapped expertly at the keyboard in front of him. In less than a minute, two parallel, very dense rows of numbers and symbols appeared on the screen.

Squinting his eyes at the screen, Peter said, "Now, isolate the geology files and get rid of all the other activity." As Jack complied, nearly all the figures and numbers cleared from the command Center side of the screen.

"What does this tell us, Jack?" Peter asked with understanding edging into his voice.

"Well, it tells me a certain set of geology files were deleted, or wiped to government standards on that date at just after three thirty in the morning from the BC1 main computers."

"Exactly!" Peter replied. "And what else?"

"Well, it also shows that your daily backup occurred right on schedule on your drive in your quarters just half an hour before, and they're still intact."

"Yes! Yes!" Peter exclaimed.

"Who deleted the files on the main computer?" Peter asked.

"The Command Center watch commander," Jack replied.

"And who was that?" Peter asked.

Jack's fingers keyed the board, and then he replied, "Toon."

"Yes!" Peter repeated. "It was on that night that we discovered Lipton's body. When I was in Lipton's stateroom, I saw that he had been into my files, collating information. Then I asked you, Francis, to shut it down before it did any damage. When I returned to my own stateroom, I was going to shut it off myself, but it was finished with its job, so I checked my own files for damage, backed them up, pulled the drive out of the computer and went to bed. Toon erased Lipton's job on the main computer, but I still have it on this disk right here."

"Yes," Francis acknowledged. "I went to shut it down, but it had completed its run and I forgot about it."

"What was Lipton doing with the geology files?" Ashley asked.

"I had no idea. The next sol, I couldn't find the drive on the clutter of my desk..."

"Imagine that," Francis interrupted drolly without a pause.

"Last night, just before retiring, I noticed the drive sticking out from under the corner of my desk safe. I remembered why it was laying there. So out of curiosity I put it in and reviewed Lipton's job. It was totally unintelligible to me. But as I began thinking about it, I realized that the coordinates on the job were the same coordinates of our investigation out on the desert on the sol of the redwind, the same sol all the trouble began. And I have a general idea that he was not looking there just for his own entertainment."

"So, Lipton was relieved of duty, locked himself into his stateroom and began to run an analysis of our site on the desert?" Ashley mused. "Then Toon decided not just to shut it down, but to erase it. That doesn't make any sense."

"No; it didn't then and it still doesn't," Peter replied. "And that's why I invited all of you here on this fine morning. Help me, if you will, figure out the link between Lassiter Lipton, my geology files and our spy, Mr. See."

"Ok, first thing we need to find out is what Lipton's program was doing," Francis offered with some enthusiasm. It appeared that after several sols of boredom, any puzzle at all was worth deciphering. "Jack, can you pull up the request?"

Jack's fingers hammered the keys anew, and a complex screen of numbers and figures appeared on the display.

"Well, I'll be a horse's patoot!" Francis mused with a half-smile. "A complex matrixed Fourier. I haven't seen one of those since graduate school."

"What does it do?" Peter asked.

"Well, we used it to analyze three dimensional atmospheric dynamics. It appears that Lipton was using it to analyze the site you discovered on the sol of the redwind."

"What could it tell him?" Jack asked, eying the glowing numbers on the screen.

"And how could Lipton manage to initiate a complex matrixed Fourier analyses?" Ashley mused.

"It was not his idea," said a voice from the back of the Command Center.

All eyes turned to see Fabian Gorteau standing behind them.

"It was my idea, and I asked Lassiter if he would not mind running the program on my behalf," the old physicist said, looking tired and worn.

"What was it? Why?" Peter asked with concern. Gorteau looked as though he was lacking rest and seemed very tired and frail.

Gorteau sighed and sat down. "When Lipton was forced out of his position, I realized that I was partially to blame for the general chaos in the community that led directly to his undoing. So I suggested that perhaps he could analyze the latest data from the probes you placed out on the desert and then propose that there might be some permafrost out there. On the remote chance that it was a success, it would have temporarily made him look like a hero and I would have been able to use the victory to pull the science and administrative teams back together. It was to be a win-win situation where everybody could have come out looking good, even you Peter. You would have been the discoverer and Lipton would have been the catalyst to make it all happen. With the whole team working as one, I hoped we could pull it all back together. I thought that even though the investigation might have shown it to be an illusion, at least the disposition of the colony would have been altered significantly to make up for my own stubbornness. Then, alas, Lassiter was found dead and the colony spiraled into war. And even there I used my God given talents for more destruction. I am afraid this has all been a rather profound disappointment, to end my life in this way."

Peter felt a surge of pity for Gorteau that he had felt for few other living humans. "Fabian, you're just wrong about all this," he said immediately. "I applaud your attempt to make things happen that way. It was a brilliant plan and it most certainly would have worked. However, you did nothing to set up the disorder here. I'm afraid that was all my own doing."

"Now wait just a minute here, boys," Ashley intoned. "I'm just as happy as I can be to hear all this macho blame-taking, but it has nothing whatsoever to do with reality."

"You are wrong, my dear," Gorteau interrupted. "As the senior scientist here, it was my personal responsibility to lead and to unify. I failed."

"Whoa, wait, hold on…" Francis stammered, eyes glued to the screen. "I think I see why Toon took such care to delete these files on the main computer. Look – this analysis clearly defines a layer of density deviations. Jack, can you model this?"

Jack skewed his lips and looked at the screen sideways. "I think so," he replied, fingers hammering the keys. As he did so, Ashley walked over to the senior scientist and embraced him tightly as the old man's eyes brimmed with tears. Minutes later, a layer of reds, browns, blacks and blues appeared on the screen in three dimensions under an image of the desert floor.

"Jack, define your layers," Peter stammered with electrifying excitement in his voice.

"Well, unless I made an error," he said pointing at the screen with his finger, "these layers here represent your typical desert profile. But this balloon here, in green and blue, represents a rather peculiar density profile different than the surrounding strata."

"Jack, can you give me the numbers, the density references, on the screen?" Peter asked breathlessly.

"Sure. The dark ones right here: 2.7 to 3.5, which is what we normally see. But here, in the green: 1.8. And here in the blue: 1.6 right on down to 1.5!"

Peter literally fell to his knees and put his hands down on the floor. "Thank you God! Thank you God!" he said in a near sob.

Ashley fell to her knees beside him. "Peter? Peter, is it… is it permafrost?" she asked.

"Yes, I think so. Yes, it has to be!" he shouted, embracing her.

Gorteau's eyes were now streaming tears. "Oh my dear God in heaven, can this be?"

"Well, if it is, then we just bought ourselves another 300 sols, at least!" Francis said, slamming Jack on the back repeatedly with his palm.

ord quickly got out and filtered throughout the colony in under an hour as Peter and Ashley prepared a MAT for their fateful run into the desert. Every colonist stood in rapt, reverential silence and even the irreligious among them managed to eek out a tiny prayer.

As the MAT began its slow first movements out of the airlock, the colonists gathered around every available window and cheered them on. In the Command Center, Francis sat in the commander's chair. "Alright, my friends, by the book this time," he instructed them through the communications circuit. "No more shenanigans like your last infamous outing into the wilderness."

"Yes, sir," Peter replied, madly flipping switches while keeping his eyes carefully on the road ahead of them. "Can you kindly close up your student deportment manual and assist me with a few vectors?"

"Whatever. It's not like your school-boy record here is exactly free from incidents, pal," Francis replied with his consistent, cocky, black humor, while every colonist heard each word broadcast throughout the colony.

Francis and Jack monitored every meter of the long trek back out into the desert. Winter had come to Elysium and in the early morning light of the Martian sunrise, the carbon dioxide snow, or precipitation frost, had settled everywhere. The thin veneer of white stood out on the landscape like a brilliant blanket, interrupted everywhere by the reddish edges of rocks and dune layers. The white contrasted with the red and exaggerated it so that the desert appeared to be a fantastically designed quilt with alternating layers of brilliant white with deep red patches.

Peter looked to Ashley as her eyes scanned the scene. Her face was lit by the brightest light he had ever seen on the surface of Mars. Indeed, because of the layer of snow, it was so bright on this morning that the sunlight almost seemed to achieve the intensity of the sun on earth.

"Tell them what you see, sweetheart," Peter urged her. "Tell them about their planet."

Ashley smiled and began to describe the beautiful snows of the Martian desert as it unfolded before them. She began simply, and then started to describe its nuances with carefully chosen words. She called out its colors, its contrasts, its infinite varieties of detail, and especially its brilliance as they drove out into the Elysium desert.

Every colonist stood in complete silence as they heard her words describe the scene. Somehow, she was connecting them to the landscape as a place of fragility, of vast and infinite beauty and as a living form, not as an immeasurable, deeply frozen and God-forsaken burial ground.

Soon they arrived at the same spot where they had been struck and blinded by the redwind just before the beginning of the incidents that had changed all their lives. Peter stopped the MAT just two meters from the last probe he had attempted to drive into the ground. As he looked out the MAT's window, he noted it had been driven only half-way in and also saw that its top had been misshapen by his repeated blows.

"Are you ready to depressurize?" he asked Ashley quickly.

"Yes, let's do it," she responded with a slight wink.

"Not so fast, children," Francis broke into their transmission. "Let's do it by the book."

Peter's hand held the decompression handle tightly. Then he relaxed his grip. "Yes, sir. Following the checklist now," he responded as Ashley gave him a thumb's up.

Minutes later, the MAT's door swung open and Peter dropped a booted foot onto the desert sand. Ashley followed and set up a camera so that everyone back at BC1 could watch their every move. Peter walked over to his probe and, with a hammer, attempted to drive it deeper. It would not budge. "Look's like the base of the probe is into a rock; over," Peter replied, not even daring to suggest anything else.

"Concur, Peter," Francis replied, his voice calm but betraying his inner anticipation. "Suggest you core it; over."

"Roger that, Base. Coring commencing immediately."

Ashley handed Peter a rather massive drill motor with two large extruding handles. On the end of the drill was a half meter long hollow coring bit. Peter stood up, pulled the probe out and inserted the coring bit into the probe's hole. He then depressed the trigger and began to drill down into the desert. Seconds later, he withdrew the bit and looked into its end.

Ashley could see the disappointment on his face through the bulbous visor of his helmet. He looked to her and shook his head imperceptibly. "Base, the probe was in a rock. I repeat, the probe was biting into a rock beneath the surface." Then he paused and added, "Not into permafrost."

There was a long, protracted silence from the Command Center. Then Francis said, "We suggest you move over one meter north-northeast and try again."

"Roger that," Peter acknowledged, shaking his head slowly. He moved to the location, inserted his bit and drilled again. This time the bit hesitated, then drilled to its full measure. Peter then reversed the motor and withdrew the bit.

"Too easy," he mouthed silently to Ashley, indicating the bit had merely sunk into a sand pocket. Peter upended the bit and looked inside the core. It appeared just like every other core he had ever taken on Mars, but it did have a slightly darker appearance.

"Investigating core," he said evenly, withdrawing a miniature acetylene – oxygen torch from his pocket. He pulled on its trigger and when its flame had evened out, aimed it at the open core which he held horizontal to the ground. To his astonishment, the end of the core sample disappeared behind a flash of steam. Some then melted like mud and dripped out of the end of the core onto the ground where it instantly refroze into a misshapen lump.

Ashley spoke first, "Oh my God! Oh, I cannot believe this. It's permafrost, base. It's permafrost! We've got water here, base; water!"

BC1 came apart at the seams. Colonists were kissing, cheering, dancing and shouting. Peter and Ashley could hear the racket in their helmets, then they stood up and embraced; not a small undertaking in their pressure suits.

"We just bought ourselves hundreds of sols, people," Peter said to Ashley and all who were listening.

"Peter, hang on a minute..." Francis voice said tensely. "Hey, tell everybody to stop the ruckus for a single damned second, will ya?" he shouted.

Everyone immediately fell silent and Peter grew to be concerned as the silence became complete and went on for minutes. "BC1, what's your status; over?"

More silence.

"BC1, what's your status; over?" Peter said with urgency creeping into his voice.

"Peter, this is Francis. We're in the middle of receiving communications traffic. I'm going to patch you over to a secondary circuit. I'm also going to patch this over live to everyone else, so watch what you say, buddy."

There were several seconds of silence, then much static, followed by a distant sounding voice over his helmet communicator.

"Dr. Traynor, are you there? I'm Aaron Seven, Commander of the Spacecraft Singleton approaching Mars orbit. Do you read me?"

Peter looked over to Ashley and they noticed simultaneously that their mouths were gaping wide open.

"Answer him," she mouthed silently.

"Yes, this is Peter Traynor, Commander. We weren't exactly expecting a call," he said simply but truthfully.

"What's your status on the ground?" Seven asked.

"It seems we're doing better than expected, at the moment."

There was silence followed by static.

"We've been attempting to raise you over your direct communications circuits for weeks, BC1. This is the first successful contact we've been able to make. We gave up attempting daily contacts and have been trying once a week."

"Roger that, Commander. We've been having many problems of late, but our communications links are all reestablished now. When do you expect to enter our orbital space?"

"In three weeks, Dr. Traynor. Where's Dr. Lipton?"

Peter paused. "He's dead, along with many others here. We'll have to detail that story to you later. What's happened on earth?"

More silence followed by static.

"There has been a great global war, as you've probably figured out by now. We'll be the last visitors from earth in a very long time, I'm afraid. We barely escaped to tell the story, and what a story it is, Dr.

Traynor. We have 14 souls on board. We lost a few on the way and on arrival we'll be down to our last breaths of oxygen, literally. But it looks like, with some luck, we'll just make it."

"How about your other supplies, Commander?"

"Well, now there's the good news. Plenty of water and every other supply you can name. We lost most of our oxygen storage and production capacity in an unfortunate, er, accident. But we also come with plenty of your regularly scheduled supplies: mail, solar generating panels, the in-situ rocket fuel generating plant that was already scheduled for this run, and even a fairly large portable nuclear reactor."

"A what?"

"A nuclear reactor. We snagged that from the Soviets on the way out. Another long story. Why? Can you use it?"

"Commander Seven, we have a saying here on Mars," Peter said in a loud voice. "Aaron Seven, you're the maaaannnn!"

If the colony had engaged in a party before, this time they erupted in a fully developed orgy of screaming, crying, embracing and simple hysteria. Peter and Ashley could clearly hear the noise through their communicators. Peter stood to face Ashley once again. Looking into her visor, he said, "I love you now, and I'll love you tomorrow, in 90 sols and even a year from now, right here on Mars, on our planet."

She pressed her helmet against his and looked into his eyes. "Now that things are so much better, I think there's one more thing I should tell you."

"At this point, I'm almost afraid to hear it," he said with a light laugh.

"I want to introduce you to the first Martian," she said with a tender smile.

"The first Martian?"

"Yes," she said, taking his hand and placing it on her abdomen. "He or she will be along in about seven to eight months, I suspect. About the first light of spring."

"You're pregnant?" he asked, with archetypal male cluelessness. What he did not know was that the cheering had subsided in the colony and his voice was being carried across the open communications channel.

"Yes," Ashley said with a beaming smile. "We're going to have this planet's first child!"

The party that immediately ensued would be remembered for a generation.

47 EPILOGUE

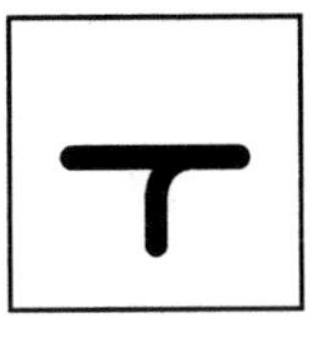

Three weeks later, the Singleton's lander touched down at Crippen Spaceport without incident. They had just enough oxygen left for one more sol. Aaron Seven managed to leave his primary cargo carrier and a Soviet space station module attached to Bob Kerry's ship which still orbited Mars.

Seven landed with a secondary cargo carrier filled with water, supplies and the last mail from earth. Onboard was also a fuel generating plant that would eventually produce enough fuel for the Singleton's lander to allow them to retrieve all the items remaining in orbit, including the nuclear reactor which would soon mine and process the permafrost waters of Elysium.

The water deposits were more valuable than gold on earth. They literally meant the difference between life and death. They were the key to the ultimate survival, not only of the young colony, but of the human species. They called this most important place the Lipton-Traynor Water Fields, in honor of its discoverers.

The colonists sent out a rescue mission to Shturmovoi, where the surviving scientists were brought food and supplies. Some returned to

BC1, but most decided to stay and conduct independent research with periodic visits from their sister colony to the north.

On the second sol of spring, the first Martian child was born to the new nation: Peter Traynor II. A week later, Rachel Lucia Seven was born, daughter of Commander Aaron Seven and his wife, Serea.

Six months after the discovery of the water fields beneath the desert of Elysium and the rigging of the new reactor, the colonists determined that they had topped the life support hill and were fully self sufficient. They would never require another transport from earth to survive.

In time, more children were born – to Kerry and Suzanne, to Brinker and Hiraldo and eventually to Rat and his wife, one of the two surrendered Soviet women, along with the other colonists and Earth survivors who had married. And thus it was set in motion; a second chance at human civilization.

On earth, there were a few survivors who managed to escape the deadly effects of the war. Many years passed before the clouds all disappeared and the sun warmed the earth again. One culture began to rebuild the earth just as another new human culture began on Mars. Many generations would pass before the citizens of earth and the independent nation founded on Mars would meet again or even know that the other existed at all.

But long before that, the colonists decided BC1 was no longer just a remote outpost on a distant planet, but a fully independent sovereign nation state.

They named it Elysia.

ACKNOWLEDGEMENTS

In the full bloom of Victorian culture, various works of writing fell into disrepute as determined by the more apposite scholars. Much writing fell from social grace during those heady days of collective literary suppression, works that were deemed loathsome written by those who were called "lascivious poetes," such as Ovid and Virgil. Rascals, deviates, hooligans all... But it just so happened that on the very day the authors of the same classics that were being labeled the "lascivious poetes", a young man of 18 years of age began his own writing career in the very city in which the verdict against his predecessors was rendered. William Shakespeare answered his calling at the precise moment when things looked bleakest for the craft of writing. You see, if Ovid and Virgil were accused of lascivious verse, then the Bard truly outdid them all and still stands today as the very master of heated, white hot passion – framed in the most astonishingly beautiful prose the world has ever known. It seems humanity's rare moments of glory are always most clearly defined as times of irony when the tiny minds of control are inevitably trumped by the power of sheer intellect and overcome by the brilliant light of purified genius.

As a writer I am continuously reminded by the masters that the state and art of the craft of writing is controlled by rules that are somewhat rigid, to be sure. And day by day, the art and craft is tilted one way or another by various and ever changing contemporary methods, formats and traditions such as rigid tense control, point of view, scene, sequel and other tricks of the trade. But the masters also remind me that they always seem to overcome these limitations to their art by somehow ripping away the veneer of regulations and substituting raw passion in its place. Hence, the reader is never burdened by the tedium of talent and is thereupon allowed the full freedom to be subsumed in the passion framed by the creative act which is ultimately formed in the collective word of the lascivious poet written just for "someone."

If you are one of those determined readers who have actually made it to this point - well past the end of the tale, let me tell you who that "someone" is – it is you. Let me say to you directly that this work was written for you, dear reader, alone. It was not written for any other reason but to entice you along to a world floating hundreds of millions of miles away. Like Peter Pan, fate, circumstance and an open window of time in your life somehow convinced you to risk stepping away from all you have known and fly along with me to a never-never-land, peopled with characters that I hope you have loved, hated and fretted over with passionate intensity. I can promise you that I had your image fixed in my mind as each word was fashioned and placed carefully on page after following page. To me, you, my precious reader, are everything – you are my closest companion, you are my friend and my alter ego. You don't remember sitting beside me as I wrote, but you were there nonetheless. I wrote just to make you happy, and I hope I have. You are why I write and you are the one whom I hope to please – not the editor, not the boss (whoever that may be) and not the critic – no one else but you. If I have made you happy, made you worry, made you love, hate, turn the page in haste or just have a good time between these covers, then I have succeeded.

No work like this is an isolated event. While the author's name is on the cover, it is not at all by his effort alone that it was created. Without the daily help and encouragement of my beautiful and awesomely gifted wife Claudia - my sweet Charlie - no one would be reading any words. Charlie, YOU are my *passionate intensity* – forever - you constitute the very fire of my being. The story was mine – its passion is ours.

I can also tell you, dear reader, that this work would not have been possible without the world's finest editing team whose ideas, suggestions and corrections are found throughout: Susan Austin, Joseph

Bishop, Claudia Chamberland and Martha Smith. These guys are incredible and their invisible mark is on every page, I can assure you.

This book could not be what it is without the artistic talent and sacrifice of three of my sons: Christopher Chamberland, Brett English and Peter Chamberland. Guys: thank-you for your gifts of genius, sweat and sweet toil even while dad was hanging around and looking over your shoulders. As always, you make me proud.

Many of you whose eyes scan these pages found this work through the efforts of Mark Ward. Mark and his brilliant promotional style is a Godsend in every respect. I truly do not know what we would have done without him and the deeply refreshing and extraordinarily creative work of Infotainment.

But I also wrote these words in the deep forests of Tennessee to honor the inspiration and genius of my mentor, boss and friend, Dr. William M. Knott III, the scientist, the man, whose vision will literally blaze the path to tomorrow's worlds and human civilizations in space and to the stars. Bill, you were so patient with me over so many years, such a model of genius and of human love, humility and inspired direction. I will never forget how powerfully you shaped my life and my profession. I believe you were one of the few humans who has ever really fully understood me – you always knew who I was and where I was compelled and where I had to go. Your selfless mark and unconstrained love has been left indelibly on me for all my days.

And finally I cannot express enough gratitude to someone who has also made a commanding and profound difference in my life: my friend Scott Carpenter. I have had the pleasure and blessing several times in my life to work with this figure of history who has repeatedly given of himself for my benefit, unselfishly and unwaveringly, every single time I have asked. Scott has always been willing to give with never ANY thought of anything he might receive in return. I have met and spent time with many very well known people, but I have never met a man of such powerful integrity and such unselfish compassion and commitment to his fellow man and to the future of human space and ocean exploration as Scott Carpenter. He is just awesome... And so there it is – the writer is out of words. Scott, I just do not have the words to express the gratitude I feel except to say, thanks – it seems so little and so inadequate.

This has been a story of human exploration, of the settlement of new worlds. There has recently been a debate in our culture as to whether some version of this story should ever happen or not. But, why there has been a debate at all is most astonishing and even a little frightening. The point of history has always been exploration. The reason for any great nation has never been its settlements or its industry, never its great buildings or its accumulated treasure - but its expeditions. The expansion of humanity has always expressed its greatest achievement and in the end, its only real expression of true power. When cultures have shrunk back from exploring, those cultures have always died. The day we forget that as a nation is the day we cease to be great. It is the first day of our terminal recession into history's formerly great peoples.

The energy that creates great empires is only found in the fires of exploration.

Dennis Chamberland
Stonebrooke, Tennessee

ennis Chamberland has been involved in the research, development and design of Advanced Space Life Support Systems and related processes considered for moon and Mars bases. He is the designer of the Scott Carpenter Space Analog Station, serving as its Mission Commander for seven missions on the ocean floor off Key Largo, Florida. Chamberland was the Principal Investigator for the first crop of edible food planted and harvested on the ocean floor inside a manned habitat.

Dennis is a former United States Naval Officer, serving as a Navigator and Main Propulsion Assistant Engineer onboard a US Navy Frigate while stationed at Pearl Harbor, Hawaii. He also served the Navy as a civilian Nuclear Engineer at Mare Island and Charleston Naval shipyards. Chamberland is a double alumnus of Oklahoma State University where he received his M.S. in Bioenvironmental engineering and has been an instructor in life sciences at Charleston's Trident Technical College.

He is an active writer and speaker, having written over 100 articles and four books spanning the last two decades. Some of Chamberland's many works have been translated from English into Chinese and Braille as well as having been selected for various college and university textbooks and over a dozen reference works. Dennis has been named a Fellow of the New York Explorers Club and has shared his adventures with audiences in such diverse places as high schools and various community social organizations, as well as the Harvard Club of New York and Princeton's Space Studies Institute.

Dennis is married to the former Claudia Schealer of Cocoa, Florida. They have six children and divide their time between Florida and their beloved Stonebrooke in the Tennessee mountains.

Readers are encouraged to visit and write the author at:

Author's Website: **http://www.Chamberland.org**
Author's eMail: **dc@Chamberland.org**

AARON SEVEN
QUANTUM
STORMS
A Novel by
Dennis Chamberland